RETURN TO A MEADOW

SHIRLEY GLUBKA

RETURN TO A MEADOW

BLADE OF GRASS PRESS
PROSPECT, MAINE
2012

Return to a Meadow
a novel by Shirley Glubka
paperback

published by

Blade of Grass Press
85 Bowden Point Road
Prospect, Maine 04981-3000
bladeofgrasspress@gmail.com

Front cover painting: *Komposition*
by artist Margret Hofheinz-Döring
courtesy of Galerie Brigitte Mauch Göppingen
and commons.wikimedia.org

Back cover author photo: Michelle Weldon

ISBN 978-0-9666481-1-9

Acknowledgments

I cannot imagine a more varied, generous, or acute group of readers. This novel, whose faults are of course entirely my own, is far better than it would have been without their responses. I listened and I revised—repeatedly. Also, I was stubborn, and refused to change what I just plain didn't want to change; so never blame them. Here they are, my wondrous readers:

Virginia Holmes, my partner
Harriet Glubka, my mother
Karen Weldon, my sister

And friends, friends, friends:

Carol Romeo Veits
Gail Roudebush
Jan Lucas
JoKasha Klest
Laura Levenson
Margaret Moore Blanchard
Rae Dumont
Susan Morse
Zarod Rominski

I am especially grateful to Laura, who read the entire manuscript in two versions and who tolerated—with enthusiasm—discussions of everything from the largest issues to the grittiest details.

My humble and somewhat astonished gratitude: to all of you.

Dedicated to Kevin
in gratitude for his existence and his tolerance

and to Ginny
life partner than whom there could be no better

and to the Pleasures of Difficult Poetry Group
which, beyond all reasonable expectation, justifies its name

Nothing could stifle my inner certainty
that a shining point exists
where all lines intersect.

– Czeslaw Milosz

Often I am permitted to return to a meadow
as if it were a given property of the mind
that certain bounds hold against chaos,

that is a place of first permission,
everlasting omen of what is.

– Robert Duncan

Chapter One

Petra Kalinowski knows this one thing: the rock she sits on. She knows its jutting places, the curve of its indentations, how faithfully unyielding it is. So much of life she does not quite grasp. Even her own face eludes her. She can use the mirror: short Polish American woman, spare but not skinny; plain dark cap of hair, no gray yet; eyebrows dominating a face neither unusual nor uninteresting. She has no complaint, but when she turns from the mirror she can't quite remember the look of herself. Ah, this is an old theme. Does it matter? Not much. Set it aside.

Necessity. She's been reading Simone Weil. No philosophy for years. Now, suddenly, Weil. *Necessity. Gravity. Decreation.* She leans her mind against the stern words. She has needed a leaning place; or something to set her mind down into, unyielding and certain, like rock, or like the vocabulary of brilliant, peculiar Simone Weil. It's that session with Helga yesterday. And yes, it's the baby, too, who comes and goes, little critter in need of care and she, Petra Kalinowski, gives the care. Only occasionally, only for a few hours at a time. Still: after all these years, a baby in her house, in her arms. Helga and the baby have sent her to this rock where she has come for years in all weathers. Once, after an ice storm, she melted out small patches with her bare hands; climbed; melted a circle for sitting. It took time, but she could sit without sliding. The world glistened under sun. No sun today. The rock rises out of dark stony sand beside the river. The river, the wide Penobscot with its tidal rise and fall, its long inhalation and exhalation, is liquid gray under the gray sky. *Rock, Sky, River: Monochrome with Variations.* Since childhood Petra has suspected that worth resides in art. She has no talent with a paintbrush unless she's pulling one along the length of a clapboard but she does what she can. Hers is a private mental art, a mere habit of giving titles. Perhaps her old paint-spattered overalls are a sort of accidental art, though. *Inadvertent Spatter.* Also—she loves this line of thought—a session with a client can become art, a lucky honing,

1

agonized or ecstatic; form cut into the suddenly clarified air of the office, stunning and momentarily eternal. Not yesterday. Not with Helga.

Those overalls, *Inadvertent Spatter*, remnant of the seventies and San Francisco and still in use though fragile, are a work in progress; also a bridge, decade to decade, west to east. She's in Maine now, but the time in San Francisco, twenty years ago, has been catapulted to nearness by Helga and by the baby.

Behind Petra is the wooded path that leads up to her house. If she turned around she'd see leaves, red and orange against the gray sky, stark, themselves. She doesn't turn around. She sits on her necessary rock and watches the gray monotone of weather and water. She presses both hands down onto the rock. Her rock, still in place.

Ready, then. Easier to start with Helga than with the baby. Helga entered the office yesterday for her first session, tall and immaculate in a beige suit, with perfectly cut blond hair. She was thirty-one years old. This number Petra gleaned from the insurance form. She can't work until she knows a client's age, a fault she long ago decided to live with. Helga's nails had been done, her cuticles were perfect. She wore high heels. Step carefully, thought therapist Petra, but the young woman was immediately human and smart, creating a matrix of well-formed sentences that gave history, life goals, an analysis of her own personality. She considered herself a little too rigid, a little too direct. She used the words *obsessive* and *compulsive*. She took a breath and set down into that matrix the essential fact: she had given up on parenting three weeks ago. Petra's pulse speeded up. Not much, just a little. She kept listening, carefully; nodding, accepting. She's sure she did that much. Ingrid is two years old and will be raised by a cousin who was planning someday to adopt an infant but has taken Helga's daughter instead. The cousin has known Ingrid from birth. She welcomed the child—here came a catch in Helga's voice, nothing more—tenderly into her home. *Tenderly*. Petra heard the word as if in a large hollow space, as if it had an echo. It wasn't much of an echo, it was almost no echo at all. "What you must think of me," said Helga. This was not a question. Petra knew, perfectly, that this was not a question. It fit into the tight construction of sentences, there were no gaps. She listened, received the sentences. Helga continued, enumerating friends who stood by her. She was not an isolated person, not alone, but she had not slept well. Her friends thought a short course

2

of therapy might help. Helga spoke quietly, so much dignity and beige, cutting into Petra's heart with each precise word. Helga's pain was firmly contained. Petra's was not. She struggled with dizziness, sweating, blurred vision. She kept listening. Her mind steadied, her body calmed. She liked the young woman despite the high heels. They made another appointment in an atmosphere of mutual respect. The session had not been high art, but it was adequate. She went on with her work, seeing three more clients, aware of deferred sensations, postponed undoing.

The tide is coming in. In an hour or two the Penobscot will surround, but not cover, this rock. Even during astronomical high tides the rock can be seen. She went down once in the middle of the night to check, flashlight in hand. The flashlight wasn't needed, the moon was full. She saw the top of the rock, stubborn solidity in a swollen river, high tide intensified by gravity compounded, by planets lined up. She was irrationally relieved, though she had prepared herself for the excitement of disappearance, a scene of uninterrupted shining water.

Helga thinks she understands her decision. Maybe she does. "I do think I have some insight into all of this, Dr. Kalinowski." Petra, lowly masters level therapist, not a doctor, decided the misconception would have to remain in place for the time being. Helga had not yet been able to leave a break between sentences. "I'm talking too much, I can't seem to stop," said astute Helga. "I want you to understand, but of course you do understand, you must have heard everything here in this office. It's a comfortable office. I didn't expect living room furniture, and the art...I want to explain my difficulty..." Helga paused, but gestured her hesitation away, a flick of the hand, a quick breath. "My obsessive-compulsive personality...I need a level of neatness. You can imagine..." Petra heard faint quotation marks around the diagnostic phrase, a subtle twist of irony. Sense of humor, then; capacity for perspective. Her professional mind was functioning. Helga's explanation helped: she, Petra, had no obsessive-compulsive traits, at least none she'd noticed. Surely she'd have noticed. "So my Ingrid couldn't quite...she's only two years old, she won't be three for another nine months...she can't be expected..." Aborted sentences, tense breathing, inability to look up. Petra waited; she was trained to endure tension. "I had difficulty...when she wouldn't...use the toilet. It wasn't right. My cousin..." Of course there would be toileting issues. The child was two years old and the mother

3

was compulsive. How much rage? Petra remembered her own rages, the foreign rush of them. Until Anya, she would not have imagined wanting to throw a child against a wall. Those two incidents of deliberately messed pants, long after the agony of toilet training seemed finished. That third late night in a row, Anya repeatedly popping out of her room, refusing to sleep. She, the mother, desperate, locking herself in the bathroom with her journal. Eyes on Helga, therapist Petra remembered the feel of the pen in her hand, remembered how carefully she inscribed sentences while Anya screamed, remembered the slumped bundle of child on the floor when she opened the door. She had bent down. Anya, still sleeping, reached up but then she was awake and her eyes darkened. She turned away and hardened herself head to toe. Petra was exhausted. She tried to lift her, but the child was rigid, heavy. She gave up. They would sleep there in the hall. She got pillows and blankets. Anya refused the pillow but by morning it was squashed under her perfect head.

The memory came in a flash, information for a working therapist, not a distraction. She knew Helga's experience would be different from hers. Empathy was fine, but she would guard against assuming similarities. "What kind of difficulty did you have when Ingrid wouldn't use the toilet?" She asked as gently as possible, aware of the mistake she might be making, aware she felt compelled to know. Helga tensed, but tried to answer.

"I couldn't...touch her. I couldn't clean her until I had...done things...alone, in a different room...it was taking longer and longer to get back to her and then..." Helga's hands shook, a fine tremor. Her pupils were pinpoints. Petra interrupted, carefully.

"Just tell me as much as feels right to you, I don't mean to pry."

"Oh. Thank you." Helga shifted in the chair, crossed her legs, and offered a paragraph declaring what a good parent her cousin would be, listing qualifications. Her hands lost the tremor, her pupils returned to normal. Petra relaxed. Helga probably did have obsessive-compulsive disorder. Her symptoms might decrease now, with the change; or they might increase. Petra felt a brief surge of pity, a sudden wind that threatened to unbalance her. She did not believe in pity as a therapeutic force. Helga talked on. Petra listened. The young woman's need not to step into the quicksand of emotion was evident. Gentle pacing would be called for. A shimmer of rapport rose in the air between them, thin,

4

almost invisible. The therapy would be successful if Petra herself did not misstep. Before Helga left they sorted out the matter of Petra's not being a doctor. Helga had no need for a doctoral level therapist, in fact she was relieved. Yes, she was comfortable addressing Petra by her first name, it would relax her. Yes, she wanted to come back, it did help, just talking about it. Thank you, Petra. Good-bye, Petra.

Here on her rock Petra wonders how Helga will be dressed the next time she sees her. Neatly, of course. More beige? This is a rock with a promising crack. She can almost wedge her hand into it. Will it take decades or centuries or millennia for the piece to break away? Would Nat know? Fifteen inches broken off will someday reveal the inner workings, how the layers formed, how the minerals mixed and melded. Lying beside the mother rock will be a piece that once fit perfectly. The fact of the fit will be visible. This won't happen in her lifetime, will it? Nat might know, or she might say, "What do you think? That I horde every fact your own mind has refused to scavenge?" Or they might sit silently, or walk, and at some point Nat would probably yield and mutter, "No one can predict that." The woman prefers not to be approached as if she knows things. Her self-image wobbles under the pressure. Nat Levesque, former lover, good friend, is the first person in Petra's circle to go gray. Also, she is another rock, another sky, another river; necessary; difficult; steady. The thought of Nat, the very stringency, soothes the uncertain psyche.

It might not be beige. The second session might call for something dark. Or, if she's feeling daring, something with a splash of color. But Helga's wardrobe is a distraction, defense against varieties of pain that wait, lined up. She puts her hand on a place where the rock juts up, feels the familiar edge, imagines Helga going home after yesterday's session. Helga, like her therapist, lives alone now. She enters the apartment where the little girl Ingrid no longer lives. She feels dread. Or she feels freedom, relief. Or she feels guilt, or waves of sorrow. The missing child is like a missing limb, it is pure pain she feels. Or, worst of all, she forgets to think about the child, remembers her later, and feels like a monster. But Helga didn't talk about feelings yesterday. She only said she was sure she was doing the right thing. She knew it wasn't good for a child to be scolded for getting her dress dirty, for making mud puppies since she was not allowed a living puppy. "She made a good mud puppy, for a two year old," Helga said, with sudden wryness. "But her hands, her dress, her *knees*..."

Petra will remember the fact that two-year-old Ingrid wears dresses. Anya had that other experience, no dresses. It was San Francisco, the seventies. None of her friends wore dresses and she never wanted one. Petra, at the zoo, the park, going to a movie, would ask her about this from time to time but practical, modest Anya always replied, "I *hate* dresses. They let your underpants show." The year she entered preschool she had seen a girl in a dress bend over and reveal her underwear with nonchalance. "She didn't even *care*." She never recovered from the assault to her world view. Petra smiles, feels the rock, lets the gray sky soothe her. Anya had such firm and practical ideas. What a convergence: yesterday, the twentieth anniversary of Anya's death; and here's Helga. Working with Helga will not destroy her. Of course it won't. Still, she'd better bring this up with Gertrude: Gertrude Benstein, colleague, goad, anchor, safety net. Last week they focused on Gertrude's clients so it will be Petra's turn. Fortuitous. Add Helga to the issue of the baby, who comes and goes, comes and goes, and a bit of clinical supervision is certainly needed. The baby is part of the convergence, of course she is. Her round face, her thick black hair. Those eyes. She closes her own eyes, sees the baby, and Helga, and Anya. They enter her body, a threesome invading. This is stern, formidable comfort. Then they're gone. All she knows is bewildered intensity. A shiver passes through her. Nothing is clear, but she feels better. She needs to move. Stretch, move, and walk.

Back in her kitchen, making tea, she is severe with herself. Helga's therapy will be damaged if she works from murky consciousness. She has known—hasn't she?—that she must tell Gertrude about the baby. Yes, she has. Known and avoided the prospect, which includes telling about Anya. Anya and Helga and this baby.

Chippie.

Of the brown bright eyes.

*

"How were you with other clients, after you saw Helga?"

6

Petra feels attacked. Gertrude is not the enemy, she tells herself. Gertrude cares. The fact seems not to matter. "Fine. I was fine." Does her voice match the shaken Jell-O sensation in her belly? She's been calibrating the level of her own defensiveness. It's rising.

"What about Kiki? She's adopted, isn't she?" Gertrude's tone is kind. Worse than kind. Careful.

"I've been consulting with you about Kiki for five years." Petra's tone is neither kind nor careful.

Silence.

"You know my work with Kiki, Gertrude."

Prolonged silence. She feels like a thirteen-year-old brat. Furthermore, Gertrude will wait her out. "I'm sorry." Gertrude waits. Petra sighs. "I do hope you never treat me this way, dear Gertrude. I was on automatic pilot. It was low-level good-enough work. Dear Kiki was just out of the hospital, one more time, because she cut herself again and her parents just can't..." Unable parents. Petra hears it. So does Gertrude. "Her parents just can't. In a different way from how I just couldn't. If 'couldn't' is the right word. I told myself it was a choice, a reasonable and free decision."

"Maybe it was."

Petra ignores this. "Helga said 'What you must think of me.' So there it is. I hereby pass it on to you. What you must think of me. I don't want a response any more than Helga did. Kiki was fine. High decibels, red high-top tennis shoes. 'I LOVE you, Petra, I'm so happy, it was a NICE hospitalization. Don't be sad for me, Petra.' She chose Raggedy Ann as boon companion for the day and left happy. Her parents can't tolerate the cutting, that's all. They can, somehow, tolerate parenting, interminably, a slow-minded loud lovable personality-disordered twenty-five-year-old. I know I'm babbling. Helga knew she was, too. I'm giving you time here, to absorb. You've known me—for how many years?—but you didn't know this. Petra had a little girl. Petra gave up her little girl. Petra's little girl died. In a minute I'll stop this. I will. We should both note that I'm mirroring precisely what Helga did in her session. I'll stop. You can talk." She blinks. Cold tears roll down her face. She reaches over, it's a stretch, and takes a tissue from the box on the table at the other end of the couch in Gertrude's clean, tasteful office and blows her nose. She hasn't told her story in a long time.

"I do need time to absorb," Gertrude says, getting up, moving the tissues close to Petra, sitting down again. "Having a child, deciding it's best to give her up, maintaining a relationship with her, having difficulty with that, and then she dies. I can't even imagine, Petra, but I don't need time to know that you're the same person, the same therapist, who won my respect two seconds after we met, so stop that part of things, it's not worthy of us." Petra just nods. She's actually crying. Life was feeling so stable, so *formed*.

"Do I need to go to therapy? I don't want to go to therapy. I hate therapy." This is an old topic. Gertrude shakes her head over incorrigible Petra. "But I'm not finished, Gertrude." She blows her nose again and tells about Chippie. "A *baby*. Three months old. Can you imagine?" More nose blowing, but the crying has stopped. "Just Sunday afternoons, so her mother—whose name is Bright Star, believe it or not—can focus on her work. She's an artist, or a would-be artist. I haven't seen her sculptures and I'm not sure I want to." She looks at Gertrude. No judgment, nothing to cringe from, nothing to guard against.

"How does it feel, having this baby come to visit?"

"I think I like it. I don't hate it, I thought I'd hate it."

"Tell me more."

"What can I say? Bright Star is a single mother, a friend. I guess she's a friend, I don't like her much. She's in our reading group and I'm the one responsible for bringing her in, this pregnant lesbian. Then she wasn't pregnant any more and there was Chippie. I remembered all the help I got with Anya. I felt that impulse thing." This is a reference to her moral life, which Gertrude knows from previous conversations. Lucky, since she's not sure she could explain today. Petra sees the world as radically complex. All data are suspect and can be counterbalanced by other data. Also, everything is gift and must be welcomed. Rational decision-making is a contradiction in terms. The only hope lies in the intuitive mind. Major decisions in her life have all been made this way: not thoughtlessly, but, in the end, out of impulse, half-blindly. One eye sees everything, the other sees nothing at all. Clarity emerges from a substrate of radical uncertainty. The important decisions of Petra's life have been: leaving Witold (father); leaving Frederick (husband); giving up Anya (daughter, dearly loved daughter); moving to Maine; sleeping

8

with Nat; not sleeping with Nat. She's aware of the preponderance of separations in this list.

"Taking care of Chippie sounds potentially healing." This is Gertrude, breaking into her thought, irritating her.

"I hate that word. You know I do."

Gertrude is unruffled. "Choose one of your own, then, but is it? Healing?"

Petra sighs. "It's disorienting. I knew I was a person who couldn't...out in the world I hardly looked at them. Kids, I mean. It was a discipline, a kind of integrity, not to deny my inability. This felt stable. Now it's all..." She pauses. She's actually feeling less irritable, less vulnerable; which is a damn good thing because the hour is ending. "Quick, before we have to stop, what did you notice about the work with Helga?"

"Gaps."

"Gaps. Damn."

"Yes. The father and the child."

Petra sighs. "I see. Major omissions."

"It's not so much that Helga didn't seem to realize her child would have a reaction to being moved, and not so much that she didn't mention the child's father. My concern..."

"Ah, Gertrude. You will now comment in your scalpel-like way that the therapist failed to notice these gaps."

"True. And you're a fine therapist, Petra Kalinowski. This will be an adventure. Next week it's my turn. I have a new couple who so bewilder me I might just tell them to go away. I thought I'd talk to you first, though."

"Good idea."

"One more thing. Parenting can be accomplished by people who have obsessive-compulsive difficulties."

"Did I imply...?"

"You did."

"Ouch. Thank you, Gertrude."

"You're welcome, Petra."

Chapter Two

Petra was twenty-one, a Minnesota farm girl who could imagine neither California nor Maine, when she married Frederick. She'd just graduated from college with a major in English, an obvious choice for a passionate reader, and a minor in philosophy. Her father had an interest in the history of philosophy, so the minor was mildly embarrassing, but she felt a stubborn certainty: her college years were not shaped to her father's form. After her mother died—she was nine years old—she'd kept track of her father's reading, quietly taking note of the titles of old, dark books. It was a way of not losing him. He never went beyond Kant whereas Sartre, *the* modern philosopher, had altered every cell in her body.

Frederick was a janitor at the college, attending classes for no charge. He'd been through most of the philosophy offerings and was about to tackle German when they met in Mr. Alton's class, Pre-Socratic Philosophy and Contemporary Physics. He wasn't interested in a degree —such a romantic, principled stance—and his paper, "Heraclitus vs. Parmenides vs. Einstein," was brilliant. Also, he was older: thirty. For these reasons, when he proposed she said yes.

"Old enough to know your own mind." That was her father's response on hearing she was engaged. He agreed to attend the wedding and returned to his book. Petra had steeled herself for this. Later, though, he looked up and said, "I'm not equipped. A daughter, grown. I'm not privy to the mysteries." A windfall of unexpected words. She was so grateful she almost cried. Witold Kalinowski, reluctant farmer, was essentially an intellectual: easy to sum up, if not easy to know. Tekla, wife and mother, was less definable even when alive. After her death the light and dark of her floated like confusing ghosts and before long she evaporated, all but the husk, the bare dry fact of her. No stories passed between father and daughter. Witold did his best with his daughter, and she with him, but conversation was not the strength of this tiny remnant family.

Witold met Frederick once before the wedding. When she brought him into the dark house (three porches and two huge shade trees blocked light) she felt as if she were pulling him, reeling him in, depositing him at the kitchen table where he would be seen and judged. She hadn't realized until they sat down to that one dark meal how the two men resembled each other. They could have been father and son, tall and thin, both slightly bent, peering at the world through thick glasses with sturdy black frames. Cleaned up for this supper, they wore matching blue work shirts, their best work boots. Both were intelligent, no question about that. Socially awkward, too. No question about that, either. Father and son, or a good facsimile thereof. The thought frightened her.

"Petra tells me you're a philosopher janitor."

"I suppose that's a way to put it, Mr. Kalinowski."

"Witold."

"Yes, sir."

She had convinced herself there would be conversation. This hadn't been entirely irrational. Witold had an enduring interest in the history of philosophy and she had reason to think Frederick had words. He had plenty to say when he and she were alone, theories spilling out of him, eyes sparking at her, then shifting inward to consider a point he got snagged on. The two men spoke that day of how the rains were interfering with planting, a sentence each, then dug into their meal as if they were serious eaters. Roast beef, dark gravy, mashed potatoes, spinach, peach pie. Petra had worked in the kitchen all afternoon. The peaches were from a tin can, but still. Eventually the men commented on the cooking, another polite sentence each. She chided herself: she should have known. After the small church wedding where Petra's friend Roo, a tall, round, comfortable bridesmaid, was the warmest element, Witold and Frederick shook hands. That was the sum of their brief relationship.

Petra left her father, moved into her husband's tiny apartment near the railroad tracks in Winona, half an hour's drive from the farm. Daughters grow up, she told herself. Daughters leave home. She made the apartment her own, painted the walls white, put up sheer curtains that framed, but did not cover, the windows. She kept the windows clean. They lived on the second floor and the path for light was clear. Sun poured in from the south and west. Still, after three months she left. Her reasons were as strong as they were unexpected. Poor Frederick didn't smell right once they got into bed. She knew of no way to change the fact or even understand it. She had no experience with sex and he had very little. They were abominable technically, not much better on other levels, but the essential obstacle was olfactory. Also, listening to this man became difficult. Frederick's thoughts were a maze. Finding the center was difficult and the fascination wore thin. The maze image was hers. He never used images, spoke in abstract, discursive paragraphs, and failed to ask what she was thinking. She had ideas, little shoots, green and tender. When she tried to show him he missed the importance, trampled. She started to write, found brevity, condensation, images with a glint of mystery. This was satisfying but irrelevant to the marriage. She couldn't control the dread when they came together for food, talk, and—worst—bed. The dread interfered with breathing. She told him she'd bought a plane ticket to San Francisco with money borrowed from Roo and was ready to leave. "When?" "Tomorrow." It was agony to see him so sad and bewildered. She was very, very sorry. No, he couldn't come with her. She wanted something warmer, perhaps even colorful. She wanted change that would be absolute, irreversible.

Roo had a cousin, Danny, who lived with a group of people in an apartment in San Francisco. There was an empty room she could rent. The Castro district. This sounded irreversible. It was. Roo called to tell her about the accident: the car had struck a tree in thick fog, Frederick was alone, the newspaper said he died instantly. Petra was stunned. She'd never called to tell him she was pregnant, to talk about divorce. When Anya was born, she called Witold. "Oh, sweetheart," he said. She didn't know what he meant, who he meant. He'd never called her sweetheart. Maybe it was the baby he was addressing, or Tekla. He was so soft and sad when he said it, he might have been talking to his dead wife. She said she'd bring the baby for him to see. He said that would be fine.

In the wet, difficult, lovely time after Anya was born, leaking milk, sweating at night, crying from sheer extreme fatigue, changing diapers, giving baths, amazed and aroused by the nursing child (Anya was enthusiastic about nursing, she pulled and pulled), Petra circled down to a quiet spot where an old ache rested. She wished she could tell Tekla she had a baby; she wished she had a mother to tell. She found herself remembering the years of her mother's illness. For two years before she died Tekla was bedridden and shrinking, dark. The Old Times had come back to her, the Old Country, Poland ripped and raped by war. Tekla's people were running, carts piled with belongings. Here were the Russians, there were the Germans. Under the boots of both, the Poles. Petra, holding Anya, yearning for her mother, thought how the long hours lying in bed sick and waiting for the end must have echoed times of unbreathing terror in the cellars and attics of Poland. Before their own time of running and hiding, before they had to leave the house and land, Tekla's family had hidden partisans. Tekla (still young and healthy) had told Petra (age five, age six) how her family knelt at night and said the rosary for these young people who stayed with them, brave young men who lived finally in the forest, emerged at night and struck blows, disappeared before daylight. Polish Catholics who gave aid to partisans were in greater danger than most, except of course for the Jews, the gypsies, the homosexuals. Sick in America on a Minnesota farm, Tekla cried, not histrionically, but quietly, day after day. Some periods were better, weeks even, but always the crying returned. Petra, second-grader, third-grader, competent student, was helpless before this. Outside, Witold doggedly plowed fields, milked cows. When he came in, his work finished for the day, or taking a long break, taking time for his wife, he sat at the bedside. He brought Tekla back to the present. America. "As free a place as humanity has learned to construct." He wiped Tekla's forehead with a cool washcloth. Petra was free then herself—to do homework, to read—before she made supper standing on a small wooden stool, or after she did the dishes, before bed. Witold reminded Tekla of their early love. He fought as a partisan but had time to fetch her, sit on a river bank, and talk about Polish freedom. "Remember, Tekla? Think of us, young and brave. Think of love in those times. You were so pretty and spunky, Tekla. So good. You cried more over a Catholic Pole being cruel to a Jew than when the Nazis...I myself learned from you. Remember how you chided me for my careless tongue? But let's not talk about all of that. Only, your beautiful tears come back to me." He reminded Tekla how she had begged and teased before the separation, trying to get him to stay in her family's attic but he said no, it was too dangerous for her family now, too dangerous for her. She wanted to stay with him, with his band, in the woods, but he took her home. She was too young, maybe next year. If they hadn't gotten their country back, maybe then. Time and again Petra heard him talk about the day he and Tekla found each other after they'd been separated, after her family ran, first to the east, thinking the Russians the more benign force, better at least than the Nazis, then every direction, away, away, looking for any safe place while the partisans, Witold among them, moved deeper and deeper into the forest. They'd lost each other, both were in agony over that, of course they were, but they found each other again. "Remember, Tekla? On the crowded platform at the train station, remember that kiss? You wore your red scarf that day." Petra, age nine, pretending to read, listened to her father pour out whole paragraphs, entire stories, at the bedside of his dying wife. She knew she was a privileged child, safe and free in America. The Nazis were not after her, nor the Russians. She'd never been raped, a peculiar and terrifying concept she puzzled over after Tekla cried out in her sleep, "Rape! Rape!" She followed the trail of dictionary entries, got lost in multiple meanings, but finally understood, or almost. She was learning. She was the daughter of a Polish partisan and his brave wife. Death was part of life. She had no right to feel alone and afraid. She turned back to her book. In San Francisco, putting Anya into her crib, Petra was impressed that a baby could rouse so much. She hadn't thought about her mother in a long time.

It was six months after the birth when she and Danny McGuire, Roo's cherished cousin, finally took Anya to Minnesota, visited Witold, and left him alone again. On that trip the two men played chess while she bathed the baby, visited Roo, or wandered down the road past fields half-harvested to where the hardwoods were turning color. The last day of the visit she picked her way carefully over the rough path to the creek, avoiding exposed tree roots. Anya gurgled, contented, riding in her blue backpack, sturdy legs dangling. At the creek she thought about Frederick. From the first moment, when Roo called, she suspected his death was the result of her leaving, deliberate; but she'd never know. He had no family other than a stepbrother who lived in Canada, someone she'd never met whose name escaped her. She was relieved not to have to contact family, not to have to tell them about the baby, express condolences. Where was Frederick buried, though? She hadn't asked—would Roo know?—and now it was time to leave. She walked back to the house, full of unnamed feelings, Anya heavy against her back. In the living room, Danny and Witold were talking about Immanuel Kant, how his ideas changed the history of Western thought. "The structure of the mind itself shapes the world, that's the radical insight," Witold was saying. There was almost a muted exclamation point. She'd never seen Witold sit down with a man the way he did with Danny that visit, one each side of the old green card table, playing chess, discussing philosophy.

"He talks to you?" she asked Danny. It was more accusation than question. She was at the wheel. They were on their way back to San Francisco. Guilt at leaving Witold made her cranky, unfairly. She glanced over her shoulder. Anya was asleep in the back seat, dark curls pressed against bright cheeks. The child had Frederick's hair. She imagined telling her daughter someday. "Your hair is so pretty, it's just like your daddy's hair. He was a good, smart man and you are a good, smart girl." And Anya would laugh and dance away to play with something she found in the tangle of growth at the back of the yard, some stone or worm or broken-off branch that she imagined into more than it was. Anya might be a writer. Better yet, an artist, making much of a worm resting on a twisted branch. But with Anya's genes, it was more realistic to think in terms of language. Petra let her daydreams fly but she could pull them back, like kites. She knew enough not to have firmly defined ambitions for a child. Anya would find her own way in the world, and she would allow it.

"Not much," Danny said.

"Not much what?" Danny laughed.

"You asked if your dad talked to me. I said, 'Not much.'"

"Oh. Sorry. My mind..."

"That's OK. Witold isn't exactly verbose, but there's a lot going on in that head. He's an interesting man, your father." Danny was more tolerant than Petra, more appreciative; but of course Witold wasn't his father. She wondered about Danny's family. Except for cousin Roo, who seemed more friend than family, he hadn't contacted relatives during this time in Minnesota. He didn't talk about the subject and she didn't ask. He was never secretive in any other way. She understood about the need for areas of privacy, her own being considerable. As were Witold's. "He's a locked box," she said. "I can't believe you found the key." Danny shrugged it off, not seeing the miracle. He said they should come back from time to time, let Witold in on how the baby grew. He liked traveling and he'd enjoy playing chess again. Petra and Danny were lovers, for the moment. They expected to be friends forever. This fit the model of their

15

time and place. Petra experienced pleasure with Danny. He listened, he was sweet, and his smell was good. He was younger than she by a couple of years, finding his way. She appreciated his malleability, how he looked up, curious, to see what life offered next. Frederick, old man of thirty, had already defined himself and that had been problematic. Danny was learning to play the harmonica—he called it his harp—going to smoky blues places, working here and there, determinedly avoiding the issues of college education and career. He'd left Minnesota the day after high school graduation, hitching rides from truck stop to truck stop. He liked hearing stories of men who rode the rails. He'd like to hop a boxcar himself but that might have to be with a friend because the prospect scared him some. Those old-time hoboes were his heroes but he didn't think he was made of the same stuff, at least not yet. He didn't imagine being tied down, ever. Petra said she didn't want to tie him down. She meant it.

San Francisco had produced invigorating, disorienting culture shock. She and Witold had lived inside silence. In San Francisco there was music, always. It went with the pot, peyote, mescaline, acid. Two of the women in the apartment played in something called the All Girl Band. She didn't understand they were lesbians for the longest time. After she stopped nursing Anya, she took some trips, but she hated the nausea that came with drugs. She had to learn the term—trips—though she found to her chagrin that it was common enough to be used by *Time* in an article on the San Francisco Phenomenon. She gave credit to LSD and peyote for revealing possibilities in her mind but what she liked best about her new life was how absolutely anything could be questioned, rethought—though this could bring on a feeling of being flung dangerously into space, unheld by gravity. Some of the roommates combined an interest in drugs with serious study of Revolution. They called themselves freaks, to differentiate: they were not hippies, not frivolous about rebellion. Petra read Mao, was told Trotsky was a better thinker, read Trotsky. San Francisco was not Minnesota. She happened into a crew of house painters and found she liked to climb long ladders. Some jobs gave a view of the Pacific. *An ocean.* Oceans were in movies, in myths. She kept working while the baby developed inside her, climbed high with a bigger and bigger belly. This was San Francisco, the seventies, there was no older generation to *tsk-tsk*, worry about safety,

16

ask why she wasn't using her college degree to make more money. She was proud of her balance, how she adapted to her changing body and kept climbing up, scraping and sanding and painting, climbing back down. Her coworkers, not universally comfortable with heights, influenced by various substances in the bloodstream, cheered. The cheers were loudest when she stepped onto a roof to get at woodwork around dormers, her specialty. It was a kind of attention she'd never had. After Anya was born she took breaks to go home and nurse her. Paid baby-sitters came and went. Danny kept himself generally separate from the child care—he felt a renewed need to make it clear he was not a family man—but he watched Anya when all else failed. People in the apartment helped out, but arrangements were fluid and Petra didn't like to leave her with anyone excessively stoned. She needed regular child care. She found Marian.

Marian was the Earth Mother type, warm and pure, older than Petra, a filled-out, comfortable person. She reminded Petra of warm, comfortable Roo back in Minnesota. Marian had the San Francisco look, colorful long skirts and shawls, wild red hair catching sunlight. She ate no meat. She took no drugs. *Not for years, honey, I'm a settled old lady now.* Marian had lived in San Francisco since she dropped out of high school, becoming a weaver. A feature story in the *Chronicle*—High School Dropout Weaves Dreams—gave her the chance she needed and now she had pieces on consignment in upscale shops. Her craft paid the rent and she understood her good luck. "But I could use more money." Having a baby come to visit and getting paid for the privilege sounded perfect. They made the arrangement. Anya was eighteen months old. She could walk and dance, but talking was in the future. Marian played Renaissance recorder music with a group of friends. When they played, Anya danced. Petra breathed relief. Marian was a gift from the Fates when the Fates were in a generous mood.

When she wasn't working, Petra enjoyed her time with Anya. She watched the solid little body operate in the world. Anya made friends with the cats and dogs in the neighborhood, the children in the park, and the housemates, a changing population. (But Danny stayed, Anya's good-natured friend, Petra's friendly ex-lover.) Anya had a ready smile and a ready temper. No one trampled her. Petra thought of her as shine, as essence. Then came toilet training. Girls were supposed to be easier, but

Anya wasn't easier. At two-and-a-half she was not yet trained. Also, she had started to talk. Petra was passionate about words. She wrote regularly, striving for clarity, for evocative images. She had expected to feel delight when her little girl acquired language but Anya's long slow process of learning to speak got tangled up with toilet training, with rages on the part of mother and daughter, with a caged feeling Petra was sure they both experienced. Anya liked to talk, wanted to talk constantly. Petra found herself shamefully bored. She wanted her own thoughts and couldn't find them. Her mind was the center of herself, she needed to feel it working. Unfocused, pulled this way and that by the demands of a toddler, her mind lost tone, a muscle weakened by disuse. Frustrated by interruptions, Petra stopped reading, stopped writing. After several months of this she was terrified. She went to secondhand bookstores, purchased old paperbacks: Henry James, Ezra Pound. The more difficult the better. She sat with pen in hand, read, took notes, tried to write. Her thoughts were dull and scattered, but she persisted. One day, interrupted for the fifth time in half an hour—she was counting—Petra learned what it was like to feel murderous, to want someone obliterated. Her daughter. This was more terrifying than the decay of her mind. She stopped reading and writing and turned to her will. If she could just strengthen her will, they might be all right. But she couldn't control her irritability. It spread to housemates. She lost tolerance for the changes, the new habits of each incoming person, the fluctuations in household cleanliness, the decibel level. She thought the order and predictability of living alone with Anya might be better, though she was reluctant to leave Danny, stable would-be hobo (he never did hop a train). Danny, her good friend, gay now. She moved to the Mission district where she could afford a small apartment for herself and Anya. The move made parenting no easier.

Paradox ruled Petra's relationship with Anya. In the worst times she felt the strongest ache of love for the child, saw beauty leaping around her like bright sprites out of old poetry, something by Alexander Pope she thought—and was pleased, irrationally pleased, when she remembered which poem. She had read "The Rape of the Lock" after her mother died and could almost see the words, feel the magic. Were the sprites there when the scissor snip broke the world apart? The lock of hair was taken, taken. It had been a new use of the terrible word rape. An

18

alleviation, a shift, a different sort of drama. *Incandescence*—her favorite word at the time—was there on the page. She thought, listening to one more question from Anya, longing for the time the child would be in bed, asleep, that she should look up the poem, see if it still sparkled, but she had no energy. The dread she'd felt inside marriage was back, the suffocation. Loving Anya was not enough. She started to meditate and attend yoga classes. She could breathe, felt hope. Anya turned three. In fifteen years the child would be old enough, on her own. Petra made it a mantra. Fifteen more years, fifteen more. Time slowed, but it didn't stop. She ripped pages from the calendar. May, gone. June, gone. July, finally gone. She could survive this thing she never should have started. Then Marian, Anya's stable, much-valued baby-sitter, told the truth.

It was a Tuesday. They sat in Marian's kitchen, just the two of them, talking about Anya. Danny had taken the child to the park. A new weaving hung on the wall, bright simple shapes crossing one another in the style of Calder's mobiles. This was a departure for Marian who tended to earth tones and symmetrical patterns. Was Marian suddenly happier? Braver? It was August now, and hot in a way San Francisco was rarely hot. Marian, fanning herself with an ad from the day's mail, confided that she had desperately wanted a child of her own but her tubes were clogged. Her uterus was not in great shape either. The two women, mother and babysitter, had never disclosed personal anguish. Petra felt a tremor. Precursor to earthquake. Imagined. Emotional in origin. As she well knew. Once started, Marian kept going. Pelvic Inflammatory Disease, she explained, a bad case of it. She had tried and tried to get pregnant, one man after another, blaming the guys. Finally she listened to her doctor and gave up hope. She told herself life was better without children, but the day she met Petra and Anya two years ago—two years! —she had gone home and cried. "That little girl broke into my heart. Made me want." It was a version of love at first sight. She was sorry she had pretended nonchalance when Petra asked her to babysit. She was so grateful. She cried, telling the story.

Marian was warmth and color to Petra's spare self. Just looking at her gave comfort to Petra who had lately remembered Tekla only as lost in illness, disappearing into death. Later, much later, the sudden wonder of Tekla's last moments would come back to her; when she could bear it. She would remember colorful toys, babushkas, Easter eggs

19

decorated in the Polish way, Tekla's strong stride through the woods, the full sure way the young mother laughed and played with her young husband Witold and with the child Petra, a little girl with a lively mother; but in this time when parenting Anya was dry duty, only the husk of Tekla remained. Even memories of the tears that were an integral part of Tekla's illness hid behind a wall in Petra's psyche along with the stories from Poland, the way Witold recreated the past for his sick, disoriented wife. Marian's tears, Marian's deep green eyes, the unexpected emotion and the strange heat of this San Francisco day coalesced. Here was fecundity, possibility. "Marian," she said, "I have to tell you about Anya and me." She told how she had set herself for the years of motherhood ahead as if she were a workhorse put into traces—the long furrows, the hot sun, plowing, plowing, interminable plowing—but she was not a workhorse, not bred for the job. If she had to choose again, she wouldn't have a child. It was her mind. She had failed to find a way to have a child and a mind both, could Marian understand that? Marian reached out, gathered her up. Tears came to Petra. *Because it's so warm*, she thought crazily. She'd been cold in San Francisco where the borderline climate did not demand central heating. By the end of the conversation she and Marian had made a decision neither could have anticipated. Anya would live with Marian. Petra would stay in her daughter's life, part-time caretaker. Like a divorced father. The child was three-and-a-half years old when she moved in with her new mother. Marian.

Petra experienced the separation physically, as if it were surgery on a battlefield, a part of herself cut away without anesthesia, but pain did not blur basic clarity, not then. Her pain was clear and her sense of release was equally clear. If Marian, godsent, had not come into their lives, she would have raised Anya, but Marian had come, and a painful choice had been made. In an agony of freedom, agreeing to what she believed was best for her daughter and herself, she survived. A long ropey scar remained—spiritual, real—evidence of severed connection, evidence of ordeal. Years later, clarity did blur. Youthful certainty crumbled. How could she have given up her child? But that was later.

Who could see into Anya? She adopted the name of the black cat, Marian's queenly Fire. "My name is Fire," said young Anya. They called her that for six months, until she said "My name is Anya, call me Anya." It seemed she had come to terms. She was still bright and spunky.

Shining. The two women were concerned, but hopeful. They leaned into one truth: the child was wanted now without reservation.

Chapter Three

Petra puts the book down. *Tender Buttons* has in the past led her down secret pathways and offered her a sense of things intercut and shimmering. Gertrude Stein: Pied Piper. The sum of the book equaled the sum of life. Objects. Food. Rooms. Domesticity, physicality, philosophy, all placeable, available, for delight—some essence of the freedom (and, to be honest, ecstasy) Petra wants from reading. None of that tonight. She turns again to the first paragraph. Surely the first paragraph...

A CARAFE, THAT IS A BLIND GLASS

A kind in glass and a cousin, a spectacle and nothing strange a single hurt color and an arrangement in a system to pointing. All this and not ordinary, not unordered in not resembling. The difference is spreading.

A tangle of words. Has she no Steinian intelligence tonight? She tries again. Nothing. She closes the book, fluffs up her pillow, turns out the light.

*

Petra ponders her plate after breakfast: an arrangement of crumbs, a smear of butter. This morning she feels alert, interested. *Crumbled Time on White with Narrow Blue Echoes.* The plate is rimmed with blue lines. The leavings of breakfast await the dishpan. Life is itself, she recognizes it. DWELL, Dykes Who Love Literature, meets this afternoon. The group was organized by Petra and Roo (Eleanor) McGuire. Roo: old friend from Minnesota, Petra's bridesmaid, that warmest element on the day she married Frederick; Roo, who lent her money to fly away from Frederick to San Francisco; Roo, Danny's cousin, transplanted to Maine, who convinced her to come to Maine when she was sunk into grief over Anya's death; and gave her a place to stay; and introduced her to Nat—Nat Levesque, former lover, steady friend—who is also in the group. As is Roo's partner, Jessie Brooks. Big, somewhat tattooed, Jessie was a Massachusetts foster kid addicted to thrills and trouble. Motherhood remade her—"part-way"—as did Roo, and (Petra loves this) tai chi classes. Now Jessie is damn-near civilized, as she herself puts it. Last winter Ricki Harding joined them: Roo's shy-bold student with the lively, earnest, somehow practical mind and the so-far-unmentioned anomalous right hand—the small hand with little stubs for fingers, a tiny stub of thumb. In the spring, pregnant black-braided Bright Star arrived: enigma, conundrum, riddle, puzzle. How many words are there for this woman? *Is* she, for example, Native American? Nat is fifty-four. Jessie is fifty. (Her birthday bash last week was chem-free and cross-cultural, biker dykes from Massachusetts dancing with tame Maine folk.) Roo is forty-nine, matching Petra. Bright Star is thirty-five. (They dragged that out of her, she tends toward secrecy.) Ricki is just a kid, a college sophomore, age nineteen. Fifty-four to nineteen: not a bad range. Baby Chippie should be added to the list. She attends regularly and contributes a well-placed *goo* from time to time, which might be an intelligent contribution to any discussion of *Tender Buttons*. Petra admits to feelings all askew about this baby. She is unnerved, she is charmed, she goes vague, she hesitates, she freezes, she melts. Talking to Gertrude changed none of that. So be it. She sips coffee, looks into the backyard and down into the woods. It is a crisp blue-sky perfect Maine day in autumn. Talking to Gertrude wasn't so bad. Maybe it will help with Helga.

Tender Buttons. Every time she picks it up she has a new experience. She read it in the spring when DWELL first tackled it and again earlier this week, before the session with Helga unsettled her mind. It can't be pulled to sweet softness, shaped neatly, wrapped in waxed paper—she is thinking of taffy—and saved for another day. This can be exasperating (last night) or intriguing (today, she hopes, though time is passing and she plans to shop and vacuum before the meeting). She takes her plate to the sink, washes it and sets it in the drainer. She pours a second cup of coffee, goes to the living room, opens Stein's book. *A CARAFE, THAT IS A BLIND GLASS.* She thinks of a container for wine, but knows carafe might have more meanings. She gets the dictionary. Carafe: container for water or wine. No alternate meanings, no mystery. However, the word has traveled. It comes to English from the French who got it from the Italians who got it from the Spaniards who got it from the Arabian word *gharafa*, "to dip." She decides Gertrude Stein knew all of this. The game with *Tender Buttons* is to take liberties, imagine knowing. Dipping; birds in a bird bath, minor immersions; a little of this, a hint of that; layering, overlapping, arranging. Stein: literary cubist, friend of Picasso. The Spaniard. Carafe: word with Spanish blood. Is this a tribute to Gertrude's friend Pablo? They must have drunk wine together. *Ah, friendship.*

Petra sips her coffee. Helga has friends, thanks be to the gods. She herself could not have gotten through the time after giving up Anya without friends. Danny, especially. Sudden sex, in the form of Sal, helped too. After Danny, she knew she'd someday turn to women. She felt at ease with lesbians by then and there would be an added benefit: no danger of pregnancy. Still, it wasn't until age twenty-five, and Sal—brief, painful, thrilling distraction from the ache of giving up Anya—that Petra had sex with a woman. Finally: sexual passion. The urgency, the intensity. Danny had been sweet, but this was something of another order. Sal was smart, raw, sexy, and controlling. She had a husband, a boyish, sub-assertive Australian who wore a white frilly apron and met Petra at the door with a plate of cookies. Everyone said he couldn't quite bring himself to yield to a man so Sal was his best bet. His best bet and Petra's adventure; until Sal moved on to her next Lady. She thinks of Sal with pleasure, the pain long past, the forgiveness complete.

Stein was with Alice B. for seven years by the time *Tender Buttons* was published. The book is full of her: Alice and sex and sewing and cooking; passion and domesticity; irritability and good humor. And writing. To take the language and rearrange it. To insist: *not unordered in not resembling.* Being different, writing differently, was not chaos. Did Alice wear glasses? Petra can't remember. The *spectacle* that this new writing will be, the *spectacle* that Gertrude and Alice, strange couple, are (but *nothing strange*, says Gertrude), could hide the final "s" of spectacles, needed for myopia. Petra could stay in this little section all morning. She sees the *pointing*, imagines Gertrude fearing the world, how it will point at her, laughing, unkind, but everything here is reversible. Gertrude herself is pointing to a way of using language, a new arrangement. There will be fame: *The difference is spreading.* Or it's the wine spreading through the body; or spilled over the table because the carafe is broken, everything is broken here. Broken and reassembled. Petra urgently hopes Helga is with a friend.

Enough. She takes her cup to the sink, gets out the vacuum cleaner, wonders what she'll bring home from the store. The week's groceries have to be gotten. Chippie comes tomorrow.

*

Sunday. The day after the strangest DWELL meeting ever. As cubist as Stein's book. Petra paces her living room with Chippie who likes to be walked while having her juice, or does today, being fussy. So Petra walks, watching the angle of the bottle, admiring the strong sucking. This little critter knows what she wants.

What *happened* yesterday?

She stops at the window. The leaves might go, torn loose by the coming storm. Public radio offers *Goldberg Variations*, Glenn Gould at the piano. Chippie, sucking, gazes at her. She returns the look, looks away, looks back into unapologetic baby eyes. The baby is better at eye contact than she is.

They made a rough circle: Nat and Roo at either end of the couch; Bright Star and Ricki across from each other, sitting on pillows on the floor; Jessie and Petra in the two stuffed chairs. Bright Star laid Chippie on the floor on a woolen blanket crowded with American Indian designs, simplicity spoiled by excess. Always before, Bright Star had held the baby, never letting her go. *Overly Blended Baby*, Petra had thought in the past, then chided her own intolerance: a normal mother might want to hold a baby close. Yesterday on the blanket, unglued from her mother but not liberated, Chippie became *Invisible Indian Infant*: brown skin, black hair, little Indian outfit almost lost in the blanket's complications. Petra wondered once again whether pale, freckled Bright Star with her currently light brown kinky hair and her perfect little Indian baby had even one drop of Native blood. The question had been there since the day they met. The breakdown of Petra's washing machine had sent her, grumpy, to the laundromat during what she had hoped would be a long noon hour spent catching up on paperwork. A pregnant woman sat cross-legged on the counter. Her dyed black hair with half an inch of pale brown showing at the roots was pulled into two braids. The sight irritated

Petra. The place was empty except for the two of them and she'd rather have had it to herself. Perfunctorily on duty, not a customer as it turned out, the woman was wearing two political buttons. The first said, "How Dare You Assume I Am Heterosexual?" The second looked homemade. It said, "Or white?" The first one roused in Petra a grudging flicker of interest. She'd worn that very button herself in San Francisco, marching for Gay Rights, and was amused to see it here, in the nineties, pinned to the shirt of a pregnant woman. She agreed, of course. How dare anyone assume anything about another's sexuality? The second felt like a warning: this woman might not be what she seemed, which was plain Maine white, and anyone around her had better take heed. The hair, straining for the American Indian look but with those roots showing, could have been another warning: this might not be the sanest person she'd ever met. The woman picked up a book and started reading. Unbelievable: the book was Judy Grahn's *Really Reading Gertrude Stein*, the very one she'd brought with her, preparing for DWELL's first discussion of *Tender Buttons*.

Some coincidences can't be brushed away. Petra invited Bright Star to join DWELL. She accepted. She arrived with freshly dyed hair, exposed roots gone, black braids firmly in place, an engaging, almost flirtatious way about her. She seemed comfortable with Stein, so playful and intuitive that Petra was envious. The others accepted her despite that fact that Petra had broken a group rule by inviting a new member without discussion. They liked the laundromat story and there was precedent. Roo hadn't consulted the group before inviting Ricki. Spontaneity—or was it destiny?—trumped consensus.

When DWELL met again in the fall Bright Star had light brown hair, no braids, and a baby who looked entirely Native American. No one commented on the hair. Chippie drew a whirl of attention and the group turned to poetry. This was a good baby who took the breast well, slept in her mother's arms through the rise and fall of energetic discussion, woke to add a gurgling opinion. She had lively eyes and with each meeting got better at using them. She was particularly adept at mesmerizing Nat. The topic of the mystery father was barely broached. Ricki tried once. Bright Star turned glacial, haughty. Ricki did not repeat the question. Petra took note.

When the bottle is empty Petra puts Chippie to her shoulder, gets up from the couch where she has been allowed to settle, and walks again. The *Goldberg Variations* continue. The baby burps.

Deep into yesterday's meeting, Chippie woke from her sleep on the floor with a screech. Bright Star looked stunned and disoriented. She hesitated long enough for Petra to think of reaching for the baby herself. When Bright Star did pick up her daughter it was an awkward operation. Awake, the baby was disengaged, her eyes wandering, her attention vague. Bright Star held her as is if she were an inert bundle, which she almost was. Petra worried she might be sick. Bright Star's own presence was inconsistent, unpredictable; but not as if she were distracted by mothering concerns, she barely seemed to be a mother. None of this was usual. When Bright Star had something to say about *Tender Buttons* it was as if she ran up to take center stage, delivered her lines a tad too dramatically, and jumped back down into the audience, self-conscious, eyes tensed, all the while holding the baby as if she were an irrelevant object. This would have been disturbing enough, but there was more. Added in were moments when Bright Star *looked* at Petra; as if the two of them had a secret; or as if imploring; or, worst, as if adoring. No one else seemed to notice. Petra felt magnetized into a bizarre private drama.

Chippie coos, contented. It is bright, reliable Mozart on the radio now. The forecast for high winds and rain has been changed. The storm will likely go out to sea, as so many do.

When Roo suggested that they each come up with an image for *Tender Buttons* Petra's first thought was *kaleidoscope*. She talked about pieces of glass, mirrors, designs that change and change. She said, "And then there's that moment—there *is* such a moment, isn't there?—when you catch the chaos of the transition, the time between patterns." No one said anything. She added, "The time *between* might be most relevant here." The group laughed. The word—between—had come up before. *Tender Buttons* could trap a reader between levels, between places that might make sense if only you had sufficient intelligence, or inspiration. Just then, Bright Star *looked* at her; and immediately withdrew, shriveled into herself. Chippie was a dormant bundle. Petra had the strongest impulse to reach out and take the baby away. Again, no one else seemed to notice. Roo took up the kaleidoscope theme. "I loved mine," she said. "I must have been about eight when I got it. They still make them. My niece got one for her birthday." She went into a little wandering riff, as she was prone to do, arriving finally at the origin of the word. "It's from three Greek words. *Beautiful* and *form* and *to aim at*. Isn't that just perfect?"

Bright Star was apparently back, mentally present, ostensibly normal. Possibly she'd never left. Chippie was simply sleeping. The baby had a right to sleep, didn't she?

Now, belly full of apple juice, Chippie sleeps again despite a sudden booming Beethoven.

Roo wandered on. "I love how it's all done with mirrors—like stage magic—just colored glass and a turn of the wrist and *chance*. Wasn't it a life passage, finding out about the mirrors? A sort of growing up ritual? When I think back..." Jessie reached to touch Roo on the arm, the lover's prerogative. Roo got the message and interrupted herself. "I guess I got off on a track. *Tender Buttons*—my image—for me it's like a walk in the woods, with paths that take so many turns you get lost but, getting lost, you *see* something."

Bright Star, too suddenly, too loudly, said, "It *is* a mirror. You look and see yourself and you look *pretty*." Which, besides being out of context was way too childlike. It didn't ring true, not at all.

Jessie's reaction was to laugh, almost to mock. "Pretty?"

But Ricki took the comment seriously. "What do you mean, pretty?"

Bright Star was miffed. "Just pretty," she said.

"Oh." Ricki was chastened. Poor Ricki.

No one else spoke. Petra felt guiltily relieved. She had *not* been imagining things. Then Bright Star, as if nothing unusual had happened and as if the word mirror had not already been mentioned, said, "To me, the book seems like a mirror. I look into it and see the entire world reflected. Time is transcended. Everything is placed next to everything else. Simplicity is achieved." It was an enclosed speech, inviting no comment. Pretentious, thought Petra, but she saw that Ricki was looking at Bright Star with—what?—respect, and something like *fondness*. A nearly *intimate* fondness. Nat and Roo and even Jessie appeared quietly interested, nothing more. Petra felt alone again, but the next moment Chippie, awake and alert, drew her attention with lively searching eyes.

The baby was herself. She smiled and Petra smiled back. Oh, hell, she thought, let it go.

Ricki, looking determined—their young brave college girl could still turn shy—started to talk. "I think the book is a puzzle. It can't be solved, but sometimes I get that feeling...you know that feeling?...of being right on the verge of solving it."

Petra said, "That feels good or bad?"

"Mostly good. Well, not every time. It's like driving around, looking for a place you've never been to, and then you think you find the right road and you'll see the place in a minute."

"That's when my anxiety shoots up," Petra said.

"I like it," Ricki said. "You might not be anywhere near the place you're looking for, you might be way off. That's OK, too."

"It is? It sounds like getting lost," Petra said.

"It only matters—getting lost—if there's a time limit," Ricki said, her voice suddenly losing timbre. She looked at Bright Star, and quickly looked away. Bright Star was blank and distant. Ricki started to massage her anomalous hand with her normal one. She hadn't done this before.

Jessie looked at Ricki, at what she was doing with her hands, took a visible breath, and said, "All right. I'll try to say this whole thing. First, this book changes. Depending. If I'm tired, it works like a monster machine for churning brain cells, making them into something like butter. Brain cells do not like this." Listening to Jessie pull her thoughts out was like watching a careful worker. This wasn't her natural arena, this literary business. In their early days together, Roo was smart enough not to push poetry on Jessie. Finally Jessie cautiously (Roo insisted to Petra that Jessie could be cautious) asked for a recommendation. Roo suggested Wilfred Owen. The young poet-soldier captured Jessie Brooks, former foster child. *By his dead smile I knew we stood in hell* was the crucial line. OK, she'd try this DWELL thing. Petra listened to Jessie and simultaneously gave herself a little lecture. Bright Star was odd today, no question about that, but her own state was hardly placid. She was probably overreacting to the mother in their midst. Possibly. "But sometimes when I'm reading this book," Jessie said, leaning forward, "the sentences have so much...I don't know, they're just completely themselves. Something goes from my gut up to my throat—it's a physical thing. It shoots down and sort of, well...takes my cunt. It's just plain sex,

29

no other way to say it. Then it travels back to my brain and lights it up." Petra found this impressive and true. Roo was smiling to herself, Jessie's fond lover. But why had Ricki looked at Bright Star so...fondly? Jessie leaned back, her energy apparently spent, but then looked at Ricki, winked, and said, "You know?" Ricki bit her lip, blushed, and stopped the business with her hands.

Roo, obviously pleased, quoted Stein: "'A green acre is so selfish and so pure and so enlivened.'" Jessie said, "Hmmm." She grinned her slow grin and said, "'All the wonder of six little spoons.'" Ricki caught on, joined in, quick and shy and bold all at once: "'The sister was not a mister. Was this a surprise. It was.'" Her steady brown eyes lit up. Resilient girl. Petra was charmed, loving everyone. *Dance a clean dream,* she thought, and almost said it, but Bright Star jumped onto the stage, reciting loudly. "'A sudden slice changes the whole plate, it does so suddenly.'" Then she took her front row seat in the audience, eyes tensed. Petra's response: I am not, definitely not, making this up. Ricki didn't look at Bright Star fondly this time. She looked down into her lap and started, again, to massage her small hand. Were they ever going to talk about that hand? Nat, who'd been even more inward than usual, looked up, looked around, smiled warmly, and said, "I like this one: 'Pick a barn, a whole barn, and bend more slender accents than have ever been necessary, shine in the darkness necessarily.' Isn't that like chaos theory? The whole book sings chaos theory. Fractals."

Now it was Petra smiling fondly. Everything sang chaos theory to Nat. "I don't know about fractals," she said, "but Gertrude and Alice are here...the plump one and the thin one, the barn and the needle...well, the needle isn't in the quote. It's probably close by in the text, or, if it's not, it should be. That phrase—'bend more slender accents'—has to be about slender Alice, and the writing, too, and it's so...what's the word?...delicate."

Petra felt happiness. A surprise burst of happiness.

Chippie, fed and burped, has fallen asleep. Petra puts her into the bassinet, a garage sale find. Clean and cheap, the bassinet seemed a sign: she had done the right thing, offering to babysit. She pulls up a chair, intrigued by her need to sit and contemplate a sleeping baby. But what the hell was Bright Star was up to? What was *wrong* with the woman?

Chapter Four

The plan was to keep everything in place. Her bed is made, her teeth have been brushed. Unbelievably, she has flossed. Only the weather has slipped into rebellion. The sun has not yet risen and already the air is warm. Warm and soft and wrong. October should be crisp.

Standing in the open doorway of her trailer, looking out into the woods, Bright Star sips coffee from her plainest mug, the pure white one. The tiny kitchen is at her back, the stainless steel sink, shape inside shape. There are no dirty dishes. She doesn't expect to control the weather, not quite, but the aberration makes her nervous. Inhale, she directs herself, and takes in the odors. Warm air, the first fallen leaves, this excellent coffee. All very pleasant, she has to admit. She should improve her attitude, decide the strangeness of the weather matches the strangeness of the day and is therefore perfect.

All right, it's perfect: Saturday morning, sunrise coming, and she's in Maine where she's always been and it's warm and the world smells terrific. Also, this is the seventh day after her final DWELL meeting. Seven is a good number. The best. And there's this: she entered and exited the group to the tune of the same song, Miss Gertrude Stein's *Tender Buttons*, and thus the circle closed. True, she missed a beat or two during that last meeting, but she participated, offered thoughts, received thoughts, remembered the baby. She was sufficient.

She likes fall. Disintegrating leaves make a good death smell, but that might not be the ideal topic for this morning. Here's the sun, sudden bright knife at the gap in the woods. Time to get started.

The heavy clay sculpture sits in the middle of the living room, a two-sided figure joined at the back like Siamese twins, two heads, two round, sagging bellies, four big arms and four big legs. Viewed from one side this is a Native American woman, from the other, a white woman. Both sit cross-legged on a rough puce base. They are not actually Siamese twins. Of course not. The Native American makes a firm oval with her empty arms, miming an invisible baby into existence. Her left

31

breast is bared for nursing and clay milk hangs in mauve droplets from the nipple. Her white counterpart is in the act of committing suicide, knife to heart. Both generous bellies rest under stretches of clayed cloth, giving in to gravity with a sigh of relief.

But now is no time for sighs of relief. The sun is up. The work begins: Bright Star nudges the clay figure into the bathroom, determined and cautious. No damage must be done. *Careful. That's it. Just a little...* She knew it would be tight. She'll manage. *Wait. Now: push!* The thing is in, unharmed. Might be good to take a break, relax. She puts the toilet lid down and sits, an artist assessing her work. She struggled with this piece during the whole of her third trimester, ignoring her growing bulk, persisting despite considerable inner resistance, and brought it to completion before labor pains started, as planned. Then she had the baby, as planned. Chippie. That was four months ago today. She is reasonably satisfied with the sculpture. Times come when she's downright ecstatic about it, in love with it, married to it, but at the moment she feels a neutralizing artistic distance. Even the white legs of the suicide, sometimes unbearable, are simply what they are, aspects of a work of art. Fallen Goddess. Sometimes the name is embarrassing, sometimes a wonder. At the moment it seems apt, nothing more.

Names have never been simple for her. A mess of embarrassment and ecstasy is often what she gets. It's that way with her own name. Born Raymona Weeks, she's been Bright Star since the day she turned twenty-one, fourteen long years ago. Bright Star: ridiculous, juvenile, narcissistic, she sometimes thinks, but the name was an elemental arrival, a sound bestowed, a word that confirmed—finally—her Native American identity. Besides, it was mandated.

Her first days as Bright Star were challenging. Imagine: the need to be Indian, exposed. She told Raymond first. Raymond, half-brother, who has to accept whatever she tells him. With courage camouflaged in nonchalance, in icy pride, she said, "By the way, my name is Bright Star now. That's what you should be calling me." Doing dishes, her back to him. She knew it was rude. Later she tried to make amends, told him about the dream, how the name was delivered by an invisible messenger, how it was carved into a piece of black rock—onyx, she thought—*Bright Star*, in silver script. There was a cool ring of fire around messenger, an aura of mission. Of mandate. "And drumming, Raymond. *Drumming.*"

He calls her Bright Star at least once every time they're together. She knows he does it consciously, conscientiously, as a kindness. She herself is not kind, that's not her way. She's used to the name now, tells it almost as if it has no significance; and hopes the listener is aware; and hopes such awareness is kept hidden. The baby's name is even more complicated, but she won't think about the baby. Today's rule against that is a necessary one. *Get back to Artist Mode.*

Fallen Goddess. Short, squat, heavy. Solid. From that foundation, freedoms: a jumble of hues and tones, a dire clashing. Reds, blues, mauves, olives, red-brown, off-white, black; splashes of pale pink and spring green. The figure itself is glazed thickly, glossily. The puce base is a dull matte. Necessary: a base that would not match the figure, would not reflect, would absorb. She remembers the decision, doesn't regret it. But pink and spring green? *What is, is.* The Pueblo woman—or is she Navajo?—is unaware her baby is missing, unaware her serene face bears war paint. Some things are clearer than others. That this is war paint is known, perhaps even researched. Ricki Harding, latest love, byproduct of the experience with DWELL, questioned the war paint, but only once. Ricki's curiosity, her freshness, her reliability, her *hand*—all of that was welcome. But the questioning of decisions firmly made was not needed. Ricki learned. And she could keep a secret. Few could have done as well.

The impulse to use war paint came during hot, slippery, distracting sex. Colors appeared: deep red, absolute black, pulsing, then bursting. A wild entertainment. She was aroused and amused, nothing more, but then the shift: red and black plunging through chaos, a terrifying, exhilarating free fall. She was alert, wary. The colors settled, became design. A chorus of voices chanted: *war paint, war paint.* The phrase made sudden brilliant sense. She answered, "Fine, yes, great." Which simple-hearted Ricki took as a comment on the sex. Those pure moments still come, it's not as if life has gone flat. Quite the opposite. Look at the quirky clarity achieved here, war paint on a nursing mother. Look at the missing child, the power of illusion. Very satisfying. Artistically, very satisfying. Just yesterday, a new idea for a series of miniatures, not that it matters. *Leave Ricki in the act of innocent sex. Do not bring her into this day.*

Right. We agree.

Not even the anomalous hand?

33

The question is mischievous, unexpected, but she can handle it. So to speak. Anomalous was a new word. She feels the syllables rolling in her mouth and watches her mind fix on Ricki's hand, the sensation of the umbilical cord wound tightly around the embryo's arm above the wrist. She remembers asking, not having intended to. "Why is your hand that way?" It was rude, but Ricki just told the medical truth. Her own unruly mind invaded the womb, felt the circulation cut, the hand struggling through weeks and months. In dreams it became *her* hand, then her whole being, struggling. Then it turned into a little art object. Awake, she would take each undeveloped stub of finger between her lips, sucking like a calf, one sweet teat after another. The hand made Ricki easy to seduce. Who else could see the beauty? Ah, Ricki, you have been damn near perfect.

Refocus. Hair. Think about clay hair.

Right. Yes. OK.

Both sides of the Goddess have excellent hair. Hours of detailed work went into texturizing each coarse strand. When she completed the hair, pride surged. This she remembers. The actual feeling isn't available today, of course. Still: damn good Indian braids and the white woman's wild locks do please a person. Another good thing: perched on the right knee of the Indian is a small mouse with shiny red clay fur, a little critter with charisma. It sits on its haunches, businesslike. Its empty arms make a circle, sweetly reflecting the empty arms of the woman. But...where's the ball of cheese?

Where the hell is the blasted ball of cheese?

Specks of cheese stick to the glossy red fur arms, proof it was once there. Looking around, she almost steps on the little orange ball. The thought of crushing it sends a shudder through her. She can't move. Damn. She cannot move at all. *This is not a crisis.* She shakes herself free; picks up the cheese; places it in the arms of the mouse. *Stay crisp.*

She puts the episode out of her mind. Time to get the Goddess rightly placed. She chose the trailer for this large bathroom but the sculpture takes up more space than she imagined. Her guts clench. Measuring should have been on the list. Her crisp mind softens and fear rushes in, again. *You know what to do.* She does. She sits down on the floor, waits, facing the Native American side, preferring not to acknowledge the white and suicidal aspect of her work. Warmer and warmer air drifts through the bathroom window. No improvement. She gets up, turns the sculpture around. Acts of courage create courage. A kitchen knife—real, not clay—penetrates the bloodied white breast. *I am Bright Star, I face what I make.* Muscles bulge under the thick gloss as both hands grip the knife. No war paint here, it wasn't even considered. This face is a simple peaceful mask of unshadowed off-white paint. As it should be. She remembers the absence of ambivalence. And the hair: olive green, a mess. She remembers the work, how she followed each twisted bit, teased the clay into shape, used instruments, fingernails, more patience than she thought she possessed, and got this great hair. *Better.* The morning presents a challenge, she notes. *Well, of course it does. Death is a major passage.* The clay white woman has no little mouse companion but she, Bright Star Weeks who intends to kill herself, will not feel pity this morning for anything, living or clay. She turns the sculpture around again and feels the relief.

She sits down cross-legged on the floor. *Legs. Think about legs.* Her own are long and strong, not short and bulky like those of the Goddess. Under these jeans they're excessively white, she knows that, but they've been great when she needed to run. The Goddess can't run, the Goddess is an essential sitter, planted in this Buddha posture. For the Goddess this is no problem. These are new thoughts. New thoughts still come. A waste? But her concern can't be about waste. Her concern is to stay sharp, do what needs doing. She contemplates the triumph of clay hair. She loves hair. Ricki's is good, always clean, soft, well-cut. Short and brown; shiny. To match her shining brown eyes. Which match Chippie's. *No thinking about the baby.* Ricki was the right choice. Raymond will make sure she survives what comes next. The baby will survive, too. *Best not to think about the baby. Look at the Goddess.* War paint. Red-brown skin. Calm.

Bright Star sits. She feels the warm air, unusual for October, just as it should be. This is on the list, this sitting and waiting, under the admonitory heading Take Frequent Breaks. Everything that matters is going according to plan. Ease is not expected. She is Bright Star. *Stay crisp.*

*

35

Raymond Weeks is working at the Bangor Public Library showing a spry little white woman with white hair and interesting wrinkles how to get on the internet. The woman says her name is Margie Stokes and she has a skunk under her barn and she doesn't want to shoot it and she doesn't want it to settle in for the winter though she supposes once winter comes she won't see hide nor hair but she's heard a person can learn all manner of thing with computers and she'd like to try.

Raymond smiles. Good to be at work. This week's been rough. Raymona—or Bright Star as she calls herself—has her plan clear now. He knows he can't stop her. What he doesn't know is when. Could be today, tomorrow, a year from now. Margie Stokes is having a hard time with the mouse. Shaky hand, maybe what they call palsy, but she seems sharp. When Raymona makes up her mind, there's no changing it. He thought about taking her to someone, but she could outmaneuver any shrink. Besides, she'd never go, says dying is the Final Quest and he should understand. Crazy. Margie's getting control of the mouse already. Good for her. He investigated the law some, thinking there might be an angle, a way to stop her. It took him back, doing the research. He didn't do much himself but some of the older kids at the Youth Center looked into the legal peculiarities of everything they could think of, in case they needed the information in the future. They had to use books, it's that far back. Staff was happy to help, figuring that if a juvenile delinquent wanted to read a page of anything that wasn't pornographic it had to be a good thing. The librarian at the Center would get you what you wanted unless it was dirty. Now, of course, there's the internet. He found out the law doesn't make it easy to stop a person from killing himself, or, in this case, herself. He'd have to catch her in the act or get her to admit her intention. No chance of either one. He grins when Margie whoops over a skunk showing up on her screen. Vinegar or bleach can take the odor away, and of course tomato juice, which she's always known, who doesn't know that? But what about the actual skunk? She sees right through advertising by folks who would do it for her and doesn't mind saying so. She hasn't come here to learn how to spend money. The very idea! Off she goes in a huff before he can say there must be more information on another site. Spunky.

Bright Star—he tries to remember to stick to the name even in his thoughts—is off to Portland to sell her unique art. Probably too occupied to kill herself today, so he should relax. If only she hadn't told him, but she had to once she went and told Ricki, probably in bed. She could have spilled the beans on herself without meaning to. Maybe Ricki was witness to a time when she got herself curled up in a ball, panicky and kid-like, unable to hold her information. Maybe she had a plan all along to tell Ricki. Hard to go out with no word to anyone. He feels bad about Ricki. She's young for this and not from inside the family where it's normal to contemplate things most people would be shocked by. She acts like she's handling it OK but that's probably cover. He hopes she'll call on him if she gets too tangled inside herself. Himself, he's known for years it was coming. Raymona used to try to get him to join her, which is probably the one and only thing he ever said no to her about. Well, that and when she told him he had to make a baby with her and fulfill his destiny. She sure can be crazy. Sane, too, and smart. She's probably the most interesting person he'll ever meet. Damn, she can bring on the worst helpless feeling. He goes back to checking out books. It's a little rough that he's only working until two today. Just can't shake the heebie-jeebies.

*

Bright Star has moved into a supremely practical, businesslike mode. She stands, arms akimbo, looking at the Fallen Goddess. Which side should face the tub? Why didn't she decide this ahead of time? Another flaw in the day. Well, it won't be the last. She closes her eyes, rearranges her energy, ponders. She still can't decide which aspect of the sculpture should face the tub so she moves briskly to the next task, bringing stereo speakers into the bathroom, setting the speakers where they barely fit, one each side of the toilet. Once things start, everything has to be contained within this room. Nothing can enter from outside, including sound. The window, now open, will of course be closed. It's crowded in here with the Goddess and the speakers and the little wooden stand she brought in yesterday. Not ideal, but appropriate. Crowding is part of the problem. Not a useful thought. So here's the Goddess. Two faces, two fronts, and a bulk of fused body. Two races, two tasks. A person does have to wonder whether the thing is nothing more than an oversimplification of what can't be made simple. Sometimes the damn

Goddess flattens unbearably. Art that goes flat is like bad caricature, lifeless. Another useless thought. The thing can leap back to life, has done so repeatedly, which is why it was kept safe when other pieces were demolished, and why it was chosen to be the focal point of the morning's event. The center.

She sits on the floor, leans against a patch of bathroom wall and corrects her thought. The Goddess will be *one* center. There are many today: music, words, tools, water, body. None more important than the others. Beware the delusion: the longing for a single-centered purity of being has never been completely extinguished. This has been a substantial longing, something to contend with again and again. She can almost see its shadow out of the corner of her eye. It was long ago personified, a fact she wishes she could dismiss. There it is, though, looking like a delicate version of herself, lying on its back, then raising itself weakly on two skinny elbows, straining to keep its head up: the old longing, Wanting-To-Be-One, waiting, pathetically, just outside bathroom door. Damn. She gets up and walks past the Goddess and shuts the door. Banished, the figure will evaporate. It's nothing but temptation under present circumstances. She sits down, leans against the cool wall. When in doubt act, distract, intellectualize. Judy Grahn, author of *Really Reading Gertrude Stein* is a big fan of the idea of many centers. She enjoyed Grahn's book but she didn't need it. Stein isn't hard to understand. Her own mind works just like *Tender Buttons*. The DWELL ladies say the little book is supposed to be a cubist piece of writing. So maybe her mind is a work of art, original as a Picasso. She giggles. Her mind *is* a work of art. It uses brain cells for paint. She takes a deep breath, warns herself not to go too far.

So. Here she is, thinking about Pablo Picasso, cubist painter, and his old dyke friend Gertrude Stein who is the author of *The Autobiography of Alice B. Toklas* and *Tender Buttons* and probably a whole lot else or why would she be so famous? Is it not amazing that on this particular morning she, Raymona Weeks, has such facts in her mind? It is. Is it not amazing that she ended up in a group like DWELL? She lights a cigarette, which upsets some of the inside aspects of herself but who could make a strong argument against it today? She never smokes when she's that other Bright Star but now she's this one. Let them lump it. DWELL. Dykes Who Energetically Entirely Enthusiastically Love

Literature. The ladies don't seem quite clear what the E stands for and they don't seem to mind this blank space in their sureness. It was Fate that caused events to converge and bring her to DWELL, though some would call it serendipity. She was pregnant, about seven months along, and working at the laundromat. Things were slow so she was reading, trying to grasp the line of logic in Judy Grahn's thoughts on Gertrude Stein. This was a different kind of reading for her, but she made it a habit to read, start to finish, any book a patron left behind. This way Fate could have a nice big hand in her quest for an education. She'd picked up romance novels, which appealed to some parts of her, and mysteries, and some really hot science fiction, but she didn't find literary criticism lying on the old plastic chairs. Just did not happen. Except that day, the day Petra Kalinowski came in, hauling laundry to be done. Talk about Fate. Stronger than God is good old Fate. She read that once somewhere and took to it.

She was on duty, sitting on the counter, reading her confiscated book by Judy Grahn, author of a poem called "Edward the Dyke," or so it said on the back cover. "Always read the back cover first, Miss Bright Star." This was advice from her favorite john, the one with a sense of humor and a mind not only educated but built large to begin with. Edgar, well along into middle age, could have been her father, he was that old. Poor guy. He had a sick and forever dying wife. Once the missus finally did die, he stopped using her services. No johns lately. Wouldn't be fitting, once the pregnancy was accomplished and now the baby... She'd like to know who left that Judy Grahn book. She suspects the scrawny woman with the two little boys, the one who bribes her kids with candy and reads text books while she does laundry. So along came this person who turned out to be Petra, small person with a strong private aura around her, dark short hair cut plain, white woman, not pretty and not ugly. Something dark around the eyebrows. Guarded. Challenging. There she was with her laundry bundled in a trash bag held awkwardly in front of her like an unwanted package she was surprised to find herself with. A stranger to Ma's Clean Clothes, not pleased to discover she left her detergent at home, looking around for the machine that dispenses packets. Got what she needed, started the machines going, then sat down and reached into a cloth bag decorated with faded Navajo designs. Just seeing the designs made the old heart skip a beat but that nonsense was stopped with a quick pinch to the forearm. Rummaging in her bag, Petra looked up, took in the presence of another human, the one sitting on the counter reading the book by Judy Grahn. Looked once, then twice, pretending not to. Took a book out of the bag and opened it. Upside down.

It didn't take long. She came to the counter. It felt right to let her stand there a minute. Finally there was a clear "Um." The woman held her book up and it was still upside down. She wishes she'd mentioned it later, when things got more comfortable between them. They could have laughed about it. Maybe. They didn't exactly get chatty. They didn't have to. The tense feeling of destiny was in the air. Petra explained DWELL, making eye contact at the point where she spelled it out, Dykes Who Love Literature. She glanced at the How Dare You Assume I'm Heterosexual button. She was making her assumptions, on the lesbian side of things. Well, the button was not a subtle cue but it's a mistake to assume anything from a person's reading material. She, Bright Star, had certainly never read *Tender Buttons*. She felt lucky to recognize the words, know they were the title of something a lady named Gertrude Stein had written. By the time the meeting came around, though, she had read the book, and then read it again, as well as *The Autobiography of Alice B. Toklas*, which was not an autobiography of anybody except Gertrude Stein herself. The title was a trick.

Sitting in the bathroom, smoking, enjoying this break, she remembers Petra's parting words. She had her clean dry laundry in that green trash bag, but now it was slung over her shoulder as if she'd learned the ways of folks who went to laundromats just by sitting in one for a while. Halfway out the door she turned and said, "Maybe this was meant to be." She waited for the answering nod, got it, and pulled the door shut behind her. She did not appear overcome with delight at the prospect.

Meant to be. Yes, indeedy. She takes a drag on her cigarette and blows three perfect smoke rings into the warm bathroom air. That night she dreamt about Petra. The woman's short dark hair became thick black braids that rested on her breasts. Her narrow body expanded to roundness. Petra, white woman, became a Pueblo potter from long ago. Chippie's path was cleared by that dream and Petra's destiny was sealed. Petra could know this through her own dreams, she has the capacity. She resists her capacities, though. Most likely she's in for a surprise. Even at this moment she's no doubt startled to find herself in charge of a baby, "for the weekend." Enough. She puts out the cigarette, stands up. Which side of the damn Goddess faces the tub? She has to decide, doesn't have all day. She seems, however, unable to choose. She's arrived at the classic metaphor: a brick wall. She looks at her watch and tells herself not to panic, then blinks. Here is the thing itself, high and old and growing moss where the mortar has cracked.

Chapter Five

Raymond looks up from the circulation desk and chuckles to himself. The discontented patron returns.

"What tribe are you from, young man?"

He wasn't prepared for a personal question. Margie Stokes waits. Something unyielding about her stance. In his youth, after the trouble the sent him to the Youth Center, Raymond made decisions. Among them: he will answer all straightforward questions. This has cost him, but anything else would cost more.

"I don't know, Ma'am."

"Call me Margie."

"I don't know my tribe, Margie." They are taking each other's measure. He's not used to this sort of thing at work. Maybe in a bar, certainly with Raymona, but not at work. Margie has one of those knobs, every white hair pulled straight into a little round bunch at the top of the head. She narrows her eyes and dares him. He has no intention of rising up against her. He waits.

Finally, she nods her head, abruptly. The knob does not wobble. "I'd like another lesson."

He follows her to the computer. "Skunks again?"

"Sheep," she says, giving no explanation. So sheep it is. She presses Enter and takes the mouse. He instructs, she follows. She finds a good site. He reminds her to scroll down. She's on her way.

What tribe are you from? I don't know. She could have pressed him, many would have. Maybe she just wanted to get her footing, make it clear she won't be sliding around while he holds his ground, he with his superior computer knowledge. He doubts she has a penchant for poking tender places. Still, if she wanted to touch a sore spot, she couldn't have chosen a better question. He has no reliable information about his father. Stella, his mother, also Raymona's mother, a very white woman, withholds information as a matter of course when she's sober. Drunk, she spouts contradictory stories. Wherever he is, whoever he is, the source of

Raymond's Indian look has never shown up. Maybe he's dead, that's one of the stories. Margie's getting some skill with the mouse, tremors coming and going. She's good at taking advantage when her hand steadies. He'll see a lot of her in the future. She hasn't whooped again but the gleam of pleasure is in her eye. "Ready to be on your own?" He knows it's a little early, but he wouldn't want to insult her by hanging around.

"You stay right here, young man. Tell me your name, please." So he tells her his name and stays in place. He could get hooked on this lady, being drawn to what's straightforward in life. When he was coming up not much was. A portion of his childhood got twisted past what most people expect. That was the dramatic part. The rest was like a tool that isn't quite true, the bent place hard to detect, but there. Take the fact that he's part Indian. Besides all the drunken stories and sober silence about his father, there was how he got treated. Special. He was adored, plain and simple, by Stella and Raymona both. You might think a person would take to that, but it was bent. He figures that, possibly unbeknownst to themselves, his white mother and his white half-sister needed an Indianness for their own purposes. Raymona would hate to hear it, but in this way she was a carbon copy of their mother. His stepfather Bede danced the same dance, but backwards. Bede declared his hatred, but Raymond doesn't think Bede despised the actual boy he was, only some idea he had about Indians. Bede is dead, so there's no hatred coming at him now, just the adoration. Even that isn't what it used to be, it's damped down. He took some years to figure this all out, how it worked, what it meant, and what he needed to do or not do about it. These days, he lets himself be used but he can put a limit to it. Most of the time.

Margie Stokes has moved on to llamas. She's proceeding from link to link, sampling a little here, a little there. He's glad it's a slow morning and he can sit with her. Why not give an old lady what she wants? When they were kids, Raymona had no shame over her feelings about the Indian part of him. She not only revered it, she wanted it for herself. When they played Cowboy-and-Indian he had to be the cowboy and she was the Indian. She was tall, taller than he was—though he was older by two years—thin and pale with freckles and short light brown wrinkly hair and nobody looked more like a poor white Maine kid, but she had to be the Indian maiden. One time the whole thing went to strangeness. Raymona wanted to be tied to the old apple tree so he tied her, using laundry line rope and his best knots. Right away she started chanting. Pow-wow-wow-wow, pow-wow-wow-wow. Quiet at first, almost a whisper. She kept at it and her voice got stronger. Eeee-iii-eeee-iii, pow-wow-wow. She was taken over by the sounds she picked up from the movies. He must've gone into a trance because pretty soon she changed to a real Indian maiden, her neck stretched up like a dignified martyr. Maybe she was the Indian version of Joan of Arc, braver than brave. Margie's neck stretched up almost like that when she reappeared. Maybe he should say a word of praise to Margie, some people like that. But he thinks better of it. Raymona made a hard kind of magic that day, or maybe harsh is a better word. For a long time he was right there with her, seeing what she needed him to see, hearing what she needed him to hear. Soft drumming got added in. Indian ghosts came and he got scared and shook himself back to normal. Raymona chanted and chanted. He begged her to stop. She wouldn't. He untied her. When she didn't move he slapped her because that's what they did in movies. When she didn't come out of it he started to cry. She looked at him with pity, chanting. Only the slam of the car door stopped her. Stella was home, with Bede. When they were going to their bedrooms that night, Raymona whispered, "Raymond, did you hear me? I got it right this time." This time? There had been no other time. He went along. Yes, he'd heard her. She'd got it right this time, yes.

"Raymond, where is your mind?" Margie narrows her eyes.

"Sorry, Margie. Guess I was wool gathering. What can I do for you?"

"You can tell me how to get out of here," she says. He's alarmed by how far away he went, but Margie doesn't appear upset, she just needs help exiting the program. After which she stands, picks up her handbag, winks at him, and leaves. At least he thinks she winked. Maybe it was the palsy.

He can't get Raymona out of his mind. He hopes the person she's meeting today admires her art objects, gives her a little encouragement in that department. It doesn't matter if her works look overly unusual to him. Something good should happen, just for the goodness of it, before she kills herself.

Behind the brick wall chaos threatens. Indecision, always a terrifying state, is unbearable under present conditions. Decisiveness is the key to a successful death. Stronger forces are needed to contain and comfort the frightened children who are starting to howl. Also, Bright Star herself needs some coaching. Help arrives. Mother Goddess Spider Woman distracts the children, wrapping them in light and turning the aboriginal flute tones now coming from the speakers into a magic carpet onto which they all pile. This should work for a while. An authoritative voice gets through. *All right. It's really very simple. The Indian faces the tub. What's on the other side won't be forgotten, we know who's white here. Now get out of the bathroom, take a real break. You know you can't relax in the presence of the damn Fallen Goddess. List-checking, that's the thing. Jesus, people, get it together.* But Bright Star can't move. The swirl of light has already dimmed and the magic carpet has lost substance. The children are falling through smoky insubstantiality. A different approach is needed. Radically different.

A brisk, unflappable part, held in reserve for the needs of this particular morning, takes over. She steps into the living room, looks around briefly. Couch, crib, wall hanging, assorted clay objects saved from The Smashing or produced since. All in order. She checks the final section of the list. Note to insurance guy: taped to the door. Note to police: sweetly brief, prominently displayed. Letter to Baby Persephone Star Chip Weeks: signed and sealed, in manila envelope. Letter to Petra Kalinowski with attached documents: in the envelope. Note to Raymond: completed and kissed, same envelope. Breast milk plus bottles of formula: in the fridge, labeled. Tools for the deed: laid out in right orderly fashion. Answering machine: cleared. Phone: off. Door: locked. Good.

Bright Star walks back into the bathroom, a little wobbly. Apparently the list has been checked and everything is ready. She planned to avoid these lapses but isn't surprised. It might be for the best. Hollow flute sounds, chant-like, a little wobbly themselves but full of the wood of deep, secret forests, emanates from the speakers. She grins a weak grin. Aboriginal sound, here in her bathroom, courtesy of American technology. What would tribal forest peoples think of this morning's

45

ritual? Would their spirits leap and dance? Would they shrink back into the trees? But women from the old time would see and nod encouragement, and the earth herself is never afraid. It's almost time for Gaia. This means stripping naked which is fine as long as she, Bright Star, now feeling a need for extreme order, is given the opportunity to deal conscientiously with each piece of clothing before the action begins. First, she'll pee, then undress and fold the much-loved Guatemalan shirt, the soft old jeans, the white bra and underpants. She'll put the clothes on the toilet lid. That is the plan. It has been agreed.

But she can't relax enough to pee. Running water in the sink doesn't work. This has happened before and is no reason, absolutely no reason, to panic. She knows how to pee. It will happen later, in the tub. All will be well. She undresses, step by step, still in charge as Bright Star, still herself. In the nude, numbed to all sensation, knowing what to do, she begins to circle the Fallen Goddess. With her back to the sculpture and her arms hanging loose, almost floating, she moves, stepping sideways, three times around the Goddess. There is just enough room for this. Bless the gods who led her to a large-bathroomed trailer. Gaia is increasingly present. Together they stop, turn, bow slightly to the Native American nursing mother. Together they bend down and accept the ball of cheese from the little red mouse. Like a priest raising a host at Mass they lift it, an offering to the Goddess. Most of the others join in, arms reaching high. Big Shorty scoffs, but that is his job. They eat the cheese slowly, a sacred act. Because she was in the grip of obsessiveness a few minutes ago, folding of a pile of old clothes so carefully, Bright Star is not allowed to remember that the cheese fell to the floor. What difference do germs make at this point? None whatsoever. Big Shorty thinks there should be a hammer. He'd like to end with smashing the old Fallen Goddess. However, he's getting sleepy. Gaia turns toward the sculpture, bends and kisses the place where the knife pierces the white breast, fighting nausea, humming along with the flute. She faces the Goddess and takes thirteen graceful steps, swaying and moving as she circles the figure, arms undulating: wings of the blue heron. She stops and bows to the Indian mother. The nausea is gone. She sees the child, a vague glow at first but solidifying, becoming Chippie: Persephone Star Chip Weeks, newborn, with a sweet little halo. She bows again. Bright Star watches, amazed.

46

Serena knew the baby would materialize, knew about the little halo. She steps to the front. All others melt away, reassembling behind the brick wall. Serena likes the brick wall. Whoever thought of it has a fine sense of history. Also, it gives her privacy. She looks around the bathroom. The window has not been closed. She forgives the lapse, takes one last look at the soft blue day, closes and locks the window. Her heart fills. Nature is perfect. She picks up the clothing, raises the lid of the toilet, sits down and urinates. There is no need to foul the tub water with unplanned bodily fluids. She wipes, stands, flushes, puts the lid down, replaces the pile of clothing, and lights the single white candle. The baby disappears while her back is turned, as planned. Only Serena knows the significance of the empty arms. Bright Star thinks they represent delusion, or simple paradox: the Native woman's impossible desire. Big Shorty calls them a stupid art thing. Gaia hardly sees the emptiness. Serena knows the secret. The white woman is not the only suicidal aspect of the Goddess. The Indian woman is not caught in the act of suicide because she is beyond it, having already chosen calm death over clinging to a baby. The ceremonially prepared face is thus appropriate, for the sacred act of killing requires war paint. Killing is sinful, but necessary.

Sin is Behovely, but All shall be well. The words of the mystic, Julian of Norwich, quoted in the poetry of Mr. T. S. Eliot who knew about hard times of the mind, are with Serena always now. One of the DWELL women, Roo The Teacher, quoted Mr. Eliot at a meeting and Serena asked Raymond to get her the book from the library. She gave the book back to Raymond last week. Returning Mr. Eliot was on the list. *All shall be well, and All manner of thing shall be well.* Death is permitted. The baby has nursed for four months, enough to give her a healthy immune system. Furthermore, there is an ample supply of breast milk in the refrigerator. Bright Star has been competent about details relating to the baby. Persephone Star Chip takes the bottle well, her body accepts formula. She is with Petra, on the way to her destiny. *Behovely.* She couldn't find the word in her dictionary but Roo knew it. Inevitable, she said.

All entities inside have agreed. It is necessary to disappear from the child's life, but Serena will not pretend this suicide is a simple matter of stepping out of the way, allowing the baby to get on with what destiny has planned for her. Death causes pain. Serena is willing to be the

47

instrument of pain. She reviews the list of those who will suffer. Raymond, Ricki, possibly Etta from the laundromat. Also, Stella-the-mother, if she ever sobers up enough to understand. Stella is Bright Star's mother. Serena herself is without a mother, being more of spirit than of body.

Chippie is not on the list. The death will be more complicated than painful for this baby, who understands the plan. It is still the time of her complete soul. She will forget, as Serena herself, Bright Star herself, every aspect of herself, forgot the essential things for a time, but will find her way back as she walks through the maze of years. A mother's suicide will be a difficult thing, a koan to solve over and over at each new stage of life. The child will accept her life, challenged at every turn. Serena understands and accepts. It is a possible way, not an impossible way. *All shell be well and all manner of thing shall be well.* This child will save the Native Peoples, as she agreed before her birth. She will be strong for her fate, and her mother will be liberated. To die is to leave pain behind and enter freer realms. Bright Star and many of the others are exhausted from obsessive reliving of their childhood involvement with demon stepfather Bede. Concocting fantasy realms of terror, fighting horror with horror, does nothing but distract; the bonds hold. Deeply, crucially, there is loneliness, and the need for a period of union with those who exist outside time, beyond boundaries. Only Serena and Mother Goddess Spider Woman understand fully how wondrous death will be. Serena knows the body is a temporary vessel, the brain a temporary constraint on the larger mind. She knows the comfort of meditating on such matters. She also knows that her hold on things is fragile this morning. She can feel the familiar force of terror building behind the brick wall. She'd better get moving.

Syringe, sculpting knife, gun: all in place.

She steps quickly back to the toilet, picks up the jeans, and takes the paper from the back pocket where she inspired Bright Star to put it, unread, earlier. Facing the Fallen Goddess, she begins to chant softly, then lets the sound become high and full, blessing the fact of the trailer's isolation on this road in the woods. "Eee-iii-eee-iii, eeee-iiii-eeee-iiii, EEEE-IIII-EEEE-IIII-EEEE-IIII."

Silence ensues, opening toward eternity. She waits, respectful. Seven full minutes pass according to the Mickey Mouse watch they wear for the children's entertainment. Everything is sacred, nothing is mundane. Serena holds the page in both hands and begins to read the Last Words. "We bow to the great Chief Joseph and honor his final message to the tribe with this recitation. *Hear me, my chiefs, I am tired; my heart is sick and sad. From where the sun now stands, I will fight no more forever.*" She circles the Fallen Goddess one more time. She kneels, arms upraised. "Eternal Mother, into thy hands we commend our spirit." With that, the Last Words are completed. Her voice is strong, she is sure of herself. She gives praise in her heart and stands and bows to the Fallen Goddess. She folds the paper into the shape of a pyramid, exciting the child parts who taught her origami. She smiles and gives them permission to come forward. They tumble through the brick wall like so many little ghosts. Together they place the pyramid in the orange ceramic bowl Bright Star sculpted just last week. Together they strike a match and set fire to the Last Words. Serena blesses the world and melts into translucence, her task completed. She will hover nearby, singing with the spirits of the universe until the others can also depart from the body. The Little Ones wave as she floats. It's magic. They like it.

Big Shorty comes to clarity, glad to see that the pretentious Last Words have been burned. His first task is to get the Little Ones into the cellar of the Castle. They hate going down the cold cement steps, barefoot as they always are, but when they get to the bottom Mama Dragon will keep them distracted, breathing fire, giving thrills and chills, their own private horror movie. They'll be terrified and brave and protected; and unable to attend to what the older ones are doing. He sure as hell hopes this works. It always has, but today is, well, different. He pulls his hair hard for doubting, and feels better.

It is the hour of practicalities. While Big Shorty organizes the Little Ones into single file and orders them down the steps, Martha runs water into the tub. She's used to being in charge while Big Shorty and Mama Dragon do their work. In times of stress she cleans and makes order in the trailer, scrubbing corners with a toothbrush if necessary, blind to internal realities. She's paying close attention to the water temperature, which has to be very hot, when one of the Little Ones stumbles and falls. The fragile line disintegrates. Child bodies careen through space and screams fill the Castle. Big Shorty is cut off from Mama Dragon who finds herself locked behind a massive iron door. The

49

sense of form and purpose breaks—a sudden crushing, a supreme force pressing down, elements flying off and darting in—and panic cleaves all being. Martha senses chaos and disappears.

While hot water rushes into the tub there is an odd interval. Only once or twice before has this happened. No one is present. No one is in charge. The terror of this is greater than the terror of disintegration. Bright Star fights her way to the front. Through flying debris and extreme heat, across great currents of black wind, she swims. If none of the others can do what needs to be done, she will do it. No one is going to sabotage this suicide. The sounds and sensations have never been more intense. Her vision is blocked, but she can feel the faucet in her left hand. Hot water runs burning over her right hand. *Too hot, Martha.* She's relieved to find herself knowing it was Martha who was recently here. She gets the water turned off and grabs the edge of the tub. Breathe, she orders her body. If you think you're getting out of this by way of a little disintegration, you're dead wrong. So to speak. Her eyes are still blinded but the noise has stopped. She can feel her knees on the floor. Christ, Martha, we never kneel, don't you know that? But she knows Martha can't hear her. The floor is dry. Which means she got the water turned off before the tub overflowed. Which means the episode was brief. Two more deep breaths. Eyesight returns. It's partial, but she can make out shapes. She stands up and slaps her face. Thank you, Stella. Without a mother like Stella she might never have learned the uses of a good slap. She looks around. Her eyesight has cleared. Everything is a little too bright, a little too definite, but this is not unusual. There are ashes in the orange bowl. She likes the bowl, her newest, but Serena surprised her, choosing to include it in the day's events. Orange? Not your usual sacred color. Maybe Serena is more broadminded than she has understood. Could Serena have had a sense of humor? *Could Serena have had...* Serena's gone? All right, she's gone. May the gods be with us. Or with me. Whatever. Look around.

The bathroom door is closed. That was a mistake. A brush with claustrophobia might have colored things here. A huge brush appears before her eyes, an artist's brush, full of some substance called claustrophobia, making rough strokes, filling the screen of her vision, coloring the internal atmosphere with a suffocating closeness. She starts to choke. Too concrete. This won't do. Think. What's going on? A feeling

50

of claustrophobia. Not even much of one. A mere brush with a feeling. A metaphor. Which is a figure of speech.

The brush disappears.

She can still think. She can make metaphors. She's a sane adult woman. She had a brush with claustrophobia and it colored her experience. Of course. When was the last time she could close a bathroom door? Decades. That's why she never uses the facilities out in the world. Doesn't everybody know this? Speaking of coloring things, her hand is bright red. Martha's assessment of sensation has always been a bit questionable. She runs cold water over the hand. Better.

The door. She opens the door and looks into the living room. There's The Knot, right beside the worn, but oh-so-serviceable maroon couch she got from Goodwill the day she moved into the trailer. The door should absolutely stay open. It might even help, being able to see The Knot from the tub. The Knot and the Fallen Goddess are her only large sculptures. Or the only ones that survived. The Knot is satisfying, archetypal, a huge snake with a head at each end twisted into a complex knot. She likes to think she conquered the devil and the penis in one efficient artistic blow with that one. She completed it the day before she conceived Chippie. As planned. The Knot and the Fallen Goddess are a linked set, but she didn't understand this until yesterday, which explains why the Knot is not on the list. It should have been on the list: Bathroom door open, Knot within view. The unconscious is such a tricky artist's partner. The circumference of each of the four thighs of the Goddess is the same as the circumference of the body of the snake. She measured, but failed at the time to grasp her purpose. Of course they're a pair, these two. Both have two heads. Both sprang from Genesis, snake and fallen woman. What could be more obvious? Both had to be completed by the time the baby was born, one before the conception, the other before labor started. Well, good. The artist in her is resurrected. Also, she supposes, the psychologist. It's a psychological necessity that The Knot and Fallen Goddess be easily seen while she tries to die. *While. She. Tries. To. Die.*

Tries?

Uncertainty is not in the plan, not that she knows of, but uncertainty is coming in like a fog. Uncertainty about whether she can succeed in killing herself. Worse, uncertainty about whether she wants to die. It's still in the distance, but approaching quickly. Was this on the list?

No. The list was about Things To Do, not Things To Expect. The realization makes her frantic. She's getting a vague sense of something...a map. Did someone make a map? She doesn't want this. As Bright Star, she never saw a map, not that she can remember. They kept it from her, advised her not to know about it, but she does know about it, doesn't she? Information is coming to her in that way she hates. On the map there was a Mountain of Doubt. No wonder they told her not to look. She did, just once. Took a good look and promptly forgot. Map of the Day of Death it was called. Most of it was interesting, and colorful, but the Mountain of Doubt was gray and barren and she can see it now, not on paper, but before her eyes. The fog of uncertainty has solidified and it is indeed mountainous. Damn, damn, damn shit *fuck*. She takes a deep breath. She really would have preferred not to...

This would be a good time for a cigarette. Where is the one who smoked? That other Bright Star. Wasn't there a Bright Star who smoked? So difficult to remember. How was everyone organized? Names float by but she can't quite... Gaia? Shorty? Wasn't there a firm plan, with tasks assigned? Today is the day she's supposed to kill herself, right? She looks at the Mountain of Doubt and thinks she can make out wisps, little entities lost in twisting paths of shadow. The paths are barely visible indentations in the barren gray rock which is like a formation on another planet, one that does not support life. She feels alone and deeply afraid. *Get a grip.* She needs to think. She needs help. If she's lost the old organization, there might not be time to find a new one. She absolutely must locate the most recent others. She has a confused sense of beings called Little Ones caught in a disaster of some sort...elements...flying in all directions...excruciating, but in the past. Minutes ago? Hours? What time is it? She doesn't have all day. She literally does not have all day. Where is everyone? She stamps her foot. Names come. Martha. Serena. Where is Serena? Even if Serena left, she was supposed to stay close enough to be recalled if needed. Is that right? Big Shorty? Mama Dragon? She can't sense the Little Ones. This is bad. This is very bad.

Chapter Six

Petra has had a divided work life for years. She's a part-time therapist and during amenable seasons she works two or three days a week at her old trade, house-painting. Among other benefits, painting gives her ladders to climb. Also, the limits of her capacity as a therapist are clear. If she presses beyond, she frays. When the weather won't allow painting, she writes. This writing remains stubbornly undefined, fitting no genre, being neither real work nor plain recreation. Hers is an undefined, unpaid, seasonal writing life and it will begin soon, but at the moment she's sitting, musing, on the warm gray asphalt of Izzie Carter's roof, taking a break from scraping and sanding. Danny McGuire sits several feet from her, playing a sweet harmonica. Both wear overalls, hers now titled *Inadvertent Spatter*. Danny's are a less layered mess. Back in San Francisco Danny became, casually, competently, a bookkeeper. He still does a bit of that but when he moved to Maine he joined her in the painting business, replacing a complicated lesbian couple with dissatisfaction issues. He's been a clear improvement.

Izzie's windows are open. Croaky snatches of song drift upward. *Rock-a-bye, baby, in the treetop.* Izzie renders this not as a lullaby but as a dance tune. *Dum-dee-dum dum-dum, cradle will fall.* Chippie produces a slide up the scale of delight. Danny adds a bright riff. Izzie is doing child care for Petra who is doing child care for Bright Star who has a "professional opportunity" and promised to "do anything" if Petra would take Chippie for the weekend. Petra, astonishing herself, said yes, though she knew this job at Izzie's was coming up, though she had no need for a weekend with a baby, though she was not inclined to feel generous toward Bright Star. Possibly this is reparation for unkind thoughts. She wonders how a meeting with a gallery owner can possibly take an entire weekend but has decided it doesn't matter. Bright Star won't be at DWELL this afternoon and the prospect sounds relaxing. This less than virtuous thought runs counter to the reparation theory but life is never simple. Well, some things are simple. Danny's harmonica. Danny.

Petra is periodically astonished and consistently pleased that she and Danny—and Roo—ended up together in Maine. This confluence is no accident. It started with Roo who came to care for an infirm grandmother with a big house in Blue Hill. The grandmother is long dead, but the house, with its view of the water and its generous grounds and its little coach house in the rear, remains. Petra lived in the coach house during her first year in Maine, after Anya died. It consoled her to see unending water, to be near Roo who knew her when. Roo remembers both the vibrant healthy Tekla and the Tekla who lay in bed for months before dying. After the funeral, when Witold, having entered the house only long enough to change into work clothes, left for the fields, the two nine-year-old girls tiptoed hand-in-hand through every room of the motherless house. Week after week, Roo was there while tall silent Witold walked from room to room reading a book, greeting no one. When Anya died, when Petra could not claw her way out of obsessive grief, she phoned Roo. "Seven. She was only *seven*." Day after day, a continent separating them.

Finally Roo said, "Come here, stay with Grandma and me until you get better. You *will* get better." Geographical cures are not supposed to work, but this one did. So they tried the same thing with Danny when AIDS took his beloved George. Petra drove from Maine to San Francisco to fetch him. He was numb, unable, exhausted. She brought him back and they set him up in Roo's coach house. He came to life slowly, like a sad plant, with a little watering and a little neglect. He pays Roo a small, fair rent. The two of them have always gotten along, each other's favorite cousins, but Petra thinks there might be no one who dislikes Danny. Here he is on Izzie's roof, a big sloppy white guy in his forties with a mess of wanton black hair and deep blue-gray eyes that have gotten more interesting with time. He plays a long riff, a little bent, a little sweet, a little funny, while Izzie catches her breath. This will be the last job of the year. Izzie phoned, humiliated. "I tried and tried but no amount of that visualization I heard about on the radio worked. I'm just too damn scared to finish the job. Fear of heights is what it is. I know it's late in the year, but the forecast is favorable. I'll pay double if that's what it takes, dear." Visualization? Izzie? All Petra said was, "Paying standard is plenty. We'll be there." Fear of heights. She should have known. All through August she watched Izzie, who must be seventy. It was an odd way to paint, bottom upward. Then work halted. The top clapboards and the eaves sat scabbing and peeling, while the rest glowed new white. Like the good Maine neighbor she's learned to be, Petra said not a word. Now Izzie starts an enthusiastic rendition of *Home on the Range*. Chippie squeals. Danny plays some punchy, low chords. Petra feels her luck.

Work at the office went well this week. Helga is sleeping better already. Between sessions she visited two-year-old Ingrid at the new mother's home, then drove around Bangor looking at people, looking at the sky, eating dark chocolate. She cried a little. She did nothing compulsive, a minor miracle. She wanted to talk about these compulsions, if it was all right with Petra. It was all right with Petra, certainly. She listened, aware of an itch in her own psyche, dread and desire rising up. What did Helga experience when she woke up in the morning, no child in the house to feel tender toward, to be irritated, or bored, or delighted by? Being a decently disciplined therapist, Petra followed her client, asked no unjustified questions.

Next came Kiki who was loud, but not off the scale, mad at her mother but not whirling in fury. The man with atypical anxiety finally agreed to talk to his doctor. Both women with Multiple Personality Disorder were sleeping and eating and going to work; neither was suicidal, and only one had harmed herself. The cigarette burn wasn't deep. Patty, child alter, had planned to spell h-e-a-v-e-n along her thigh, but she stopped when, for the first time, "it *hurt*." "You felt pain. That's great. It *should* hurt when you burn yourself." "*I don't like it*." "I know, but it's good." Petra advised other parts of the self to reach out to Patty, try to understand what she wanted to accomplish, find another way. A good-natured, slightly cynical alter took control. "Petra dear, nothing substitutes for self-harm. Sublimation just ain't the same." "I know. Nevertheless." "We know. We're working on it." All very collegial. Someday Patricia might experience herself as a single individual. For now this is good enough. After work: Chippie, delivered by a brisk, businesslike Bright Star. All night, a baby in the house. How did that feel? Neither traumatic nor ecstatic. She, Petra Kalinowski, slept well with a baby in a bassinet beside her bed. She might make it through the weekend. Izzie will take the brunt, today and tomorrow both, because she wants the painting finished. DWELL will help.

Izzie chatters at Chippie who chatters in return. Danny starts a raucous tune full of chords cut short, steep changes in pitch. He slides his eyes at her, their brightness glinting. Petra smiles, looks at the view. From the rooftop they can see a fair stretch of the Penobscot beyond the descending woods, the pine and spruce and the bright dying deciduous leaves. Dark green, orange, red, yellow, and...she reaches into memory...burnt sienna.

Burnt sienna: from the Crayola box of her childhood, sixty-four colors, the ultimate Christmas present. Witold had wrapped it in red and taped a bow on top, slightly askew. She feared they might not celebrate Christmas, Tekla being gone. When Petra saw what she had not dared hope for, so many colors, she hugged her father. Awkwardly, he patted her head. She ought to call him. It's been too long. He relies on no one, refuses to leave the farm. He'll die there alone someday. She loved those crayons, used them down to nubs. Anya liked crayons too, better than magic markers. The thought brings back her dream, Anya working in a coloring book, applying pure tinted light, pink and purple and blue light, to a surface that shimmered. With great competence, she stayed inside the lines. Then Anya wavered, becoming less substantial with each stroke of the crayon. Petra watched, silent, separate, helpless, as her little girl threatened to disappear. Then, in the inconsistent way of dreams, the scene turned solid, secure. Anya ran around a racetrack beside a black horse, matching him stride for stride. The rich brown of the track's dirt was a wonder, the large green field in the center a vibrant joy. Anya, running easily with her gangly legs, laughed and conversed with her horse without actual speech. Petra leaned on the white fence, one foot on the lower rail, relaxed. Each time the pair passed her, they turned and looked at her and nodded briskly as if to say, "We see you. We are completely here and you are completely there." The repetition gave her a spiraling sense of well-being that stayed with her when she woke up, while she tended to Chippie, while she ate breakfast, while she scraped and sanded Izzie's highest clapboards and peeling eaves. She feels...gratitude?...reverence?...a purity of joy? Along with this, an ache. She'd pray, if she believed in such a thing, right here on this roof beside Danny whose tune is now unbearably bent and tender. She'd pray for Helga. Elizabeth Bishop's poem comes to mind, her Man-Moth, his single, precious tear. If attention is paid, he will offer it; if not, he will

56

swallow it. When Helga's tear comes her therapist must be ready with clarified, uncontaminated attention.

Danny puts the harmonica into his overall pocket and unwraps a Snickers bar. He has the least healthy diet of anyone she knows. "How goes life?" he asks. "We're at anniversary time, right?"

"It was twenty years as of Monday."

"That's what I thought."

"It's been different this year. Better."

"Good. Why?"

"I'm not sure. Maybe sadness wears out."

"Maybe."

She hesitates. "I had a dream last night." She stops, shy.

"Tell me," says Danny, casual, easy, not looking at her.

So she tells him about Anya and the horse, how they could communicate without words. Danny listens, nods. "They were on their own in a fine, radical way. I was released...into..." But she feels too self-conscious to continue, though this is safe, tolerant Danny. No one could be safer.

"Into what, Petra?"

He's interested, not prying. This shouldn't be so hard. She gathers courage. "Separateness. Freedom."

He nods and looks out over the trees, sparing her. "I like the horse."

"I like the horse, too. It was a great horse."

They sit. They watch the river. Everything is quiet in the house below. Are Izzie and Chippie napping? "And then there's Chippie Dippie, daughter of Bright Star."

"So I noticed."

"I suppose I never told you I was taking care of her."

"You failed to mention the fact."

"It's just been for a couple of hours on Sunday afternoons, until now."

"And now?"

"All weekend."

"And how is it?"

"It's good. Good enough. Sort of normal."

"Hmmm."

57

"Right. Hmmm. Good response. You wouldn't get away with anything more definite."

"I suspected that."

"Isn't Izzie a sketch?"

"She is. You aren't getting involved in a loverly way with Bright Star, are you?"

"Ye gods and little fishes."

"What *is* it you have against her?"

"I don't know."

"Hmmm," says Danny.

"Now you're pushing it."

"Is that what you do in sessions? Ration yourself, one *hmmm* per quarter hour?"

"Shut up, Danny McGuire." They sit, companionable. "So it's helped, I think, having this baby around. Don't say a word now."

Danny chuckles and moves closer and gives her a quick hug. "We should get back to work," he says, and stretches and yawns. "Nice day, huh?"

"It is," she says, and moves with him down the roof toward the ladder.

*

Inside, primal energies rise and fall in desperate noiseless rhythms disconnected from meaning. Gritty remnants of form are swept up and thrown around. The brick wall is gone. The Castle with the steps leading down to Mama Dragon is gone. Even the Mountain of Doubt has disappeared. Individual alters are so completely absent they might never existed.

Bright Star—or should she call herself Raymona now?—is alone.

She desperately needs a cigarette, but will she know how to smoke? Where are the cigarettes? Stop this, she tells herself. Breathe. Listen to Bach. Brandenburg Concertos. Not a bad choice—cerebral, with a deep emotional structure, or so she read somewhere. Where are the damn cigarettes? Stuffed behind the toilet tank, as she very well knew. What else does she know? She knows she's a white woman. Plain

Maine white. She walks to the mirror. White skin. Freckles. Flyaway light brown hair, recently unbraided. When did that happen? She lights a cigarette, blows smoke at the mirror, lets it clear. *Raymona Weeks. So you never went away.* Face: bit horsy. Not beautiful. Plenty for a sculptor to work with. Strange she's never done a self-portrait. Not of this self. She takes another drag, blows a couple of rings, watches them collide with the mirror, disintegrate; the face remains. She opens the bathroom window, looks out at the changing woods, feels the warm soft air, turns and looks at the Goddess, big round white woman, knife to breast, trying to kill herself. "Sweetheart, pressing that big dull knife into your breast just ain't gonna get the job done." Another drag on her last cigarette. That was the idea, wasn't it? No way to kill the white woman. No way to get rid of the white skin. She's the daughter of Stella Weeks and never mind the father. The point is: Raymona Weeks has not one drop of Native American blood. Only Raymond got that and, no matter how Indian he looks, half his blood is white, too. She lifts the toilet lid just enough to drop the cigarette in, hears the sizzle, lowers the lid. The pile of clothes is undisturbed. Raymond, like it or not, is a half-breed. So is the baby. Chippie looks purely Indian and that's luck beyond luck but white genes are hiding in her somewhere. Persephone Star Chip Weeks, daughter of Bright Star and one gorgeous Indian named Chip, tribe unknown, just passing through, and therefore perfect, is a half-breed. She's always known these things, just as she's always known that those inside who took over when life was rough were paradoxically more fragile and temporary than she, Raymona, is.

The baby looks so very Indian. Can a half-breed be destined to save the Indian peoples? The question is beyond her. She slumps to the floor, the cold porcelain reality of the toilet bowl, unyielding and necessary, at her back, her naked white legs splayed in front of her. She pushes hard against the bowl, hurting herself, then sits forward. She knows two things. One: she has made the decision to die. All the doubt in the world isn't going to change that. Two: the baby will be better off with Petra, no matter what her destiny might be. Two rock-solid facts she can plant her feet on. How convenient: one for each foot. She sees her tall, white, serviceable body standing over a stretch of desert, feet planted firmly. *Colossus.* This is a metaphor. She knows a metaphor when she meets one, at least right now she does. She has tendencies to slip into the

Slough of Insanity, which is on the Map of the Day of Death not far from the Mountain of Doubt. Beyond the Mountain of Doubt, is the Castle of Last Decision. It sparkles, crystal, under sudden sun. She has no need to turn it into a hallucination. It's the right and necessary image and she has reached it. She gets up and walks back to the mirror. Yep, still white. *Impressive circles under your eyes, White Woman.* Her energy is leaking fast. She remembers to leave the bathroom door open. She'll be able to see The Knot. Some part of her has been afraid the snake will come alive, straighten itself, attack. Juvenile, crazy thinking. She looks at the Fallen Goddess. "One more time, Old Girl." She turns the sculpture around. The white part faces the tub. She picks up the sculpting knife and gun and gets into the tub. She doesn't need the syringe. She'll do this straight.

Chapter Seven

Saturday morning. 11:25. Dave Robichaud pulls onto the shoulder of the road, stops the car, leaves the radio on. He wants a minute to reconnoiter. Not that he's in a bad frame of mind. Good to get away from Bangor's pavement, for one thing. Sure would be a relief to sell a policy. Since the accident he's found it hard to get in the groove. Good thing Etta's helping him out with this girl from the laundromat. He knows these words. *I will lay me down.* Shouldn't have to rely on Etta so much, though. He made the whole drive with the windows open, listening to "oldies," which seem to be from his very own younger years. The trailer's about half a mile down the road. He doesn't always get good directions, but this Bright Star lady—strange name—was very specific. Truth is, he needs directions, isn't one of these fellows who has the instinct, can find a place by following the scent like a dog. Wouldn't want to be a dog anyway, would he? Sure is a nice day.

He clutches, shifts, starts down the road. He'll have to get the real name if there's a sale. Here it is. Nice little trailer. Not new, but it's been kept up. Sweet old Volkswagen's in good shape, too, but somebody went and gave it purple doors. Green and purple, what's the point of that? He climbs the steps and almost knocks, but here's an envelope taped to the door, FOR THE INSURANCE AGENT. Damn. He opens the envelope. "Please call the police. Do not enter this trailer. There is a dead body inside. No insurance will be needed. Thank you." What's this? He knocks softly, listens. He reads the note again, tries the doorknob. Locked. What if it's joke? It's not a joke. He looks around, but who does he think is going to rescue him? He ought to have one of those newfangled cell phones but of course he's not up to date. At least he had his hands on a computer once or twice. Times change. He looks at his watch. 11:30, right on time. If she'd been here. He'd like to sit on the step, get his mind settled. Would this be the sheriff's territory? Pretty dooryard. Not a speck of trash. The nearest store is what he needs, or a neighbor. Is this a real emergency? Crazy question. He gets back in the car, drives as fast as he dares, sees the pay phone at the gas station. He gets his instructions to go back to the trailer, someone will be there soon and yes, sir, we give dead bodies high priority.

The officer arrives, all alone. Just a kid, twenty-one at the most. Knows how to break into a place, though. Dave follows him, holding his breath. Is this dangerous? The officer tells him to stay right there, sir, and goes to investigate. A door closes. Is there really a body? Etta told him the lady was an artist of some unusual kind and he sees what she meant. First thing that catches his attention after the empty baby's crib placed right in the living room is a clay statue that looks like a snake tied up in a knot with a head at each end and colors that go with the car outside. Not much to his liking. Was there a murder here? 12:16. Down on the floor next to the walls are little clay forms sitting side by side by side. You might say the room is outlined by them. The officer is talking quietly. A pause. More talking. Must be making a call. He'd have that cell phone gadget for sure. 12:20. Time stretches out when a person's waiting. He stoops down. Tiny bowls, not very regular or smooth. Looks like she took colors from the snake and parceled them out, but then here's a little man on a black turtle and his sleeve is red but the rest of his jacket and his hand, the one not in his pocket, are blue, so that's different colors entirely. Ugly little guy. Better not touch, this might be a crime scene and what if they found his fingerprints? He's trying to breathe quietly. Should he call out, see if the officer needs help? No, better wait. 12:26. He looks at a monkey curled up like a baby on a purple pillow, painted with stripes of green and brown. Terrible colors. Maybe she was a bad artist. 12:28. Tacked onto the wall is something that must be art because it isn't anything else. Sewed-together feed sacks with objects glued on. Feathers, beads, quills, straw, and three bird's nests with broken open robins' eggs. She did a good job securing the nests. How did she do that? Not exactly pretty. Interesting, though. The young officer comes out, looking pale. Maybe a person should have been more active here, gone and helped him somehow. "Ambulance will be here soon," is all the fellow says. They stand side by side, waiting. 12:32. 12:38. Dave sits down, thinking this might help the officer sit, too. It doesn't work. He gets up and stands beside the officer again. 12:45. 12:57. The sirens are a welcome sound. He steps back to let the paramedics rush in. A body gets carried out on a stretcher. Must be dead because it's covered over, head and all.

Then they're gone. The young officer pulls out a tablet to write on, asks him who he is, takes his information. He wonders why this didn't happen before, with all those empty minutes, but it makes sense when he thinks about it. One thing at a time. When the officer closes his writing pad and puts it in his back pocket Dave asks if the dead person was a lady. The young officer breaks down. Now Dave knows what to do. He says maybe they should sit down on the couch for a minute and the officer nods. The paramedics didn't care about shutting any doors, so he gets a quick look into the room where it happened, whatever it was that happened. It's a bathroom, and there's some blood that looks overly red, like a scene in a movie. Then they're sitting. The officer hands him a piece of paper. *Officer, if you're reading this, I certainly hope I'm dead. I assure you this is a suicide. I enclose birth certificate and driver's license to help with quick identification of my body and my signature. Next of kin is my half-brother, Raymond Weeks. If you act quickly you should be able to locate him at his place of work, the Bangor Public Library, where he'll be until 2:00. The urgency is about the baby. Please extend my apologies to the insurance agent. Death is never easy, but it is wondrous also. Be comforted. Sincerely, Raymona Weeks, a.k.a. Bright Star*

Dave looks at the officer. We're both in over our heads, is what he thinks. "Hard day at work," he says. "She's my first," says the young man. He starts to cry again, but it doesn't last. Then they just wait. Is the note maybe a little strange, being so businesslike and almost upbeat? It makes Dave uneasy to be included in someone's suicide note like that, but also proud. He feels recognized. This certainly is an unusual day. Before they leave, they go into the bathroom together, and then through the entire trailer, investigating like a team, but quickly, because the officer has to get to the brother, or the half-brother, at the library. They don't find a baby.

When he tells Etta the story she comments that it might take a while to get pictures like that organized into a reasonable place in his mind. She's sweet to him, as if it were *his* hard time. The girl who killed herself is her employee and she should be the one getting upset, but that's Etta. They drink some whiskey that's just for colds and such and they go to bed. He shivers, though the day never turned cold, not for a minute. He holds Etta close all night. She jerks a little from time to time but seems to sleep. He sleeps, too. A little, not much.

Raymond sees the two young officers approach the circulation desk and speak quietly to Charlene and his gut tightens. When Charlene nods in his direction, he knows. Raymona isn't in Portland trying to get her art work recognized.

"Are you Raymond Weeks?"

He feels sorry for them because their job is hard today. Right away they want to know if there's a baby somewhere. He's glad he can explain Raymona's plan, how the baby will be all set, though he's unable to give the location. It seems to make them feel better. At the morgue when he says Yes, that's her, the one who was at the trailer gives him a manila envelope all sealed up with his name across the front in her most careful writing which is not easy to look at. He doesn't open it. He worries Ricki might be at the trailer. The officers say nobody was there except this poor insurance guy, Dave somebody, but Ricki might've gone over there after they left. "Would I be allowed to go in?"

"Yes, sir, you would. If you really wanted to." The officers look at each other. He tries to appear strong for them but most likely fails.

When he catches himself speeding he slows down. He isn't inclined to play the radio. You never know what might come over the air waves. Raymona's Volkswagen sits in the dooryard and he feels sorry for it which is probably not a normal response. Ricki's truck is nowhere around. He could leave, he wouldn't have to go in there. He goes in. He makes sure the crib is empty, but of course it is. The kitchen is the place he wants to sit in, just for a minute. He has to work up his courage for the bathroom. Some strange meals took place here. There were laughs, and fights. Well, her fighting and him trying not to. It was a long time she lived here. He remembers the day she declared her new name, all abrupt, then gave him the information about how it came to her in a dream. She was trying to smooth things, so he listened and tried to be nice in return. He walks over to the refrigerator and opens it. At the morgue nothing was real. He starts to understand she's dead from the baby bottles lined up with their labels. "Breast Milk." "Formula." She made a big attempt to leave things right. He feels tears trying to get shed but isn't ready for that yet.

He remembers now. Raymona made sure he knew there was a meeting today. He should have known something was up. Dwell, is what it's called. It has to do with lesbians and what they read together, is that it? Ricki will be there, but where would it be? He's missing some important pieces of information. He knows Ricki's not the new mother, but who is? Raymona liked secrets so much, ever since she was little. You could see her work hard to keep one from bursting out. That thought makes him feel tender and torn, but he can't let his mind go soft, has to think what to do next. Two things are important, Ricki and the baby. He might as well look in the bathroom, get it over with. He lets himself throw up in the toilet and brushes his teeth. He should remember to tell Ricki about the toothbrush, how he used it, in case it's hers and not Raymona's. He knows she stayed here some nights. At least she didn't move into the trailer. Think what that would be like. He leaves a note taped to the trailer door to keep Ricki from going in but he sure hopes she doesn't come anywhere near. He shouldn't worry, she'll be at the meeting. Maybe Gertrude will know where it takes place.

Back to Bangor. A few more pieces of information would've come in handy. Gertrude's last name, her phone number. At least he's been to the house and knows it's where Ricki lives, renting a room or something such. What's it like to live with a psychologist? A person could feel observed. He still doesn't want to play the radio. Raymona had a kind of economy about her lying, so he's pretty sure Ricki will have the gallery lady in mind, which might make her day like any other. Until he arrives. He hopes the Dwell meeting's a good one because after this it might not be the same for those ladies. A lot of things will be different but there's no time to think about that because here's the house. This would be harder if he'd never met Gertrude. The thought of her hair helps him. It's a type of hair you don't often see on a white person and it would never let itself be put into place. It's the opposite of what Margie Stokes, elderly internet explorer, combs out and buns up every morning of her life, or so he has to imagine. Gertrude'a maybe in her forties. Not old like Margie, but old to start being a mother. She's probably not the one. He presses the doorbell.

Chapter Eight

Ricki Harding used to feel solid and sure. Smart enough. Ordinary. She did have a bad time when she was fourteen and hated every girl who liked a boy and hated her anomalous hand which she knew even then was a symbol for hating her entire self but all of that melted away the afternoon she went down to the creek with Lionel and they tried to have sex. Lionel had a philosophical interest in her "streamlined" hand, thought Plato would say it was closer to pure form than a common hand, and thought it might be able to get his stubborn "member," thus far unresponsive to girls, to harden. No hardening was achieved. They caught a few trout with the poles they had carried as cover and marched back to Ricki's house, giggling and singing. *Deck the halls with boughs of holly, fa-la-la-la-la.* It was August. They were buoyant with insight: sexuality was irrelevant, for both of them. They talked about career plans. Lionel was headed toward physics with the modest hope he might be the next Einstein. Ricki would be the best high school English teacher Maine had ever seen. She planned to introduce Advanced Grammar into the curriculum. The structure of language needed to be understood. It was bedrock. Lionel and his family moved away that fall. Dear, smart, wandering-eyed, pigment-deprived (he has albinism) Lionel. Ricki missed him terribly, but she studied; and there was family life—gathering eggs, chopping wood, talking to her mother, going on occasional short runs with her father. She was the youngest kid, the only girl, the tag-along. Her brothers were plumbers, loggers, handymen, except for Alvey, their artist, who waited tables at Dysart's. Maybe it was seeing their father gone so much from home, their mother on her own, that kept the boys from becoming truckers like Peter. They were a domestic bunch. *She* didn't intend to marry and have kids. The summer after The Fishing Trip—that's what she and Lionel had called it, locking eyes and grinning and never telling anyone what *that* was all about—she went on the road with Peter. He'd hurt his back, needed help. She was the one to do it. Except for missing Lionel, life was good. She was using both hands, both arms, lifting, carrying. She had more upper body strength and better balance than she'd ever had. She felt fit. Then in a small town in Massachusetts she saw a man murdered. She and Peter had stopped for the night. They went for a walk to limber up their legs. They passed a bar and out poured the murder, two men falling to the ground, a blinking blue neon light catching and losing the arc of the knife's progress. Peter was on top of the aggressor, yelling, pulling at him, but the knife descended, slow motion in the blinking neon. Then it was in the chest of the man on the bottom, a huge Indian lying flat on his back, not struggling, his long braid settling beside the knife. He turned his head and looked at Ricki. He narrowed his eyes and she had the crazy idea he would spit at her but instead he winked. At her. People rushed out of the bar, the police arrived, an ambulance. Later came the trial, which she and Peter, witnesses, returned to Massachusetts for. Peter's back, not helped by the incident, was still hurting. She had the wink in her mind, a private thing, a mystery. The murderer was a stringy little white man. Convicted, he got himself killed before he could be sentenced; another knife fight, this time in the local jail. It was more than the small town was used to and certainly more than Ricki was used to. She had a lot to mull over. Gradually she turned the Indian's dying wink into something hard and real, but still mysterious, inside her. She could feel it near her heart. Lionel would say this was alchemy, that she was making gold and it would take a little time, alchemy takes a little time. She could hear him say it. He came back to visit later that summer. She told him about the wink. No one else knew. A dying man's wink is a metaphysical event, they decided, and she was right to guard it. "Can I still be ordinary as sin, with this inside me?"

"Yes. This deepens the ordinariness," said Lionel, exuding wisdom. They laughed but then he sighed.

"What?"

"Big news time." He didn't sound happy.

"OK," she said, and waited. It took a while. They were down at the creek. No fishing poles this year, no need for cover. It was hotter than Maine usually gets. Some of the low growth was already dried up. They needed rain.

"It's just that I'm gay," Lionel said, staring at a rock.

67

"Wow," she said. She could hear the hollowness in her own voice.

"Yeah." He kept staring at the rock, barely wet by the creek.

"Just like that?"

"Well," he said. She knew what he meant. He meant it hadn't been plain and simple. They talked about it through the rest of his visit. He'd gotten his heart broken and the person who broke it was male; ergo, he was a faggot. "Albino and a faggot. Jeez," she said. That started them giggling and the words became part of their private culture. They sang them, operatically, when they were out in the field with no one around. *Albino and a faggot, Jeez.* They made a chant. A*l-BI-no-AND-a-FAG-got-JEEZ.* They could hum the rhythm without the words and crack each other up on Main Street in Bucksport, Lionel with his thick glasses and floppy anti-sunburn trademark hat and new uniform of striped tie, ragged T-shirt, and designer jeans; Ricki hatless in old non-designer jeans, her T-shirt in good condition. The night before he left he looked at her, his wandering eye under control for once, and said, "What about you, Ricki?" They were sitting side by side in a neighbor's field, under the stars. Rolls of baled hay were their company. She was stopped by the question. She hadn't imagined it. This was the Summer of the Wink, wasn't that enough? It was true that girls seemed sexier to her than boys, but she was busy, she had a career to think about. *Et cetera.* "That's OK," Lionel said. He meant it was OK that he was out there by himself in homosexual country. He was letting her off the hook. She leaned against him and whispered, "Thanks."

She got letters detailing his sexual adventures. He had no trouble with erections now. She learned about penises, circumcised and uncircumcised, flaccid, hard, half-hard. The focus was too narrow for her but she answered the letters. Her answers got shorter, her response time longer. Then Lionel said his family was moving again. He never sent her the new address. In a way, it was a relief. He'd started to question intellectual pursuits, higher education, the idea of a career. Love was everything, he said. Sex was what he meant. They'd gone in different directions.

She started college, young in many ways, aware of the fact. Her second semester biology lab partner was twenty-one and from New Jersey. Julia: impossibly attractive and firmly engaged to a star hockey

68

player. What happened to Ricki's innards when she leaned over a microscope with Julia was unexpected. Suddenly she needed Lionel but had no way to find him. She went to her most admired professor, Eleanor McGuire, and confessed. Professor McGuire listened and thought and listened some more and then, smiling warmly, invited her to join DWELL. Dykes Who Love Literature.

"There's a group called that?"

"Yes."

"I could just come...I mean, not have to prove anything...I mean..."

Professor McGuire smiled her sympathy. She seemed to understand how a person could want and not want to be in a group like that, feel honored and feel like running away fast. "In the group I'm known as Roo, Ricki."

"Roo? Am I supposed to call you that?"

"Yes, of course. Welcome to DWELL."

Scared to death but so full of curiosity she tingled with it, she walked into Petra Kalinowski's living room. Did she belong here? Only Professor McGuire—Roo—knew she'd never had sex with a woman; or man, unless you counted The Fishing Trip. Sitting on Petra's couch, looking at these women who were so settled and confident they could call themselves dykes, she ached for sweet albino Lionel who knew all about sex. In the middle of the night her mind had gone wild. These women would make her prove she was a lesbian. One of them would make a pass at her. Someone would casually display a dildo, she'd heard of dildos. But they welcomed her without much fuss and started talking about whether they should put more gay male poets on the agenda. Not yet, but soon, they decided amid banter and humor while Ricki watched and listened and said not one word. They'd already read T. S. Eliot, prejudiced toward theories that his longtime roommate was his lover. She'd never heard *that* theory. Ashbery, of course. Duncan was a possibility. Bidart. Others, none of whom Ricki knew a single thing about. Petra favored Robert Duncan, something from *The Opening of the Field*, but not yet. Then they began to discuss a poem by a woman named Stevie Smith, "Not Waving But Drowning." Nobody claimed Stevie Smith was a lesbian, but that didn't seem to matter. Maybe only men had to be gay to get on the list. When she'd been in the group for a few months, when she no longer felt dangerously at sea, when she was swimming well enough, waving quite happily, and certainly not drowning, Bright Star joined DWELL. Finally, someone made a pass at her. It was a polite and nonphysical pass, more of a beckoning than a pass, made while they were standing in the driveway after the meeting. "Ricki, come over to my place and have a cup of coffee."

"OK," said Ricki, gulping air. By this time she suspected there was nothing in life more important than lesbian sex, which she had not yet experienced. She wasn't disappointed. Sex turned out to be even more...what?—fun, exciting, *necessary*—than she'd imagined. She became part of Bright Star's daily life and then, step by quick step, found herself involved in a death drama. Bright Star, her first lover, was planning to kill herself.

Now, this week, in the middle of a special breakfast—French toast, three mini-scoops of vanilla ice cream, a sea of maple syrup— Bright Star served up the announcement that her death date was set. "I'm excited, Ricki Dicki," she said, stooping to kiss her quickly on the cheek, pouring coffee into her cup, neither activity interfering with the other.

"When?" She wasn't ready.

The suicide was to be "soon now, sweetie." It was best if Ricki knew only that much. End of discussion, no questions tolerated. Her eyes were hot with sudden tears, her hearing felt clogged, and there was way too much sugar in the breakfast that lay half-eaten and repulsive on her plate. Practical, smart Ricki, who's always been able to cope—with a hand she learned to call anomalous at the age of six, with a dying stranger's last wink, with Lionel's disappearance from her life, with being a lesbian—isn't sure she can cope with this. She thought she could, at first. After they were together for three days Bright Star casually mentioned she had a fatal illness. Nothing more specific, just some unnamed fatal illness. They were at the Shop and Save. Aisle two, pickles and olives. "So I'll be killing myself, of course," Bright Star said, and put a jar of sweet pickles in the cart and went on down the aisle. Ricki trailed after her, stunned.

That night, lying awake beside the woman who was going to commit suicide, she remembered the wink of the dying Indian. She felt for the hard, eternal thing the wink had become. Lionel would say, "The wink will help you." A sense of life and death clear as the water in a good dug well, solid as the well's wall that separates earth from water, stayed with her all night. In the morning, Bright Star asked, seriously, formally, if she would accompany her to her death. She said yes. It was the only possible answer. Then they made love, solemnly, and Bright Star's pregnant belly became an altar. They both thought so and there was no embarrassment when one of them, she can't remember which, used the word *holy*. Then they went shopping for yet more baby supplies. That was over four months ago. There have been whole weeks when death has receded into the background. Not this week. Probably never again. "The date is set." That fact, those words, changed the air. She tells herself as a joke that the world's oxygen supply has been reduced by some evil conspiracy, possibly by extraterrestrial beings, which explains her difficulty with breathing, but she's not laughing, she's scared now unless she's with Bright Star. When they're together it only seems natural that one of them is going to kill herself.

Last night at supper Gertrude looked up from her plate: "Are you OK, Ricki?"

No. No, no, no. "I'm having trouble with a paper. I'd be fine if it weren't for my mind." She thinks she smiled a rueful smile, made good eye contact. Therapists like good eye contact. Her paper on Marianne Moore's "An Octopus" *is* a hopeless snarl. Nevertheless, she was lying. She felt riled and guilty, wanted to come clean, tell Gertrude everything, but she'd given Bright Star her word. Gertrude must know about the sex since she's gone most nights, but that's all. Only Raymond knows most of it and even he, for some reason she's not privy to, can't be told about the illness. All this secrecy. Will this meeting *ever* start? Here she sits in Petra's living room, another DWELL meeting. "Man-Moth" this time. Elizabeth Bishop is poet of the day. She'd rather be with Lionel. She'd tell him everything. No, she wouldn't, she'd keep her word. If she *could* tell, Lionel would help her, ask the right questions, say smart things, start a good argument. How will she ever write that paper? "An Octopus" makes sense for a minute, then breaks into pieces. She's left feeling outmaneuvered by a poet. Bishop was Moore's friend. If she can pay attention, this meeting might help her.

Chippie, in the kitchen with Nat and Petra, burps. Nat tells the baby that such behavior is rude, but forgivable considering her age. Ricki feels calmed, just hearing Nat's voice. At least she, Ricki Harding, who

71

never wanted kids, doesn't have to be Chippie's new mother. *Not your responsibility, sweetie.* She's never even changed a diaper. She could do that much. She offers, gets turned down. Does Bright Star think she couldn't manage, with her hand? Bright Star's interest in her hand is confusing. It's not like Lionel's interest. Sometimes the woman seems to want, or *need*, her to be disabled. What a mean thought. Anyway, her hand has nothing to do with the plan for the baby's next mother. Someone was chosen long ago. "Who?" she asked, once. "Don't bother your handsome little head about it," Bright Star said, too quickly, too sharply. She calmed herself in an instant, she could do that, and added, "It's all taken care of. This baby will be raised by the best person possible." Then she led Ricki to bed, a common ploy, one that brings uncomfortable or forbidden conversations to an end. Ricki likes the results. She can't understand why sex, which is a very strange activity when you think about it, feels so good, but it does. Also, she respects a person's need to change the subject, to keep areas of privacy. Bright Star is a complicated puzzle, which is part of the attraction, but the number of missing pieces is frustrating. She'd like to know about the Weeks family, for instance. "You're for the present, Ricki, not the past." As if family existed only in the past. Then a distraction, ice cream that time; strawberry cones, they *had* to be strawberry. Sometimes Ricki feels older than Bright Star. "Age is a matter of chaos," she was told one day. She didn't think she should ask what that meant. Bright Star would like her to relax and yield now, waiting for date. "Be happy for me." *Oh, right. Happy.* But she keeps her mouth shut. Bright Star says they have to be reverent toward Fate, it's one of the gods. She bows from the waist, then, her hands pressed into prayer mode. Maybe this is a game, or it might be serious. It's followed by skipping or bed making or baby tending.

Ricki can accept Fate, too—by this she means the fact that her first lover is about to commit suicide—when she thinks about the illness, about taking control, not being a victim; but it's the hardest thing she's ever tried to do. Bright Star has lectured and lectured: "Live in the moment. Don't anticipate. Don't make yourself suffer." This would be sensible if it weren't impossible. Being sensible is one of Bright Star's aspects. She has so many aspects. Ricki's never seen strobe-lighting but from what she understands it would be a good image for life right now. Sudden illuminations one after another, dark times in between. She tries to be grateful. Not many people her age get to be part of something this important.

When *will* this meeting get started? Roo is in the bathroom with Jessie. She's still not used to this: her teacher in the bathroom with her lover. She recognizes the music Petra put on. Bright Star has been playing Bach. The notes, the chords, so definite and determined, make her heart hurt. She used to think the hurting heart was a metaphor.

Roo and Jessie come out of the bathroom talking about the connection between Gertrude Stein and Paul Cezanne. Last week's meeting, still in the air. At least it doesn't look as if they had sex in there. Well, it never does, does it? Roo turns the music off and everyone settles. Chippie's bright brown eyes go from face to face, studying and moving on. Petra is holding her, looking relaxed. This was one tired baby at last week's meeting. "Up all night," Bright Star explained curtly. Bright Star's place, where she puts her pillow on the floor, where she should be sitting, is like a missing tooth, but Roo, all rosy and ready to go, starts right in: "Isn't this poem so perfectly vertical and straightforward? Such a contrast to *Tender Buttons*, the Man-Moth making his way up from underground, climbing the side of the building, trying to reach the moon, 'his shadow dragging like a photographer's cloth behind him'—what an image!— thinking the moon is a hole in the sky, thinking he can get *out* through it, then falling back down, 'scared but quite unhurt.' It's just up, up, up, and then down. It's like an old-time movie, visual and simple. Then I reread it and see how it's been holding out on me, has more to give. I love it when that happens."

"Yes, so many *perspectives*," says Petra.

"From above, from below, from places in between. Intuition and reason. Striving. Insight," says smart Nat. "Besides the Man-Moth, there's the rational man, who 'has no such illusions.' *He* doesn't believe you can get out through a hole in the sky. He knows a cold hard chunk of matter when he sees one. But he's like a doll, so diminished."

It's early for Nat to talk. Every meeting Ricki waits for her first words. Nat is her idea of a real lesbian, a thing she'll never tell Bright Star who might be hurt. Bright Star wouldn't fit into the "Before Stonewall" pictures in that book of Roo's. Nat would. Wearing a tie, she'd be sitting in a booth in a private bar with a group of women, her arm around someone's shoulder and that someone would be a "femme." A few meetings ago she talked about washing her hands in a Ladies Room and the woman at the next sink gave a look, as if Nat didn't belong there, as if she belonged in the Men's. "It shouldn't bother me so much, I should be used to it by now," Nat said. Roo and Petra let out sympathetic sighs but Ricki noticed that only Jessie had a story of her own to add, about sneaking into the men's room once, "passing," and what a charge it gave her. She *wants* to be taken for a man sometimes. Jessie scares Ricki, is the truth, whereas she's half in love with Nat. Not that she'd want to have sex with her, what a thought. Terrifying. She'd like to *be* Nat. She imagines getting herself a fedora, starting to wear a tie, but of course she'd do no such thing and Nat doesn't even dress that way. She should be listening. Jessie is talking. "...so I admire the little guy, trying over and over to make it up the wall and out through the damn hole in the sky."

"Like a child."

"Like a fool. A wise fool."

"Like a monster."

"What? Not a monster."

"Well, he *is* part human, part insect."

"A chimera."

"But not horrible. Endearing!"

"He's more like..."

"Like a poet?"

"Well, yes, that's probably what Bishop meant."

"Or like a mystic."

"Does anyone know what she thought about God?"

"She was probably agnostic."

"An intellectual agnostic but experientially an embarrassed mystic is my guess."

"Nobody knows?"

"Nobody knows."

"Nobody here in this room or nobody at all? Ricki? Have you run into Bishop, doing your paper on Moore?"

Ricki hardly hears the question. She's caught in the litany of similes. *Like a suicide*, is what she wants to say, but can't. To the deluded Man-Moth she would like to shout: *The moon is not a hole in the sky. You can't get out that way, so STOP TRYING.*

Chapter Nine

It's Raymond and his truck. They're doing the day together like two guys with a tough assignment. Now he's on 1A, on his way to Prospect, to the home of Petra where the DWELL ladies meet. The first letter stands for "dykes." He remembers that now. Raymona giggled when she told him. Gertrude offered to drive him but no, he has to do this himself. She didn't insist, just gave directions. It was a help, how she stayed calm. He met Petra once—at the baby shower, an event he hesitated to go to but of course he went because Raymona wanted it. She said he'd be glad later which is turning true right now. He won't be a complete stranger knocking on Petra's door. He's trying not to speed but what if the meeting ends and Ricki goes over to the trailer? He could have phoned from Gertrude's but this is nothing to make a phone call about. It went all right the other day with Ricki. She might be a college student but she's also a girl from outback Bucksport, daughter of a trucker. Easy enough to talk to, all things considered. Raymona was her very own self that day, walking up to the two of them in the parking lot of the cafe, all jaunty. "OK, you both know now, so sit down, have a cup of coffee, and talk to each other." Then she gets into her painted up Bug and drives off. Leaves them and their two trucks all alone. Nice surprise. Damn, but she could manage a situation to her own liking. Ricki was holding up pretty well that day. At least they've sat once, talked about the hard thing. Suicide. He doesn't really grasp it yet. He's speeding again. Wouldn't do to get a ticket.

*

Nat, Jessie, and Roo have left. Ricki has not. It was a good meeting. Petra loves the climb and fall of the Man-Moth, his single tear, the turns of language through which the creature emerges and reemerges. Bright Star's absence and Chippie's bright availability were both such a relief that it took a while to notice Ricki's half-presence. Petra, on impulse, invited her to stay for supper. What will they eat, though? She shopped, but not with an eye to company. In return for the meal to come, Ricki is changing Chippie's diaper. While this operation takes place on the living room rug, Petra stands in the open driveway door looking across the road at the stubbled blueberry field, glad for the sun which is now low in the sky. She's trying to conjure a menu and give Ricki privacy in case she's fumbling. An old pickup, loud, in need of a muffler, pulls into the drive and parks behind Ricki's. The trucks are a matched set, dusty, red, dented. It's strange, this way of parking, because there's a space closer to the house. Is one beat-up red truck compelled to park behind another? The man at the wheel, a Native American by his looks, takes a minute before he gets out of the truck. He seems troubled, and vaguely familiar. Walking toward her, working at his breathing, holding a manila envelope to his chest, he calls out her name as if to let her know he's not a stranger walking up her drive; as if to reassure her. Wait, yes, they met at the baby shower. Bright Star's brother. One of them must be adopted or maybe it's just different fathers. The introduction was irritatingly cryptic. Bright Star ended it by saying, "Remember this one, Raymond." Some distraction must have occurred or she'd have asked why she'd become a mandated memory. She puts out her hand and he shakes it. Just the right firmness, but he's a troubled man. "Raymond. Something's wrong?"

"I'm sorry to show up like this. Gertrude...I don't know her last name, I'm sorry...she told me Ricki Harding might be here and I see her truck..."

As they enter the living room, Ricki's eyes widen. Petra picks up the freshly-diapered baby. Ricki hardly seems to notice. Raymond looks at Chippie for a quiet moment. "I'm glad to see this little girl," he says with understated emphasis, then takes his time turning toward Ricki who meets his eyes. Petra feels in her own body the effort this takes—for both of them.

It's obvious that Ricki knows Raymond. Which means Ricki and Bright Star spend time together. Given who Bright Star is, this means they're lovers. Or is it Ricki and Raymond who...but she can't imagine Ricki with a man. Such a classic baby dyke. Maybe the phrase is out of date. She wants to whisper into Chippie's ear, "What about it, Chippie Dippie? Do they still use baby dyke for the cute butchy young ones?"

This is anxiety, this silliness. Someone should break the silence. It's Ricki who speaks. "Was it today?" Raymond nods. Ricki nods back, then keeps nodding. "OK," she says finally. So Ricki knows why Raymond is here, and it's for nothing frivolous, nothing light. "That's OK. That's good, right?" Ricki says. She's the one breathing hard now, Raymond is barely breathing.

In Raymond's response, Petra sees intelligence at work. The man makes a lightning calculation and restructures whatever his approach had been going to be. "Yes, this is what she wanted." He turns to Petra. "I'm sorry to have to tell you this. My sister, my half-sister, Bright Star, committed suicide this morning."

What?

Ricki puts her hand over her mouth as if to stifle herself. Her face crumples. Yes, she "knew" but to hear the words...

Petra, stunned herself, sinks into the nearest chair, hugging Chippie. *Suicide?* Suicidality is part of her work life, not part of her personal life. "Please, sit down, both of you. I..." Petra Kalinowski does *not* invite disturbed people into her personal life. But she did this time and she's known it from the beginning.

Raymond and Ricki sit next to each other on the couch. They do not touch. Nobody says anything. Petra calculates. Ricki knew this was coming, which means Ricki *has* been seeing Bright Star. Why the secrecy? And what was that about this being *good?* She starts rocking, though the chair, overstuffed, is not a rocking chair. Here is Chippie, whose mother is dead, asleep in her arms. She hums a tuneless set of sounds and glances at the pair on the couch. They have similar shapes, short and stout. Raymond is the softer one, rounder. More vulnerable? He's older, well into his thirties. Ricki's only nineteen. *Nineteen.* That bitch Bright Star, how *could* she? She should say something. "I'm so sorry," she says to Raymond. "Ricki?" She doesn't mean to put her on the spot, but this is too strange. She needs clarification. Ricki just looks confused.

Raymond intervenes. "I'm glad you have the baby."

"I take her once in a while, to give Bright Star a break." Is this insulting to Ricki? If she's the lover? But she might feel uncomfortable, bringing a baby into Gertrude's home. Does *Gertrude* know about this relationship? Ricki needs a tissue. Petra goes for the box which should been have gotten sooner. She carries Chippie with her. It occurs to her she's monopolizing the baby. Raymond will take Chippie with him. Maybe there's a father. Well, obviously there's a father. She has to admit she'll miss the little thing. *Bright Star is dead. Suicide.* She hands a clump of tissues to Ricki who blows her nose, grins bleakly at the noise, and says, "It's good, really it is. What she wanted, like you said, Raymond."

Raymond nods, then looks at Petra. "You'll need papers. I think they might be in here." He starts fumbling with the envelope. "I haven't had a chance to open this." Papers? Raymond takes a small black Swiss army knife from his pocket, cuts through layers of tape. Petra gets fixated on the fact that his knife is like hers, classy black, not common red. She has an aching need to comment on this. Inside the envelope Raymond finds smaller envelopes and takes them out, handling them as if they're fragile. There are three, one addressed to Raymond, one to Persephone Star Chip Weeks, and one on which her own name is carefully printed in capital letters, PETRA KALINOWSKI. She closes her eyes. This is not happening, of course it's not. Raymond is looking inside the manila envelope as if he expects something more. He turns toward Ricki, a question in his dark, beautiful eyes. Mahogany. Ricki looks back with matching eyes. *Pain.* "Maybe she put something in the mail for you," says sensitive Raymond. Ricki nods, stricken. So she and Bright Star *were* lovers. Petra doesn't like it. It's wrong. Wrong, wrong, wrong. Raymond hands her the envelope with her large, stark name. "She told me it was all set, all legal. I don't suppose you expected it to happen today. She said she hadn't told anyone except Ricki and me about having a date set so I don't suppose she informed you. I'm sorry."

"A date? To kill herself?" Raymond nods, carefully. "Christ," she says. Then, "Sorry." Ricki looks at her, looks quickly away. Raymond and Ricki look at each other. "What do you mean by 'all legal'?" She feels irritated; scared in the pit of her stomach; kid-like. "What's going on, Ricki?"

Ricki says to Raymond, "She doesn't know. But she must be the..."

Raymond nods, sighs, closes his eyes. "OK," he says. He's regrouping, she watches him do it. He knows what Ricki means. So does she, but she's sure as hell not going to admit it. Somebody's going to have to say it. Raymond just says, "Let's just go through these papers here, a step at a time." Which is a reprieve. He opens the envelope addressed to him, skims the page. "Nothing here. You'd better open yours, Petra."

There's a whole sheaf of papers. The first page says only: *I sent you a dream. I hope you got it. Respectfully yours, Bright Star, a.k.a. Raymona Weeks.* Her response, which she does manage to keep to herself, is, *No, I didn't get any dream. I have my own goddamn dreams.* Chippie wakes up, yawning. Petra puts the papers down and positions the baby on her lap, facing outward, toward her uncle and her dead mother's lover. This is awkward, trying to hold a baby and deal with papers. It occurs to her the scene is a bit surreal. Her arm, where the weight of the little body rested, is numb. So, these papers. *Last Will and Testament.* How very formal. "This would be for you, Raymond. She must've put it in my envelope by mistake."

"I don't think it's a mistake. Maybe if you read it out loud..."

"What about other family members? They should hear the Will." But she's stalling, and shaking.

Raymond says, oh so gently, "I think she meant for you to see it first."

So she reads it. Chippie accompanies her, cooing. *Cooing.* "'I, Bright Star, also known as Raymona Weeks, being of sound mind and body, do herein declare my last will and testament. After my death all belongings of mine will go to my half-brother, Raymond Weeks, of Bangor, Maine, with the exception of what is listed below. Upon my death I give custody of my child, Persephone Star Chip Weeks, to Petra Kalinowski, of Prospect, Maine, and I give to said Petra Kalinowski all belongings of mine that pertain to this child, including crib, clothing, toys, books, and all items of mine that will assist in the care of this child. I give to my child, Persephone Star Chip Weeks, one clay sculpture of my making, titled Fallen Goddess. This sculpture of two fused women will be found in the bathroom of the trailer in which I live.'"

The neat, handwritten document has been witnessed. It's notarized. *Crazy. She was crazy.* Chippie shifts abruptly and Petra nearly drops her. She watches her mind search out the precise professional description for her physical experience. *Fine whole-body tremor.* Under stress, a body will respond this way. It's expected. She closes her eyes.

What comes is the horse, Anya's dream friend—so black, such a *being*—
and it rears up and whinnies. The green field is too bright to look at. Is
that Anya doing a handspring in a circle of pure light? All this in a flash,
between breaths. She takes firm hold of Chippie and looks at Raymond
and Ricki who are staring at her like a matched set. *Salt and Pepper
Shakers on Blue-Gray Couch.* Whatever.

Ricki says, "You really didn't know."

"I did not know." She separates the words. I. Did. Not. Know.
She feels a confusing surge, an electrical charge associated with Anya
and the horse. She can hear an overtone of awe, faint but discernible, in
her own voice; along with the anger, the helplessness.

Raymond and Ricki say, in unison, "She said it was all
arranged." They might have rehearsed it.

"In her dreams," says Petra, nastily. Then, "I'm sorry. This is..."
Her mind is splitting. There's the terrified, hostile part that just spoke;
and the part that appreciates the performance of Raymond and Ricki, the
theater of it; and the part that will remember that hint of awe.

Awe?

Ricki says, "I didn't know it was you. She wouldn't say who."
She looks at Raymond. "Did you know?"

Raymond shakes his head. "Not until I saw you with the baby,
Petra. She said the new mother would have the baby, not to worry. She
liked secrets. She really liked secrets, from when she was a kid, but I
never imagined she wouldn't tell..."

There's a copy of the baby's birth certificate, no father named.
Other papers, all handwritten. Petra has stopped listening, she's gathering
information from a dead woman and keeping her own breathing going.
Pediatrician. Inoculation schedule. A long letter. *Dear Petra.* It blurs
when she tries to read it. Something titled *This Baby's Destiny* which will
offer more evidence of insanity. Scorn rises up. *None of this will stand up
in court.* The thought calms her. Her life is not going to be mangled.
"Raymond," she says, "take this baby. She's yours. Unless there's
someone else in your family..."

"Maybe you could hold her a little longer. If you would. Please."
Raymond speaks quietly, carefully. He looks at the floor, sits with his
knees spread, his hands clasped, his shoulders...

She's seen shoulders like that in the office. Men burdened beyond their capacities, forced to come to a therapist, someone having convinced them they can lay down their heavy loads. These Maine men —from the paper mill, or construction workers, or lobster fishermen, or men who take whatever work comes, odd jobs; men cautious with words, used to their pain—but something too sudden or too intense has bewildered them. The women are different, less afraid to put pain into language; usually. No wonder she keeps her therapy schedule to a minimum, takes to ladders in the summer, scrapes off old paint, repaints. She thinks of Danny who almost never leans on her emotionally. She pulls Chippie in tighter against her stomach, but keeps her facing the nice man who's her uncle and the young woman, her mother's lover. She puts the papers back into the envelope, lays it on the end table, notices a triangle of dust. She keeps herself from getting up to find a dust cloth and takes a deep breath. "What do you know about this, Ricki?"

"She said it was all arranged, that there was a new mother, that Chippie would be with the mother when she..."

"You knew she was going to..."

"I didn't know it would be today. She said something about meeting a woman who owns an art gallery in Portland."

"Right. Raymond?"

"I knew what Ricki knew. Same story about today, too. I believed her. She could always do that, make me believe her."

"So, Ricki, you and Bright Star...?" This is interrogation, possibly cruel, but she can't stop herself.

"We got together right after she joined DWELL. She didn't want me to tell anyone. I think it was sort of a test." Ricki looks at Raymond and he nods. "To see if I could keep a secret." Ricki starts to cry again, but stops herself. "I didn't think it would be so soon. I didn't think it would be today."

"God, Ricki."

"Yeah. But it's OK."

"No, it's not." At that, Ricki cries fully. Raymond's eyes fill with tears.

Good. People should be crying. This is—

She turns Chippie toward herself, looks at her round face, pulls her close, feels her firm little body. The baby starts to root at her breast.

81

This happened in that other time, when she was doing her bit, baby-sitting for a few hours on the weekend, a stage of things that seems to have ended. *Damn.* The child will need a bottle soon, there's just enough milk left to get them through the day. She should keep her another night, give Raymond a chance to make a plan. She can do that much.

Ricki cries. Raymond wipes his tears. Chippie stops rooting. So she's not hungry after all; or she's accustomed to having her needs ignored. Ricki blows her nose. She uses both hands. Bright Star was probably attracted to Ricki's hand; that, and youth. The girl is *nineteen*, for God's sake. Suddenly, and for no reason she could name, she decides Chippie will be more comfortable lying down. She gets up and lays her down—she's sleeping again, what a good baby—on the couch beside her uncle. Raymond puts his hand on the edge of the couch, a protective gesture. He'll take care of this baby, of course he will. He starts to say something but Ricki gets up and walks to the window. Which stops him. What he meant to say is fragile, can't survive the smallest other thing. *This was his sister who killed herself.* As if she were sitting with a bent-shouldered client, Petra feels suddenly tender and calm.

Ricki stands looking out the window. Finally she speaks. "She'd hate it that I cried."

Petra can hardly stand this. "Oh, Ricki."

Ricki turns around abruptly and says to Raymond, "Would you tell us?"

"About what she did?"

"Yes, please."

Raymond looks at Petra, as if for permission, or courage. She nods, feeling very much the therapist. Or the older woman. She must be almost ten years older than this sweet, gentle man. Raymond tells the story, including details, which he handles with care. The methods were cutting and gunshot.

The woman was serious, at least there's that, thinks Petra. Ricki looks as if she's folding all of this up, putting it away for future pondering. She nods when Raymond mentions details, the pieces of clothing set neatly on the toilet seat, an orange bowl, a sculpture. Yes, he tells Ricki, the one where the woman has a knife to her heart. A suicidal piece of art? This is what Bright Star wills to her *child?* Raymond describes the refrigerator. Baby bottles lined up and labeled. Petra can see them. All of this is real, then. Bright Star committed suicide. She had an overload of pain, a determined will, sufficient clarity, enough guts. The death is real. This baby is real. The future is blasted apart, or might be. Who will take this baby? Clearly Uncle Raymond is not jumping forward.

Chippie, beside her uncle on the couch—Persephone Star Chip Weeks, who must be all of four months old by now—starts to squirm. Petra goes over and picks her up. She should have heated a bottle, what was the matter with her? She jiggles the baby and whispers in her ear, "Shh, shh, not quite yet." She listens to what Raymond is saying and thinks about what he's not saying. He doesn't say there was blood. Obviously there was blood, brain matter. She tries to imagine the sculpture; fails. In the bathroom? Chippie falls asleep, a heavy head on her shoulder. The story is finished. Enough details given, enough questions asked. Raymond seems numb, Ricki looks stoic, and Petra's own mind is a ragged sponge. Ricki doesn't look worse, at least there's that. What time is it? They should eat something. But now Chippie's sound asleep. Maybe she needs sleep more than food. Her mother is dead, let her sleep. "Raymond?" She gets his attention easily. Not a self-involved man. "Will you be taking the baby? Or someone in your family? Or the father?" This little series of questions, uncalled for, conjures Wile E. Coyote—or was it the Road Runner?—who had a habit of running off cliff edges. He was perfectly safe on thin air until he glanced down.

"No, no other family. The father—his name was Chip, that's all I know—he was just passing through."

This is not a man who pleads, but look at him. *He's more honest than I am and he needs me to take this baby.* Her mind veers. Chippie is Chip Junior, daughter of Chip Senior. She is not therefore a little chip of Big Bright Star as she, Petra, has assumed in her periodic, irrational hostility toward the woman. She's little Star, perfectly appropriate. Also, just for good measure, she's Persephone, lost daughter of Demeter, and she will grow up to become Queen of the Underworld.

While her mind skitters, while she lurches between scorn and kinder feelings, she understands: she's being asked to take a child into her life. *A sudden slice changes the whole plate, it does so suddenly.* Thank you, Gertrude Stein. That was Bright Star's final DWELL meeting. Should they have known? She takes a deep breath and turns in the only remaining direction. "Ricki? You were her partner." This is not her best moment. She thinks of Sartre, of bad faith. Also, deep in her psyche, or her body, a weird excitement stirs. Which is ridiculous.

"Partner? No, I don't think that's right. She said I wouldn't have the responsibility, or the privilege either. That diaper I just changed was the first one. She was so definite, Petra. I never imagined...I thought there was someone who...do you think I should?"

Petra stops her. There's no need for this. Her own cruelty appalls her. "I suppose it's the same with you, Raymond."

"Yes, but if you can't..."

Petra understands, finally, that she's in charge. She knows what to say, of course she does. "We don't have to decide anything today." Unable to stop herself, she adds, "I can't believe she did this. Any of this." She feels hunger. Abrupt, gnawing hunger. Chippie cries. This motherless baby is hungry, too. She gets up quickly and moves toward the kitchen. "We should eat something," she says over her shoulder. No response comes. "Or at least drink something," she mutters to herself. She warms the baby's bottle, opens the refrigerator. Leftover meat loaf. She thinks of lined up baby bottles and wishes she were dreaming. *I sent you a dream.* Christ Almighty. Was that really Anya doing a handspring? The human mind is a frightening, astonishing thing. She sets the microwave timer. Hot meat loaf sandwiches, best she can do.

Chapter Ten

Ricki ate a sandwich she can't remember tasting but Petra was right, she needed to eat. She feels more real. She's not happy about making this trip, but what else would she do? Petra has them going to the trailer for supplies for Chippie. Besides, "Bright Star's mess" has to be cleaned up. Thirdly, none of them is permitted be alone yet. One, two, three, ready, set, go. The bed will be there, made up, not rumpled. *Everything in order, sweetie, everything in order.* But order broke down, Petra hadn't known about Chippie.

She's in the truck's cab between Raymond and Petra, all of them like sardines who got caught in a net and taken from one place to the next, every new place a less familiar element than the one before and now they're packed tight, their eyes stunned blind. The next time air hits they'll get eaten. But no, they'll be climbing out of Raymond's truck and into the trailer, which is nothing like getting eaten, and nothing like spending your life inside a sardine factory, which is what Aunt Helen did. "It's fine. You get used to the smell. I like the girls." Ricki had a strong ambition from a young age not to end up working in a sardine factory. She could have refused, said death was beyond her capacities, she was too young, too scared. She didn't know, though, did she? She wants Lionel. The center line here was recently repainted, strong yellow dashes, passing permitted. Raymond doesn't pass the slow car in front of them. He's taking them there, but not any faster than he has to. *She's gone.* She doesn't really believe this. The woman was like a firefly, a point of light against a night sky, disappearing, reappearing, you can't stop watching, where next? Petra holds the baby against her breast. She looks downright motherly. Ricki understands puppies, even baby chicks. Not babies. She told Bright Star that, but it was irrelevant, the arrangement had been made, it was all settled, *et cetera*. It was *not* all settled. Tears well up but she's already tired of crying, tired of her hurting head, tired of the dense mess in her chest. She was pretending, stupidly, that there was more time. "Time's up," Bright Star said a couple days ago, and grinned and winked and ran out of the trailer and rushed around the dooryard and rushed back in and grabbed her by the waist and made her dance, but never touched her anomalous hand, the one that was supposed to be so special. The road disappears under the truck. Her mind flattens against the pavement. Raymond drives. What was it like for him, going to the morgue? One day Bright Star said, apropos of nothing, "You'll be fine, Ricki. People like you can't be rearranged." She feels rearranged. There won't be anything in the mail for her. The envelope was the place for final messages. "I don't split essential energy, Ricki Dicki. Don't ever ask me to split essential energy." She requested clarification on that one but it wasn't forthcoming. Here's an example, though: all final messages in one envelope, and none for her. Maybe no message *is* the message. "Courage starts here. You're on your own now, girl." Bright Star could get preacherly, not her best mode. "Trust your wisdom, sweetie," she'd say, doling out wisdom. Convolutions were built into their situation. Bright Star told her she had "solid peasant wisdom." At first she felt insulted, but later she understood. She is, or was, unified, real, plain, unpretentious. Bright Star was—*was*—luminous and unpredictable and she broke apart readily. Here's the turn. She'll have to get out of the truck, climb the steps, go through the door.

The trailer looks unaware of itself as a place left behind. The familiar old painted bug sits quietly. *Nothing happened here.* One unusual thing, though: a note attached to the door. Will there be blood? Yes, there will be blood. She steps into the living room behind Petra who holds Chippie. She's following a gentle snoring baby sound, letting it pull her. Behind her comes Raymond. They make a little parade, doing what needs to be done. Raymond has the note in his hand, he took it down from the door, it has her name on it. "I didn't want you to go in there, Ricki. If you came..."

"Oh."

Petra puts Chippie down in the crib. Bright Star would say the baby knows, that she's still close to the spiritual realm and understands the miracle of death. Ricki stares at the crib. She smells blood and wonders if she has to...

"Ricki, would you stay with the baby? I'll do some cleaning up." Petra, in charge. Like a mother.

She sits down on the couch. It's Bright Star's blood she smells. Raymond stands there. Petra tells him he can collect the baby's things and get them into the truck. He heads off to do his task. The bathroom door closes. She feels shut out, left alone. It should be her business, not Petra's, to be in there where more happened than suicide. The two of them in the tub, giggles, sexy playing around. She sits. Chippie sleeps and snores. The trailer is itself, a little crazy, still special. Nothing bad shows. Petra shut the blood in the bathroom with herself. Raymond comes and goes, gathering baby things, taking them to the truck. Where is Bright Star? In the morgue.

Ricki rubs her small hand. She broke the habit the summer before fifth grade when her brothers started chanting "rub-a-dub-dub" every time they caught her at it. It was a reminder, not a mockery. There's a special Harding tone they used, upbeat. "You should stop, we're helping you," the tone said, and they were. Also, they were embarrassed to have attention called, and embarrassed about being embarrassed, having been "raised right." All week, though: rub, rub. Bright Star never touched the hand after she made her "announcement." No last letter. Because Bright Star was finished with her. She might have to throw up. Where would she do it? But the urge passes, all she has to do is sit here. There's The Knot. It has a big meaning, but what? Everything Bright Star said, every word, could disappear like champagne bubbles bursting. They had champagne once in that bathtub. She rubs her hand. It's starting to chap. She stops.

There's Patchwork, the little grotesque, divided into his red and blue aspects, sitting on his shiny black turtle. There's something significant about turtles, something Native American. She wishes the baby would wake up. It was OK, changing the diaper at Petra's. She feels like cement set into a shape, sitting, doing nothing, being obedient. Petra's taking forever. Raymond stopped coming and going. Where is he? Smoking in the truck? Does he smoke? Bright Star smoked—sometimes. Other times, the idea was anathema. *Anathema, Ricki Dicki. Great word, huh?* "I saw you smoking this morning." She knew better, but she said it. Bright Star's eyes glazed over, but then she was joking about the religion of inconsistency and how she was high priestess. She seduced Ricki on the spot. The spot, that particular time, was this sofa. It arouses her to remember, which is embarrassing, a sin maybe, if she "believed." The high priestess of inconsistency was very sexy that day. She looks at the monkey, guaranteed turnoff. He's curled up in fetal position on a pillow and could have been sweet but the colors ruin him. *His name is Honey Monkey. He got christened before the paint job. Don't say anything.* Bright Star laughed a terrible rough new laugh while Ricki held the day's creation, a green and brown and purple thing, then put it down as instructed. Ricki feels like curling into a fetal ball herself. She wants to see her mother, be a kid. A little kid.

Chippie lets out a screech. She jumps up, tries to get the squirmy creature out of the crib. Petra materializes from nowhere and she's caught in her awkwardness. Everything goes blurry, then overly definite. Petra seems to be reaching her arms out. Chippie gives off diaper-filling noises. "So that's it," Petra says. "You stink, little baby." Her tone is forgiving. She pulls a fresh diaper from the bag, competent, flushed. Raymond appears. "Finished?" he says. "Yes," Petra answers. They look at each other. Seeing them look at each other that way, seeing how they acknowledge what they're talking about by a plain look, makes everything less strange. "Thanks for doing the cleanup." Raymond says. "It would've been a tough thing for me. I was sitting in the truck, imagining." "It wasn't as hard on me." But Petra doesn't look well, her face flushed one minute, drained the next. Still, she bends over and kisses the freshened baby as if she's inside some easy routine. She *should* be the next mother.

Petra looks toward the bathroom. "Ricki, do you want to..."

"Should I?"

"Let's all go in together. How would that be?" They take a deep breath, all of them together, and start toward the bathroom. No one's pretending this is easy. It's Petra first, with the baby. Petra, Ricki, Raymond. This is how them came in today, this is the order of things, she can do this. She smells bleach which is the smell of cleaned-up blood, better than blood not cleaned up. The Fallen Goddess sits still, she was here when it happened. The bathtub is too white, too clean. Chippie squirms and mewls and Ricki feels like squirming and mewling, too. The question she has kept inside spurts out. "Was there a lot of blood?"

Petra pretends this is an ordinary question. "Quite a bit in the tub. Some splatter on the wall. A little on the floor."

Ricki looks at Raymond, but he seems to be holding up. She started this, she might as well keep going. "Did parts of her brain...and bone...?"

Petra sighs. "Oh, Ricki. Have you been sitting out there imagining?"

"No. I couldn't, but now I'm in here. What about her brain?" She's pushing her sentences out, hoping this isn't rude.

Petra hesitates, but answers. "That was the hardest. There were tiny bits of what must have been brain matter, and fragments of bone, but not a lot, Ricki. I think most of her brain must be..." She made a mistake. Her ears are full of pressure. Petra says Bright Star's brain must still *be*. So it's all right, everything's fine, except she feels a little strange. Raymond is putting his arm around her and guiding her out of the bathroom. Petra is following, trying to quiet Chippie, saying soft cooing things. This parade is backwards, so the order of things must be different now. She wants to go home, but where is home? She wants her Mommy.

Time gets choppy. Back to Prospect, to Petra's house, the three of them plus Chippie in Raymond's truck. Goodbye to Petra and the baby. Start her own truck, clamp onto steering wheel with normal hand, press hard against it with anomaly. Going to Gertrude's house. That's alliteration. Raymond behind in his truck, keep him in the rear view mirror, he has to follow. *For safety, Ricki, you don't look so good.* Raymond's forgiving smile. Everybody forgiving somebody now. What about *him*, he's in such great shape? Can't stop shaking, but Gertrude's house is achieved.

Is this home? She sleeps a little, tense and wired; gets up, packs, writes a note for Gertrude. She wipes tears away and forgets to play the radio but she gets to Bucksport, Bright Star flattened like a paper doll against the side wall of her mind. Maybe this is home. She takes her shoes off, goes on tiptoe, avoids the boards that creak, but her mother comes out anyway, blinking and concerned, pulling on that old chenille robe. Her mother, Mary. Her father is on the road. Daughter Ricki and mother Mary have warm milk and cookies. She tells everything, starting with the fact that she's fallen in love. *With a girl. In the spring.* At dawn, she crawls into her childhood bed, settles under the worn and lumpy quilt, and lets herself suck her thumb, the normal one. A thing she hasn't done since first grade.

Stella doesn't look drunk to him and she doesn't smell bad at all. "I'm sober, Raymond."

"That's good, Ma. How many days?"

"Twenty-two."

He nods, looks around, counts. Five new doilies, more than one a week. She's been struggling. When Stella falls off the wagon she takes her doilies to the Goodwill. One beer and they all have to go, that's her rule. When she gives up the booze she starts crocheting again, uses it to steady herself. Raymond admires the doilies. Rectangular, a clear shape, they lie flat. Electric blue this time, a satiny thread, and the designs are more intricate than usual. He hates to rock the boat.

His own boat isn't as steady as he'd like it to be which is why he stopped downstairs at Bitta's. Stella really shouldn't live above a bar, but here she is. Bitta's helped. Pool and Pepsi: Saturday night ritual. He considered passing on it, the night not being normal, but he saw he needed it. He doesn't always choose Bitta's. He feels guilty if he's so close and doesn't go up to Stella's. Sometimes she's down there herself, making his Saturday night a little complicated. Truth is, he's been going other places most weeks recently. But it appealed to him to park the truck and be done with driving. Pool, soda, and up the piss-smelling stairs, and here he is. "Ma, I have something hard to tell you."

"No, sweetie, not today."

He isn't surprised at this, tries again. "Ma..."

"You should walk more, Raymond. Did you even notice the warmth of the day? It was lovely down by the river. I'll make coffee. I have cinnamon buns from the Shop and Save." She talks at him, rolling her words out over his intention, her pitch a little high. "Tell me about work, Raymond. Did you work today?" Fussing with the coffee, shaking a little. Maybe he shouldn't tell her yet. He searches for a topic and pulls up Margie Stokes, researcher into the matter of troublesome skunks. She's a part of this same day.

"You don't happen to know somebody named Margie Stokes, do you, Ma?"

"I believe I do, Raymond. From when I'm homeless, you know. I think she comes by the shelter bringing baked goods. Is she a bit elderly?"

"You're amazing, Miss Stella. Yes, she's a bit elderly. She came into the library today. Wanted to learn how to use the internet. Quite a character."

"Yes. Well, she has those bright bird eyes. Like a tufted titmouse, I'd say."

He's tempted. They could go on like this. She'd let him. But he knows what he has to do. "It's about Raymona, Ma."

"That girl is no longer my daughter, as you well know. News of her would not be my concern. Excuse me, dear." She heads to the bathroom, upright as Margie Stokes. Two proud and stubborn women in one day. Not to mention his proud and stubborn half-sister, laid out at the morgue. He feels stupid, getting taken in by that story about the gallery lady. She's such a damn good liar. *Was* such a damn good liar. The clock on the wall ticks. It's the angle of her face, how her chin was higher than her forehead, that he can't get rid of. Reminded him of sex, the climax. The back of her head gone, shot away. At least her face was whole. He turns off the coffee, pours a cup, wonders how long his mother can hold out in the bathroom. The baby's settled for the night. Maybe Petra will take her. He doesn't want to think about what might happen if she refuses. No alternative comes to mind. Not a thing out of place here, not a speck of dust. Stella's trying hard.

It's half an hour before she emerges from the bathroom. "I suppose that coffee's cold," she says. "I'll heat it up and then you'll say what you have to say. You might have to stay until Bitta's closes. You understand that."

"I plan on staying the night. Sleeping bag's in the truck. Sit down, Ma."

When they've said all there is to say for one night Stella takes her fourth cup of coffee to the bedroom. He spreads his sleeping bag in front of the door, turns out the light, gets in. He fingers the doily he took from the back of the couch. It's a good talent she has, pulling strings to a shape.

Chapter Eleven

Petra's not much of a drinker but she keeps a little something around. Now, at the end of this very strange day, is the time to indulge. As she sips amaretto the brutal facts of the day recede. A deep, buzzing fatigue takes over. She gets herself up from the couch, walks to the bedroom, stops to look thoughtfully at the baby asleep in the bassinet, climbs onto the bed, and falls into a vague web of dreams.

Toward morning she dreams in a more defined way, split and lucid, aware she's dreaming, and here is the Man-Moth, a creature of varied and shifting identities. He is Helga who has given up two-year-old Ingrid. He is Bright Star a.k.a. Raymona Weeks who successfully managed a suicide. He is Petra Kalinowski, a woman impelled to climb. The creature emerges from underground and makes his way up the side of the skyscraper, determined to get to the moon which he perceives as a hole in the sky. Aware of being watched by an alert, engaged, observing Petra, he turns his complex head toward her, slightly enlarging his shadow which is made of actual black cloth. Critic Petra declares the real cloth to be a non-subtle touch. In the poem the cloth was appropriate simile, the shadow "dragging like a photographer's cape behind him." Looking at Petra over his shoulder, dream Man-Moth says, "This is the sudden slice." Then he falls. Landing unhurt, he sheds a single tear which he offers to her because, despite artistic distance or perhaps because of it, she has been watching carefully enough. The tear rests on her open palm. It has come from Helga, and from desperate, determined Bright Star, and from her own bewildered-by-longing self.

She wakes up, or thinks she does, her pillow soaked, her face wet. Sounds of a singer, a jazz contralto, emerge from the distance and come closer, closer until the lyrics are clear: *a sudden slice changes the whole plate / and he trembles / and he must investigate / and high / and so / and falling / slicing into the silver / of six small spoons / and onto the three-ringed plate / and over the moon he goes.* The voice layers the beat, going deeper, deeper, each layer pulled out of the one beneath and they are now violently colored scarves pulled from a hat. The magician, who seems to have been there all along, bows. Petra, critic and victim, tricked into pleasure, reluctantly applauds and now bubbles float from daughter Anya's happy mouth, each bubble holding a letter of the alphabet. This is a cartoon dream. Petra is bent over, breathless, laughing too hard. She straightens. The bubbles spell nonsense; then—the child is learning—C-h-i-p-p-i-e; then, C-h-i-p-p-i-e D-i-p-p-i-e. Petra catches her breath. Anya disappears. A cloth diaper, the kind that needs pins, must be changed. When she completes the task and holds Chippie up to be viewed, Raymond, her audience, applauds and then everyone in the auditorium is applauding because Petra Kalinowski has successfully changed a diaper.

*

Sunday morning. Petra thinks of this as the day after Bright Star blithely tossed a baby into her arms and proceeded to kill herself, but she could revise that. Yesterday her friend died—she *was* a friend, of sorts— and left a will entrusting her only child to Petra Kalinowski.

Impossible.

Petra is walking toward her faithful rock, a woman with a baby on her back. Her own name means rock. *Remember that, Petra. We named you strong after the world broke apart.* This is Tekla, mother, referring to World War II, referring to Poland. Chippie rides in Anya's blue baby carrier. *Held Eggshell, Bright Blue.* Petra watches every step. The path is rough with gnarled tree roots and old water ruts. She remembers a small triangle, bright blue, a chip of painted eggshell from her Polish American childhood. Easter. The rest of the broken shell has been discarded but she finds this overlooked piece. She takes the treasure to Tekla, excited. Tekla stoops down and together they contemplate beauty. That night young Petra takes the chip to bed with her, puts it under her pillow, hopes a fairy will come. In the morning the triangle is broken in two. She throws the pieces to the floor, stomps, and runs to Tekla and Witold, sobbing. At bedtime the tiny mess is gone. She knows it was her mother who cleaned it up, no fairy would want a *broken* triangle. Oh, dear, thinks present-day Petra. The tide is right. There will be time before the river rises and surrounds the rock. She climbs onto it carefully. This is a risky venture, coming here to think the thoughts she plans to think with a baby on her back, but she's certain—unreasonably —that Chippie, currently sleeping a deep baby sleep, will cooperate. She begins in the usual place: George, his big molded girlie body shimmering in a long silver gown, his wild golden hair a ten-inch halo, his beautiful face. Just George, standing there, looking good.

Returning to the night Anya died is a discipline, almost a spiritual practice; necessary, though only rarely. Today, the imperative is intense. The story begins in the elegant apartment George put together long before he and Danny became a couple. Danny had only recently moved in, he wasn't used to such niceties as cloth napkins held firmly in wooden rings. "What a trip," he'd say, grinning, besotted with his Beautiful Boy. George's old oak table was permanently set with good china. The centerpiece was frequently changed, often elaborate, but simple on this evening. A single rose stood in a tall crystal vase, honoring their one-month anniversary. It was George who bought the rose. Danny, would-be hobo, wouldn't know to do such a thing. They were going to a ball, a benefit. Not for AIDS, AIDS had not yet been named, but for some other good cause. George was a figure in the gay community, a talented female impersonator. It was almost part of his job to go to such events. He was doing fussy last minute things, wearing his silver gown. Sometimes Petra forgets she wasn't there when Danny, ready to go, went to turn off the television, saw the news. The reporter, shouting above sirens and whirling red lights garish against the San Francisco night, gave the address, no names; woman and girl, apartment building on Fair Oaks. "George, come here," says Danny.

Yesterday's warm sun is gone. Petra and Chippie are bundled for the cooler weather. Twenty years ago, October in San Francisco was unnervingly consistent, mild and clear all month. She was told the stars were in a terrible place. She had gotten used being asked what her Sign was. She had learned to say Scorpio, and watch the raised eyebrows. Anya was an Aries: fire sign. *My name is Fire, call me Fire.* It took years to make the connection, astrological sign to the child's chosen name. Silly, but it felt like a hint of order behind events when it finally became obvious.

Anya, Fire Child, died that night in San Francisco.

Chippie, Maine Cancer child in need of a home, is being sweetly cooperative, sleeping and snoring.

George came to the television. The camera scanned faces of the gathering crowd—curious, excited, appalled faces—then swung to the building and held the focus long enough for certainty. "Oh, God." They reached for each other's hands; clasped, released, moved into action. The building was two blocks away. George plucked the rose from the crystal vase as they rushed out, Danny in clean jeans and a new white loose cotton top, George in his long tight silver gown and silver heels. They ran. George pulled the gown above his knees and he was proficient in heels. Still, he was hampered. Danny wore modest sneakers. He paced himself to stay with George. Petra almost remembers running with them, but of course she wasn't there, she was settled in her own living room, some book in hand, Bach in the background, or Mozart. It must have been one of the two. It disturbs her now as it always does that she can't remember which. Nor can she remember what she was reading. She knows, knows for sure, that she wasn't thinking about Anya. She was relaxed that night, untroubled.

Danny and George, part of the crowd, saw the covered bodies carried out on stretchers. They saw which apartment. They ran back to get the car. Danny drove, speeding. George held the rose. The rose was red, like the whirling lights at the scene, like the blankets that covered the bodies. Petra is in the back seat of the car at this point, she's with them. They're breathless, horrified, silent; sweet and caring; frightened by what they have to tell her. She runs up the stairs with them. The bodies were the right size for Marian and Anya, the apartment was Marian's, but none of it is real yet. The real thing for these boys is how Petra will feel, how they have to be good friends to Petra, though George hardly knows her yet. They knock at her door.

She's been fearful in San Francisco since she started living alone four years ago; since she gave Anya over to Marian. She doesn't like to admit this so she won't ask who's there. If someone knocks, she opens the door. There they are, looking far more frightened than she is. George's hair is electric, alarming. Danny's white top is excessively bright. The light in the hall has good wattage, a fact generally appreciated, but it exaggerates this whiteness absurdly. She can hardly look. "Come in. What's wrong?" This is like being in a play. She isn't sure her intonation is effective. George gives her the rose, such a sweet, thorough faggot, always managing the lovely gesture, but what's *wrong*? They make her sit on the couch and they sit, one on each side of her, very close, and she can't imagine. She's holding the rose, careful not to prick herself. They tell her. Break-in. Stretchers. Red blankets. Bodies. Her mind stops working in any normal way. Deep cold comes, starting at the solar plexus. She takes yoga classes, knows the terms, solar plexus, chakra, she has a good life, her journals are starting to make sense, she's twenty-nine years old, adult, everything's working out, it's just that it's harder to spend time with Anya, the child has gotten so long and thin, so awkward, distant, but this is just a stage and life is so interesting now, everything's working out, really it is. The cold spreads, she can measure it, one micrometer per second, two, three, four, five, six, seven years old her baby got to be—

Danny offers a glass of water and keeps saying her name. George rubs her back. How sweet they are, these boys, and they want her to drink this cold water. They want her to add more cold. One. Two. Three. Four. Five. Six. Seven.

Enough.

She's on her rock, Chippie sleeping against her back, and this is enough. Enough going back. She might mean, too, that seven years were enough for Anya, enough for a complete life. A new thought, the kind she tells no one. She lets a shiver pass through her body and Chippie stirs but settles again, cooperative child. The rock is cold and hard. It holds her.

The facts. She, Petra Kalinowski, gave up on parenting and her little girl lived a very few years in the care of Marian Kelly. Then that little girl was raped and murdered, stupidly, along with Marian, by a couple of ridiculously young boys high on drugs, prodded and dared by companions who waited outside the open window until the deed was done. Too noisily as it turned out. The police found the little group not far away, sweating and hysterical, disabled by fits of giggling and crying, out of breath, two of them with blood smeared over their young white hands, thirteen and fourteen years old.

A swirl of rearranged lives. Two fresh bodies at the morgue. No signs of torture, of prolongation. Get in, rape, slit throats, get out. Except for getting caught, it all went so well, the high from the drugs holding, the task completed with aplomb, efficiently. Or so she has to believe. A

96

considerate official told her the knives were well-sharpened. The whetstone was, absurdly, evidence.

This is how she can do it: acidly summarizing. She has a softer way, a way of wishing. She wishes she could believe Anya and Marian had no time to wake up. They were both in bed, the apartment was dark, the boys needed flashlights. The flashlights were confiscated and labeled, evidence. Of course one doesn't sleep through. She has never imagined, not fully. She, the lucky one. Tekla was raped in wartime Poland and died young of disease. Anya, child of seven, was raped and murdered in peaceful San Francisco; as was Marian. Petra lives on, alive, healthy, unviolated. All this air, hers to breathe, and another baby on her back.

She's thinking of accepting this baby. Raising her. It's embarrassing how chosen she feels, how this dangerous sense of destiny has expanded hour by hour since the moment she saw the envelope with her name, the careful, deliberate printing, the capital letters. Even before she read the words that *presumed*—she's still angry—to will a child back into her life: this sense of destiny, too exciting to trust, or even, at first, acknowledge. She shifts her body to change the configuration of pressure from the rock. She listens to Chippie's breathing. No snoring at the moment. She ponders her scandalous new thought: seven years can make a complete and sufficient life, something other than a torn off piece of time. How inhuman is she? But despite obvious possible interpretations —callousness, avoidance of guilt, pretense of enlightenment—she thinks this might be a worthy and respectful way of regarding the life and death of her daughter. She looks at the leaden sky, feels its good weight and the good weight of this baby against her back. Anya, Chippie, Anya. Turning her attention back and forth, child to child, is all she can think to do.

One person would accept this new thought. Marian. *Seven years, a complete life. What a lovely thought, Petra. Yes, I know what you mean.* But Marian is dead. Still, she'd be interested. But there'd be too much air, too little gravity, in her response. Marian read books with pale blue covers with white clouds and sun rays fanning out, books that proclaimed everything perfect. Maybe everything *is* perfect. Would it be perfect to take Chippie? Does this feeling of destiny running around inside her like a wild thing signify? Is she making a decision? When Anya came last night, a silly dream child, a cartoon character, she gave

97

permission. Goofily, but she gave it. Which only means she, Petra, gave herself permission.

How crazy am I?

She doesn't feel crazy, not exactly. Here is her good rock, and not far from here, constantly receiving the waters of the Penobscot, is the ocean which determines the weather so much of the time, a satisfying fact. A low wind off the ocean is working with the tide which comes in like molten pewter. Chippie sleeps, protected from the wind by her potential mother's slight but substantial middle-aged body. Protected enough? If Anya's short life was complete, what might this mean about Chippie's? Is there a path out of every tragedy? Can she, Petra Kalinowski, be the one to find it, hack it out of the wilderness, for this little being, or is she the worst possible candidate? Raymond will inquire, gently, "Have you thought about details?" No, that will be Danny, Nat, Roo. One or all of them. She'll snap back, "Diapers were never a problem." Danny, who witnessed her time with Anya, will say, "I know. It's more a matter of tiny painful tears to the fabric of your mind. Interruptions, for instance." And she'll say, "Fuck you." And cry, and plead: "What about maturity? Haven't I matured?" And he'll put his arms around her and say, "It's up to you, of course it's up to you."

All of which settles nothing. The river is rising, Raymond will be coming. She eases herself down off the rock, cautious, but Chippie wakes up, startled and fussy. Raymond will be driving his dusty red truck, twin to Ricki's, along 1A at this moment. The coincidence of the two trucks is a source of comfort, one of those glimpses of possible order in the whirl of improbabilities. Chippie settles down. Petra feels the solid little body against her back. She wishes, not for the first time, that she understood Chaos Theory. Nat has explained and explained. She follows, or thinks she does. She glimpses the elegance, but ten minutes later the whole thing falls to pieces. Possibly it's demonstrating itself. At least she's picked up the vocabulary. Now, for example, as she walks toward this meeting with Raymond, her mind is composed of shifting fractals: stern, principled uncertainty; dark, wild excitement. Halfway up the hill Chippie cries, and keeps crying. The child needs to be fed.

Chapter Twelve

Driving down to Prospect again, Raymond plays the radio. Country western. The plainness can settle him, or it reaches in, pulls on his heart. Right now it's bringing tears, sending them rolling. He doesn't mind. Everything feels sad this gray day. He blinks, straining to see through the film, glad there isn't much traffic. Raymona was no fool. If she trusted Petra he will too. Will Petra be willing?

He slept several hours, doily in hand. Stella didn't try to dislodge him from his post and even slept a little herself but mostly she crocheted, finishing up one doily, starting another. Rose-colored this time. Three buds will decorate one corner. She showed him, proud of herself. She's still sober and planning to stay that way with help from AA. Should he let himself hope? "I'm fine, Raymond. Get it settled about that baby. You'll be back tonight." He never had to hold the baby yesterday. It's hard enough just seeing her, bright little thing that she is. Raymona would understand his position. There are aspects to his life no one will comprehend now. More tears. Sorrow for himself this time. The sadness travels this way and that. To her, to himself, back to her. Probably be this way for a while. He parks.

Petra's right at the door, towel in hand, looking electric. He feels unprepared for how actual she is. Yesterday nothing was real, everything unfamiliar, Petra included. Today she's familiar, though different. They've been through things, they have matters to decide. She offers soda and they get settled, Chippie on a bed of blankets on the floor, entertained by plastic toys he recognizes. Petra wants to know how he is and what about Ricki? He tells what he learned from Gertrude, how Ricki ended up leaving in the middle of the night, went to her parents' house. "I hate to see her go through this. I tell myself she's solid enough."

Petra knows what he means. "I've been doing some serious thinking, Raymond. First I have questions." Right down to business, then. Good. Best way. She asks about family, about the father of the baby, about his own situation. Must be aiming to see who else could raise

Chippie. He discloses the existence of Stella, feeling cautious, protective, just saying she's not well enough to take on a child. Petra nods. Her real interest appears to be the father. She's been through the papers and there's no mention. She wants to know about other writings, whether there might be more, where they might be. Chippie falls asleep, a sudden thing. He's seen it before. It's sweet and startling, both, how it happens. Maybe any baby would do it that way, what does he know? "The father will have rights," Petra says.

He lets himself sit there, breathing. Is he forgetting something Raymona told him? An Indian named Chip, fellow passing through. Good looking, she'd say, and grin her funny secret grin and shut the conversation down. He doesn't see a need to tell Petra about the grin. As to writings, he doesn't know. They agree there wasn't anything in plain sight in the trailer. They both know without saying it that there could be something hiding. "She was always scribbling, ever since her teenage years. I was gone for some of that time and she'd send me..." He stops. He wasn't intending to go in that direction. When he starts up again he tries to sound a little steadier. "You might be right. Words she wrote down might give some hint about the father. She could've been holding out on me, or shifting the story. She didn't always stick close to facts." But his mind drops down to the past like an elevator with a cut cable, out of his own control. Raymona and her words. She put her words onto the page so carefully, but all those letters she sent him when he was in the Youth Center, and her spoken words, too, needed a certain kind of reception. You couldn't count on truth. She liked to give a piece of information a new shape. It was part of her and he was accustomed to living with it. Now he won't be living it. He's starting to feel her being dead. Petra hands him a tissue. She makes this easy. She's a therapist, he knows that from the baby shower. She's used to people's feelings spilling over, which is a good thing today. She has her eyes on him in an intense way. He doesn't mind, which is interesting enough to dry him right up. He didn't mind when Raymona kept him in her line of vision like that either. Still, he wishes he hadn't come so close to mentioning the Youth Center.

"Let's go now." Go where? He might have missed a beat. But she gives him her complete thought, he doesn't have to ask. "To the trailer. To see if we can find more papers." He's reluctant but she puts a sense of rightness around it, as if there's no choice except to go back in there.

It's Petra who knows where to look. She has an instinct about her, goes right for the bedroom. She stands a minute at the foot of the bed, then gets on her hands and knees, pulls out the stacks. Notebooks, maybe thirty of them, all green. Three separate piles. They're placed this way and that, alternating, so the spiral bindings won't get them off balance. They're marked by dates. The organized part of Raymona is coming through here. On top of one pile is a piece of paper with some printing, clean and neat. Petra offers it to him but he asks her to read it please. He'd rather not touch it, feel what it would make him feel. Chippie's noises, happy and squawking, are coming from the living room. Maybe she thinks her mother will be home soon. Petra sits down on the bed and starts to read aloud. The words sound unusual, even for Raymona. *"Aha! You found us! OK. This mess of writings is by everybody and you better not believe half of it if you want my opinion. I know you have a big question and I have to tell you I don't understand why "she" didn't think of this and put it in the letter to Petra but here is your answer and I swear it's the truth so help me God."* Petra says they should move to the living room, that they both need to sit down. What kind of writing is this? Petra thinks they should be near Chippie.

"OK."

Chippie says hello, or her baby version. They sit. Petra looks him straight in the eye with a question she doesn't express in words, then reads the writing that comes from Raymona and nobody else. *"That baby has a father but you can't find him so give it up. His name is Chip and he's not from around here and to tell you the truth I don't think he even said where he was from but he was Full Blooded not that he said so but you could tell by the look and someone inside can smell it too and that's all that mattered at the time. As for now, since he never told a last name and why should he because 'she' didn't either, well there's nothing to be done. You're stuck, Petra, ha! ha! You can read all the words in all these 'journals' if you want to but I don't see why anyone would unless you don't believe me but you should because the only thing I was made for was Last Minute Desperate Truth-Telling, so THERE. I am the End. There isn't any better truth than what I say. More truth is that not a single one of us cares or is sorry about not knowing the name of the father of Persephone Star Chip Weeks because we ALL agree with 'her' about one thing. You, Petra, are the Chosen Mother, and that's just your Fate. At least I answered your question, right? Very sincerely yours, Teenage Truth-Teller, age thirteen-and-one-half. P.S. Do you like my alliteration? They let me name myself."*

It strikes him that Petra is a good reader, putting feeling into the words but at the same time holding back. She's sensitive about reading the words of a dead person. It further strikes him how hard he's trying not to notice the unusual way the message is written. Petra turns the page over. *"Addendum: To whomever shall find this document: Despite its obnoxious tone, you—whoever finds this—can trust this message. The full name and whereabouts of the father of the baby are not known. To Petra: It is my sincere hope that you will find it in your heart to accept this baby as your charge. Sincerely, The Legal Adult of Raymona Weeks, Also Known As Bright Star."*

It's quiet except for two kinds of chirping, the kind that comes from chickadees outdoors and the kind that comes from the baby in her crib. When did Petra put the baby in her crib? He's missing beats here, more than one. He watches Petra turn the paper over, look at the front, then look at the back again. He feels incompletely set into present time.

"Raymond, do you understand the signatures here?"

He looks at her. He'd be willing to bet his helplessness comes through. He shakes his head, no. She's up and heading back to the bedroom. It takes a minute before he understands they're going to bring the piles of writing to the living room. It takes longer to understand they'll be going back in time.

They're sitting close to each other on the sofa and can approach their task together. Somehow Petra has made this happen. The first notebook has START HERE printed on the cover in letters a six-year-old might write. Petra lifts the cover and he sees an envelope. More printing: RICKI. The hand here is confident, not at all young. "Well, that's good," he says. "Really," Petra agrees, picking up the envelope, looking at it, not opening it. She's careful when she sets Ricki's message aside. They read silently in the notebook, Petra making sure he's ready before she turns a page. They have about the same reading speed, a comfort. The writing stops. Blank pages follow, then there's more. They don't try to read past the blank pages; enough is enough.

*

The Journal of Raymona Weeks
(Parts Saved)

DEAD. DEAD. DEAD. He is dead, really and truly dead, and I get to keep every word I write from now on. No more secret bonfires in the backyard after everybody's asleep. I can't believe Raymond loved me enough to kill him and go to the Youth Center for me or maybe for the People. That's OK, too. I can't stand to think about if old pasty white stubbly skinny stepfather Bedey Boy Weeks got me pregnant. Ugh. My baby is Destined to have an Indian father, everybody knows that. Somebody had to kill Old Bede the minute I got the Curse. It couldn't be me. The mother is not the murderer, they said. They meant me, the Savior Baby's mother. Raymond is the Holy Murderer. He will be honored in History. SCARED, SCARED, SCARED. GHOSTLY GHOST. BAD BOY BEDE. Shut Up. I am writing in permanent ink on purpose. It will never get washed away. Every dream honored. It is not easy to have your brother get arrested, especially one who never committed a crime but only followed Destiny. He is a hero and loves me enough. I saw his hand shake, he was so scared, but he did it. He was brave. Old Bedey Boy never knew what hit him. Passed out drunk at the moment of pain-free death. That's OK, he just needed to be blown off the earth. No more messing with me. I learned the word for what he was. Sadist. Now I have a word. Fucking sadist. No one will ever do stuff like that to me again. Just Raymond, and he's only gentle. Raymond will never be a sadist. Pretty soon we have to talk about who the father of the Baby will be. Raymond hasn't figured that out yet. I hope he gets home soon. When the judge hears the story he'll understand and let him out. Mama won't be so sad then. This is the first Official Writing for History. Not torn up and burned in the wood stove like the beginning writings. Not burned in fires in the backyard like writings from spring and summer and into the Time of Now. We start the Saving of the Writing and the Saving of the People. Good. Written by Raymona Weeks, age 14.

This is the Second Official Writing for History. I miss Raymond, I want him to hold me in bed. The shaking is worse than I thought. I wish Mama wouldn't drink for just one day now. When can I see Raymond?

103

Did he tell the police I was there, Willing the Act? Will they come to arrest me? I refuse to leave this room. They'll have to carry me out of here like a sack of dog food. DOG FOOD! GOD FOOD! GHOSTLY GHOST FOOD! Stop that. Nobody here believes in ghosts. Got it? Screaming in my head, but I shouldn't write about it in the Writing for History. Yes, you should, dear. Everything. Nobody knows the beginning and end of what needs Saving. When they carry me out to Accuse me I'll make myself heavy and hate them with my strongest hate like a suit of armor. I will be a Knight in Armor. Hard and heavy, but not shining. I can't find shining in the life of being here. I miss Raymond. I am NOT going to school. Mama won't even know if I stay in this room forever. I had to masturbate today. DON'T WRITE THAT. Write everything. No one can know what needs Saving. All those silly whimpers in my head. I refuse to hear them ever again. I don't like the picture inside me of Bede all bloody. I refuse to see it. Maybe I'm Destined to see it. I wish I could tell Mama. He should not have been a sadist, that was wrong. I won't have to get his baby inside me now. We did a sacrificial killing, Raymond and Raymona together. My Will. Raymond's hand on the gun. God wants that sometimes, as in the Bible, Holy Sacrifices. Why won't they let Raymond come home? I wish somebody would tell me something. I had to take three bears to bed with me last night even though I am fourteen years old and (yes!) have my second menstrual period. Raymona Weeks

*

Her mind speeding, Petra gets up, puts the notebook on the pile. She sits back down on the couch, but not as close to Raymond as when they were reading. She hopes he can feel this as a natural move, no comment on what they just read. He looks like a man gathering his strength after a blow, which no doubt he is.

The journaling is utterly familiar, as if her work life barged in, an unwelcome, determined visitor. Her own feelings are unwelcome visitors. Fear, irritation, pity; a stony distance. But here is Raymond. Poor Raymond. Murder? Incest? She tries to find her place of professional discipline. She mustn't make more of the writing than is warranted. She watches her mind skitter to curiosity, distaste. Is this writing based on fact? She fears it is. What's in the envelope addressed to

Ricki? It could be anything, including words that would shock or hurt or confuse. Of course it might be a responsible loving final message, but the trick, the *cruelty*—leaving a message for Ricki where it might not have been found for days or weeks; or, if no one opened the notebooks, ever.

"Raymond." He appears to be focused on the area of Bright Star's old, braided, remarkably clean rug between his feet, but turns his head toward her at the sound of his name. "I don't suppose this murder is some kind of fantasy..." He shakes his head, no. He's looking at the rug again, but present. She decides to keep going. She watches herself, recognizes the mode. Nothing will stop her now. "We should talk about this." He nods his head, yes. "And then I'll have to tell you about something from my own past." This gets him to look up. She can see he takes it as a kindness. It's not a kindness, it's simple necessity. What a strange scene. He swallows, then starts talking, his voice only slightly lower than usual, his words only slightly muffled.

"Raymona—she wasn't Bright Star then—she had the idea we should kill our stepfather." Petra feels herself nod, like a therapist, and she watches Raymond take deep breaths, one after the other. "I had my own gun, for hunting. Everything was a mess." He stops. She can imagine the chaos he's trying to shape. The conversation needs structure. She moves into the familiar gear.

"Your stepfather, Bede, was approaching Raymona sexually?" She hears how formal she sounds, how clinical and tense.

"Since she was a little girl. Not just sex. Other things, things that made her crazy. Weird, painful...activities...he called them games. They got more and more violent." This would be easier at work, a delicate interview, the eliciting of difficult information. At work she's prepared to pull such facts from people, a good midwife. In her personal life, never. But that is apparently no longer true.

"And it seems from this writing that you and Raymona..." He sighs, looks her in the eye. He doesn't speak. She can wait. They got here very fast. He looks over at the baby, steadily, then back at her.

"I was two years older. It was my fault. Yes, we had sex." He's covering, she thinks. He's not telling who wanted this, who started it. She knows the murder scenario, the young girl toughened by terror, how it was her idea to kill the stepfather, how Raymond's hand shook while he tried to get himself to pull the trigger; so probably the sibling incest, too,

105

was the girl's idea. But she's making things up. She's still angry. She orders herself to stop this, and proceeds with the strange, displaced, necessary interview, aware that her turn to be questioned will come.

"You were sixteen?" He nods. "You went to the Youth Center? Or were you tried as an adult?"

"They took it into consideration...the circumstances..."

"Were you in the Youth Center for the whole time, then, until you were twenty-one?"

"Yes."

"Have you been in trouble since?"

"No."

She indulges in a period of silence, watches herself experience a flurry of professional reactions. She has sat so often in her office with "nice" men who've done terrible things. Time might reveal whether innocence of spirit is feigned or not. Here there's no time. She closes her eyes, shifts herself, opens her eyes, looks at Raymond. He's so *real*. "God, Raymond, what a life." So she trusts this man.

"Maybe this would make you hesitate, Petra. About taking a baby from a family like ours. About getting involved." Chippie stirs. She goes to pick her up and receives a full baby smile. What a good-humored little tyke, thinks mother-to-be Petra. Someday, though, a disturbance will emerge, thinks therapist Petra.

"It doesn't matter. The past is irrelevant," she says. *Murder and incest, irrelevant. Oh, my.* She begins to change Chippie's diaper. Raymond sits, containing whatever he needs to contain.

"What I have to say about my own past raises questions that are more to the point, Raymond. Should I make my confession now?" She looks up, looks him in the eye. He looks back. They can do this. She picks the baby up, tells her she smells good, takes a breath. "I had a daughter. Her name was Anya." She stops, gives Chippie a squeeze. Raymond listens steadily as if he's able to put aside the fact that his life has been laid open. "I raised her until she was three years old. I was young, but not terribly young. It was my choice. I was having a hard time and Marian, her name was Marian, was there, wanting to take over. I let her."

"Now you want to..." This is a gift, she thinks, this quickness he has, this acceptance.

"Yes," she says.

"Are you sure?"

"Almost. Yes. A kind of clarity comes to me sometimes. I just sort of know." He nods. "That doesn't mean I'm the right person."

"I'm not wading deep in alternatives."

"No, I gather that. There's the State."

"No."

"Or your tribe?"

He flinches so subtly she's not sure what she saw.

"I don't know my tribe." She can see this is a shame he has lived with, and managed.

"And we don't know the tribe of Chippie's father," she says.

"That's right."

"And her mother was white," she adds, just for completion's sake.

"Yes. Anyway, they'd be strangers. If there was a tribe." He looks at her, clear, direct.

She's stunned and pleased by the implication that she is not a stranger to him. "Thank you," she says, but immediately realizes he must have meant she wasn't a stranger to Bright Star, or to Chippie. How embarrassing, to have assumed unmeant intimacy. He nods, pulling the conversation through the glitch. Is she blushing? At her age?

"She trusted you," Raymond says.

"I don't know why."

"Oh, I suppose it was a kind of clarity that came to her."

"Right," she says, and they smile at each other, old comrades. "Change of subject," she says. He nods. She likes their rhythm. "Do you know if Bright Star—Raymona—had a number of different..."

"Personalities," he says. He doesn't seem thrown by the idea. "It's a new thought, since the signatures."

"Yes, for me, too."

"I don't know." He's thinking. She waits. "She never came to me wearing unusual clothes or talking in a strange voice, saying 'I'm Sarah Jane.' I guess I don't know enough..." He's so earnest. Is she torturing him? What difference does it make whether he thinks his sister had MPD? But he asks, as if it matters to him, "Do you know about that? About people who have different personalities?"

"Yes, from my work life."

"I guess you couldn't tell..."

"With her? No."

"She'd curl up in a ball sometimes, and sort of whimper. Like a puppy. I might knock on the door of the trailer and she wouldn't answer and I'd go in and find her hunched up under the kitchen table."

"That wouldn't be unusual with MPD—multiple personality disorder—but she might have been having a trauma reaction, nothing to do with personalities. Maybe she saw something on TV, or heard a noise, that brought a painful event back to her, like the guys who came home from Viet Nam and hid in the bushes when a helicopter..." He nods. She doesn't say, Maybe she was just plain crazy. Still angry, she notes. She decides to ask, since she's in this far, about the grandmother.

"Alcoholism," he says, smiling fondly to himself. "She's sober at the moment. At least I hope she is." He looks at his watch. "I should go. She'll be getting out of an AA meeting, or if she didn't go to meeting she's been alone for some hours. It's a lot of stress for my mother, Raymona dying like this."

"Yes," she says. Then adds lightly, as if it weren't the point of the conversation, "I'll keep Chippie for now," thinking about the genetic component, alcoholism, the likelihood of a variety of mental health problems. And dismissing the thoughts.

Raymond looks right into her. "OK," he says.

"OK," she says. And thinks, "Amazing."

"Yes," he says, and she realizes she said the word aloud. She's aware of elements of past and present, internal and external, stable and unstable, stirred and blended by the big stick of Bright Star's suicide. *Revelatory Soup, Crazy Cook.* She's a little dizzy. She has a baby on her lap. The baby's looking at Raymond and he's looking back at her and they look alike. She hadn't realized. Out of the whirl, to her relief, comes a practical question. "Raymond, what about a memorial service? Will you let me know?" She's not surprised when he says he hasn't thought about it and he doubts his mother has.

"To tell the truth, my mother's doing all she can, staying sober. She and Raymona haven't talked to each other for some years..." He looks stymied. It's obvious what needs to be done.

"Do you want us...DWELL, the reading group...do you think your mother would..."

"Would you? Raymona would like that. It'll be fine with my mother."

"You'd better get back to her."

"Yes."

"Raymond, these journals..."

"Would you take them?"

"Of course. How would you feel about my reading them? I still think she might have written more about the father."

"Someone should read them. I can't be the one."

"No, of course not."

Raymond puts the journals into the bed of the truck while she prepares a bottle for Chippie. *Mothers of Questionable Value. Unlikely Would-be Mothers. Irregularly Stippled Mothers.* The picture can't be neatly titled. She hopes this baby brought something of her own, something sturdy, into the world. Raymond drives them home and leaves immediately, on his way to tend to his mother. He, at least, seems to know what he's doing.

Chapter Thirteen

Monday evening. The water in the tub is as hot as Petra can stand it. She's here to relax and to collect herself before this strange DWELL meeting begins. "Collect herself." As if she were scattered, pieces here, pieces there. Accurate, she thinks, sinking deeper, catching at a little vision in her mind, a grainy scene on a cobbled street where a lone woman in babushka and sweater and shabby boots picks up street things, puts them in basket, plods along in black and white and wind, disappears around a corner.

Vanished Babushka.

This is not a figure from an old newsreel, though it has the look. Must be her own great-great grandmother, never spoken of, never known, come to visit this steamy bath. Also herself, she supposes, not caring much. How tired she is. Is she falling asleep?

Kiki appears, ghostlike, picks up Teddy Bear; kisses, drops, chooses Raggedy Ann, tosses up, catches triumphantly, shouts, PETRA, PETRA, I'M HAPPY TODAY. Not so ghostlike, really. A person could float here forever. Like that old soap, 99.44% pure. *Ivory.* Floated as advertised, but left a scummy ring. No scum in this tub, so pleasant, soaking, letting go.

Oh my God, Ricki. Forgot all about—

Petra rises up, sheds the cooling water, dries herself, puts on her robe, and the doorbell rings.

Ricki says, "Hi," looks around, nods as if affirming that things are in their proper places. Petra, toweling her hair, asks how she is. "My foot had trouble finding the brake. Strangest thing. Felt shrunk to a stub. Fate bestowing another anomaly. So my hand wouldn't feel lonely."

"Oh, Ricki." *She mentioned her hand.* Petra is insanely pleased.

"The bridge was a problem. Vertiginous. She taught me that word. You'd think I'd be used to the bridge. Shouldn't bother me. Water under the bridge, let it go, it's all over now, *et cetera.* Sorry about the babbling brook of my busy tongue. Too much coffee. She said that one day, babbling brook of a busy tongue. Liked a bit of alliteration from time to time, games with language. Sorry, Petra, I..."

"God, Ricki, you have a right. I'm so angry with her myself. Here it is." Ricki looks, hesitates, then receives the envelope as if it were sacred, both hands reaching, eyes filling up. Petra feels wildly protective. *Whatever's in there had better be both kind and sane.*

When she returns, dressed and thinking how very satisfying a cup of coffee would be—but it's too late in the day for that, she's no longer young, her sleep would suffer—Ricki, who seems to have acquired an extra dimension, offers the page.

The Naked Drop

Once there was a liquid pyramid.
It hung there upside down in space,
lowest drop trembling, aching to fall.

When I was a kid in Bangor,
manholes opened where I walked,
infinity for falling into.

Alice of Wonderland fell.
I never remember the landing.

If the last drop held,
if the manholes closed,
if I ever remembered the landing,

some surround that would be, eh?

Ricki Dicki Darlin', you were a success. Is this thing a poem? It has some lies, so maybe. And stanzas, if you can believe. Manholes scared me bad but they were covered, mostly. Holes brought on terror, Babes, but don't you worry, it's all over now. Signed, Bright Star Who Smokes

Petra notes the signature, thinks about this view of suicide, the ultimate and presumably naked drop to infinity.

"She says I was a success, Petra."

"Is that good?"

"I think so. I hope so."

"I didn't know she was a poet."

"I didn't either. I don't want to read it at the meeting."

"No, I don't suppose so.

"There's more on the other side."

Petra turns the paper over.

Little hand, little hand,

Jesus loves you, you're so grand.

Little hand, little hand,

you are anything but bland.

"She's saying this to me to make me feel better. Sometimes I felt like that, bland, next to her. She liked it...my hand." Ricki blows her nose. She has a large handkerchief today. Her father's? "Now I have to tell you what Mom told me. I know the others will be here soon. Bright Star really liked being in DWELL. But I have to tell you. Mom just looked at me when I said Mrs. Weeks' name. 'Stella,' I said, and Mom stared at me. It's about when Bright Star and Raymond were young. There was a tragedy, Petra, I guess you'd call it that."

Petra orders herself to be cautious. And calm, if possible. "I think Raymond told me about it, Ricki." *But it's too much, all of this, all at once. She's too young.*

"About the murder?"

"Yes."

"It got into the papers. Their stepfather..."

"Yes, it would have, I suppose. It was before my time in Maine."

"So you know."

"Yes."

"OK. Good. I still think Raymond's a good person. I had to make sure to say that."

"I think so, too."

"That's good, then. Look how she signed this. I guess she divided herself up. She was different when she smoked. Cynical."

Petra takes another deep delaying breath. The last topic needed today is Bright Star's possible multiplicity.

"You saw more than we did, Ricki."

"Maybe, but I didn't know about the murder, or being molested. Mom knew Mrs. Weeks and she knew Bede, too. The stepfather. Both of them were named Weeks. They were cousins, second or third maybe. People talked about that. Inbreeding, they said, but Stella and Bede never had kids, so it wasn't inbreeding, was it? The three of them, Mom and Stella and Bede, were in the same grade. Here I am, living up in Bangor, going to the University, feeling far away from home, thinking I have this complete life of my own."

"And it turns out your mother knows your girlfriend's mother."

"Right. I'm not going to say anything about all this...from the past...at this meeting."

"There's no need, Ricki. You must still be getting used to..."

"That she did it. At least I'm not breaking down every two minutes. How are *you* doing, Petra?"

"It looks as if I might have a baby to raise. It's all...I'm OK, but..." The doorbell saves her. It's Nat and Roo and Jessie, none of them looking cheery. Well, of course not. Roo goes to the kitchen. Soon she's emerging with a tray of glasses and cups, then another with juice and soda and—Petra loves how Roo-like this is—a pitcher of warm milk.

Roo is taking over, listing tasks. Where should the service be held? They'll need to have food somewhere. Jessie's place, unless someone has a better idea. By the way, pen poised over tablet, does anyone know Bright Star's legal name?

"Weeks," Petra and Ricki say in unison. "Raymona Weeks," Petra adds.

Roo puts down her pen and paper slowly. "What?"

Petra says it gently. "Raymona Weeks."

"I can't believe it." Roo looks at Jessie. "She was that *girl*."

"*That* girl?" Jessie says.

Roo pours herself a cup of the warm milk and tells them, starting with the day Bright Star first walked into Petra's living room. *Déjà vu.* Meaningless, she thought. "But now I see. She was that *girl*." The story goes back decades, to Raymona Weeks, eighth-grader, pale, stringy, oddly courageous. Petra looks at Ricki who seems to be coping by quietly rubbing her anomalous hand. The precious final message has been tucked into a book she brought with her. Petra's heart is wrung, but she can't deny her curiosity, alive and reprehensible as it is. What will Roo add to what they know?

Roo holds her cup in two normal, plump, kind hands and looks off to her left. Retrieving details, Petra thinks. "She wasn't my student, but there she was." It was winter, Roo says. She was student teaching, preparing for her first career, grade school teacher. She sat correcting papers, classes finished for the day. Except for the ticking of the clock on the wall, the room was silent. She looked up and there stood Raymona, notebook against chest, pencil in hand, the large window behind her. Outside, fresh snow clung to every tree branch. "This was a girl in a picture, a ghost girl. The strangest aura..." Roo closes her eyes. Petra glances at Ricki who catches the glance and shakes her head: they won't stop Roo, she can handle this. "Her words were abrupt, graceless. *I heard you know about Indians.* I was teaching a unit on American Indians, calling it Geography." Petra wonders how far into delicate territory this story will reach. Chippie, bless her heart, sleeps. Yet another bit of news about her absent mother is coming. What a good idea Roo had, heating milk for the undone adults. "...so when I finished student teaching, when I was leaving, I gave her a book about Anasazi cliff dwellers, the stone cities they left, the southwest landscape. I loved that book, almost changed my mind about giving it away, but the girl needed something. At least I did that." Roo's eyes stream tears. "Shit." She pulls a tissue out of her pocket, blows her nose. *I know you will do it right, Petra. The southwest landscape surrounded you in my deep magic dream. Soft red-brown rock-face. Your hands will mold my Baby into the Indian she is. Good Pueblo pots you once made, and now you will make her.* The letter was dated one week after Petra and Bright Star met at the laundromat.

"...kivas, stone structures, no roofs. I suppose the roofs were made of wood and earth and didn't last. Raymona and I pored over those photographs. I remember dreams I had...this is awful...about the two of us hiding, listening in on old rituals as if we had a right, as if we were a pair of old souls making our secret visitation. God, I hated student teaching. But Raymona was a point of pleasure. She wanted to learn. She *needed* to." Roo finishes her milk, puts the cup down, moves from couch to floor and rests her head against Jessie's knee. Jessie massages her neck, leans forward, kisses the top of her head. Jessie, big tough tattooed biker dyke from Massachusetts, who loves Roo well. "Now there's this baby," Roo says. "Where *is* the baby?"

"She's here. Sleeping," Petra says. *Leave it at that, for now.* Ricki is completely still, eyes wide. This is going to be a long meeting.

"I should have put it all together," Roo says. "Once the baby came, I certainly should have. Of course she'd fall in love with a Native American. But I haven't told you the worst part." Ricki takes a ragged breath. Also, Nat is looking worse. Roo tells about reading the article in the paper—Boy Murders Stepfather—the names coming out despite the fact that they were children still—"Children!"—and how she finally understood that this was that *girl*. Petra feels her own attention swerve and settle around Nat: rigid, encased, distant, not herself. Chippie cries. Petra picks her up, soothes her into a calm bundle of baby and proceeds to change her diaper on the floor in the middle of the room, what an expert she is, while Roo talks. Poor Roo, captured by the Weeks family way back then. "It's one of my sins, that I didn't contact Raymona then. I thought about it, but life moved on, I got distracted. It was just a story in the paper and then it wasn't. Then she walked into my life again, right here, and I didn't *know* her."

"Do you think she recognized you?" This is Jessie, speaking slowly, her hand on Roo's shoulder.

"How can I know? I'm so different. I was young and thin. Well, thinner. Good Lord, I wore make-up. I was Miss McGuire. It was...what?...twenty-two *years* ago."

Petra is carefully not looking at Nat. Whatever it is, it's nothing to bring attention to. Later, when they're alone. Tears slide down Ricki's cheeks. She's taken the envelope out of the book and laid it on the couch. She opens the book, but Jessie says, "I just have to..." She looks into the distance, then looks at each of them: Petra, holding Chippie; tense, gray-haired Nat; young, young Ricki. She has her hands on Roo's shoulders. "I'm *pissed*. The woman has a baby and then right away she exits. I don't care how hard her damn childhood was, and if she *knew* you, Roo— people don't have to be that fucking *weird*." Petra's never heard Jessie this angry. How satisfying.

Roo smiles tolerantly. "Jessie's been sputtering since she heard about the suicide." She turns and looks up at her partner. "I'm amazed you kept quiet so long."

"I'm finished. Just had to say it." Roo smiles to herself, head down. "And I don't want to see that damn little smile about how cute I am when I'm mad," says Jessie, but already she's softening.

Roo keeps smiling the little smile. She reaches around and takes Jessie's hand and kisses it, then asks, "How are the rest of you?"

"Dammit, woman," Jessie cups her hands around Roo's head.

"Rub," says Roo. Jessie massages her head, gently, professionally, physical therapist and lover melded into one. Roo sighs a long sad sigh.

Ricki nods, as if things are right again, takes a visible breath, and says, "I need to read these lines from H.D." She stops herself, looks around. "Is this OK?" Everyone nods yes, even Nat, though hers is more of a stiff jerk of the head. What *is* this? Petra is almost dizzy with alertness.

Ricki, valiant, determined, says, "It starts in the middle of a sentence and I'll just...'*we last sat in this room / with other people who spoke / pleasant speakable things; // —they didn't know // how my heart woke / to a range and measure / of song I hadn't known—*'"

Petra hugs Chippie since she cannot reasonably get up and hug Ricki. Chippie appreciates her hug and says so. *Glisksh.* "In the poem," Ricki says, "two women are in a room...and the other people...the other people don't know about them." She stops.

Roo says, "What?"

"About their *relationship*." Ricki is pleading.

Petra sees Nat flinch. *After all these years, Nat chooses Bright Star?* She can hardly believe it.

"Goddamn," Jessie says, her soft eyes reaching out to Ricki.

"...a secret, that we were together. That's what she needed, I guess. What she had, her disease, I don't know what it was, but it was going to kill her."

Disease? This is a new piece. Petra doesn't believe it. "So she..." Ricki stops and wipes her tears. "So she decided to do it herself. It made her feel better, to be in charge. We couldn't tell anyone. That secret made sense, I guess, but it was hard not to..."

Somewhere in the middle of this, Nat unfreezes. Petra watches age and misery take over, then a sort of chivalry. Nat looks directly at Ricki and says, "When you love a woman, something—a force—pulls you over the edge of how things were before. You drop to a place that feels, I don't know, untamed maybe. There's an order to it, but it can't be grasped with the usual mind. It's physical, cellular; and beyond that. You're young for it. You saw things you're young to see."

Ricki's fresh tears fall into the space Nat has created. Nat, suddenly their elder lesbian, kind, wise, profoundly ethical. The whole room relaxes. They're in the realm of mystery and Petra lets herself slide into the phenomenon. Soon, however, she intends to have a conversation with Nat Levesque. Curiosity might wait, but it won't disappear. Certainly not. Meanwhile, this patient baby needs a bottle. It occurs to her that a child tethers a person and that this is a *good* thing.

*

Tuesday evening now. No clients for Petra this morning. Chippie instead. Emotions came and went like intense weather. Still, the two of them did eerily well. Then Izzie took over and Petra went to the office. Helga starts to grieve, questions her decision, but Ingrid seems fine with her new mother. "It's just hard. I remind myself I'm not suited to parenting. I'm glad I came to talk to you, Petra. I can see in your eyes how you want good things for me and for Ingrid, too. You don't forget Ingrid." What Helga apparently couldn't see was how her therapist, who had also defined herself as not suited, stepped back, took refuge in her professional mind, and warned herself not to make too much of parallels. It was a relief to leave the office at the end of the afternoon.

Now this trip to Danny's. He has been given no warning. Chippie gurgles happily in her car seat. Petra, in the unlikely role of mother number two, has been well-supplied by mother number one: car seat, diaper bag, blankets; even a baby swing, which hangs suspended in the doorway between Petra's kitchen and living room. Soon she and Raymond will get the crib from the trailer. Bright Star, gone, is so *present*. It's not so much the baby, who came on her own somehow, as it is the possessions, the high chair, stroller, hand-sewn clothing. The bedroom floor is crowded with notebooks, so far unread. She did read the statement titled This Baby's Destiny and the pages devoted to Care and Feeding of a Baby and the Letter to Petra Kalinowski and the crazy, touching last message for Chippie. *Little Chippie, you are The People's*

117

Dove. And mine. Mine, too. MINE, TOO! Me, too, Baby Doll. In a variety of handwritings, some of them young, young, young. It will worry Danny that she might take Chippie. Or does she already *plan* to? She'll need his help. In the years before menopause, permitting herself the wildest thought, she fantasized: sex with Danny, just enough to achieve pregnancy. She'd be a satisfied, successful mother with help from mature Danny who no longer had to preserve himself for riding the rails. It was pure fantasy, or so she thought; but was it, instead, a primitive, confused, quite real, vestigial *longing*? Odd that she'd choose Danny for the father. Or maybe not. So few men in her life. There was Frederick, briefly her husband, but he's gone. Witold, dear distant father. She should call him, he gets forgotten. Now, suddenly, there's Raymond. She has no resistance to Raymond, no need for self-protection, a fact to take note of. He exerts no pressure, she tells herself. Then remembers the one small exception: the man wants her to raise his niece. She feels almost leisurely about the project of getting to know this man, clarifying his role with Chippie, a baby who is at the moment—she turns around to catch a glimpse of the little creature—slumped in her car seat, snoring, very cute. Exceedingly cute. Beautiful.

Tears come. She widens her eyes to keep vision for driving. It's impossible, what's happening. It's right and it's terrifying, in equal parts. An old image comes. A bright globe spins, its crystal points of light stabbing out in every direction. Here is every possible emotion, every possible scenario, every being, everything reflecting everything else, no facet incomplete—one of her images for God, if there is such a thing as God; that difficult, that astonishing. Also one of her images for life. Life, which includes the gift of dreams. She finds herself humbly grateful for recent dreams: the world applauding the diaper well-changed; and her own child, no longer alive, giving unexpected, undeserved permission.

Thank you, Anya.

No one knows she speaks to Anya. She does it only *in extremis*. "Can we do this?" she whispers over her shoulder to Chippie who whistles in her sleep and repositions her head, managing to look simultaneously awkward and relaxed. A car seat is not the best bed for a baby, but a baby makes do. This baby is making do quite well. Petra admires the trust, the self-containment, the existence. She feels a surge of pure awe at the phenomenon: that she is able, is allowed, to feel such tenderness again, and toward a *child*.

What a whirl. Her responses to what's happening feel like transgression, and like humility. Is any of this trustworthy? She turns into the long drive and passes the main house. Roo's car is not at home. Good, because one person at a time is enough. She takes a quick look at the view. Blue Hill Bay, wide water, deep blue under a crisp early evening sky. *Here we are, Chippie Dippie.*

Danny opens the door, puts his harmonica in his shirt pocket. "Hey," he says, to both of them. "What's this?"

"Let us in."

"Coffee?"

"Thanks. Decaf. I need to heat a bottle."

Side by side they busy themselves. It brings back their life in San Francisco. She gets a saucepan from the open shelf, runs water from the single tap at the rusted sink. Danny doesn't press her. She gets the temperamental gas burner going and tries to begin. "I'd say 'You're not going to believe this,' but I suppose you will. I suppose that's why I came here."

"OK," Danny says, interested, bemused, attentive, ready.

But she herself isn't ready. "Give me a minute."

He nods, takes the harmonica out of his pocket, rubs his thumb along the metal. That gesture. She and Danny beside the dying George. She'd flown to San Francisco. Danny moved his thumb tenderly over the silver casing, back and forth, back and forth while George slept. He has a number of harmonicas, ten-hole diatonic, various keys. He explained this at some point when they were not chained into silence, holding their breath for fear of waking George. She memorized it, *ten-hole diatonic*. When George died she had a dream: a huge, benign, clean thumb rubbing, rubbing, against a gleaming piece of washed whalebone. She looks out the window at the strip of ocean beyond the edge of the field, now almost lost in evening light. She looks down at Chippie, who sucks vigorously; at the wood stove which gives good heat; at the posters Danny finally framed, to protect the fragile edges. She's fond of the one of Forrest City Joe Pugh with a harmonica—harp, Danny calls it—in each hand. On the stool between the man's knees sits a bottle of gin half empty, a glass half full. He looks ready. The walls are covered. Robert

Johnson, Muddy Waters, Little Walter, Sonny Terry. Danny practices a form of tempered worship, just a step beyond admiration for the old blues guys, tries to breathe their music, in and out, feel that thing *they* felt. It makes his eyes shine.

"Something about this baby?" The question startles her, interfering with her reverie, her escape. She feels unprepared, as if she forgot to study for a test.

"How did you know?"

"Had to be. Here you are together and weekend is over." She focuses on feeding the baby, watching bubbles form in the bottle. Soon they'll be out of breast milk but Bright Star left bottles with formula. More will have to be bought. What kind? No information in the voluminous instructions from the dead mother. Another hole in the pretty picture. Danny gets up to put a log in the stove. His back is to her.

"Bright Star killed herself Saturday. She left a will and I get Chippie. There's no one else. I'm going to keep her. Don't tell me not to." By the time she finishes this efficient set of sentences Danny has turned around.

She lets him look, astonished and kind. She lets him say, "Oh, boy," and come and put his arms around her and the baby. "Well. Wow," he says. She even lets herself drop her head against his chest, creating an arch over the baby, who tolerates this, and start to sob.

Between sobs she says, "Do you think I can do it?" Which she definitely did not plan to say.

"She's a real cutie, isn't she?" he says.

"Yes. I can hardly stand how cute she is." She reaches for the handkerchief he pulls out of a pocket, wrinkled, no longer white, but clean. Somehow, in the exchange, he ends up with the baby.

He, too, remembers how to hold the bottle at the correct angle. Chippie swallows the last bit and Danny, attentive, puts her to his shoulder. She burps. He sits her on his knee, facing him. She gives him her rudimentary smile and reaches into his mouth with four fingers. He sucks them for a minute. "Yum, gurgle, gurgle," he says, tactfully leaving Petra to her nose-blowing.

"She likes you," she says, taking a deep not-overly-ragged breath.

"She seemed quite happy with you. Are we going to talk about this?"

"I have to. You saw me with Anya. You're the only one who..."

"So tell me." He hands Chippie back to her.

"OK." She holds Chippie in the crook of one arm, picks up the cup of coffee with the other, sips. It's still warm. She kisses Chippie on the forehead. "It was like a reversal of those old events."

"With Anya."

"Yes. I'm glad you're here. Sorry I'm so difficult."

"I like you difficult. Anyway, you're not that bad...today." He's teasing.

OK, we can get through this. "I'm glad you were *there*, too."

"I know. It's like you knowing George. It's good, this history thing."

"Remember how it was when I talked to Marian? How it seemed obvious Anya would be better off with her and something just broke loose in me and I didn't even feel I had to decide, it was all decided?"

"Yes."

"Then there was all the time after that. Getting used to what I'd done. Anya getting older. Four, five, six. How she got so awkward when she hit seven, I hardly knew how to..."

"I know."

"Then the deaths."

"Yes."

"And all the time since."

"Long."

"Yes."

"Long enough, maybe."

"Yes. I think so. I hope so," she says.

"So this is like reversing that history?"

"Exactly. Like a film played backwards at high speed, the colors and sounds. The feelings. Rushing by, a blur, and then it stops and there's a picture and it's just there, it's just the way things are. Clear. Only this time it's about *taking* a little girl."

"I think I..."

"Don't tell me I'm crazy."

121

"I was going to say I think I understand, a little. Some kind of strong thing happened."

"Yes. Not very rational, though."

"You want me to play devil's advocate, Petra?"

"I want you to tell me it's obvious I'm completely grounded and utterly rational and know exactly what I'm doing." She roots around in the diaper bag and pulls out a baby blanket. Black against red and brown. She lays it on Danny's worn rag rug, not as clean as Bright Star's but not bad. She puts Chippie down on her stomach and gives her plastic toys to reach toward, geometric shapes in primary colors. She picks up her coffee cup and sits beside the baby on the floor. "Damn. Is this completely irrational, or only partly? I vacillate."

"More coffee?"

"No thanks. What a crappy position I'm putting you in."

"How has it been with her?"

"I've been so busy. I cleaned up Bright Star's blood and brains on Saturday, for example, and I've been meeting with her brother. Her half-brother. Nice man. Yesterday and today I went to work. Izzie took her. We're limping along. Nothing's final."

"When you've been alone with her...?"

"Oh, it's nuts. I'm so *into* it. This morning was the first stretch of hours, just her and me, since I knew about the suicide, and the will. I operated between satisfaction and ecstasy, all the while fearing the crash. This is a very calm baby, God knows why. She just did her baby thing. I was competent. I was also in thrall to her. Her dedicated slave."

"Slave."

"Yes. If her breathing changed, I decided she needed something. I was run ragged. I won't do it like that when it's real. It's not real yet."

"I don't suppose so."

"I couldn't stop watching her. Think, Danny, how much she's *learning*. Those little wheels turning. She probably knows more about the smells and sounds and sights in my house than I ever..."

"Sounds entertaining."

"Exhausting. Thrilling, too, but definitely exhausting. She took a nap and I got a break."

"Good."

"Well, yes. There was another layer. I got obsessed with observing myself do this thing, take in this new little human being, coo and sing to her. There were layers and layers..."

"Intense."

"Yes, but I'm not...there was...all this *softening*. Sometimes I got teary, sometimes I felt like dancing. Like Izzie. There was a jazz thing on the radio, something you'd recognize, and I danced with her for a minute. I felt ridiculous." Chippie cries. Petra picks her up and puts her over a shoulder. Chippie burps, once, twice. Gurgles, smiles. Grabs her shirt collar. Danny laughs.

"Good burper. What does Nat say?" He gets up and pulls the chain on the standing lamp.

"Let there be light," says Petra.

"Indeed. What does Nat say?"

"I heard you the first time. I haven't told her."

"Oh. Since Saturday, you haven't told her."

"I know. You had to come first."

"I'm honored. Still, it's Tuesday."

She doesn't want to talk about Nat.

"What do *you* think, Danny?"

"I think this one's your call, but tell me why. What's different now? I'm not aware you were considering...wanting..."

"I wasn't."

"Now you are."

"Now I am."

"You wouldn't be able to write a dissertation, make an elegant and well-reasoned argument as to why."

"Right."

"Nevertheless, you want to raise this baby."

"Yes."

"This baby landed in your vicinity and she looked cute and you picked her up and she felt good."

"Maybe."

"Well, maybe you're crazy."

"Yeah, maybe."

"Maybe you know what you're doing."

"Maybe."

"Guess you might have to try it and see."

"It's not as if I could return her."

"Nobody to return her to."

"Do you like her, Danny?"

"I like her, Petra."

"Will you help us?"

Danny looks at Chippie who's working hard, chewing the corner of a green plastic triangle Petra is holding for her. "She's an earnest little thing, isn't she? Will I help you? Yes, I'll help you, but I helped you the last time and it wasn't enough."

"I know. Maybe I'm more grown up."

"You're quite fully grown up. That might be a problem? All these years you've accumulated before this baby came your way?"

"I figure if I can make it to when she's eighteen, that will do. I'll be sixty-seven. That's not so old. Then she can take care of me."

"Petra Kalinowski, you are refusing to consider certain things seriously."

"That is correct."

"Well, I don't think it's a worry. Grandmothers raise their grandchildren." Danny reaches down and puts his finger near Chippie's hand. She grabs it. He pulls her hand this way and that. Her bright eyes follow. She coos. He coos back.

"I could *be* a grandmother by now. You, too. Grandmother or grandfather, whichever you might choose."

"Grandfather, I think, to keep the scandal factor down," Danny says, not taking his eyes off Chippie. "Wouldn't want the neighbors to talk."

"You'll help, won't you?"

"Sure. It'll be a trip. This time I'm not even afraid you'll try to get me to settle down behind a white picket fence."

"Danny McGuire. After all that protesting, you went and domesticated *yourself*. Or George did."

"George did."

"George." Petra sighs. "He seems relevant to this. What you did with him." Danny nods. Nursing George changed him. "I don't mind that we're of the grandparent generation," Petra says. "It might be a good thing."

"It might."

"Are we going to do this, Danny?"

"Are *you* going to do this, Petra?"

She picks Chippie up and moves to the couch. She sits the baby on her knee, facing her. "Are we going to do this, Chippie?" Chippie looks thoughtful. Petra looks at Danny. "I'm not so good at translating her messages yet, but I think she just told me to go ahead, and if I can't manage it she'll find someone else. Maybe a big hunk of a white guy with a harp."

"No, no, no."

"Are you sure?"

"Are you that scared?"

"Of course I'm that scared."

"Good. You should be scared, but I can't be your backup. Not like that."

"No, of course not." Chippie starts to fuss. Petra pulls a fresh diaper from the bag, lays her on the couch and changes her, glad for the distraction.

"Really, I mean it," Danny says. "Don't go into this thing harboring thoughts like that."

"No. I'm not. I'm embarrassed I said it. It's not a thing to play with."

Danny moves close to her, puts his arms around her and makes a little clicking sound for Chippie who's reaching toward the harmonica while she endures being diapered. "You're just a little terrified," he says. "You need to let Nat know about this." He gives Chippie the harmonica but she drops it.

"Her mouth is stronger than her hand at this point," Petra says.

He puts the harmonica to the baby's mouth. She chews at it and then astonishes herself by exhaling a chord. They laugh. Chippie looks from face to face. She doesn't know what to do. She decides to smile.

"I will," Petra says.

"Will what?"

"Talk to Nat."

"Soon."

"Yes, soon. It's a strong thing, Danny. I have to do it."

"I know. I'll help. I won't make myself as scarce as last time. "

"Good. Now that's enough of that. Let's stop talking."

"Wait a minute. What about Bright Star? How are you feeling about that?"

"Oh, I don't know. Irritated. Chippie takes precedence. Some day I'll sort through my reactions to this damned suicide."

"Seems like kind of a big thing."

"It is. There's a complicated story, more than a simple suicide."

"Simple suicide."

"Some are less complicated than this one, but that's for another day. Play something for Chippie. For me. Something sweet and not too sad."

He plays for a long time and she relaxes. The baby falls asleep. The sky goes dark, the water invisible. "I love you, Danny," she says.

"I love you, too, Petra, but talk to Nat."

"I will. Maybe I should go."

"When you're ready."

"Soon," she says, and falls asleep against his shoulder. By midnight she's on her way home with Chippie. The world is a dark wonder.

Chapter Fourteen

A white cloth covers the table. The creases form neat squares which give a sense of order and somewhere for his eyes to go when they need a rest from Raymona's things. The little clay pots, the wall covering with bird nests, and the photos, especially the photos, are tolerable for a bit and then not. When they were snapshots on his dresser, that was one thing. Here, made large like posters and meant to be looked at by everyone, they give a looming feeling. There's Raymona, a kid in a dress, squinting into the sun, arms hanging down, with a scraped knee. In the snapshot he barely saw the little wound but here it's noticeable. In the other picture she's posed with her biggest clay creations, Fallen Goddess and Knot, squatting between the two, adult but not acting it. She must be embarrassed because her eyes are crossed and she's sticking her tongue out. When she finished with a piece of work Raymona would make introductions, "Raymond, meet So-and-So." Honey Monkey or Patchwork or such. You'd think it was a person and not something he'd watched from a lump of clay. The day he was introduced to Fallen Goddess, she told him how the colors didn't want to behave and then all of a sudden they did, and about the glaze and a number of other artistic decisions. It had been a long time since she'd discussed her art, though he was always allowed to look. When she finished talking she twirled in a circle and came close and whispered in his ear. *I'll tell you a secret.* Her secret was that the goddess was a self-portrait. *Don't tell anyone. Isn't that a good word, self-portrait?* Then she ran and crawled into bed and covered herself, head and all. *Go away, go away.* Before he got the truck started, though, she was there asking what was the matter, the soup was getting cold. So they ate lunch, thick soup, lots of vegetables. The conversation was a lively one, jumping here to there. They fell into giggling, then the baby kicked from inside, hard, probably saying it was ready to come out. Her labor pains started that night. She gave him the photo after she told him her death date was set. She didn't like her picture taken but Ricki had managed it. *She got around me that day. I don't know how. You might as well have it, since it exists.* "Not easy to get around you." "I know, Raymond." She kissed her fingers and touched his forehead. It was the last touch. He feels it now, a real thing, her cool fingers, and looks up at the poster of herself and her art. The looming feeling is strong. In a pew alone further back would have suited him better but Petra pulled him forward. Now they sit side by side but not too close. Petra doesn't crowd a person. The lady named Nat—he met her at the baby shower, along with Petra—also tried to sit in the back but Petra brought her forward, too. "Nat, this is Raymond. Raymond, this is Nat." They reached across Petra and the baby and shook hands as if they'd never met. Nat has one of those dry, good handshakes, respectful, and she seems like a fine person but he'd rather have been left to himself. He could tell she felt the same. He'll be calmer once Stella arrives. He planned on bringing her but she had ideas of her own for how to get here. He's left with a lack, like a suitcase he's assigned to carry but inside is plain air and nothing else so what's the point? He tells himself she'll be fine, she'll come, she won't drink, but the minutes keep passing. The ladies had a good thought, making the chapel into an art gallery. Having a showing, Raymona would call it, something she wanted but didn't get around to, dying on time apparently being more important. The smallest creations, she called them her Thimble Pots and Little Fellows, give a satisfaction to the eye that was missing when they were lined up on the floor at the trailer. He's glad to see Patchwork whose colors are understandable, red and blue. Does Patchwork's black turtle stand for death, though? Death is why they're here today but it's hard to grasp the fact in a circumstance that's so public. Stella could be at Bitta's getting drunk. It would even make sense. Chippie cranes toward him. Petra gives a questioning look but when he shakes his head she distracts the little critter with a set of beads. There are pitfalls in different directions here. He'd like to keep walking through this day without falling into one. Roo, who had a relaxation and friendliness to her when they met at the shower, looks tense and sad moving to the front with papers in her hand. She explains how things will go, inviting them all to speak. He'll speak himself, he has his idea in mind. If only Stella...

She arrives, whispering to her friend who is none other than Margie Stokes, the skunk lady from the library. The two of them settle into the back seat. Roo, the introducer, waits, giving them time. He never quite grasped the resemblance folks talked about but he can see it now, how Stella is Raymona rounded down with wrinkles added in and hair turned gray, what Raymona was bound and determined not to become. He can't smell alcohol, but would he, from this distance? She has her crochet bag with her. Must be all right. She waves and he nods. What a day for her, her daughter's funeral, and suicide the cause of death, but from her manner she might be settling in for a nice school production. She tried her best to make it to those. Sometimes she smelled from the drinking and wore her clothes in unusual combinations but she got herself there, looking pleased and parental. She made her efforts.

"Why, it's Raymond!" says Margie Stokes in a whisper loud enough for everyone to hear. "And he has a wife and baby! Cute little thing, looks just like him. Was he a friend of your daughter's, Stella?" Raymond can't make out Stella's answer. Margie talks again, quieter. He hears her last words. "*Just* like him." Chippie's straining toward him again but Petra folds the squirming baby up in her own arms. He hopes Margie's thought isn't an offense. Him and Petra, a lesbian, married, having a baby. What an idea. Stella's had her first look at her granddaughter. What effect will that have?

Now it's Ricki up in front looking determined. Her voice is too loud, sign of how hard she's working. Someone named by initials only, H.D., wrote the poem she's reading. "*Now let the cycle sweep us here and there, we will not struggle...*" Her voice quiets little by little. His mind starts to follow. Without warning, a bird enters in.

> *somewhere,*
> *over a field-hedge,*
> *a wild bird*
> *will lift up wild, wild throat,*

The bird is Raymona. Her wild, wild throat. He pulls himself back from a verge he's not ready for. *Indians have words of power, Raymond.* She was always trying to teach him Indian things. *Poems are the white folks' version. That's what we read at DWELL*—she grinned and whispered—*just us dykes.* Punching at him from across the room, teasing, playing. Maybe she thought it made him uncomfortable, that word dyke. Maybe it made her uncomfortable. Ricki sits down. He should go next.

Up here in front of people, he can almost feel her. *Go, Raymond, go.* Like a kid, excited. Or his very own cheerleader. He looks at Stella. She catches his look, nods, businesslike, and goes back to crocheting. "My sister liked to take Indian things and make them into something for herself. 'Today is a good day to die' was one of her favorite Indian thoughts. I want to thank you for making this service happen and for being her friends. She had a spark in her. I believe she wanted to put it out." He sits down. That wasn't too bad. He didn't forget to look at Stella.

Roo's up again, explaining how she was a student teacher in Raymona's school, a fact to file with the other surprises of this period in time. She says the next poem has "mythical implications that Bright Star would appreciate," and something about going to the underworld and then she says, "There was passion in the heart of that little girl." What does Stella think about that? He knows it to be a true statement and it sounds fine. Roo gives the poet's name, Sonia Gernes, a good name with roundness to it. When Roo starts to read, he's struck by her gentle, intelligent manner.

> *I dropped the little I was holding,*
> *turned my face upward as we had been told.*
> *Glowworms clustered somewhere above us –*
> *a newly constellated heaven*
> *of blue and equal stars –*
> *and long before the passage widened,*
> *I knew the rhythm of the river,*
> *long before the light came,*
> *I was ready to float free.*

He can feel the quiet, a full thing. The absence of Raymona is here. It takes him like a sudden wind. He wants to call her back and let her go on, both. *Ready to float free.*

Petra, looking held inside herself, stands at the front with Chippie and says something about complexity and death which he doesn't try to follow. Ramona is dead. Now Petra is sitting down and getting a bottle out of the diaper bag. It's the same bag Raymona used. Raymona, all around, but gone. Petra takes a deep breath and then she's looking at him like a friend, which is a little present she's giving to him on this hard day. Or maybe the present is from Raymona who arranged all of this, who set him down next to Petra where right now he belongs.

Roo and Jessie—the names from the shower stayed with him, she wanted it—go up to the front together. Roo is taking a big role in this ceremony, starting it, then reading a poem by herself, and now going up with Jessie. They read lines back and forth to each other, like a conversation, only it's a poem. Words of power. He can see the power shining out of the two of them. Together, they're stronger than Roo was alone, and she was strong enough then.

Before Nat gets up to say her words, she looks to the back with a question. Stella smiles at her politely and shakes her head, No. Then, sitting a little straighter in her pew, never stopping her crochet work, she adds her words. "You go on, Nat Levesque, I'm just fine here." So his mother knows Nat. It's the small world of Maine right here in this chapel. Stella might be at any old social occasion, she looks so comfortable, but right after this service will be a time of danger. Maybe he can help her through. Nat has a plain poem to read about loving for a short time only but something raw about the way the words rub against each other makes it hard to listen to. He can hear Ricki crying which is a good thing, or he hopes it is. Coming back to the pew, Nat has her chin up. Petra tries to catch her eye but fails. There are dramas here beyond his comprehension and Nat appears to be the key to one. There are some people in attendance he can't identify. They don't appear to want to speak. He turns around to see how Stella's doing. The empty pew just sits there, nothing to say for itself.

*

"Is the baby here?" Nat asks.

"She's sleeping."

"Cranky on the way home?"

"Yes, but she fell asleep. She can drop off in the middle of great protest. Quite a talent. Beer? I bought beer, thought we might need it."

"Yes, thanks. What's she doing here, Petra?"

"We'll talk about that, but you're also on the agenda. When were you going to tell me? Such a crazy week." When there's serious talking to do, it's done in the kitchen. The wallpaper offers a delicate, precise set of vegetable relationships, slightly abstract and quite calming, broccoli

131

nodding to celery, carrot leaning against eggplant. The square oak table adds solidity.

"Tell me about the baby, Petra."

"Bright Star left a will." She stops there, hoping Nat will just know.

"And?"

"Well, it's all a tad surreal." Petra is lightheaded from just a few sips of beer. Also, she's plain scared. Nat won't be as gentle as Danny.

"Petra, are you taking this baby?"

"She was willed to me, unlikely as that is."

"Bright Star said in her will that you inherit a baby."

"Intensely strange, yes?"

"Did you know?"

"Of course not."

"Did she know...?"

"About Anya? I doubt it. I didn't tell her."

"You babysat. Maybe it was as simple as that."

"I wish. The will was written before Chippie was born." She watches this information take hold.

"So..." Nat runs her fingers through her neat, gray hair. It falls back into place, well-trained.

"She wasn't very stable, Nat." *Gently, gently. O ye gods, whoever you are, let me be kind.*

Nat's fingers trace the grain of the table's wood. Her eyes follow her fingers. "Do you believe she had the illness Ricki talked about?"

"No, and neither do you."

"Do you think Ricki does?"

"Yes, for now."

"You want this baby?"

"I think I want this baby. Week number one went quite well, despite those surreal elements."

"Hmm. Well. A lot going on. Did you see me talking to Mary at the reception?"

"Mary. Ricki's mother? Yes, what was that all about?"

"We were in school together."

"God. We're in some kind of weird web, aren't we, my dear old Nat?"

"We are. Connections, tangles, whatever. Mary was a kind and very normal teenager. I was...whatever I was. Introverted. Alienated. Gay, of course. I didn't know Mary was Ricki's mother. So many Hardings around here, I never put it together. But we're off onto me..."

"A relief, frankly. We'll get back to me. Were you ever going to tell me..."

"You saw."

"I saw. I could hardly stand it. After all these years, Nat."

"From the first time she came into the room. It's always been like that for me, so juvenile. It's like a physical fall, the time in the air before hitting the ground that everybody imagines. Slow motion. It was the same with you. I must have told you."

"Actually, you never did. But *Bright Star*. Nat Levesque."

"I know. I feel so stupid. There's more. As long as we're confessing."

"We are, aren't we? I love you, Nat."

"I know. I'm used to the way you've decided to love me. I still think you're wrong."

"What else do you have to confess, besides that you fell in love with a woman who...I'm so mad at her, Nat."

"It was my mistake, falling for the wrong woman. Again. But, Petra, she must have had some indelible agony."

"I *know*. That doesn't keep me from being furious. Make your confession."

"This is as embarrassing as anything you could be doing by agreeing to raise a baby."

"I doubt it. Tell me."

"You saw Stella, Bright Star's mother."

"Saw and heard her. And her friend. Now I'm Raymond's wife as well as Chippie's mother. She knew you."

"Stella was in our class, too."

"Wait. Ricki told me. Her mother and Stella and that Bede person...and *you*? You didn't say anything when Roo told us..."

"Too much going on. Ricki was about to burst. Also, I wasn't exactly focused on the past after Ricki told about their relationship."

"Of course not. You were great. Really, you were so kind."

"Do you want to hear this confession or not?"

"Sorry. It's about Stella? Oh, Nat..."

"Yes, in high school. A huge crush. I was totally private about it, or I think I was. Maybe she knew, but I doubt it. She was in her own world. I imagined it was an interesting one. I wanted in. Then, when Bright Star joined DWELL..."

"Did you know she was..."

"No. I just..."

"You didn't make the connection, you just had a visceral response."

"Old, deep, and mistaken."

"You didn't see the resemblance."

"She had that black hair."

"Then, after that, she was just, as Roo said, one of the group."

"Maybe I was ready. It's been a long time, Petra."

"I never asked you to..."

"I'm not accusing you."

"Sorry."

Nat takes a deep breath and folds her hands on top of the table. Her knuckles whiten, then the color returns. Petra has never stopped being thrilled by Nat's hands, which is not something she intends to say. "Were you going to...with Bright Star..."

"I thought I might ask her if she'd like to have coffee."

"Oh, dear."

"It's so *stupid*."

"Well, it is." Petra says this with a smile. She does love Nat. Nat is nodding her head, agreeing, how stupid, and then shaking her head side to side, rueful. Then they're both smiling, old friends, and they start laughing, hard, and can't stop, tears streaming down their faces.

"*Why* are you taking this baby?"

"God, I don't know," Petra says, her gut aching. "It's so *stupid*."

"Well, it is."

They start to recover, taking deep breaths. They both blow their noses with identical handkerchiefs. "I can't believe we still have these," says Petra. They bought cotton handkerchiefs when they were a couple, unable to tolerate the statistics about trees and tissues.

"I know. How many do you have left?"

"Three."

"I've bested you. I have five," says Nat.

"I don't believe you."

"They're precious, a remnant of our glory days, but they do just disappear, don't they?"

"I suspect the washing machine eats them, for a change from socks."

"Probably true."

"Nat, are you all right?"

"The worst part is how I've complicated my ability to respond to a friend's suicide. I bet it's the same for you, from quite a different perspective."

"Yes. So much *self* rising up when any normal person would be feeling sad for her."

"Well, she's dead."

"Nat, Nat. You practiced that in front of a mirror."

"What a crappy therapist you are."

"You did."

"Well, you're almost right. I rehearsed in the middle of the night, in case a need arose. She really *is* dead. She doesn't need us to feel for her."

"What did it do to you, realizing you had a crush on the daughter of the first girl you...maybe you didn't focus on that."

"I did focus on it. It threw my feelings into another...how can I explain?"

"You don't have to. Is this too private?"

"If I can't talk to you, Petra..."

"OK, talk."

"All I have is an image. A very old painting, a fresco maybe, with cracked paint, so the picture is broken into bits."

"Is that you? Broken like that, but not exactly broken apart?"

"Not me. Not that personal, not that basic."

"Your feeling for Bright Star."

"That's closer. What I'd built up around her was suddenly distant —old, cracked—as if it were some ancient memory. More about Stella than Bright Star, and so damned embarrassing."

Petra reaches across the table but Nat's hands move. She's patting her shirt pocket, an old, old gesture. "Nat, dear, you quit smoking years ago."

"What? Oh. Was I...what a ridiculous..."

"Automatic," Petra says.

"And to let myself...profoundly ridiculous, don't you think?"

"Oh, I don't know. I doubt I'd say *profoundly*." They look at each other and smile and shake their heads. They pick up their glasses and drink from them. They put their glasses down. "Did I do this to you, Nat?"

"Indeed you did."

"Oh, well."

"Right."

"Nat, I never liked her much."

"I know. I hope that's not why you're planning to raise her daughter."

"You know me better than that. I have trouble summoning a seemly quantity of guilt over giving up my own child. And no, I don't think *that's* why, either. It's irrational, perhaps profoundly so."

"Join the club."

"OK." They sit, sipping beer. Petra wonders if she's going to get by this easily. "Are you hungry, Nat?"

"No. I haven't been, much."

"I have to pee, and take a look at Chippie. Maybe she's not real."

"She's real. Go."

When she comes back, she says, "You were right. She's real. She snores. I wonder if I should worry about that. I can't remember Anya snoring. Are you not going to grill me?"

"I should?"

"I don't know. Maybe."

"Why *are* you doing this?"

"I don't know."

"That's what I thought. Why do you want to be grilled, Petra?"

"To see if I can take it, maybe. To see if I'll buckle."

"I'm not vitally interested in the role of griller. The setting is a bit too pleasant. No bare light bulb."

"A lot of help you are."

"You just don't want to be alone with your decision. Too existential for you."

Petra is stopped by that. After a while, she says, "Oh."

"Oh?"

"You're right. It's very, very existential."

"No certainty available."

"Right. That's it. Thanks, Nat."

"You're welcome. Let's move to the living room." They go through the doorway, Petra first, pushing the baby swing aside, holding it for Nat who looks up to see how it's attached. "You could take that contraption down and no one would know it was ever there. No screws."

"I thought about that."

"Change of subject. You said there was more, about Bright Star."

"It's not simple, or light."

"Tell me."

Petra tells and tells, stopping only to get them more beer. She tells about the will, the rest of what was in the manila envelope, the message left for Ricki. Nat listens and nods. "What else?" She says there are signs that Bright Star had multiple personality disorder. Nat squints and shakes her head but all she says is, "What more?" She tells about Raymond, who he seems to be. Nat says, "You like him. You trust him." "Yes." "OK. More?" She decides to tell about Helga without naming her or giving much detail. "So I had to tell Gertrude about the client, and about Anya, I'd never told her about Anya. And about babysitting Chippie. That's all it was then, just a bit of babysitting."

"Oh, my dear poor Petra, what a lot. Was Gertrude nice to you?"

"Gertrude was nice to me." She doesn't tell about the journals, thinking they might hurt whoever touches them. Or is she hoarding them for herself? She says, "When I met Bright Star at the laundromat, she was wearing two buttons. One said, 'How Dare You Assume I Am Heterosexual?' Which was nostalgic, but also a nice touch on a pregnant woman. I think I told you."

"You did. The other one?"

"It said, 'Or white.'"

"Oh. That you didn't tell me."

"I tried to find an interpretation I could feel good about. You remember how a few straight people would wear the one about assuming heterosexuality, trying to show solidarity, during demonstrations, or after Charlie Howard was killed."

"Those kids are out now, free to roam," Nat says.

"Not kids any more."

"No. I wonder if they still torment boys who carry purses. Do you think she *was* part Indian?"

"I think she was crazy."

"Petra Kalinowski."

"Perfectly good word."

"Are you getting drunk on two beers?"

"I might need food. The point is, I knew she was strange from day one." Making sandwiches while Nat is in the bathroom, Petra names the moment: *Crystal Infant Mysteries*. She counts the *i's* and *y's*. *Y's* are *i's* traveling incognito. "I" four times, then. Is it only unadorned ego that compels her to try parenting again?

Nat comes back with red eyes. Petra puts her arms around the small strong bony body of this decent woman. She loves their equal height. "Have you lost weight, Nat?"

"Probably."

"You saw something in her that I missed."

"I don't know. I wish I felt more real grief about a real person." Nat cries. Petra holds her. They stand beside the kitchen counter, sandwiches half-made.

"It's that you opened yourself up again, to wanting."

"Yes," Nat says, and breaks away. "And it's still you I want."

"I know." They look at each other. This is a return to old helplessness for both of them. Petra can do nothing but endure the long moment, keep herself from cutting it short. Finally Nat reaches into her pocket and pulls out her handkerchief. She blows her nose and says, "Let's eat."

Chapter Fifteen

Ricki made it through the memorial service and survived the time at Jessie's: food, conversation, her family mixing with lesbians. She got herself back to Gertrude's where she's determined to stay, unpacked her suitcase, changed into her oldest, softest pair of jeans. She sits on the bed. *This is where I live, this is my life.* One shirt and one jacket hang in the closet, one good pair of pants. Other clothes are folded and arranged in dresser drawers. *Order.* She gets up, goes down the long staircase, joins Gertrude. The wine has been poured, it seems rude to leave, but the tall, delicate glasses are impossible. Gertrude isn't offended. "Should I wait up, Ricki?"

"Oh. Oh, no. No, thanks." Embarrassed.

She puts the key in the ignition, reaching with her left hand, a familiar, awkward, comforting maneuver. She listens to the engine's struggle, poor old thing, and how it succeeds once again, all pistons put to work. Her own little world, this truck. She backs out the driveway. When she and Bright Star had wine they used heavy tumblers. Bright Star said their wine was proletarian, a word she rolled out like a carpet to be walked on. "Like you, Ricki. Like me. We are of the proletariat." She had found a book at the laundromat, *Introduction to Leftist Politics.* Turning a corner, relieved to be driving, Ricki thinks of Lionel who would probably know about the proletariat. She abandoned him to a solitary quest, exploring gayness. Nothing to do with her, she thought. Wrong. And now? Does it still feel right, being a lesbian, with your first lover dead? Yes. She's avoiding bridges, avoiding the Brewer side of the river, determined not to wander down to where her parents and her old bed wait. The bed where she let herself suck her thumb. By the fourth night it was wrong. She stopped doing it. She has to get back to school. She tried last week, driving from Bucksport to Orono, thinking what a strong link the river was, liquid steel linking childhood to college life. Class was Derrida and gaps and erasures: ideas that stopped her mind. *Infinity for falling into.* She turns the radio on and takes a right. Poor

Raymond. His mother's disappearance upset him. Had to. But he went to Jessie's, ate a little, thanked everyone one more time. He did the courteous thing instead of making a drama. Raymond and Bright Star, two different people. She wishes she could get back to the dying man's wink. It feels like something she dreamed, not her very own real life eternal alchemized event. She turns into an unfamiliar neighborhood, tries to get lost so she can make a project of finding her way back, but she knows where she is, right above Main in a very proletarian neighborhood. Kids holler back and forth across the street, in tee shirts, unsupervised, younger than they ought to be. It's dusk now. Cooler. Her jeans jacket is on the seat beside her, the one Bright Star instructed her to buy at a lawn sale. Dense embroidery covers the back, an American Indian design. *Splurge, Ricki.* Then a giggly whisper in her ear. *Turn me on, babes.* She picked up the jacket and pretended to consider its worth with a critical eye. *Hey, no blushing.* She wore it to bed that night, nothing else. Bright Star wore nothing at all. A fun day, start to finish, Chippie in a sling against Bright Star's breast and the three of them out in the world instead of in the trailer which could get a little tight. Walking along, looking around, commenting on life in the neighborhoods of Bangor, they managed to get briefly, cheerfully lost. They asked a man in a business suit for directions. He was formal with them but his good-bye was a grin and a limp-wristed wave. They loved this. She was allowed to drive that day, allowed to demonstrate that she could use a stick shift perfectly well, thank you. Bright Star played mother-wife, sitting politely in the passenger seat while she, Ricki, made decisions about which way to go. Is she trying to retrace...? This might be one of the streets.

There she is. Raymond's lost mother. Bright Star's mother. Stella. Or it could be the woman sitting on the curb only *looks* like Stella. She circles the block, pulls over, parks across the street. The woman bends over her handiwork. Beside her is the distinctive cloth bag. Ricki gets out of the truck, crosses the street, stands at little distance. Stella ignores her, or maybe she's too involved in her work. Finally she looks up, nods, and pats the curb. Stella crochets and Ricki sits beside her counting cars and trucks. She hasn't looked at vehicles from this angle since she was a kid. Tires are more varied than she would have predicted, if she had tried to predict. *Now let the cycle sweep us here and there, / we will not struggle.* She had to wait like this in silence for Bright Star more than once.

"The black is for spite," Stella says at last. Matter-of-fact, explanatory. Ricki doesn't know how to answer. She nods. Maybe Stella sees the nod, maybe not. "One entire doily made of spite is my plan." The idea of a doily didn't occur to her. She assumed at first that the black shiny thread was a sign of mourning, but when she saw the shape the piece was taking she thought this might be a work out of control. A doily made of spite? Against Bright Star? "The problem seems to be coming soon, dear," Stella says. "I can feel it like a large truck looming at the crest of a hill. Myself I see sitting in the middle of the road. The curb won't keep me to the side of things. It's a center I'm at now. It will be a small one." Small? Stella looks at her. "The doily. It's nearly completed and then what turn will things take? I have a little urge to get myself to Bitta's. You wouldn't happen to have time?"

*

"We'll be sitting at a table, Bitta," says Stella. Ricki sees relief on the bartender's face, as if where Stella sits has meaning and she made the right choice. This is a neighborhood place, not much populated but not empty and not sad. They sit at a square table near the cleared space. People must dance on the worn wooden floor, but no one is dancing now to Johnny Cash who will walk the line. She hears the click of balls. The room beyond must have a pool table. She feels nervous about her age, but maybe being with Stella, who pulls her crochet-work out of her bag, will make it OK. She sees the restroom sign and excuses herself. When she gets back to the table a can of Pepsi and a glass with ice cubes are waiting for her. Ten minutes pass. Stella crochets. Maybe the Mack truck —is that what Stella said?—can be avoided by sitting here saying nothing. The clock on the wall is a plain one with black plastic around its face. A few people talk quietly, murmurs with private meanings. Dolly Parton sings about family and sad tender pride. A familiar-looking man and woman come from the other room, declaring their thirst. Another pool game starts. No one can predict, listening like this, blind, when the click of the balls will match the beat of the song, Hank Williams now. She's never learned to play pool. She could, left-handed, or maybe if she held the stick right-handed from the underside she'd have more control. She'd find a way. Nat would be good at pool, leaning over the table,

141

intent. The idea of Nat and Stella and her own mother all knowing each other from school is such a prickly fact that she keeps forgetting it. The thirsty couple have joined a man in a green golf shirt. Now she remembers, they were at the service, long ago, on this very day. Not at the reception, though.

"I've decided to extend it some," Stella says, startling her. She must mean her crochet project. Ricki nods, Stella keeps crocheting. *I'm sitting with Bright Star's mother in a bar.* Does Stella know who she is, that she was Bright Star's lover? Laughter from the other room. A woman making fun of her own bad shot, a man saying she gets the prize for progress made. Back to the clicking of balls. Stella said six words. Six is better than none. This bar is a world of its own, away from that other world where a person might decide to take her own life before it gets taken from her. Ricki feels under a spell and the thought comes that she might be sitting in a bar in the future with a Bright Star who lived. For decades they've been drinking Pepsi and listening to country music while the click of pool balls keeps things fresh and current, keeps Bright Star calm and silent and crocheting items that will never lie flat and aren't expected to. "What if I'd arrived a little early?" This is the man from the memorial service. "Dave, stop that. You couldn't have done anything," says the woman. "What? What are you talking about?" The man in the green shirt is asking. Stella finishes her Pepsi and looks toward Bitta who is talking to a man at the bar. Bitta wears jeans and a flannel shirt and a wedding ring. She misses Stella's signal, pours a drink for the man, answers the phone. "Etta doesn't want me to talk about it," Dave says. "That is not true, not true at all," the woman responds.

"Bitta?" Stella calls out. Ricki decides to keep up with her, finishes her own Pepsi. Bitta comes over.

"Stella, I just heard."

"Well, yes," Stella says.

"I'm sorry for your loss. I didn't even know you had a daughter."

"Well, yes."

"What can I get you?"

The two women look at each other. "Maybe another Pepsi would do, one for each of us. Ricki here was my daughter's close friend. She's had a day of it."

Bitta looks directly at Ricki and nods. "Pleased to meet you, Ricki. Two Pepsi's, then." She hesitates before she leaves, as if she has more to say, but turns and walks to the bar.

"...this young fella," Dave is saying. "He was about as shaken up as I was. Being an official person makes you do a thing, carry out your duty, but it doesn't make it easy."

"So she was dead already then?" the other man asks.

"Must have been. Her face was covered when they carried her past me."

What? Ricki looks at Stella, but Stella is crocheting as if there's nothing in the world but her own handiwork.

"Dave was pretty shook up," Etta says.

"I'm not used to blood. Especially like that."

"It was bad?" the man asks.

"Bad enough. The smell got to me worse than the sight, but the sight wasn't something you want to see every day. They drained the tub. What stayed in the bottom was diluted, but on the floor was a pure thick puddle. Red. I don't know how the fellows avoided stepping in it. I suppose they're trained. I figure she had her wrist out for a time and it dripped. Then there was the spatter, some of it not blood. You know what I mean."

Ricki feels dizzy, tells herself she shouldn't jump to conclusions.

"Dave can't stop thinking about it," Etta says, and reaches out toward Dave.

Dave says, "Why would a person who calls herself Bright Star..."

She wants to cover her ears. She might throw up. Stella keeps crocheting, like a deaf person. Or maybe a deaf person would feel something, know something.

"It was a lot for Dave," Etta says.

"Etta's the one should be upset. She hired her, to work at the laundromat."

"So you knew her, Etta."

"I did. Maybe that's why I'm not quite as upset. I could tell she wasn't a stable person. I tried to help her out. Of course, I didn't see the blood. Maybe it just hasn't hit me."

"That's what I think," Dave says.

"It would take something, to realize a thing like that," the friend says.

Ricki isn't going to vomit but she has to breathe to keep herself under control. It's only reality, what Dave is saying; nothing she didn't already know. Stella's hands keep moving, fast, knowing their job. Bright Star got carried out with her face covered like a body in a television show. This man, Dave, must be the insurance agent, a person who happened upon a death, or maybe he had an appointment.

"I had an appointment, you see."

The words make her feel dislocated, as if she joined the conversation, as if she left Stella behind with her calm face and her crocheting. A picture of Bright Star's wrist comes, blood dripping to the floor.

The friends says, "She made an appointment with you and went and killed herself?"

"She left a polite note, right to the point. It said to call the authorities and how there was a dead body inside. The operator and the dispatcher were good at their jobs, very quick about things."

Ricki pulls herself back to the silent table where she's sitting with Bright Star's mother. Stella stops her work and seems to become a statue, crochet work held in the air, a stitch half-finished, staring ahead. But she's not a statue. She makes a sound like a baby animal, a wild whimper, and drops her work and slaps the table with both hands. "Bitta!" she says, looking sharply in the direction of the bar. Her glass is half full of Pepsi, but she probably wants a real drink. Ricki's head is already spinning, but she'll have whatever Stella has. Alcohol might help. "Bitta!" Stella says again, and Bitta turns and walks in their direction, a kind, worn, Maine woman who will take care of them.

*

Raymond is walking the streets of Bangor, shivering and sweating in the night air. After the service he made a quick trip to Bitta's in case Stella was drawn to drink. Not there, not home. He wants to decide she's in good hands with Margie Stokes. Hours have passed. There was the reception at Jessie's, then he started walking. He hasn't been back to Bitta's, nor to the apartment, which is how he knows this

144

walking isn't about finding his mother. His worries were piled up by the time he got to the reception. What if Petra had the idea the baby was his, put the little critter in his arms and walked away? She was the one who answered the door for the reception, though, and he could see his thoughts were off. She looked at him in her acknowledging way, as if they had a mutual experience in progress, which they do. She told him Chippie was fine before he asked. He could see it was true because the baby was being passed from Roo to Jessie like a treat to be shared. Ricki's eyes were full of tears when she turned to him. "I wanted to see you, Raymond. Could I keep on seeing you and Chippie?" He nodded, unable to find his voice. Maybe his time with Raymona's friends was just beginning, not at an end. Nat approached and offered condolences in a way that took him to a firmer place. Now he's walking, unsure of his purpose. His truck is waiting in front of Jessie's where the reception was. All week he went from one thing to the next while his worries rose up and settled down in a rhythm that didn't seem to have much to do with him. He did what he could at work, calling his mind back to his tasks. Stella stayed sober but that was her own doing, unconnected to his vigilance. He wasn't surprised when she started expressing annoyance at being watched over "like a naughty child." Right now is a time when she might need watching over though; might even want it. But his own mind won't quiet. Raymona's death is like a thing with teeth, waiting in the dark part of him. He gets pulled back to when he shot Bede, and called the sheriff on himself. He and Raymona argued about that, whether to run away. She hadn't made a plan beyond the death. He never put the gun down. He was holding it when the sheriff came. For a while, walking, he was in stopped time. No sound. Nothing. Then came a block or two with a sense of crush, too many things to be done, himself an impaired giant unable to accomplish any of them. His dishes are piling up. He's been eating fried egg sandwiches breakfast, lunch, and dinner, loading them with pepper to get beyond the cardboard sensation. Three boys came up behind him a while ago. They were whispering. He didn't think much about it but then he heard the word—*Indian*—repeated on a regular basis. It turned into *dirty Indian* and they came closer. An urge to let things happen as they would, let himself be played with, even get beaten up, took him like a drug, but he did an about face, saw how young and small and afraid they are. They ran and he went back to his own world. They seem more like hallucination than reality but he knows they were real. What's he trying to accomplish? Maybe he's only walking time away, not an easy thing to do. His skin feels activated, as if it stands out separate from his body. The world under his feet turns and turns. It's hard to keep up. He has the idea he could get thrown off backward and spun out into space if he stopped. The needs of another person could anchor him but Raymona is dead and Stella's missing. Stella wouldn't be missing if he found her. He's been keeping her in the missing category with his blind walking. He might have passed by her without knowing. *Passed her without knowing?* He stops right there, in the middle of a block. This is a nice neighborhood. Porches with lights on wait for someone to come home. Lit windows show folks sitting down together to watch television. His thoughts have gone down a strange track. It won't do. He heads back to his truck. His jacket will be there and he'll be glad to put it on. It's cold as the devil now. Is the devil cold? He'll go into Bitta's, see if Stella's there. She won't be. He'll climb the stairs and knock until he wakes her up. She'll be irritable or friendly or just plain blank, but she'll be real. It takes a while to get the engine started, though. Nothing wrong with the truck, but his own mechanism isn't working. Can't get himself to turn the key. He can see a portion of the moon coming over a nearby house if he leans forward, peers through the windshield. He's shivering even with his jacket on, but that seems unimportant to the moment. What's important is waiting. A dog walker comes by, and a young couple holding hands. No one seems to notice him, maybe he's invisible. He leans forward again just to prove he can move. The moon's progress is a comfort. Everything in order in the skies above. Then it's time to turn the key and drive. Nothing changes, it's just time. Bitta's is closed. He won't have to go in there. The stalling might have been for this, to spare himself the sight of his mother sitting at the bar. He opens the door. Here are her stairs. He stops, not going forward, not letting the door close behind him, between worlds.

He starts to climb. He's been climbing these stairs all week. He gets the feeling of an escalator now, and he's climbing up the down part. He's never done that, made his way up an escalator whose own movement was downward, certainly not at Freese's in Bangor where even going the right way was a thing that challenged his childhood best-clothes dignity. He'd step on carefully and keep from stumbling and step off carefully, scared every time. He saw a movie that made things worse. There was a chase, a man was running up the down part, not making good time. The movie was a comedy, but the idea of running up something that keeps taking you down agitated his child mind. He had nightmares. He didn't have one nightmare about shooting Bede, but he had nightmares about that.

He's more tired than he wants to be. He hardly remembers why he's here. He raises his arm for the job of knocking on Stella's door but she opens it. "It's about time," she says, and turns her back on him and walks right through the kitchen to the living room. A bad sign. She's not going to offer coffee.

"I thought you'd be with Margie."

"You thought no such thing, Raymond Weeks."

They're sitting down now, he forward on the couch, she on the edge of the easy chair, and they look at each other without speech until he gives in and puts his head down into his hands. He's had time to take in the fact that the doilies are removed from their places. He's seen the neat pile on the floor in the far corner. He's seen that Stella is not crocheting, not planning to, her supplies nowhere in sight. Still, he can't smell alcohol. Maybe this is the hiatus. "I had to walk," he says.

"Well, yes, I suppose you did. While you were walking, I held out, but you can see that by morning I might not be doing well. Bitta nearly pushed me out the door at closing. That nice girl was with me."

Nice girl? But what he says is, "That's good, Ma, that you didn't drink yet. Maybe you can make it."

"No help from you. Why didn't you tell me that child was yours?"

This is so unexpected his mind goes blank. He can feel his hands stretch out into a helpless position, like a person being held up at knifepoint. His mind clicks back a notch. "What nice girl?"

"The one Raymona took advantage of at the end of her pitiful life."

"Ricki?"

"Ricki Harding. She's a very intelligent, very nice girl who should not have been used by your sister in such a way, but that is beside the point. I have no patience for you tonight, Raymond."

"She's not my baby, Ma." He feels the weakness in his words. His hands have come down on either side of him. They hold to the edge of the couch.

"She's the spitting image of you, can't you see that?"

"To tell the truth, no. Do you really want to talk about this? I can't make you believe me."

"That's a true set of words. How could you father that child? Did you do it into a bottle, at least? I hear that's how it's done with women like that. Into a bottle and then a turkey baster. It's still not a forgivable event, Raymond. The child will not be right in her head. Not that she has any chance, being the daughter of Raymona, but this complexifies the situation. That's probably not even a word, but you know what I mean. All I want to know is why you didn't tell me. You have a baby now, so I have a grandchild regardless of the mother of it, and I would want to know a thing like that and I am mad as a hatter about it. What if that girlfriend of yours had never brought it to the memorial service? I would not have seen my own grandchild and would not know to begin making plans for more."

He's unsure he caught the latest turn. If he's the father, she wants contact with Chippie? He's distracted by the phrase mad as a hatter. Doesn't that refer to mental unbalance? And how did Ricki and Stella end up together at Bitta's? And Petra is *not* his girlfriend. But he keeps the thread. "More, Ma?"

"More of seeing your baby. Where is your mind, Raymond?"

"Ma, she's not my baby, but she *is* your grandchild. I'm sure you can see her whenever you want to."

"I intend that. That is not the point."

"What is the point, Ma?"

"It's the blood."

"I'm not the baby's father. I don't know how to help you with that."

"I need no help about the baby. That was just steam. A person has to let off steam. You should have told me. Letting me go to the service with no preparation was not right. I was embarrassed in front of Margie who is becoming my friend and needs to see something beyond sickness all about me."

"I'm glad you and Margie..."

"That is not the point, either."

He's starting to relax, a little. This sparring is familiar. If he stays, she won't drink. He wishes he had the sleeping bag, but the couch pillows can be put down near the door. "What's the point again, Ma?" He's almost smiling. He feels an urge to lie down on the couch, let her rant at him while he sleeps. It takes real effort but he keeps himself upright.

"Blood, Raymond."

"What do you mean?"

"That nice man David, who sells insurance, was telling about it." Dave. Insurance. Raymona. Raymona's blood. But the connection might not be accurate. She's upset enough without him bringing in things she can't tolerate.

"David?"

"That had to call the police. On Raymona."

"Oh, Ma. Where was this?"

"While I was having my Pepsi Cola and that nice young Ricki was staying right with me even to the point of having Pepsi herself and not a drop of anything different and not talking. She knows how to keep herself quiet, that girl."

"At Bitta's? The insurance agent was at Bitta's talking about blood?"

"Well, he didn't know we were there, not at first. I went over and told him I was sorry for what my daughter did to him. He was harmed by her. The numbers of *that* club are increasing rapidly."

"I'm sorry you had to hear about that, Ma."

"This is another thing you didn't tell me about, Raymond. There was a quantity of blood left over from her death and I think you knew that."

"It's a hard thing to have in your mind."

"Well, yes it is. It was washing over my entire brain for a while. I was afraid to lie down. I had my solution."

"Would you like to put the doilies back in place?"

"In time we might get to that. You're right that I'm calmer, having you to discuss things with."

"Why don't I make some coffee, Ma?"

"I could do with a cup. Thank you, Raymond."

149

"You're welcome, Ma." Maybe it doesn't matter who she thinks the father is. At least not tonight. The little critter should have some blood relation around and now a grandmother is interested. He can't do it himself. Stella hasn't messed up her kitchen yet. She could still refrain. He's bone tired. Right here is where a saying like that fits the situation. Bone tired. It doesn't matter. This will be another long night and he has to be ready for it. He almost is. Caffeine will help. "Coffee, Stella," he says, going back into the living room. "Are you going to tell me where you went after the service? I know you didn't go right to Bitta's."

"No, dear. I'm not that predictable. I suppose it would be easier for you if I were."

"Less interesting, though."

"Thank you, dear. Margie brought me here. I didn't stay, of course. I did some walking of my own. I would rather talk about the blood, if you don't mind." He does mind, but he nods for her to go ahead. "That insurance agent, David, is living with some gruesome details in his mind. What do you suppose we can do about that? I've been thinking that a cake would be a fitting gesture. I wrote down his address. I've not baked in a number of years, but there's always an exception. Nothing too sweet because these are not sweet times, but I thought it would help. Lemon, I mean. So you'll deliver it, won't you?" He takes a sip of coffee and looks at her. *I will deliver a cake to Dave, who came upon my sister's suicide.*

"Yes, Ma. It's a good idea."

"Well, of course it is," says Stella.

Chapter Sixteen

When Petra's mother was finally, after months of fatiguing uncertainty, diagnosed with cancer, a new way of life began in the family. Each of them, Witold, Tekla, and Petra, found a place of dark privacy. For Tekla it was simple: shades pulled in the daytime bedroom, the bed itself in the center of the room. Witold wrapped himself in thick black silences. Petra began practicing blindness. When she climbed the stairs each night she closed her eyes and manufactured bravery, step by blind step. *Anybody can lose anything*, she whispered again and again. The molded wood of the railing was cool under her hand, her toes found the next rise, her leg muscles worked against gravity. There was almost a thrill, blindness spicing the family tragedy, but the exercise wore itself out and she took the stairs with open eyes, adjusted. This was inevitable, she thinks now, sitting on the edge of her bed with Bright Star's final notebook open in her lap. People adjust.

It's past midnight, Saturday again, two weeks since she inherited a baby. When life's timeline folds back on itself, segments touch each other in extraordinary ways. A shudder and a gap and then the raw rubbing. *Timequake*. But she wants an image more subtle than an earthquake. She closes her eyes. What comes, surprising her, is lace: old and yellowed, from the wedding gown of a woman from a previous century. Upright and classic, the woman descends a staircase with open, flirting eyes. She is not yet as old as she will become, not yet unable to negotiate stairs. *Stairway Lace* is this story's title. Lace is mere thread wound around itself, and holes. Good image for the pages in this notebook written during Bright Star's pregnancy: a moth-eaten version of lace with unintended holes and in need of delicate handling. Petra sat down on the edge of her bed over an hour ago, thinking to glance, skim. She was too thoroughly tired for more than that, wasn't she? But she read the notebook through, the entire last year of Bright Star's life lumped in clots of words. *Clotted Verbiage*. She's aware of vacillating between respect and repulsion.

Bright Star dated every entry. It was easy to locate sections that might reveal the identity of Chippie's father. "Chip" gave no last name, no place of residence, said he was in town for the weekend only. Bright Star seduced him because he was Native American and, what luck, looked like a clone of Raymond. Perfect, given that Raymond himself had turned down the job. Chip would father a singular child, not that he knew about his role as progenitor of the Savior of the Native Peoples. The delusion of the girl who wanted her stepfather killed had staying power. Not that consistency ruled. According to some passages Chip wasn't real. Even the baby is All Spirit on one page, but her physicality is immediately, angrily asserted on the next. The notebook offers numerous references to Raymond, of course. Petra found these alarmingly interesting. Sitting on the edge of her bed, not comfortable but not inclined to move, she faces the truth. She found the passages about Raymond stimulating. Sexually. In her work with clients with multiple personality disorder, she sometimes feels aroused. She doesn't experience this with other clients. She and Gertrude have evolved a theory having to do with intense and poorly contained energies and the fact that anything can be experienced as sexual by such clients. An old boot, sidewalk graffiti, an irritated tone. Anything. And why not? When abuse began they were, most of them, exceedingly young humans, unequipped for making distinctions. Sometimes sexual energy leaks into the therapy room, a mesmerizing fluid. The therapist takes it in through her pores. Unscientific, but descriptive. The Bright Star of these journals has been boldly diagnosed by therapist Petra. Multiple Personality Disorder. Are the pages saturated with free-floating sexual energies? Has she simply absorbed those? Does that explain the effect of the Raymond passages? Is this idea a weak and obvious defense against her own unruly, inappropriate hormones? One passage was written the day Bright Star, already quite pregnant, tried, not for the first time, to seduce Raymond. She, perhaps as a child alter, was convinced it was not too late, Raymond could still become the baby's father. Something to do with magic. Raymond declined the honor. The entry was written in great disappointment and confusion. Tears fell. Ink blurred. Petra thinks this ridiculous attempted seduction—or sad, of course it was sad—did happen. Raymond's response was so Raymond-like. Patience, kindness, firmness. He put his half-sister to bed as if she really were a disappointed child, covering her, head and all, as she requested. He tiptoed out when he thought she was asleep. His sister heard him, the caution of his departure, but waited quietly until he was gone, then got up and wrote the story. Which Petra, voyeur, has read. So she's been there; seen. She doesn't know what to do with this fact. She's embarrassed to have felt aroused, but the feeling has passed. The embarrassment is unimportant. So is the strange sexual response. No father will come to claim the baby sleeping peacefully in the other room. That is the crucial fact. The peace is worth noting, scarce as it has come to be. This is her baby now, this suddenly cranky baby. If she wants her.

Too existential for you. She's been avoiding Nat's words all week. I'm busy, she told herself. Existentialism is irrelevant, she told herself. Avoidance, denial, blindness, all week. Also, though, a hum of alertness vibrating under everything. Bright Star's notebook might be strobe-lit with contradictions, but so is Petra's mind. Has she been dull? Yes. Has she been keen? Yes. *You just don't want to be alone with your decision,* said keen-eyed Nat. *Too existential for you,* said blunt, loving Nat. "It is a fault to wish to be understood before we have made ourselves clear to ourselves," wrote Simone Weil, to whose unrelenting pages Petra has been compelled to return in recent days. What to make of all of this?

She opens the lacy, moth-eaten verbally clotted notebook at random. *All right. Ricki will do. But how to soothe her ethical little mind? Maybe we should have a Mystery Illness. Allison would like that, wouldn't you, Allison? Yes! I will be the Heroine with palest skin, fainting at the Ball. The tall dark Stranger will step from the circle of people who helplessly surround me. He will warm his stethoscope with his sensitive fingers. Don't we love to make Allison happy? All right, everybody, we have a Mystery Illness which requires the courageous Final Action. Don't tell Raymond, he wouldn't buy it for a minute. Tell only Ricki. That's a rule. WHAT, Allison? I think the hero is a Red-haired Wild Man, from Far Away. Everybody is afraid of him, but not me. He lifts me from the floor and puts me on his horse. We ride away and I never see any of you again. Fine, Allison. Just don't tell Raymond.*

Good Lord. At some point she and Raymond will have to talk. Should Ricki be told there was no fatal illness? Does it matter? Is she, Petra, longtime lesbian, attracted to Raymond? Surely not. Besides being the wrong gender, he's too young. To say nothing of the fact that she's not

153

suited to sexual involvements any more, not since Anya died. The failure with Nat proved that.

Somehow it's become inevitable, almost mandated, that she think her way through. Tonight. Sex is not the point. Raymond is not the point, except in his role as the person who will end up with Chippie if she can't follow through. The point is this baby, who needs a parent, a committed parent, not a parent as deluded and temporary as the biological mother and not a parent as unsuited as her own younger self. *Is* she still unsuited? Perhaps even more unsuited? Chippie whimpers and has worked her way to a sustained scream by the time Petra gets to the spare room where the bassinet is currently placed. She looks at the clock. 12:45. Late, late, late. This is a baby who slept when she was supposed to until three nights ago. No fever, no other sign of illness, but all is not well. A fresh diaper, a bottle, half an hour of walking, humming, and jiggling result in a sleeping baby. Carefully, carefully, Petra eases her, this stranded child, into the bassinet, and stands, not moving, not breathing, waiting. But Chippie is asleep and perfect. Back to sitting on the edge of the bed. She picks up Bright Star's final, quite well-written, occasionally courageous, very crazy, sometimes stunning, notebook. There, that's a better and more balanced attitude. It's time to *think clearly*. Anya was a good baby. She mothered her good baby with ease. It was only later, when talk and toileting undid her, that she weakened, gave up. Now she feels worn, jittery, prematurely undone, nearly ready to give up again, this time on an infant. She hasn't admitted this. She's sweating, hot and cold. *This is not a catastrophe even if true.* Of course not. But she feels heavy-headed, as if her head is irregularly weighted and could fall in any direction. Ridiculous. She can calm herself, she can think. She can breathe: *one, two, three, four, five, six, seven.* Seven. The number of years in Anya's life. That is a fact. She can live with this fact, *has* lived with this fact. Now there's Chippie, who comes with her own set of facts, including the one about a dead mother secretly slipping her into the life of a certain Petra Kalinowski. Can said Petra K. live with this? She thought she could, thought she wanted to. Something happened. What, though? Eight. Nine. Ten. Eleven. Twelve. Thirteen. Fourteen. Fifteen. Sixteen. Seventeen. Eighteen. She has to get to eighteen. That's all. Eighteen. Hasn't she been here before? Everything is fine, though, she just has to *think*. She told Danny—when was that?—

how fascinated she was, even obsessed, watching, knowing that every smell, sight, and sound was forming the baby's mind. She remembers talking to Danny about it, but she doesn't remember her own intense— ecstatic?—experience. The dulled blur came so soon. Is this true? When she studied child development, not an easy subject for a mother whose child has died, a mother who gave up on parenting, her mind wandered, but she remembers some things. A baby must make a coherent whole from the elements of her caretaker's face. It's a task the brain is wired for, preferring curves over straight lines, liking the symmetry of the right and left sides of a face, the acute angles at the corners of the eyes, the contrast of the pupil against the white of the eye. Babies are drawn to putting the elements together, seeing faces. *This is good, thinking is good.* Babies study faces, learn to interpret changing expressions, learn they can *do* something about those expressions. Most babies do their work with gusto. She remembers relishing that thought. Pain about Anya did not keep student Petra from savoring such an idea. Now, in less than two weeks, she has begun to give up. What *happened*? Babies develop what is known as The Gaze and around Chippie's age they begin to insist on *mutual* gazing, intense mutual gazing such as will not happen again until they are old enough to fall in love, or so someone claimed. Ordinary mothers love this gazing thing. Chippie is awfully good at it. Wasn't Anya? The baby is learning to control human interaction, said the books. The baby uses the gaze.

Eye to eye she goes, says Petra to herself. A boxing ring comes to mind. Big gloves on the baby. Not everyone thinks of this as combat, says a part of the mind. Well, no. Not everyone would.

She *can* think this through. Her hands are cold but she's no longer sweating and her head feels properly weighted, aligned over her body. She can breathe. She can even contemplate moving from this position. Why is she not in the living room where sitting is more comfortable? She might have had a plan, unknown to her conscious mind, to lie down, to sleep through the rest of this night. She gets up and intends to go to the living room but veers back toward the spare room. Chippie is restless and hiccups in her sleep. Petra, frightened caretaker, holds her breath. This child *must* not wake up. She can't parent this child. What made her think she could?

Chippie settles into regular breathing, no hiccups. Petra stands over the bassinet, watching. She can't remember Anya's babyhood in detail. Was she distracted, living in the whirl of San Francisco, somehow ignoring the intensity of Anya's gaze, the demand of it? Is that how they got through the first year? Chippie's gaze tends to pull her into a watery world where nothing is solid, where she can't get her footing and breathing is dangerous. *Too existential for you.* The words mean more than Nat intended, or Nat intended more than it seemed she did. Maybe she *should* be sleeping instead of standing over the bassinet of a baby who might wake up if not left to herself. Ridiculous. Chippie has sunk into quintessential baby sleep. The room is filled with lovely baby peace. Even in her riled state she can feel this, a miracle, but she can't stay in the room. She turns away and strides, yes that's the word, strides into the living room and sits down in her comfortable chair. But she can't stay there, either. She gets up and walks, deliberately, energetically, purposefully, and enters the kitchen and turns on the light and runs the water until it is icy cold and fills her largest glass and turns off the tap and marches, now she's marching, back to the living room and sits on the couch, upright, and drinks half the glass of water without taking a breath. She notices she left the light on in the kitchen. She decides, firmly, that it doesn't matter. She puts the glass down and settles back into the couch, comfortable and upright. She takes note of her ridiculous exaggerated movements and declares them effective.

So. She was fascinated by Chippie. Then she was not fascinated. This was expected. She expected the acute (unnatural) interest to become simple daily interest. Of course she did. Is this what happened? No. Does she understand what happened? Not yet. Petra is in a Socratic dialogue with herself. Also, she's remembering how Chippie smiles in her sleep, turning unbearably sweet but also somehow self-sufficient, but no baby is self-sufficient and the sleeping smile is only from gas. She continues, determined now, a lawyer making her case, gentle inquiry turning accusatory: *Then there's this business of the gaze. Demanding, dangerous, so intimate it's boring.* Boring? The intimacy of the gaze is boring? She hangs her head because, yes, the baby's gaze is frightening, but, worse, much worse, it's boring. This is the unexpected thought, the insight avoided, the existential pit. She, Petra Kalinowski, hates nothing more than being bored. *Babies are boring?* Well, not entirely. But, yes, after the first electrifying insanity, for this woman, at this stage of her life, this baby began to seem less interesting. Yes, even a bit of bore. Unworthy as the thought is. She drinks the rest of the water. Surely she'll have to pee now, a biological necessity. She'll be allowed to get up, saunter to the bathroom, pull her pants down, feel the cool toilet seat, let go the good stream. Somehow a rule has been made that without an adequate excuse she has to stay here, think and feel and think and feel until she has clawed through this whole damned mess. Time crawls along. She doesn't have to pee. *Damn.*

*

"Still for spite. You mustn't think I've passed into mourning. I'm sorry, dear, but facts are facts." Stella, emerging from long silence. If five nights of doing the same thing can be called a ritual, this is a ritual. Ricki drives, Stella crochets. They do not go to Bitta's. They'll drive around Bangor until Closing Time, Stella crocheting spite into increasingly strange three-dimensional black doilies. Once in a while on these drives, Stella speaks. For example, the other night: *I like a series, for satisfaction.* Or the monologue on Margie Stokes who's decided to feed the skunk under her barn, which decision could only be made by a person from away, you know, and Margie is one of those, though acclimated now after her fifty years here but not completely for who feeds a skunk? *Still, it's a kindness, isn't it?* Tolerant Stella. Next came commentary on the bakery at the Shop and Save as opposed to one's own lemon cake. The Shop and Save came off well. There was a businesslike statement of gratitude for the service Ricki provides. A talkative night that one, an exception.

Ricki has been to classes this week. Her mind agrees to focus, but thoughts of Stella enter in. Hiding behind Stella is the ghost of Bright Star. When she's alone in bed, Bright Star comes forward. Sometimes they blend, mother and daughter, one person. *Stella* means star. Latin. So said a professor this very week. Did Bright Star know? So many unanswered questions. Stella or star: what you see is a brightness from long ago, nothing to do with present time. Still, brightness. "After midnight is worst," Stella said. So from midnight to two a.m. they drive, stop for a while and sit together, drive some more, avoid all bars.

157

"Porches provide an opening toward the world, which is an advantage for a person in my situation," says Stella. Which situation, though? Her daughter or her drinking? Ricki takes a left onto Broadway, for the porches.

When Raymond came to Gertrude's to talk to her, he commented on the doilies. "They used to lie flat. They had a sense of order about them, to my mind." The doilies were a way into telling her. "You need to know, my mother is an alcoholic." He said it kindly. The kindness spread like a blanket, covering her and Stella together. Wherever Stella was then, she was covered over with her son's kindness. "I'm not asking you to take a role," he said. "No one can stop her drinking if she has a mind to." She nodded. She understood this. She believed it. Also, she knew she'd try to prevent Stella from drinking, take a role. She's almost a substitute daughter now, she's been feeling it more and more. "I figured you had to know. You might feel bad if you invited her to drink, being left in ignorance." "I appreciate it, Raymond. Bright Star never said much about..." He nodded and said, "She didn't always own Stella as her mother. Maybe you hit a stretch like that." "I knew Stella was the name..." "I know how it could be. Things wavered at times for Raymona. Stella knows I'm here, the purpose of my visit." Raymond is so respectful it almost makes her feel like a complete adult. "That's good. No secrets." The words slipped out, a cliché. Stupid. Bright Star loved secrets, Raymond loved Bright Star. "My mother goes to AA," Raymond said, moving along, saving her. "It's a demonstration of how close she came the other night, how much she wanted to drink, that she didn't inform you." Maybe this was the time to tell him. "Raymond, there's something Bright Star...Raymona..." She got stuck there, not knowing what her plan was. Raymond waited. She thought how good he was at waiting. Then something, it was like a crack in his surface, told her this ability might not hold. She regretted what she was doing but kept doing it. "There's a secret I haven't talked to you about. She wanted me..." His eyes closed so briefly she could have imagined it. He had to be worn out, but she thought the information would help him, not add to his burden. "Raymond, she was sick. She wanted me to keep that a secret, along with all the rest. I couldn't even tell *you*. It was a fatal illness. I don't know what kind. That's *why* she..." He looked at her from his place on the couch in Gertrude's living room. He'd closed the crack, was back to being careful of the other person. She was the other person, not being careful of him. "I'm sorry," she said. "Nothing to be sorry for, Ricki. I appreciate your telling me." He ended the conversation soon after that. Had to get to work, he said.

She wonders if this was true. She drives beside the Kenduskeag Stream now, the truck a sturdy container holding Stella and herself and silence. *Stella is the alcoholic mother of a daughter who killed herself. The daughter who killed herself was Bright Star and she was my lover.* Holding to reality is the only way Ricki knows to get through this hard time. *Ricki, honey, of course it's hard, it would be for anyone.* It helped when her mother said that. It was no help to Raymond to hear about the illness, she could see that. Would it help Stella? But they can't talk about Bright Star. It will be good to see Nat tomorrow, at DWELL. Gertrude at home and Roo at school are both so generous, so considerate these days, it's almost too much—too soft. Nat is like a rougher towel against your skin.

Stella sits upright, crocheting. Stella could be a rich woman and she would be the rich woman's chauffeur. Or she could be a cab driver, it might be an interesting job, in which case Stella would only be a proud person down on her luck without a car of her own who needed to be driven somewhere, which is exactly the case. *This is Bright Star's mother.* Stella has a beautiful complexion for a drinking woman. There's something about her that doesn't fit being a mother, though. Innocence, maybe. Like a child. Like her daughter. An unusual version of innocence, a complicated version, old and young at the same time. Sly. Defiant. But innocent, both mother and daughter. *Why* would they stop talking to each other? She wishes Stella would tell. She can imagine it: Stella crochets spite into yet another doily and the words begin to float out of her mouth. At first it's impossible to follow because Stella proceeds from wherever her thoughts happened to be, but eventually the story makes sense. Things *will* make sense. But not tonight. Stella stays inside her stubborn silence. Except for her declaration that she has not started to mourn, the woman has said nothing. Ricki sighs and takes a left.

*

159

Raymond sits on the edge of his bed in the deepest part of the night holding in both hands a copy of *Black Elk Speaks*. He's afraid to open the book. He needs to open the book. The lamp on his bedside table gives enough light for reading, if he can get to reading. The dim outer circle of the light picks up the basic shapes of Raymona in the photos propped on the dresser. He can't see the little wound on her girlhood knee and he can't see her adult crossed eyes and stuck-out tongue but he knows the details. Before he allowed himself to come to the bedroom he did his dishes up. For the second time since Raymona died he managed to run hot water, make it soapy, work away the dried food. He ran the vacuum and swept the kitchen floor. These were his preparations. Then he got the book from under his stack of T-shirts. He never told Raymona about Darlene. By the time he got to the Youth Center he understood Raymona needed to be the one who knew about Indians. If he tries to read now, tonight, she might be angry and turn the words to code, something resembling Chinese characters, each complicated drawing telling a story, but not to him. This is a crazy thought but it has a pull, like the inclination that comes when a person gets close to the edge of a cliff, to step onto the air. What is he really afraid of? It might be the presumption. Even holding the book is a comfort, but does he have the right? It's only an unknown father from an unknown tribe who added Indian blood to his makeup. A purely white person could read the book and that would be fine, he doesn't mean otherwise. It's the way he reads, how he enters in as if he had a claim, that makes a problem. When Black Elk sees the two men coming from the sky headfirst like arrows, he feels they're coming for him, Raymond Weeks. He's the one who gets lifted to the place that's all cloud, sees the bay horse and the twelve black horses. This has nothing to do with becoming a teacher to a tribe, that was Black Elk's job. Still, feeling so taken up, maybe he's an impostor. Darlene was the best teacher he ever had. She was short and tough and had been at the Youth Center forever, trying to get kids to feel at ease with a book in their hands. She was Penobscot, grew up on Indian Island not twenty minutes from where he is right now. When he was leaving the Center, finished with that part of his life, she walked out with him and handed over the book. He was on his way back to living with Stella. By that time Raymona was gone from home. He was twenty-one years old. "It's not the story of Maine Indians," she said, "but it's a necessary book." She wrote onto the title page her good wishes and the date. No one had ever given him a book or taken the kind of interest she did. She didn't mind his tribe being unknown. "You're probably some kind of Wabanaki," she told him. "Maybe you're my cousin." The kindness of a person can make a difference. Like Roo with Raymona back in school. It's been two entire weeks. He feels the absence. He knew this would happen but he didn't predict it would loosen all his connections, do away with his sense of shape. He wishes he had a habit to hold to, smoking or drinking, but he made his decisions. Being wrapped around Raymona was his habit. Even when he didn't see her for a few weeks he kept himself in position, ready. He let her control him except for the sex. He held the line there, for both of them, once they got to be adults. Good thing. He could be Chippie's father, or maybe not even know if he was. That baby opens an avenue of terror he can't approach. He's missing Stella or maybe it's her needing him that he's missing, not exactly Stella herself. Must be five weeks she's kept sober. She has Margie and Ricki and tells him not to fuss, which leaves him floating. Wisdom poured in from an old story might weight him. The Grandfathers, the horses. At least he's gotten this far, holding the book. Sitting here isn't too different from sitting on the edge of the bed with the gun in his hands the night he killed Bede. He rubs his thumb over the grain of the cover and wonders why the thing that keeps overtaking his mind is the call to the sheriff. Why not the shooting? Or the minute before the shooting, Raymona behind him whispering orders? Or the blood spreading slow and irregular onto the mattress ticking? Stella washed sheets that morning and hurried off to work at the hospital laundry before they were dry. Funny, he never thought about it: how they both worked in that same line, at least for short whiles. No one made the bed all day. Raymona said, "Why waste good sheets?" The dramatic aspects of that night are part of a well-known story, but his call to the sheriff and the interval before he came are like slices of time that open up and swallow him. He can fight his way out but it takes an effort. Raymona isn't hovering, waiting to change words into code, he knows that. All of a sudden he sees his real concern. He might find the book has gone flat, like a balloon that's been punctured and can't get its fullness back, or like a dead thing with the spirit departed. If he could pull his courage into line, he could open the book. Without quite deciding to, he opens the book. *My friend, I am going to tell you the story of my life, as you wish; and if it were only the story of my life I think I would not tell it; for what is one man that he should make much of his winters, even when they bend him like a heavy snow?* It takes a minute to hear the knocking. He tightens himself up, walks to the door, asks who it is. There's a pause, then two voices cross over each other.

"Raymond, it's Ricki and..."

"Open this door, Raymond. It's your mother." His first thought is the book in his hand, but he opens the door. "Good. You're up." Stella walks past him, goes through the kitchen to the living room, sits down on his couch. She pats the place beside her, showing Ricki where to sit. Ricki sits. He puts the book on top of the refrigerator. He doesn't think anyone notices.

"Coffee?"

"Well, of course," says Stella.

"Ricki?"

"OK. Thanks," Ricki looks uncomfortable. Probably thinks it's not polite to show up in the middle of the night.

"I was up," he says, trying to set her mind at ease.

"I already noted that, Raymond," Stella says.

"Yes, Ma, you did." He starts coffee, glad for the task. Change can come any moment, sneaking and pouncing, which is not always a bad thing. He's in a new part of this night.

"It's not much of a night for sleeping," Stella says, as if she's making conversation in line at the grocery store except that she throws her voice from the living room into the kitchen where he's stalling. He comes and stands in the doorway between the rooms while the coffee's making. This is how he's situated when Stella comments that she thinks it would be lovely to see that baby and where is she just now?

"Now, Ma? It's the middle of the night."

"Well, I know that. I had an urge, you know, and I thought...she isn't here, by any chance?"

"Oh, Ma. Petra Kalinowski has her. You know that." Ricki's just watching, one face, then the other.

"Also, I thought you might need to see me," Stella says. This statement sends shivers through him. Once in a great while Raymona would appear at his door. "Need a bit of family, do you, Raymond?" She'd step into the kitchen, all jaunty. It never happened unless he was

162

having a blank or uncertain time. Unless he needed a bit of family. He brings the coffee in and they all sit holding their cups and occasionally one of them takes a sip and comments on the merits of a hot drink. The silence is the main thing, though. It has no awkwardness to it. He wonders what time it is, but this is only curiosity. He feels easy now. Maybe he needed company. There's a small knock at the door. All three of them look toward the kitchen and then at each other. A group feeling has come over them and it's as if they've been waiting for this. It's Petra and Chippie and a good many of Chippie's belongings that come into the kitchen. Petra hands things to him one by one.

"Coffee?" he asks, leading her to the living room. Stella has moved to the middle of the couch to make room for Petra. Petra nods to him, yes, she'll take coffee. They're leaving his chair for him and they're lined up, three women and a baby on a couch. Petra hands Chippie to Stella. They don't need words to make this happen. He goes to the kitchen and while he's pouring coffee he hears Stella say, "Now, isn't this nice?" How does she do it, is what he wonders, shaking his head. He's glad to see Petra, though her state worries him some. She has to be here for more than giving Stella a chance to hold her granddaughter.

Chapter Seventeen

"Night hauls itself to morning's dooryard, its burden on its back." Ricki's mind has gone so strange it's almost poetic. Long time since she slept. She sits in the back seat of Petra's car beside Stella, who, having declared the car seat an unsafe device, holds Chippie and makes grandmotherly noises. Chippie makes corresponding baby noises, earnest about her part in the duet. Petra drives stolidly. Patient Raymond sits beside her. When they turn off the road onto the long curved driveway the sun lays a knife of light over the still water. No matter what, the sun comes up. Petra points out Roo's big old white house. Ricki is seeing the home of Professor McGuire who is sleeping, or taking a shower, or maybe it's breakfast time. Maybe she's out for a morning walk. She might be in Bangor, at Jessie's. But, no, her car's here. Petra stops the car at the coach house so this must be where Danny McGuire lives. Danny is someone Petra knows well or she wouldn't have consented to drive a car full of people to his home unannounced at this hour. Whether she consented or just let herself be drawn along is a question, though. This isn't the Petra who took charge the day Bright Star died. This new Petra is someone Ricki doesn't know how to think about, except that she can see when a person has hit a wall. Stella isn't the same either. She's become the director, leading them through this night, and she's the first one out of the car. Even with a baby in her arms, she's quickest. Everyone else hesitates. Ricki certainly hesitates. Petra lets her head fall onto the steering wheel, but she straightens right up, gets out of the car. Stella has stepped aside, so it's Petra who knocks, calling out Danny's name. He comes to the door with a steaming cup in his hand. These men, first Raymond, now Danny, are up and dressed no matter what time they're interrupted.

"Company!" says big, soft, mussed, kind-looking Danny.

"Here we are." Petra's entire complicated apology is in her look.

"So I see." Danny ushers them in, another parade entering another home, this one belonging to a person who probably won't commit suicide. The trailer must be sitting there all alone. A family of mice might have moved in. She hopes they have. "Maybe I'll make a new pot of coffee, this one's about empty," Danny says. "Have a seat."

More coffee. Ricki's thoughts already have a jagged edge. Not enough places to sit. Stella chooses the floor, never letting go of Chippie. Raymond sits beside her. Ricki ends up on the short brown couch, embarrassed to have the comfortable seat while gray-haired Stella has the floor but there's nothing to be done. Petra is on the couch beside her. A strong tender feeling about Petra keeps rising up and spilling over into confusion. They leave the chair for Danny who is gathering up cups, milk, sugar. She feels as if she's in a play, a minor actor, a beginner. Or maybe she's the audience, because the script is a mystery to her. This is a peculiar intermission, a silent one. Even Stella and Chippie have nothing to say. Everyone taking a break from the drama. Bright Star would do that. One minute an intense event would be in progress, then, no warning, the air would empty out. At first this hit Ricki like a vacuum, a time of uncertainty, but she learned to sink into the softness. It helped to think of her grandmother's feather bed after a day of hard work in the orchard. She doesn't believe, not completely, that Bright Star is dead. Lionel would be severe with her. "Never deny death," he'd say. But does that sound more like Bright Star? Now she has two people gone from her life. Petra wants Chippie gone from her life. No, that's not quite right. Danny is in his assigned seat. The intermission is over. Petra says, "You can guess why we're here."

"Better tell me," says Danny. "Maybe we could have some introductions first."

"Oh, Lord. Sorry," Petra says, and stops. There's a blank space. Stella isn't being the director, she's fixated on Chippie who's looking at Raymond with a curious tilt to her head. Danny is the one who talks.

"I suppose you all know I'm Danny. Danny McGuire. I'm not sure what's happening here, but I guess I'll find out soon enough." He looks pleasantly around the room, but when he gets to Petra there's a question in his face. Petra gives no response. Danny doesn't press her, even with a look. He relaxes back into his chair. He might be the director now, setting a gentle pace. But they're not in a play, this is real. Ricki can feel the potential of what might happen, electrical potential, electricity running around looking for something to connect to, or do damage to. Maybe she doesn't understand the science, though. She wishes someone would answer Danny, wishes Petra would help. The bottom nature of Petra must still be there. That's Gertrude Stein: bottom nature. A good thing to have. *Someone should answer Danny.*

"I'm Ricki," she says finally. She doesn't know what else to say.

"Raymond Weeks." The sound of Raymond's voice changes everything. They'll be all right now. "I'm this baby's uncle. I understand you've met her already." Danny nods, friendly, waiting for what comes next, his eyes on Raymond's face. Raymond finds his words. "Thanks for tolerating this intrusion." He stops. Danny waits. Raymond adds, looking down with a small private smile, "This is good coffee." Then he looks up again. The two men look at each other. Ricki wonders what passes between them. The thought of her brothers comes to her, how men take each other's measure, but this is different. Or maybe not different.

"Well, now it's my turn," says Stella, rearranging Chippie. "My name is Stella Weeks and I am the grandmother of this baby and we are here—"

Petra interrupts, as if she woke up. "It's OK, Stella. This is my job."

"Well, I know that. You were absent, though."

"I know. I'm here now."

Stella's eyes fill with tears. Ricki can't grasp the nuances of this scene, this reality, but feels her own eyes respond. Sadness under everything, this much she understands. Danny and Raymond are dry-eyed but Petra is silently crying, tears shining on her cheeks. She looks at Danny and says, "I can't do it."

Danny nods, and takes a breath. "You want me to do it."

Petra smiles through her tears. "I do. We do."

Danny puts his head down into his hands. Nothing is settled, but some plain words were spoken. *I can't do it,* Petra said. Everything is different, simpler, more possible. The morning light is strong and warm in this room and they might be in a church, a church with a restrained and tolerant God. It hardly matters if Ricki never understands Petra again because Petra understands herself.

Stella speaks into the silence. "It was the word companionable, of course." The sentence sounds domestic, task-like. It reminds Ricki of her mother cheerfully unpacking groceries from a plain brown bag onto the kitchen table.

Danny looks up. "Companionable?"

"Petra informed us about your day with this baby. You said it was companionable and of course none of the rest of us is in a position."

"I see," says Danny. Just that. He must be a calm man deep in his bones. Her own parents are calm down-to-earth people. Even learning his daughter is a lesbian, her father stayed quiet, kind. She should have known he would. She can hear birds calling. Danny says he sees. *There are grow-ups here.* Sometimes with Stella Ricki feels like the adult, sometimes like the child who gets ordered around. The word cherish, an old-fashioned word, has been coming to her. Is she starting to cherish Bright Star's mother? Her feelings toward Stella shift and sway. She wants to shield Stella, and shield herself from Stella. This might be a new kind of love, or maybe just a temporary spill from Bright Star's death. *There will be some unpredictable spillage. We can't prepare for everything, Ricki.*

"So one companionable day qualifies me for parenthood," says Danny, finally.

"It certainly does," says Stella.

Petra is crying again. "I'm so sorry," she says, and looks at Danny, then at Raymond, then back at Danny. Ricki wants them to pour forgiveness over Petra, but they're absorbed in their own thoughts and barely look at her. Stella goes back to playing with Chippie.

"Well," says Danny, starting to get up. "Should I make more coffee?"

That brings everyone to attention. "No," they all say, then look at each other and sort of laugh. "We've been up all night, drinking coff—" "We've been drinking coffee all..." A chorus of identical explanations. When Danny sits back down everyone goes silent again. No one looks at anyone else. Ricki knows what would happen if she offered to take responsibility for Chippie. She tried it at Raymond's apartment. Stella said, "What nonsense, my dear." Petra and Raymond firmly agreed. She felt like the group's child who'd said something inappropriate. She doesn't want a baby, they were right about that. She's just like Petra that way.

Petra moves to the arm of Danny's chair. His elbows are on his knees and his head is in his hands again. Petra bends over his shoulders and puts her arms around his big body and says, "I know this is insane. I don't know why it's happening this way. Coming here like this, I mean."

Stella interrupts. "You certainly do. I had that afternoon nap, so I prevailed. This friend of yours seems able to handle it, so you must stop chastising yourself. You've done what you could and now we're here for the next stage of things and it's fine with this nice man, isn't it?" Danny is still holding his head in his hands and Petra is rubbing his shoulders. Stella looks at the top of his head, as if willing him to take this cue, but he's not that easy. He doesn't answer. He sits up, though, and Petra moves back to the couch. Danny looks at Chippie who's been chirping along with the birds and drooling and smiling and generally making herself into an appealing prospect. Ricki can see he's charmed but that doesn't mean he wants to raise her. Everyone waits.

The next thing that happens is embarrassing. Her stomach growls. Danny becomes the good-humored host again. "I'd serve breakfast, but it would be Cheerios, and I've run out of milk. I have orange juice, though. Orange juice on Cheerios isn't as bad as you might think." She wants food but when everyone else turns down the offer she does, too. She and Bright Star used to eat dry Cheerios in bed after sex. It was one of the few things they did based on her own suggestion. Bright Star didn't take suggestions easily, she could be downright rude about another person's ideas. Critical feelings about Bright Star, sometimes marching right beside memories of fun, have been a problem for the last few days. Petra's face is wet with tears again. Chippie has given no sign of distress but Stella gets up and walks over to the diaper bag. Chippie, lying on Danny's faded rug, watches Stella with great baby seriousness while she gets her diaper changed. Stella seems up-to-date about diapers, at ease with the sticky paper tabs. Ricki would have thought she used only cloth with her own babies, but when did Pampers come in? Could Stella have afforded them? Will she ever ask these questions? She's intrigued by the thought of Bright Star and Raymond as companion babies, a little white girl baby and a little brown boy baby. One of them must have been older, though. She's taken by surprise when Stella, up on her feet, gives freshly diapered Chippie to Danny who doesn't miss, or refuse, this cue. He takes the baby and cuddles her to himself. Stella goes back to the diaper bag and gets a bottle. "Do you heat this?" she asks Petra. Petra nods, blowing her nose, and Stella walks into the kitchen as if she's in her own house.

Danny looks at Petra long enough to get her attention. He's worried about his old friend. He has an easy way of holding Chippie who sits in his lap and looks around the room. Petra says, "I can't believe I'm doing this to you, and in this particular way."

"Nothing's been done to me. It's more what you've done to yourself." Danny shifts Chippie around and looks her in the eye, man to baby. She starts to cry. He laughs and pulls her closer to his chest and tells her a bottle is coming. She quiets.

"I made a big mistake," Petra says.

"Looks that way," Danny says, friendly and kind. Pretty soon Ricki will start loving Danny the way she's been loving Petra and Raymond and Stella all night. No matter how confused she feels about Petra, this loving feeling keeps coming, It never leaves Petra out.

Raymond's head is lowered. He sits on the floor like Bright Star's Fallen Goddess. The weight is not off him yet. Stella comes from the kitchen and gives the bottle to Danny. Chippie starts sucking. Ricki's stomach growls again. "We could go out to eat," Danny says. She hasn't had this much appetite since the day Bright Star died. She's aware of Chippie's stomach filling up with milk. She wills everyone to say yes. They say yes.

The few other customers at the diner are solitary and quiet. The waitress is a good one, courteous and efficient. No one says much of anything until they are well into their eggs and home-fries when Danny comments, almost as if he's talking to himself, "I'll do it, I suppose."

"Oh, God," Petra says, and starts to cry again. Raymond looks at Danny. His own world just changed shape, and Danny's, too. Stella, who's been tending to Chippie's needs while eating her own breakfast, takes a minute to understand what Danny said. When the sense of it comes through to her she nods her head slowly, up and down, up and down, not looking at any of them. Does Danny mean to be making the commitment they think he's made? Ricki feels awkward and presumptuous, but she might be the only person here with her feet on the ground.

She looks at Danny. "Do you mean you've made a decision?"

"I guess I have. Fast, isn't it?"

"I don't mean to..."

"That's fine. I wasn't taken by surprise. Not completely. The situation didn't seem entirely stable to me."

"What?" Petra says. Her tears are drying.

"Well..."

"You were watching me."

"I wondered."

"And never said a word."

"Guess not."

"Danny McGuire."

"You didn't have much of an opening around you, for comments."

"I thought I could do it."

"I know."

"Damn. Damn, damn, damn."

"It's not so bad, you know."

"I don't know. I don't know anything. You'll do it? Are you sure?"

"Seems to be the thing I'm handed."

"That's why you can do it, I suppose. That attitude."

"Think it will help?"

"I think if I had that thing you have—what *is* it, anyway? I remember when I first met you, I thought of you as perpetually looking up, curious about what came next."

"I have some room in my life. You're off the hook."

"You said I shouldn't think of you like that, as the one who would do it if I couldn't."

"I meant that, but now we're here." They take time to look at each other. Finally, Petra looks around, as if she realizes there are other people present. She appears about to say something, maybe to draw everybody in. That would be her way, her old way. Maybe Petra's coming back to her self. But Danny has more to say. "Not entirely off the hook. I'll need help. I mean that." He's looking at Petra and at the same time accepting from Stella—they have to reach across Raymond—one hiccuping baby.

"You'll have help," Petra says. "I owe you. I don't know what to say. I didn't really think you'd..."

Stella interrupts. "I am an alcoholic." She looks at Danny until she has his full attention. "Whenever I'm sober, I intend to act as grandmother to my son's child. That should help." Ricki isn't sure she heard right. Her *son's* child? Chippie still has the hiccups and Stella's words got muffled. Her own caffeine-laced brain balks like a revved, stuck engine. Raymond's child? She sees Petra signal No to Danny with a subtle movement of her head. Danny bends and kisses Chippie's waving fingers and then glances toward Raymond. Raymond's face is in his hands. So she must have heard exactly what Stella said.

"It certainly will help, Stella. Thanks," says Danny with a light, calm assurance. The conversation turns—is steered, Ricki thinks—to the weather. A beautiful, beautiful day, they all agree, but she herself says nothing. *Raymond's child? But that would mean...* It's not long before Raymond asks if anyone knows what time it is. He has to be at work by noon, he almost forgot. Petra remembers the DWELL meeting. Ricki wonders if anything ordinary can belong in this day. As they file out of the restaurant, Raymond's shoulders in front of her, she thinks of Elizabeth Bishop's armadillo walking away from the fire, "rose-flecked, head down, tail down." The armadillo is just something in a poem, though. The fire. The armadillo. The bent, hurt aloneness. Or did it all really happen? She remembers saying to Petra only two weeks ago, "I still think Raymond is a good person." Does Bright Star see what's going on here? See, or care?

*

"Stella must have gotten the idea at the service, Ricki. Didn't you hear her friend? She made me into his wife, too, but that's beside the point."

"I was in a fog, I guess. She does look just like him."

"I know, but he's not the father."

"What makes you so sure, Petra?"

171

Bright Star's writing. Which is an annoying secret. A Pandora's box. "Think about Raymond. Who he is."

"I have been. Chippie's always reaching toward him. She *studies* him."

"She'd drawn to him, you're right. I think it's just the family smell." Petra gets up and turns off the phone, as she does before every DWELL meeting. She'd like to be more helpful to Ricki but can't see how. Her own composure is partially restored. Danny has Chippie and Chippie's belongings except for the crib which has to be gotten from the trailer. In the meantime the bassinet will do. She just walked away, though, leaving the man with a baby in his arms. At least they're good arms. She should call him, tell him she'll be back after the meeting, go over details. How To Parent a Motherless Child. But here's Ricki. And in a few minutes Nat will arrive, who once loved Stella who was somehow more babyless than Petra herself on the trip to back to Bangor, trying to finish her doily but falling asleep, irritable when they woke her up. Petra finds Stella appealing in an odd way. *Irregular* might be a better word. She can understand what attracted young Nat. What about now? Will Nat and Stella get reacquainted? While she, Petra Kalinowski, has been revising her parenting life, other lives have been eventfully proceeding. Stella, for example, declared as she got out of the car that she wouldn't need to be driven around Bangor this particular night, a declaration apparently for Ricki's benefit. Now there's this business of Ricki's suspicion that Raymond and Bright Star copulated to produce Chippie. *Ragged-Hearted Hours.* "Ricki, I don't know what to say."

"I know. It's OK."

"Well, it's not, but it will have to do for now. Why do you suppose we haven't called this meeting off?" This gets a smile from Ricki.

"We might not be thinking too clearly."

"I don't even feel tired. Do you?"

"It's more like going past it, into something eerie."

"Well, this should be an interesting meeting," Petra says.

"Are you going to say anything?"

How can she not say something? On the other hand, what is she supposed to say? *Well, folks, I blew it again, just dumped another kid.* "I

172

don't know. I just don't know, Ricki." She *is* tired. Every cell abruptly sags.

"Petra, I..."

"I know, Ricki. You've been great. Really. Somehow you seem able to...I don't know...just *take* all of this." Nat's truck pulls into the drive. She hasn't seen Nat since that difficult talk, the two of them, looking at each other, helpless once again. *We really should have canceled this damn meeting.*

"Except for the thing about Raymond," Ricki says.

"That will be all right. You'll see."

"You sound like a mother."

"Well, that's ironic, isn't it?"

It turns out poetry is what Petra needs. Today it's Elizabeth Bishop's "The Armadillo." Fire balloons ("illegal") are sent into the sky where they "flush and fill with light / that comes and goes, like hearts." *Like hearts.* Nat says this is the key to the poem. She says it without innuendo, without rancor, without apparent pain. Jessie admits she didn't notice the hearts. "So this is a love poem?" She's not sold. "Multi-valenced," says Ricki. Everyone smiles at the jargon, including Ricki, who must have put her doubts about Raymond away for the moment. But no. Look at the set of her mouth. She's just trying hard. "This is love that comes and goes," says Roo.

"And can destroy," says Petra, determined not to sit silent and fragile just because she's yielded up her second child.

The fire balloon hits the cliffside behind the house. This has to be the house where Elizabeth and Lota lived in Brazil in the 1950s and 60s. The cliffside catches fire. The creatures are burned: the owl, the armadillo, the unbearable baby rabbit. Roo, who has no way of understanding what she's doing, reads aloud the passage about the baby rabbit, "*short*-eared, to our surprise. / So soft!—a handful of ignited ash / with fixed, ignited eyes." This is where Petra's composure cracks and she starts to cry, so predictable, and annoying. She wanted a *normal* DWELL meeting. Apparently she can't have that. She tells about Chippie. The women of DWELL are enragingly supportive. They leave the poem behind, the baby rabbit on the broken dusty road. She, Petra, is being carted away from the little creature, human or rabbit, it makes no difference, who is stranded on the other side of the awful gap. They tend

173

to her, fallen mother. Even Jessie, damn her. Jessie, foster kid, who should be baring claws, ripping at the face of this twice-failed mother. But she's saying something about having the guts to, and her own mother, and how much better... And Ricki, of course, who just lost her lover. Ricki, who's in a crisis about the dead lover and her supposed incestuous baby-making relations with poor, innocent Raymond, but the crack in *her* composure seems to have closed nicely, thank you, and she's only generous, concerned. Possibly she knows, really, that Raymond wouldn't... And Roo, who went through this earlier, when it was Anya's turn to be foisted onto a substitute parent. Roo, who will no doubt become another grandmother to Chippie, child of Raymona, her long-ago lost student, carefully secondary to Stella but more faithful than Stella. This will happen naturally, with Chippie living as she does on Roo's land with Cousin Saint Danny, but right now Roo is all Petra's. And Nat, unshakable Nat, who has come to sit beside her. Nat, who offers a shoulder and she, Petra, takes it, clinging and sobbing and saying, "Dammit, dammit, dammit," while Nat just holds on. When she can, she sits up and blows her nose. She never did put the tissue box away after all the recent communal tears, so here it is, right here, isn't that handy? And looks around and says humbly to this circle of good friends, "Thanks." Then, unable to stop herself, "Sorry." Which evokes a flurry of declarations that she has nothing to be sorry about, which she endures quietly like a good girl.

Nat stays on after the meeting. Petra has spent her little rage coin and is planning to dig into her supply of greater reasonableness. She'd like to do this, have this necessary chat with Nat, efficiently. She has called Danny and promised she'll be sane enough to get to his house soon. He, of course, is fine. "Don't hurry," he said. This did not rouse her anger. She must be "better."

"Tell me," says Nat, who is making peanut butter and jelly sandwiches.

"Peanut butter and jelly?"

"There's nothing wrong with childhood food," says Nat firmly.

"To match a certain immaturity."

"Or real pain. Stop doing this to yourself. Tell me what happened."

"A whirlwind crisis, I suppose."

"You seemed all right, for a while. Not that this is a real surprise."

"Not a surprise," says Petra.

"Not entirely," says Nat.

"You were watching me."

"Of course I was watching you."

"You and Danny. I hate you both."

Nat hands her a half sandwich. "Tell me."

"It was one of those late night things. You're right, this tastes good."

"Late night crisis."

"Yes. Did I tell you Bright Star left stacks and stacks of journals?"

"You did not."

"Sorry. I shouldn't start there. Are you still...?"

"I'm all right. A little tender, but not mortally wounded."

"Oh, Nat. I'm so sorry."

"I suppose you've been apologizing at every juncture, to everyone."

"I have. I can't seem to stop."

"Bright Star left journals."

"I read the latest one last night, looking for information about Chippie's father. Not much there. His name was Chip, no last name, no home town, just passing through, and happened to be seduced by... Oh, dear. I still get so mad at her. But something happened to me, reading the journals. A lot happened. First, if there was no way to find the father, it was real. I had a baby to raise."

"Which scared you."

"Once I let myself know it, it was a bit like terror. It didn't help that she'd been cranky. Sweet as could be, though, once she got into the arms of Stella, and then Danny, but that's superficial. This isn't about whether she's an easy baby or difficult, at least that's what I'm telling myself."

"It's you."

"Right. Unsuited still, and what made me think otherwise?"

"I'm not sure *thinking* was exactly..."

"I know." They bite into their sandwiches. "Something about reading that journal was so...I don't know. There she was, planning suicide through all these pages, before she ever got pregnant."

"Before she got pregnant, she had a plan to kill herself?"

"Yes, my poor dear Nat. Ever since we've known her and a long time before that." Nat closes her eyes. Petra reaches across the table and takes her hand. "I'm sorry. I shouldn't be..."

"You should. It's just...my judgment is so bad. I thought I was attracted to vitality."

"You were. Alongside, even *inside* the plan to die, there was vitality." This brings color back to Nat's face. "And ruthless honesty. Intelligence, creativity, acuteness. Also, insane denial. Notable obtuseness. It's all in the writing. It's impressive. In the middle of the night, I have to say, it was very impressive. I thought about my constricted little efforts, how I censor and hone. But that's not quite the point."

"Maybe it's more the point than you're admitting."

"Dammit, Nat." Her own writing is the thing she refused to consider when she decided to take Chippie; or undo the taking.

"Petra..."

"I know. Danny and I were doing our last painting job and I was about to start again. I had ideas. I hereby admit that I don't know what would have happened..."

"Mothers do write, though." Nat said.

"Some. Those who can juggle. Multi-taskers, I suppose."

"So don't you think—be honest—that the writing..."

"Maybe what the writing means, what it *is*, for me."

"Which is crucial."

"Is it?"

"Stop that."

"I mean it. I don't know."

"When you've had a night's sleep, you'll know."

"I picked up Simone Weil."

"Speaking of writing."

"Yes, she's got that bone-clean style. That's what I'd like to..."

"See? You have ambitions you won't admit, even to yourself. Especially to yourself. And there's nothing wrong with discipline in one's writing."

She waves Nat's comment away. "I turned to the 'Necessity and Obedience' section of *Gravity and Grace*."

"Obedience?"

"It was Necessity that drew me. I have a client in a situation. Oh, I already told you about that."

"That convergence. The woman who just recently..."

"Yes. I must be tired, to bring her up again."

"You don't usually talk about..."

"No, and I don't need to now."

"Simone Weil. Necessity."

"Yes. Something comforts me about Weil's vocabulary. Not just Necessity. Gravity, too. And Decreation. You read her years ago, didn't you?"

"Yes," Nat says. "She does have a keen mind. Original. Though I think she might have been mentally unstable. She starved herself to death out of principle, or that's the impression I have."

"I know. Still, there's something compelling." She has in mind a particular passage, the one that sent her into the night to return a baby to her uncle. Weil took her to the level of ethics she needed. Despite reflexive self-flagellation, Petra feels reasonably sure it was right to take Chippie to Raymond's apartment, and Weil helped her do that. It's almost a matter of honor to give her credit, but she feels embarrassed. Or shy. Deeply, childishly shy. She might even be blushing. She's certainly being too quiet.

"What are you thinking?" Nat asks. Petra's nasty, defensive thought is that a person cannot have one private moment in this woman's presence. *Unwarranted. There are few people more respectful of privacy than Nat Levesque.* "What did you find in Weil, Petra?" *Nat is curious, not demanding, not prying.*

"I'll get it. I want to read it to you. It's so *interesting*."

"And important," says Nat, raising her voice so that it reaches into the bedroom, which is currently dubbed *Baby Chippie Crime Scene*, the crime being taking Chippie or giving her up, depending on the moment.

"Yes, important to me," she calls back, and picks up *Gravity and Grace*.

Nat is wiping the table when she gets back to the kitchen. They look at each other. Petra reads, "'We should not take one step, *even in the direction of what is good*, beyond that to which we are irresistibly impelled by God.'" Nat sits down quietly, dishcloth in hand. "Do you see?" Petra asks.

"Yes, I think I do."

"It's not the God part."

"I know."

"I did feel impelled, at first."

"Then came reality," says Nat.

"It's not that reality was awful."

"It was awful for *you*."

"It was boring."

"Petra. Oh, Petra, that matters."

"Does it matter enough?"

"Apparently," says Nat.

"Or Danny wouldn't be sitting over there waiting to be instructed as to the care and feeding of a baby."

"I doubt he's sitting there waiting for you."

"No. That's the point, I suppose. He's probably just living his new life. He took care of Anya at Chippie's age. He did a good job."

"He can probably manage for a while yet without you." Nat is teasing now, gently. Still, the words hurt. Petra can feel her eyes filling with tears. "Must be complicated," Nat says.

"It's irrational. I want him to need me. But he'd better not, in any big way, or I'll kill him."

"Justifiable homicide, needing a woman like that." Nat gets up, comes around the back of Petra's chair, and massages her shoulders.

"I shouldn't joke about homicide. Raymond killed his stepfather. Murder is real. Like parenting."

"Exactly like parenting," says Nat, straight-faced. Petra knows because she turns around and checks. A completely straight and honorable face and a dry, dry sense of humor. She loves this woman. In a certain, circumscribed way, of course. Perhaps just beyond that, if you think primarily of her hands.

"Don't tell Ricki there are journals, Nat."

"No?"

"A topic for another day. I do have to get over to Danny's."

"Want me to drive you?"

"I can do it. You've put me together with enough glue to hold for a while. Thanks."

"You're quite welcome. I like the Weil quote."

"It does *mean* something, doesn't it?"

"Of course it means something. It's even relevant to the situation at hand. One more thing. Boredom is a threat to the *mind*, Petra. It matters. Now get thee to Danny's house."

Chapter Eighteen

"It's really OK," says Danny.

"I don't want to put you out," says Raymond.

"You're stuck. There's no other way."

"I wish you were wrong."

"I'll collect later." Danny smiles. Chippie is bundled into her car seat and Danny starts the car. Raymond would rather be alone in his truck but his truck has let him down. They might have dealt with the situation earlier, when there was time, though neither of them owns jumper cables, but he forgot himself and his obligations. He has to get to Bangor, pick Stella up, and be at Dave and Etta's for supper by 7:00. He tried to call Stella. No answer. He doesn't have Dave and Etta's number and he can't look it up because he can't remember the last names. He's not used to living a life beyond work and family, having to know the full names and phone numbers of people he just met. There's no getting out of this supper and no getting out of imposing on Danny. So here they are, Danny in the driver's seat. An accumulation of awkward moments— that's what would just about describe this day. The first came at breakfast when Stella referred to Chippie as "my son's child." He could see this upset Ricki but couldn't figure a way to clarify things. Then at work Margie Stokes appeared. He was on the phone with a patron who failed to understand why a notice came in today's mail about overdue books he returned this very morning. Margie stood waiting and he felt sweat run inside his shirt. He was that nervous, worrying she'd start a conversation about his wife and baby. When the time came she just said his name, giving a brief nod. He reciprocated in kind. Maybe he should have thanked her for watching out for his mother but he worried that would sound patronizing. Margie got them out of difficulty, said she wanted a book about giraffes. "It's the long neck that interests me. I imagine it's useful for eating from the high parts of trees but perhaps there's more to know. A book I could read in the evening before retiring would suit my need." Along with every word came a signal from her eyes. *We have a bond now outside this library, but I needn't bother you with that at the moment.* He was sure she had the skills to locate the book herself. After a short work day—he was only filling in while Charlene took time for something personal, which probably meant doctoring—he headed to Danny's. When his truck coughed and died, he hardly cared. The quiet coasting into the dooryard suited him. He had nothing in mind past the moment. Here was his truck saying this is as far as we have to go. He sat. The sun came through the windshield and he could hear the sound of a harmonica. He put his head back. Sleep would be the best thing. He roused himself and walked to the door and knocked. That stopped the harmonica. Then came the next set of awkward moments. "Oh," is what Danny said when he saw who was at his door. Just that. The two of them alone were not like the society that gathered in the morning when Petra and Stella and Ricki were there to fill up a room. He stood in the kitchen while Danny hunted for pencil and paper—they needed each other's phone numbers—and threw comments over his shoulder about how Petra would have writing materials at hand and wouldn't find herself in such a spot since she was a writer, and then about how he shouldn't be saying that, that was her business to tell. He himself offered up information about Raymona's writing as a way of evening things out. They were using the women to make the moment easier. Even the baby might have helped but she was having a nap which Danny told him as he came up with a stub of pencil and an old newspaper. They wrote their numbers in the margin. They tore off the bits of paper, exchanged them, put them in their pockets. "Well," Danny said. They were sitting in the living room by then.

Raymond thought he could use a cup of coffee to help him get on with things, but there appeared to be no coffee this time around. He took a deep breath and started in. "Well. Yes. I..."

Danny interrupted right away. Now came the offer of coffee. He accepted so quickly his desperation must have shown. Chippie started to fuss from another room and Danny asked if he'd mind checking on her. He hesitated. The baby swing was hanging in the doorway. He couldn't make his mind agree to go past it.

"Oh," Danny said, as if he'd gotten an explanation for why an uncle wouldn't go right in and pick up a baby in distress. He felt himself go off to the side of things, then found the coffee pot in his hands. "This is ready except for the burner," Danny was saying. They were standing in the kitchen together. "Matches are over there." He got the burner lit. It was good to have something to do, even the smallest thing. He sat down at the table which was a solid object. He was back to himself then, but wanted to put his head down. It wasn't so easy missing a night of sleep any more. He'd be forty before he knew it. What would Raymona think about the new arrangement, Chippie being raised by a man? If that *was* the new arrangement. Danny wasn't at ease. Maybe he meant to back out. No one could blame him. Danny came back and went to the stove and turned off the coffee. He poured them each a cup and sat down on the other side of the table. "She's fine" he said. "One last burp and a dry diaper and she went back to sleep."

"I appreciate this."

"I know. It appears you aren't in a position, as your mother said."

"That's right, but are you?"

"You came to see if this situation is going to last."

"That's one reason."

"I'm getting used to the idea. You shouldn't be worried."

"No? I wonder what it would be like, not to be worried."

"I gather there's been a lot."

"Yes. Well. That's not why I came. I must be tired, to say that."

"Have you had any sleep?"

"No. I had work."

"That's right. I knew that. Sorry."

"That's all right. Why should you remember?" There was a pause. They drank from their coffee mugs.

"Not normal times, in your life," Danny said.

"No. Not in yours, either, as of today."

"I don't think you're the father, if that's what it is."

"You're quick."

"Petra let me know."

"You mean that little shake of her head? I thought you might think she meant not to go on with the topic."

"She meant both, but she mentioned it on the phone, in case I had doubt. She'll be over, maybe soon, to orient me to my new job." Raymond nodded his head, thought about Petra walking in. He had to keep going with this conversation, finish his business before she came.

"I don't know what you know about our family, what you might want to know about us, before you get too far in with..."

"Not much. I mean, I don't know much and I don't need to know much, but if you think..."

"I wouldn't want to burden you."

"It wouldn't be that, but I don't need to know." They fell into quiet, but not a comfortable quiet.

"I do thank you for the coffee." He took another sip. "I should get going."

"Being up all night...I guess you want to get back home. Don't worry about us. We're fine. Unless there's something else."

He didn't get up. He thought about being in his bed. Nothing could be better, if he could sleep, but he might not. He remembered sitting with the book in his hands, trying to get to where he could open it. *Black Elk Speaks*. Did he ever get it open? The drive home didn't sound inviting. Hard to stay awake. Here was Danny, looking around his kitchen, not appearing comfortable.

"I should be going, if you're sure, about Chippie."

"Maybe you're not sure yourself," Danny said. This brought him awake. Was he going to have to make his case? "I mean about me," Danny said. "Maybe you're not sure about me being the one." This relieved him so much he almost cried.

The words that emerged from him next were a surprise—to himself. "I trust Petra." Danny's answer took a while to come. When it came, it was slow and careful.

"Petra's a good person. None better. The best friend I have. Still, she hasn't been...lately, I mean...since your sister..."

"I know. But underneath, she's solid." Danny nodded, but he didn't relax. They had to wait through another silence. Raymond didn't know what to do to help. They finished their coffee.

"More?" Danny said, as if the idea of his leaving wasn't in the air. He shook his head no, no more coffee. He wanted to get going, but something additional needed to happen. This is when he remembered he didn't have a working truck.

"I might have a problem. My truck quit on me. I had to coast down your drive. I should have said something earlier. Done something. The truth is I forgot. Maybe it'll start now." Danny looked at him and took a breath. He's going to say it, whatever it is, was Raymond's thought. He could see that his truck dying on him wasn't going to get attention yet.

"I have to tell you something before you go," Danny said. "Maybe Petra told you, but I can't count on that. It's awkward, and you don't have to say anything about it, but you have a right to know."

"OK." He felt sorry to see Danny struggle like this. He was wide awake now and part of his mind was wondering how he could get his truck going. Maybe Danny has jumper cables, was his thought.

"It's just that I'm gay," Danny said, looking him in the eye.

"Oh." Danny wasn't an obvious fairy type of man. He wanted to put him at ease, so he said, "That's not a problem."

"You're sure?"

"My sister was a lesbian. At least she was at the end of her life. I don't understand entirely. But it might make her happier...than if you were..." He felt good to come up with this thought.

"Oh. Well."

"I'm not worried."

"I just thought you had a right..."

"I'm sorry if you had to be concerned."

"No. Well, yes. That's not your fault. It's part of being gay."

"I suppose." *Was* he worried? Should he be thinking this over? He looked at Danny who appeared more relaxed. He had a calm feeling about Danny. "I'm just grateful."

"Grateful," Danny said. He was looking down at the table. Then he looked up and his face was soft. "I'm grateful, too, I guess. Maybe I fell in love today. I like your little niece." In the middle of getting used to this idea, and thinking how well things were working out, Raymond remembered his mother and his obligations.

"Oh, no," is what he said. He saw Danny freeze. "Oh. I don't mean about you falling in love with Chippie. That's...well...only good. I just remembered I have to be somewhere, and I have this broken-down truck." What followed was a quick time of determining that the truck was not just flooded. Maybe it was the battery. No jumper cables to be had. Humor about ineptitude with cars, an easier feeling growing between the two of them. Danny convincing him he had to accept a ride after he was unable to get Stella on the phone. Now they're on the road together,

Chippie asleep in the back, strapped into her baby seat. They left a note taped to the door for Petra who didn't answer her phone, which made him think of the note he left for Ricki the day Raymona died. The trailer is sitting there this minute, no life inside it, but here they are, moving along the road, three live human beings in a car, going somewhere. Danny's a good driver. The fact seems important. *A gay man will raise this baby. Well, all right.*

*

"Chocolate is a good bet, don't you think?"

Dave agrees, not really knowing. This meal is costing her some. New wine glasses from the Shop and Save, special wine, her good roast beef—and the nervousness over strangers coming—all to return a plate on which another cake, this one chocolate, now sits.

"Those people have had a hard time," Etta says.

"You're a good woman, Etta Jennings." He goes behind her and gives a squeeze. She wiggles her soft backside. He's a lucky man, a new woman at his age, and a real peach as his father would say.

"You're a fine man yourself, sir." She gives him a lick of frosting, which is good, and her finger's even better.

He can tell something's wrong the minute Stella Weeks walks in and sees the table. She turns to Raymond, her son who brought cake over in the first place. Good lemon, it was. Raymond follows the look. You can see he's resisting a request but when Stella stiffens up Raymond nods and explains how his mother has a hard time with alcohol and could we maybe just take the wine glass from where she'll be sitting. Etta whips every glass off the table, good-natured, apologizing where there's no need. It makes a naked feeling, all the little circles on the good table cloth. They get past it, though, and have a nice meal. No difficult topics come up. The women enter into a discussion about cooking and complicated recipes compared to simple ones, both favoring simple. Next comes shopping and a good hoot about items brought in for the summer people, foods they couldn't identify, much less cook with. "It's worse in Ellsworth, not that we don't get our share of summer people here," Etta said.

"Clog up the aisles, don't they?" Stella said.

185

"All those particular requests, what they're accustomed to at home."

"And at the check-out, asking directions only after you've waited through their entire credit card transaction."

"Or acting cozy with the clerk to demonstrate they're willing to speak to locals."

Everybody laughs. We're in a friendly dance here, is Dave's thought. He learns that a bit of coffee added to a chocolate cake brings the taste out. While the women are washing up in the kitchen, all gossipy and familiar, there's the next step to take, himself and Raymond alone in the living room, no drinks in their hands and neither one of them a smoker.

"That was a good meal," Raymond says.

"I feel lucky I found a good cook." That doesn't sound complete, so he adds, "Not just a good cook."

"It's the best meal I've had in a long time," Raymond says. That about covers that and it looks like neither one of them knows where to go next. They're just waiting for the women. Maybe he ought to offer a word about the sister.

"It must be hard, about your sister."

"It's harder than I thought it would be. I knew it was coming." Knew a suicide was coming? What could a person say to that? He nods his head, as if he understands, as if they're in this together. They go quiet again. He hopes the women wind things up fast in the kitchen. Raymond sits back in the easy chair, so he does the same with the couch. It's not that he dislikes Raymond, not at all, but he can't stop thinking of questions that might give offense. Why would a girl kill herself at all, not to mention writing such a formal and considerate note beforehand? Then this brother who's Indian, was that an adoption? He wishes he felt more comfortable. That day at the trailer never quite leaves him, the covered body, the blood, the baby bottles, and here's the very family involved.

"Are you bothered by what you ran into? At my sister's trailer, I mean."

Dave is startled to find his mind read. Maybe it's the next obvious topic. He isn't always sure how people find their topics.

"Oh, not too much." He thinks that's a pretty good response, taking the middle way between crying about the thing and pretending it's nothing. He likes to find a middle way if he can.

"I guess I was the next person in the trailer, after you and that officer," Raymond says. "It wasn't an easy place to enter into. Of course, I knew what I was going to find."

"I sat in that living room for a while. I looked around." Raymond nods and smiles a little so maybe this is where they can go forward with the conversation. "She was quite an artist, your sister. Not that I know anything about art." He hopes this isn't avoiding the thing Raymond wants to talk about.

"She took her work seriously, with the clay," Raymond says.

"I could see that, or at least guess at it."

"Yes."

"It seemed she produced a good number of objects."

"I think she was glad about that."

"Good. That's good." They fall to silence again. It's better now, though. They had a little conversation of their own. Finally the women come in, both looking satisfied.

"All finished," says Etta. He'd like to be released now, go tinker with that lawn mower, drain the oil and gas for the year. He can do that much for Etta. He's living off her now. Not a single bite for a policy since that day. It can't go on. The women sit down but Etta jumps back up. "I just remembered something," she says. The three of them, himself and Stella and Raymond, wait. She comes back with a book in her hand, sits down, and turns herself to Raymond. She looks to be carrying out a plan that makes her feel shy but it's important to her so she'll go ahead. She's like that.

"Raymond, you coming here gives me an opportunity. I hope it's not an offense and I did hesitate but I decided...well, maybe I should explain first. A distant relative of mine, Fannie Hardy Eckstorm, wrote this book. It's signed by the writer herself and I have my own copy. All these years I've been wondering what to do about the fact that I have two and last night it occurred to me that you'd be the person..."

Dave knew nothing about this. His eyes are stinging with tears of love. He can see Raymond gathering himself to respond politely but Etta's not finished, she's just catching her breath and finding her next words while she holds the book against her big soft breasts. He never had the opportunity to rest against a large woman before. None of them can see what the book's title is. He catches sight of Stella in a struggle with herself over that, straining forward and holding back at the same time. Poor lady is trying to keep herself from getting up and demanding a look, or that's his thought.

"This book is called *Old John Neptune and Other Maine Indian Shamans*, Raymond," Etta says. "Maybe you're familiar with it."

"No, Ma'am." Dave wonders *What's a shaman?* But the question is off to the side. Etta is at the center, and Raymond calling her Ma'am and Stella stretching forward to get in on things. Raymond appears nervous but there's not a thing he can do about that. They got on a train, the four of them, and have to stay on until their stop.

"Mrs. Eckstorm had a curiosity about the local Indians," Etta says, "so that's what she wrote about. I don't have occasion to sit down in a room with many Indians. I thought about your loss, and I always like to say that when something is taken away another thing comes. Oh, dear. I don't mean to imply that a book can replace a human life."

Of course you don't, Dave wants to say, but he keeps quiet and lets her proceed. He and Stella are the audience here, or maybe the congregation of a church, though he hasn't been inside a church for a long time so it's possible he doesn't have the feeling right. It could be Stella's hands folded so tight in her lap, making him think of white gloves, that bring on the idea of church. Etta gathers herself up. He can see how she does it, pulling air into herself for courage. She walks over and offers the book to Raymond. He reaches to accept it and thanks her and the surprising thing is how tears are running down his face and he just lets them and looks at Etta, straightforward and grateful. Dave admires that. Maybe everything's all right here.

*

Petra wakes up when Danny comes in. It takes a minute before she knows where she is. At his house, on his bed. She was obedient to the note. "Come in. Do not drive. Raymond, Chippie and I are off to Bangor. Back soon. Use my bed."

"What time is it?" she asks the big man with the baby in his arms. *Marshmallow Male Madonna.* She's still inside her dream. Anya, again. Seven years old. Dark, dark eyes. Accusing?

"8:30. P.M.," Danny says. "Saturday." She smiles. She can well use a bit of orienting. Her mind is starting to clear, though. She remembers this day, what she did. Gave another child away.

"How are you?" She needs to know.

"We're fine. Go back to sleep. I'll get her down. I'll sleep on the couch."

"I don't think so. I'll get up in a few minutes." She yawns. Something luxurious about this situation. The middle of the night, or it feels that way. All the ordinary structures of life fallen away. They might be in San Francisco sharing a joint, music from the stereo offering dimensions beyond. Danny turns to go, good Danny with his quiet baby. Then a little squawk comes, a moment of baby distress. Not her responsibility. Can this be true? Again? Overtaken by nausea, she runs to the bathroom, vomits, tells herself this is crazy, wonders what *this* means, rinses her mouth, splashes cold water on her face, uses Danny's towel. The towel is a comfort. She buries her face in it.

"You all right?" Here's Danny at the door of the bathroom which she apparently left open. She's sitting on the toilet seat, not knowing where to go. "Petra?"

"I don't know."

"Maybe we should go to the living room." He takes her hand, leads her, his grownup child. But she was never a child, was she? Only the others are children, thrust into her arms. She feels seriously stoned. Here it comes again. She breaks away, runs to the bathroom. Danny follows and does the thing that tells her she was in fact once a child. His cool hand holds her forehead while she vomits, exactly as Tekla's hand did long, long ago. Now she's crying while vomiting, a challenge. "Here," Danny says, softly, kindly, giving her a cool washcloth. She flushes—vomit swirling down, down—and closes the seat over a pool of pure still water. She's on the toilet seat again, Danny kneeling, his shoulder a place to put her head. She puts it there. Her arms are dead things ending in her lap, but his come around her. Time passes. *Too dead to weep.* Eventually she revives enough to cry again. She cries hard, holding onto Danny. This too passes. She collapses against him, present,

189

not absent. "Goodness," he says. She sniffles. "Sorry I wasn't home, Petra."

"Bet you tried to call, so I wouldn't come and find the house empty." She feels real again, but sad.

"Bet you had your phone off, because of the group."

"Aren't you smart?"

"Occasionally," he says. "Do you think you could make it to the living room?"

"Are you tired of kneeling here with an insane woman on your toilet?"

"There's my Petra."

They sit on the couch and he lets her rest against him. She could almost fall asleep, but suddenly she's curious. "What was Raymond doing here? Why is his truck still here?" Danny says nothing. "Danny?"

"Oh. Raymond. He came to visit. His truck stalled."

Danny has something to tell and he's not telling it. She sits up. "What's the matter with you?"

"What?"

"Danny, what about Raymond?" He doesn't answer. "*Danny*. Has something gone wrong?"

"Oh. Sorry. No, he's fine. I think he came to convince me he's not Chippie's father. Maybe he was worried, too, that I could change my mind."

"Have you?" She didn't know she needed to ask, or had the courage. Her hands are cold. She makes them into fists and presses against her cheeks. Her cheeks are hot.

"No. No, it's all right, it's fine, it's great. I fell in love."

"Fell in love? With Raymond?"

"Oh. Well, no. I was talking about Chippie."

"Really? You'll do it, then? You like the idea?"

"I think I might even like the reality." He grins at her.

"Whew. In that case, I have to pee." When she returns, he's standing at the window. The night is clear. The sky, the stars, the water, the shine of things.

"Beautiful, isn't it?" she says.

"Yes. Are you OK?"

"I think I could have another little breakdown any time, but for the moment I'm superb. You really fell in love with her?"

"At least with her."

"Danny? Are you kidding? Raymond?"

"It's just that I haven't met anyone—of the right gender, that is—in so long. It's probably nothing. I had to come out to him. Because of Chippie."

"Oh, dear." She wants to wrap him up and hold him like a baby, an ironic impulse in the current situation.

"You could have done that for me, friend Petra. You could have told him about my sexual orientation."

"It didn't occur to me. I was remiss." She bows her head.

"I might forgive you. Perhaps you had other things on your mind."

"Perhaps I had no mind."

"You had a mind. It must have been hard-worked in recent times."

"I should have told him, so you wouldn't have to go through that. Was it awful? How did he take it?"

"It was awful. He took it fine. I haven't had to do it in a while. It's just as hard as it used to be. I thought I might lose Chippie." His eyes fill with tears.

She feels like laughing, from relief, and joy. "Danny McGuire, you really do want a baby."

He wipes his eyes. "I want this particular baby. Forget what I said about her uncle, it's nothing."

"Well, I suppose he's straight," she says lightly, wondering if she's finding the right tone.

"He'd better not be closeted considerin' as how I turned me own self inside out for him."

"Indeed not, Danny Boy, though your midwestern Irish accent leaves a bit to be desired."

"Now, now, lass, no insults."

"Surely not, m'boy. I'd not insult a lad such as yourself. Certain as the sea shines, he has to be straight."

"He must surely be straight as a twelve-inch ruler but your accent is worse than mine, ye Polish lass."

"Want me to find out?" She can't believe she said this, even joking.

"OK," he says, not missing a beat. "Go all seductive on him, see what happens." He puts his arm around her shoulders. They stand looking out the window.

"I haven't done so well with women in recent years," she says. "Might as well try a man."

"Just a little test run, though. If he has inclinations toward The Life, we'd hate to straighten him up."

"We would indeed. I'll use a delicate touch."

"That's what I'm afraid of," Danny says quietly.

"Danny, are you serious? I mean are you *seriously* attracted to Raymond?"

"Are you?" The question catches her by surprise. She looks at him and can feel herself blushing. He drops his arm and they move away from each other, breathing as if they've been working out, or running.

She says, "We're too old for this."

He says, "I don't think so." Chippie cries, loudly. Danny turns and is gone. She goes to the couch and keeps herself there, a statue seated, focused on a poster of Robert Johnson. He looks back at her, stunned and full of the music they say he got from the devil. His large, large hands hold the guitar. He crosses his knees and wears his hat at an angle. Danny has told her the story, how he died, poisoned for sexual indiscretion with some man's woman. She tries not to hear the cries from the other room, not to feel her body's urgent maternal response.

She does not rush in and take over.

*

Stella dozes beside Raymond in the cab, her head against the window. Etta's gift, this compact little book with its firm brown cover, is in both his hands like a prayer book on First Communion day. He feels unable to put it down or relax with it so he lets it take him back. When Bede forced the family into the Catholic Church Raymond was seven years old and determined keep his heart safe from nuns and priests, Bede's new friends, but on the day of First Communion he knelt with the others, holding his prayer book, God inside him. Each young convert received a shake of the hand from Father Perrin. The congregation congratulated them. They got their picture taken, dressed in white, down to their shoes and socks. All of them, him included. The simplicity, how it wasn't bent, how he wasn't singled out, carried him through the months of Bede's enthusiasm. He learned to swallow the flat dry wafer at Mass, allowing saliva to gather, never letting the Body get stuck to the roof of his mouth. He coached classmates who had trouble. It's the only time he can remember being a teacher to anyone. When Bede yanked him and Raymona from their respective pews one morning, Raymond knew life was changing yet again. He hid the prayer book with its white shiny cover in the back of the closet and declared it lost when Bede came to burn the Refuse of God. In the night he got up, sat in the closet with the book in his hands, and fell asleep. Luck, or God, saved him. In the morning Bede chose not to wake the children at sunrise for the new regime of calisthenics. Instead, he pounded the kitchen table and demanded fresh-squeezed orange juice from Stella. Raymond in the closet was startled awake. He put the prayer book in its hiding place and quietly returned to bed. Raymona saw and giggled. She didn't know about the prayer book, only that he'd been where she sometimes slept. She'd never tell. *Old John Neptune and Other Maine Indian Shamans.* His second Indian book. Maybe he needs it.

*

Petra walks into her bedroom and undresses slowly, alone for the first time in two weeks. No baby in residence. Chippie, after almost an hour, stopped crying. She left them, new father and exhausted baby, paired and quiet, and drove home feeling released. The last notebook of Raymona Weeks lies open on the bed next to Simone Weil's *Gravity and Grace*. She closes the notebook and puts the words of Weeks and Weil together under her pillow. She feels dislocated but not distressed. She sleeps. It is midmorning and the sun is strong when she wakes up to the next stage of her life. Curled on her side, fetal but brightly conscious, she holds Raymona's notebook against her chest. Must have pulled it from under her pillow while she slept. The corner of Weil's book, still partly under the pillow, juts into her cheek. *Making its mark.*

She has a plan, suddenly known. Eating breakfast, she reads a paragraph of Weil, a page of Raymona, back and forth. She's determined to unmask Raymona, who hides behind Bright Star. She shakes her head from time to time. *Raymona, Raymona.* Raymond, a definite presence as she reads, is part of today's plan. More precisely, not to have contact with Raymond today is part of the plan. Unless he calls, unless he comes.

The pressures of time and fame have given Weil's words a hard, clear edge. Petra needs these sentences that carve thought, this rigorous vocabulary. Raymona meanwhile goes on tossing herself indiscriminately over the pages. Her truth is a wild sprawl decorated with lies, saturated with innocence, coupled with experience, written in a hand that slants this way and that, childishly earnest, alarmingly cynical, agonized, hilarious. The writing is impressive, raw, uncarved, unruly, with tiny obsessive stitchings across the whole, as if decisions could be made. Decisions *were* made and actions were carried out in a context of pain denied by reader and writer alike, the denial so obvious that together Petra and Raymona have to glimpse it; one eye seeing, one eye blind. She goes from Weil to Weeks and back again, remembering occasionally to take a bite of toast, a sip of now-cold coffee, all the while wondering what she's doing, what the real plan for this day is. Her own writing waits. Her discipline, then, is to leave the dishes in the sink, fill a bottle with water, take it with pen and tablet and no reading material and no baby, and walk down to the river.

And climb onto her rock.

Nothing happens except that the river is in constant motion, and the air is stirred and the birds are restless. Fallen leaves skitter around the base of the rock. She's alone and unfamiliar to herself. Movements in her mind and body are no more hers than the dance of the dead leaves. She holds her pen. She even scribbles against the page, round and round, to get the ink moving. She can't think of a word worth writing down. Maybe she used her mind up, reading. Maybe she let a boulder roll over her soul, and then another one. Simone Weil. Raymona Weeks. She climbs down off the rock and walks to the water's edge and stoops and puts her hand flat where the ground is barely covered with returning water. How she loves this tidal river. Cold water is good, the rough feel of the fine gravelly shore is good. If she starts to write, a torn thing might be pulled from her. She's afraid of herself, and unused to knowing this. It's as simple as that. Besides, she's never been good at writing outside.

Back at the kitchen table, she sits and looks at the scribble. Round and round and round it goes. *Tail-chasing Inky Beast.* She needs a cup of coffee. After that, a nap?

Chapter Nineteen

Eight o'clock Monday morning. Roo, hurrying in with cake: "It's been in an airtight container, should be OK. You like chocolate, don't you? Ultimate comfort food. I'm so sorry, Ricki, I should never have gotten you involved with DWELL. There are lesbians your age, but their group was a mess so I thought...never mind. Let me get this ready, then you'll tell me." Roo finds spoons in an overcrowded drawer, pulls packets of sugar and powdered creamer from her pocket, pours coffee into stained, but possibly clean, mugs. Ricki watches her sink down into the battered desk chair, take a deep breath, and appear to forget what comes next. Finally, she offers a napkin with its burden of cake.

"It's not your fault, Roo." Ricki bits into dense chocolate. "This is great."

"You don't mind, cake at this hour?"

"It's perfect."

"How *are* you, Ricki?"

"I'm O.K. Sort of. I found something out." Roo nods and reaches for her coffee, keeping eye contact. *Roo is a good person.* "It's..." This is harder than she thought it would be. She looks at the floor. She wants the dirt to make a pattern, but it's just dirt. Roo is looking over the edge of her mug. Her eyes are blue. The mug says Aged to Perfection. She should ask how Roo is. "I know you feel bad yourself, Roo."

Roo sighs. "I just let her get lost. Or I didn't find her again when I heard about the troubles."

"You gave her what she wanted. She needed to learn about Indians. And the book."

"It's been a shock, but I'm better, Ricki. *You* wanted to talk."

"I can't put everything together, Bright Star and what I found out. Raymond..."

"He seems like a nice person."

"That's what I thought." Roo takes another bite of cake. So does Ricki, but this one sticks to the roof of her mouth. She drinks some coffee, manages to swallow. She thinks she might cry. "Shit."

"I never heard you talk like that."

"I don't."

"What did you find out about Raymond?"

"He's Chippie's father." There. Just plain words.

"Really?" Roo is putting her mug down, wiping her mouth with a napkin, never losing eye contact.

"Weird, huh?"

"How did you find out?"

"His mother. It was just dropped into a conversation. She said, 'my son's child.' She meant Chippie."

"Could she have misspoken? She's under terrible stress."

"She meant Raymond. I saw him when she said it."

"Have you talked to Petra?"

"Petra says it isn't true. She has her own stress, though."

"I know." Roo stops, sighs, looks off to the side. Ricki waits. Roo sits up straighter. "So you think Bright Star and Raymond..."

"Had sex. She got pregnant." She feels hard from the truth of it. Angry. Strong.

"They have the same mother, but not the same father," says Roo.

"Right."

"God, Ricki."

"Right."

"This on top of everything else. I've been thinking so much about you...keeping secrets...knowing she was going to..."

"Die."

"I suppose you're starting to get it, that she really did die."

"I'm starting to get a lot of things. She told me it was some guy named Chip, a stranger, but it was Raymond, wasn't it?"

"You must have doubt, if Petra said..."

"Petra is...I don't know what to think about Petra, either." Roo looks at her, soft and sad. Softness and sadness fill the room. Not what she wanted. Maybe she shouldn't be talking to Roo, Petra's old friend.

"Ricki, I don't know what to say."

"That's OK. Nobody can make it right."

"How well do you know Raymond?" Good question. Roo waits, drinking her coffee, looking patient.

"I guess I made assumptions." A bitter taste in her mouth. "Just because he was her brother. Half-brother."

"You trusted him, didn't you?" *Yes, I trusted him.* But she can't say it because here she is, crying, and right inside the mess of crying the strangest thing is happening. Her life is passing before her eyes as if she's dying and she sees everyone she knows, her family, Lionel, DWELL, Bright Star, Raymond, with his kind, lying eyes. Then, stranger than anything, Chippie, yawning. The biggest little yawn in the world. A yawn means you need more air. Maybe this is what it feels like when you're going to faint because Roo is saying "Put your head down into your lap, Ricki." Her shoulders are being rubbed. She's coming apart in the office of her best teacher and, look at that, the very last bite of cake is lying in the dirt at the end of the toe of her shoe. *This school needs more janitors.* "I wish I could say it'll be all right, Ricki. I just wish I could say that." Roo sighs. She's a big sigher. It feels good, Roo rubbing her shoulders.

"I'm sorry, Roo." Pretty soon she'll sit up.

"Isn't it funny how we all say that, how sorry we are, when we ourselves are feeling the worst?"

"I guess." She thinks she can sit up now. She sits up.

"Better?" Roo asks, sitting back down in her worn old chair.

"Yes, thanks." She does feel better.

"Oh, your cake!"

"I know. It was the best cake I ever had, Roo."

"And there it lies, in the dirt. This floor is a disgrace."

"Oh, well," Ricki says, and they're smiling at each other. She feels nearly normal.

"Maybe it will just take time, Ricki." Ricki doesn't know what "it" is. It's OK, not knowing. They sit. Roo looks at the clock. "Oh, God." Roo has to go. She's probably already late for something. Roo says, "I hate to say this but I have a class."

"O.K." This sounds weak, stupid.

"Will you be all right now, Ricki?" Roo needs her to be all right.

"I'll be all right. Thanks, Roo."

"Are you sure?"

"I'm sure." Suddenly, she is.

"Good."

"Maybe it doesn't even matter." A new thought. It made itself while it was coming out of her. She saw it make itself.

"About Raymond?" Roo's such a good listener.

"And Petra and everything else. She *had* to do it, Roo." An urgency, to say that, before Roo leaves.

"What? Oh, Bright Star."

"Otherwise it would've been out of her hands." *Roo has to go. Let her go.*

"I know, Ricki. Still, it's been awfully hard on you."

"Maybe it was just my fate. She liked to talk about fate. It was something she respected. But you have to go."

"I do. Come back and we'll talk more. I won't always have cake to give you and you won't always almost faint. We'll just talk. OK?"

"Thanks, Roo. Really." Thankfulness spreading through her. She can let Roo go to her class. She can get up and leave this office, leave the filtered sun, the good clutter.

"Stay here as long as you like, Ricki. Just pull the door shut when you leave." Roo leaves. Time passes. She lets it pass. The dust in the air floats and sinks and floats. There are patterns. All those questions about Raymond don't matter. She finds a box of tissues under a pile of papers and cleans up the dropped bit of cake. She can't clean the whole floor though she'd like to. She pulls the door shut when she leaves. Outside, she breathes fresh air and thinks about Chippie's yawn and how people yawn when they're *bored*. Innocent, new, smart Chippie would be bored by all of this. Bright Star and Raymond made a baby together. So what? Petra keeps getting kids and giving them away. Who cares? Well, maybe she does, Ricki Harding who almost fainted in her teacher's office. Maybe she should stop caring. Maybe it really doesn't matter, any of it. She starts up the wide welcoming steps to Fogler. She loves this library. She loves books. She loves learning. She loves to know. Up to the second floor. She gets a comfortable chair looking out over the campus through a tall window. She's exactly where she should be, with work to do. *Do your work, Ricki. Don't let this stop you.* Bright Star was serious that day. Tired. You could see how sick she was. Maybe they had sex just a few minutes later, though. If they did it was almost violent. Is that right? Yes. Bright Star wore her long soft white dress. The sex didn't match the dress. *Deceptively reserved and flat,* writes Marianne Moore. Which means not flat at all. Not what it looks like. The glacier isn't a plain ice sculpture shaped like an octopus. It's big and complicated. Every move you make changes what you see. In the poem this is only interesting. *Twenty-eight ice-fields from fifty to five hundred feet thick / of unimagined delicacy.* Ice, five hundred feet thick, and Moore thinks to write "unimagined delicacy." Perfect. Bright Star is free and safe, isn't she? Raymond probably thought it was a *good* thing to create a new life. Petra made a mistake. Anyone can make a mistake, even a second mistake just like the first. There are fir trees with huge roots in this glacier's park. *The rock seems frail compared with their dark energy of life.* Petra's name means rock. Bright Star tossed this fact into the air one day, never letting on how she meant to choose a new mother who would be a rock. But rocks can be frail.

She looks out the window. Time passes. She feels terrible. It's all a mess, isn't it? Petra let herself fall apart when Chippie needed her, which is either selfish or weak or both, and she's supposed to be a *therapist.* Raymond and Bright Star had sex, an ugly fact. Raymond is Chippie's father and too cowardly to admit it. *Completing a circle, / you have been deceived into thinking you have progressed.* She slams the book shut. One more fact: Bright Star is *dead.*

*

"Well, truthfully, I'm glad, dear. It was the most engaging thing but I couldn't have kept it up, helping you out that way. A baby's more work than I remembered. My own two are grown so long. Did you find, too, that a baby was more work than you anticipated? Why, Petra, I didn't intend to bring on tears." That was Izzie. Yesterday. Today is Monday, a simple work day. No Chippie to make arrangements for and no writing to struggle with. Not a word got written yesterday. She finished her coffee, stared out the window, decided against a nap. The kitchen cupboards are now organized. The refrigerator shines. Her mind is another matter, but here she is, Petra Kalinowski, professional assistant to the minds of others. She feels unexpectedly ready to work.

Kiki walks in heavily, slowly. No whirlwind. She chooses Good Old Teddy Bear Blue and crushes him to herself. She sinks to the floor, sticks her legs out in front of her, a great V ending in red high-top tennis shoes, black-soled. Petra sits on the floor across from her. They've been here before. "Sad day, huh?"

Kiki nods. Tears roll down her face, spreading and washing.

After a while she looks up and says, "But I got a new shirt."

"This one?"

Kiki nods, sniffling.

"It's a good color on you, Kiki."

The shirt is bright orange. Kiki smiles a sly smile. She's gotten what she wanted. Petra feels passive, contented. They sit together quietly.

They play checkers. Kiki almost wins.

"I almost won."

"Yes, you did."

Petra feels clean in the work. In the past she would have chided herself for not working harder, not ferreting out what was behind the tears. She's learned.

A new client comes next, Andrew, tall and thin with a receding hairline, a little nervous. His marriage just ended, his wife took the kids and moved to Arizona where her parents have a large house. *His wife took the kids, of course she did, it's the normal thing, the mother takes the kids.* "I teach at the university," Andrew says. "Philosophy. Last week I missed a class. Didn't even call to make an excuse, then spent the hour imagining how the students would wait, talking quietly. Boyfriends, music. Finally, the one confident extrovert, she's a skinny little thing with a nondescript wardrobe, would suggest they go ahead and they'd have a fine discussion, idealism versus realism, no need for me." Petra listens, waits. He's gathering confidence as he talks. *This will be about his agony over his wife. This will not be about parents and children.* "In reality, they probably dismissed themselves after ten minutes." Andrew manages a wry smile. Petra smiles, too. Says nothing. She's just listening. This is her work. Andrew says his students will be kind when he goes back. They'll make a mild joke or ignore his lapse entirely. He's a lucky man. Life treats him well. His wife—Iris—well, she seems to have decided she's a lesbian. He hopes Petra isn't uncomfortable with that. She assures him she won't judge, tells him she's glad he came to therapy, lets herself think how easy this is. When he runs down, his introduction of himself achieved, she picks up the lead. Sleeping? Not much. Eating? Enough to keep going. Weight loss? About ten pounds since Iris left, since they all left. Eight days ago. Yes, trouble concentrating. No, no history of depression. Life treats him well, as he said.

"Tell me about your own philosophy," she says. This is her first probe, well-timed, she thinks. But he hesitates. She backs off. "Or does that question make no sense, Andrew, at least not today?" He's looking out the window.

"My philosophy is as dry as the leaves out there. It has a tendency to crumble." She likes this, of course. An image. Dryness. Crumbling. He'll need to cry. They're doing fine.

"Is there anything that helps?"

"If there is, I haven't found it." He looks right at her. He wants help and is undramatic about it.

"Tell me the story," she says. He takes a purposeful breath.

"I think the trouble began...but I shouldn't call it trouble, it's a sort of liberation for Iris...you might be able to understand." She nods, yes, she can understand. Do others in his life have difficulty understanding? "Yes," he says.

"It matters to you, that Iris not be thought the villain."

"Yes."

"You respect her choice, to explore her sexuality."

"I do."

"But it's not easy for you." He looks at her, tears in his eyes.

"Do you have children, Petra?"

She imagines the blood draining from her face. *Does* she have any children? But she has an answer to this question. She's used it many times. "I had a daughter. She died years ago. Is it your children you miss most?" She gets away with this. He doesn't apologize for asking, doesn't freeze at the word, died.

"You asked about my philosophy." He starts to cry. "My children..." She hands him a tissue and he thanks her. Maybe he doesn't notice how her hand shakes, how she can't get her breath. Chippie's bright eyes loom, then disappear, scaring her. The room darkens for an instant. It might have been a cloud, a small cloud covering the sun, but she doubts it.

Here is this man, crying. "Tell me what your children mean to you," she says, gently, inviting. She can do this.

And she does. She nods, understanding, when he describes what it's meant to him to have young *beings* in his daily life, the liveliness and solidity and color. The insistence. "They can't be controlled. They can't be made into abstractions. Do you understand?"

"Yes," she says. He cries quietly, without drama. "And now they're far away," she says, almost in control of her voice. He cries harder. He blows his nose, thanks her, says he hasn't been able to cry, then cries more. She does understand. Deep in her being, she understands. Children can't be made into abstractions. Anything else, not children.

He's almost finished crying. It's nearly the end of the session. "Andrew," she says quietly. He looks at her. He blows his nose again and wipes his eyes. He doesn't apologize. Short-term therapy, she thinks. He's so healthy. She likes him. She made no major errors, she's almost confident of that. He drops the tissue in the wastebasket and smiles tentatively.

"Whew," he says. "What were you going to say?"

"You're doing very well with this. Do you know that?"

"I can stand to hear it."

"We're going to stop soon. Would you like to come back?"

"Should I?"

"It's really up to you. I doubt you'd need to come many times, but a it might be helpful for a while."

"Helpful would be good."

"Let's go week by week." It's only after Andrew leaves that she remembers who her next client is, though she knew, of course she knew, as she drove to work under the clear sky.

Helga looks dreadful. She's overdone her makeup. Garish accessories call attention to themselves. The beige sweater and slacks hang as if lacking a body to give them shape. She fingers a circlet of worry beads, dark brown beads that look tempting, like coffee beans, a new element. Either Helga needs the beads desperately or she's relaxed enough now to allow herself this aid. Petra wishes she had some for herself, or at least a cup of coffee. Helga's ragged cuticles almost unhinge her.

"It's a bright day, Petra. Driving here, I knew that. The sky was pure blue. But the world felt like a cardboard thing, a backdrop to a play

I was taken to but wasn't interested in. The rituals—from the OCD—are getting longer and helping less. I missed some work last week. I'm not sleeping more than two or three hours a night." Helga looks tense but perhaps a little satisfied with herself, having completed her list. "I think that's everything," she says. Petra would like to get up and shake her hand, congratulate her on a job well done, and usher her out of the office. She sees them, Helga the client and Petra the therapist, two unsuited mothers, constructed of exceedingly heavy cardboard and held together by oversized nuts and bolts that permit stiff movement out the door. *Cardboard Wish.* Can she work with this woman today? At least she has supervision tomorrow, but is this the week for her clients or Gertrude's? She's lost track.

"Petra?"

"Oh. I'm sorry, Helga."

"It must be hard, listening to problems all day."

"I generally do a little better than this. I liked your image, the cardboard backdrop. I mean, it expresses a feeling very well. Why do you think life has been so hard this week?"

"Has your life been hard, too? Maybe I'm not supposed to ask that." The worry beads slide quickly through Helga's fingers.

"The last couple of days were a little rough for me, too. It's OK to ask. I appreciate it, but this is your time. Do you know what's been so hard?" The beads slow down. Helga looks at her. *She's trying to decide if I'm able to do my job today.*

"I suppose I do know," Helga says. Know what? Petra can't keep track. She waits. Waiting is a fine therapeutic intervention. Unless it's a matter of stalling. Should she confess, stop the session? "I'm glad you're here, Petra. I needed to see you this time." The beads are clutched now, held tight.

Helga feels a special need. She's leaving space, not filling the room with long, competently constructed paragraphs. She's ready to enter into the therapeutic relationship; which requires a therapist. Petra gathers her forces and resigns herself to her chosen work.

"That's different, isn't it, Helga? Really feeling the need to see me?" Gently, but not sparing her client. Helga's eyes fill. She fingers the beads slowly now, breathes deeply. She doesn't speak. Petra speaks: "Looks like there's a lot going on." Helga nods. *Just stay with her. Give her time.* When she was a younger therapist she had to instruct herself like this. It got her through. Her breathing now matches Helga's. They're swimming in the same water, side by side. That either of them can tolerate this is astounding, Helga inside her make-up, she herself inside her own roused state, her now terrible suspense. *Where is Ingrid? What happened?*

"I never told you the whole truth, Petra." *Ah, a secret.* So nothing happened with Ingrid. It's only the hidden element of Helga's story, ready to surface like rocks sometimes do, breaking into view in a field after long years underground.

"Do you feel ready to tell me more?" Helga nods and fingers her beads, one by one. But what if the secret brings their stories closer?

"It's about Ingrid's father." The father. Fine. Even if he, like Anya's father Frederick, drove himself into a telephone pole, that will be fine. She can do this.

"Ingrid's father?"

"Yes." The worry beads stop moving. Helga holds her breath, looks frightened, and determined.

"This will take courage, won't it?" Helga nods, a child, her eyes big. "There's something important to tell, about Ingrid's father?" Helga nods. Petra waits, ready, attentive, perfectly able.

"Rape," Helga whispers.

"He raped you? Oh, Helga."

"There's more," Helga's voice is barely there.

Petra leans forward and says, as gently as she can, "Tell me."

"More of them. There were more of them." The worry beads make indentations, tight around knuckles.

"I'm not sure I..." Petra says.

"More men." Helga's voice cuts across Petra's, suddenly raw and rough. Her breathing is audible. Petra waits, her own breath stopped. "It was a group," Helga says. It was a group. As with Anya. As with Marian, Anya's second mother. *Stay with Helga and her new raw voice and her loud breathing and her terrible ragged cuticles.* "I was leaving a party. I wasn't drunk. They followed me home." Helga, angry and committed, needs no prompting now. "They tied me up in the basement. They gagged me." *Which is not the same, not the same as Anya and Marian at all.*

"You couldn't scream," she says to Helga, but her comment is irrelevant, unrelated to the core of the story. Helga glances down at her lap where the worry beads are held taut, then raises her furious eyes to meet Petra's.

"She looks like one of them, so he's the one."

"Ingrid's father?"

"Yes." The word is a hiss. In a compartment inside her mind reserved for the purpose Petra knows the scene is playing itself out: Anya and Marian are being raped and killed. She's never watched it, not really, not with attention. But this is different. Helga's story is different. A woman raped into pregnancy, a daughter made in the image of the rapist. A basement. Ropes. It's all different. Good. It's all different. Her compassion crawls forward, pulls itself up, takes over: *Oh, Helga.*

"Have you talked about this before, Helga?"

"No. No, I have not." Each word a carrier of rage.

"It takes courage."

"It takes several sleepless nights."

"A kind of desperation," Petra says.

"Yes," Helga says.

Petra nods. "So Ingrid looks like one of those men."

"I couldn't stand it any more."

"Looking at her, being reminded of him?" Helga nods. "And that's part of why you..."

"Gave my kid away. It didn't even work." A harsh, bitter flavor to the words.

"It didn't work?"

"It's worse. What you counselors call flashbacks. *Worse.* Since Ingrid isn't with me."

"You must be so angry."

"Finally."

"Should you have been angry earlier?" Helga doesn't answer. The question seems to stop her.

Then: "I wasn't thinking, earlier. I *thought* I was thinking. Such a big decision." Petra waits. Helga needs time to think now. She herself needs not to think. "What I told you about my compulsions was true." Helga speaks slowly, looking at her therapist who listens, grateful for the distraction. Compulsions are nicely neutral, no compulsions in *her* story.

206

But did she think through her own decisions? Does anyone? "I do have OCD. It was getting worse. I thought Ingrid was making it worse because she was old enough to have a mind of her own, because I couldn't control her, but the rape, anger about the rape, *any* feeling about it...I decided it was better not to think about that. When the flashbacks got worse I thought it was Ingrid looking more and more like...like that..." She stops, her jaw clamped, beads squeezed inside one fist.

"That rapist," Petra says. *That goddamn fucking rapist, and his goddamn fucking rapist pals.* But those words are back in the compartment that holds the past, almost theoretical. Here, today, is Helga. She loves Helga intensely. This happens when the hidden pain pours out, this tender surge. What a privilege, to have such work.

"Yes. And look at me. I need worry beads now. Believe it or not, they help." Helga loosens her fist and runs the beads through her fingers.

"I believe it," Petra says.

"Well, good," Helga says, sounding lighter. She even smiles a little.

"Well," Petra says, mirroring the tone. They sit quietly. Helga looks thoughtful as she gently fingers her beads. This is almost comfortable for therapist Petra.

"Thank you," Helga says after a while, as if closing the conversation. As if they've worked something through. Petra looks at the clock. She's startled to see it's time to end the session. Some clients keep track. Helga, of course, is one of those.

"Do you think you'll sleep better tonight, Helga?" Perhaps they *have* worked something through. These things are mysterious.

"Maybe."

"We'll talk about this more another time, if you want to."

"Do you think I should?" Helga is being a good girl. Clearly, she wants this rape topic over and done with. Petra laughs gently.

"It might help, but we'll only do what feels right to you." Helga nods.

"And there's Ingrid."

"Yes," Petra says. *Do we have to talk about her?* This is a last-minute curve Helga is throwing. Petra had almost left the batter's box.

"The whole problem of Ingrid," Helga says, sighing.

"Are you having doubts?" Petra asks, bravely returning to work.

"It's more that I *ought* to be having doubts."

"Is she all right where she is, for now?" Surely this is a reasonable question.

"I think so. How would I know?" Helga puts the worry beads into her purse, businesslike. She's finished for the day, not asking a real question.

"You feel like you don't know much, right about now," Petra says lightly.

"You said it."

"No major decisions until we talk more. How does that sound?" says Petra, counseling prudence she herself has not been practicing.

"That sounds like a reprieve. Thank you." They make another appointment. Helga walks out of the office, steady enough in her beige attire but still thin, unbecomingly accessorized, and living under makeup too thick. This therapy might take a while.

*

Raymond is stirred to disorder in himself. Electrical wires with no coating and crossing each other every which way might be a good description for his inside state. Maybe that's an exaggeration. He had no trouble opening the book about Maine shaman Indians. It wasn't like the other night with *Black Elk Speaks*. He got through the introduction and a good deal of the first chapter before this electrical feeling came on. The book by Mrs. Eckstorm is about Indians her grandfather knew in Brewer, right across the river, back in the 1800s, and at first it felt sort of homey, but then...

It could be the Native magic that has him trembling, or it could be how the magic is made strange because it comes at him through the intention of a white woman. All these white women are mixing in. Raymona's everywhere now. She won't let him read this book without watching. And Etta. She gave him the book. Number four is Stella and how she turned, getting out of the cab, and said he ought to be cautious about "that book" because she had a feeling. He didn't even try to ask what she meant. He feels drunk and sober in equal parts, that might be a way to put it, though he hasn't been drinking. He almost understands what it would be like to inhabit two worlds because while all this trembling and leaping around in his mind is going on he's sitting at his own kitchen table and bringing a cup of coffee to his lips and his hand is as steady as it's ever been. A sure aspect of himself is in place, which might be the most surprising fact of all.

It's Monday afternoon. He's glad to have the day off. He slept fourteen hours and woke up wanting something. He thought he might get it from this book. He got what he wanted and more. He wanted, though he didn't know it, the story about the fellow who took a ray of sunshine, pulled it like molasses candy, then hung it across the backs of two chairs and laid an ax on it. He wanted stories from here, from Maine, with woodchucks and sea monsters of no consistent description. They give a plainer feeling than the horses and Thunder Beings in Black Elk's story, though he appreciates both ways. He wanted, too, Old Molly Molasses, John Neptune's lady, a shaman herself, "feared by all she frowned upon," as Mrs. Eckstorm put it. This has to be the same lady he sees glaring at him from the library wall. Beside her on the wall is Old John Neptune himself. Raymond has information in him now that wasn't there before. Maine Indian information. Which he might not have a right to. When he couldn't take the reading any more, he went grocery shopping. The walk was a help. Now he's back to sitting at his table and he's read a little more and stopped again and the book is lying here in front of him. He wants to pick it up but if he's honest he has to say the book wants to *be* picked up, as if it's a living thing with a will directed toward him. He puts down his cup and picks up the book but it's time to make lunch. Mrs. Eckstorm says right out she can't put the information all together for him. He wants and doesn't want the incompleteness of her telling. It messes up all his Indian knowledge to read this book. He can't sort what's silly from what's sacred or what's superstitious from what's true. Black Elk's story was more complete and knowing. A poet wrote up that one, which might be the difference. The problem is there's an Indian part to himself, and it could even be a Penobscot part, that wants these old stories with a craving, but he can't stop thinking that a father, unknown at that, isn't enough since the line comes through the mother. He'd be afraid to let a real Indian know how he's sitting here today, what it means to him. Maybe a better word than afraid, and a worse word, a harder word, would be *ashamed*. Stella could be right to caution him, but the book feels good in his hands, old and brown and small, like an object a person

209

can hold and the holding will do him good. How did Etta discern he needed it? He gets up and starts to peel his carrots. He made a decision to cook some decent food today. What to do about Stella is a question on his mind. Now she says he's never again to contemplate sleeping across her doorway, thank you very much. An end to babysitting is what she wants and he can't blame her, but he worries. Bitta will serve whatever Stella orders, following a rule of her own about not messing in customers' lives. He puts the carrots to boil. Then there's this business about Raymona having a fatal illness. Ricki believes that. He doesn't. Should he? A picture passes through his mind, Raymona at the morgue, her head dropped back in that way he doesn't feel easy seeing, but he does see it at least once every day. There's a chance, maybe a one per cent chance, Raymona did have an illness. That would put a turn to everything he knows about her dying plans. Mrs. Eckstorm thinks a book by a man named Joseph Nicolar is important. *Life and Traditions of the Red Man*. He feels a need to get it into his hands today which is a little crazy since he hasn't finished *Old John Neptune*. He's following something here, step by step. The night he kept walking time away instead of searching for Stella felt similar, nothing quite where it belonged and the only thing to do was whatever he found himself doing, all of it out of kilter and at the same time right. The carrots are turning a new orange in their boiling water. He's never stopped to watch a carrot get cooked before. It's a strange meal, a whole pot of carrots and nothing else, but he has an appetite for it. Butter and salt and pepper will bring it to perfection. It isn't until he's draining the water off that he remembers this was the menu one day at Raymona's. It wasn't just any day, it was the first time she had him over after he got out of the Youth Center. "Carrots, for seeing in the dark, Raymond." She was only nineteen then, Ricki's age. She worked up her courage, you could watch her doing it, and asked if he blamed her for his time away. She didn't relax when he said No, so he added more words. "I don't blame you, Raymona." She just looked at him and said, "Well." He remembers that. "Well." As if something would follow, but nothing did. He dishes up the carrots and raises his first forkful in a holy salute to his crazy dead sister. He loved her. The carrots taste good, better even than he thought they would. The tears are rolling down and he's eating and he's reading the words of Mrs. Fanny Hardy Eckstorm which are really the words of Clara Neptune, Penobscot

Indian. Here's Clara, telling old stories for supper and a bit of money and Mrs. Eckstorm writing it all down, letting it be, not trying to make smooth what comes rough out of Clara. The feeling of First Communion is in him, his young self right here with him, special and good, not bent. Maybe Raymona is here, too. Maybe she's not even mad. This is what he thinks, making his way through carrots cooked just right.

Chapter Twenty

Lunchtime, Tuesday. The day after she almost fainted in Roo's office. Ricki heads into the Bear's Den to get a soda and sit, anonymous, inside a miscellany of sounds. Student voices, scraping chairs, African drumming, a television no one watches. The floor is far from clean, as usual. Lone students pore over textbooks inside the chaos. She's found an empty table and is pulling out a chair when Lionel takes her elbow and turns her toward him.

"*Lionel.*"

"Hey, Ricki." They hug. He's skinny, taller, but himself. This makes her cry.

"Hey, hey. Not that bad, is it?" She can't stop crying so they stand there holding onto each other and he pats her on the back until she absolutely has to blow her nose.

"Damn, Lionel, where've you been?"

"Ricki, meet my Old Lady." Standing behind Lionel—but he, grinning, pulls her forward—is a woman who might already have borne two or three kids though she can't be very old. She has that dumpy poor woman look and lives behind her face like a few of Ricki's cousins except that this face is Indian. And this handshake is unlike any other. The woman takes the anomalous hand and creates a normal handshake with no hesitation, no embarrassment. Can she really be Lionel's Old Lady? Isn't he still gay? "Ann Marie Redfeather," the woman says, introducing herself properly while Lionel steps back and twirls in a little circle that might not even have happened, since now, the handshake still in progress, he's standing quietly. Beaming, but not too brightly. As if trying to be modest about what he's accomplished just by being here, or by bringing together two people he likes. "I'm not his Old Lady," says Ann Marie Redfeather, not as if she's contradicting Lionel, but as if she saw Ricki's confusion and thought to reduce it, that being the business of the moment. Lionel bends from the waist in glee. He's quietly whooping and giggling to himself and Ricki wants to kick him. When he comes up for air he wipes his eyes, glasses off and dangling in one hand, and comes at her. She gets another hug, almost more vigorous than she can stand. "Damn, Ricki. Damn, I can't believe we just walk in here and find you." They stand and look at each other. His wandering eye isn't behaving well, but he's looking at her all the same. They turn toward Ann Marie, including her, breathing hard, shaking their heads.

"Sit. I'll get you something to drink," Ricki says. She takes a step away, stops, turns back. "What, though?"

"Pepsi," Ann Marie says.

"Ginger ale," Lionel says. He's obediently sitting down.

"Anything to eat?" They shake their heads. By the time she gets back she's stopped trembling and has had time to warn herself. Lionel might be here just for the day. "How long are you here for?" First things first. *Just tell me, I can take it.*

"I'm home, Ricki," Lionel says. "We're going to be University of Maine students." Which is too lucky. Impossible, in fact. She decides to ignore it.

"What's this Old Lady business?" Second things second. She's feeling quite organized.

"Don't worry, I'm still the faggot you know and love."

"Well, that's good. I guess. But..."

He just looks at her, beaming, so she turns to Ann Marie, who says, "I'm twenty-one. He likes to pretend I'm old." She can't tell if Ann Marie thinks this is amusing or irritating. *Just the facts, ma'am.* They sip their drinks. Lionel beams at Ricki, looks around the room, beams at everything. He doesn't seem to notice the quick stares he gets as people walk by. He's a picture: his albinism and his cowboy hat and cowboy shirt and string tie, his thick glasses, his wandering eye, and how he keeps grinning. Ann Marie sits, quiet, unreadable. Like Ricki, she wears a plain shirt and jeans. Bright Star would sit at the table this way, unspeaking and opaque. You'd think she was far away until you went to leave and you'd hear, "Stay." As if you were a dog. She didn't mean it that way. She meant she needed you near her, though the meal was finished and there was no conversation and the dishes were waiting and you really wanted to get to that assignment due next week. Bright Star herself, however, did not stay. She left. Died. But here's *Lionel.*

213

"Will you major in physics?" He barely hears her, only looks vague, then grins. He might be over-stimulated. The drumming has intensified and someone has turned the TV up to hear the local news. Two car accidents, one fire, a foster home scandal. No one she knows. Then the drummers are packing up, walking out, efficient and colorful in dashikis and blue jeans. A girl turns the TV's sound off, evoking scattered applause. More people leave. Afternoon classes begin soon. Does she have a class? *Panic.* "What day is this?" She's asking Ann Marie since Lionel is walking away. *Stay*, she wants to shout.

"Tuesday." Ann Marie says. "He's going to the bathroom. He'll be right back." It's not right, Ann Marie interpreting Lionel to her, and without even being asked. Still, he'll be back, he's not going away. Can this be true? It's Tuesday, no afternoon classes. A good day to have an old friend show up with his pseudo-old-lady who gives signs of being an interesting puzzle, alert behind her face. And that handshake.

"Do you have to be anywhere?"

Ann Marie almost smiles at the idea. "Nowhere to go, nothing to do. You?"

"No, I'm free." They sit with that. The lone studiers stay on. Pages turn. Someone shouts to a friend across the room. The friend throws a wad of paper in response. Then more quiet. Lionel comes back and gives her a strangling hug from behind and messes up her hair. He's all energy.

"Ricki, Ricki, Ricki," he says.

"Are you really here? I mean here for real. To stay."

"Yes, Ma'am."

"Well, I missed you."

*

"I think you helped her," Gertrude says. "The work sounds fine, Petra."

"I was shaken."

"You were *with* her."

"I was, but more with my roused self. I'm not sure Helga would let me know if I made the wrong move."

"Not immediately, I suppose, but you'd know eventually."

214

"They do always let us know, don't they?"

"I'm afraid so," Gertrude says. "Which is a good thing, of course. I think you should relax. In fact, you look more relaxed than you ought to. What have you done with yourself, to be this fine?"

It's true. Petra feels fine. She came through a piece of her own dark woods after the session with Helga which forced her, finally, to confront Anya's last hour, and Marian's. To imagine: waking in the dark, an assailant with a knife, penetration by a clumsy but bone-hard penis. Anya's vagina so small, so unready, ripped. Marian's vagina, informed and horrified. Their agony doubled by worry for each other. The scared crazy drug-induced danger-induced hilarity of the boys coming at them, an ooze of sadism around the edges. Cold knives against their necks. The final cuts, not necessarily quick or clean. Death. Having imagined, Petra learned the unexpected: that it was all pretense for her, no matter how she gave herself to it. She could not know. Nothing in her life compared, or prepared her to understand. She was here, alive and for the moment safe, and for all foreseeable moments safe. A chasm separated her from Anya and Marian's final experience. Also, from her parents' wartime years. From Helga. From Raymona Weeks. From Raymond. In bed, drifting to sleep, she thought of Simone Weil, her concept of grace. Radical, unsentimental grace. She thought of Anya and her black horse running around the dirt track, green shimmering grass at the center. *We see you but we are completely here and you are completely there.* Which was not painful but liberating. Still, when she woke in the morning she remembered Helga, raped into pregnancy; Helga, giving her child away, which might have been a mistake. Should Helga be running to her friend's house, reclaiming her child? Gertrude has banished the hysteria. It is Helga who determines what happens. She, Petra, follows, listens, does her job. Gertrude's question—what has she done with herself, to be so fine?—is easier to answer than she would have thought.

"I came to terms with Anya's death. Working with Helga got me there. Forced me there."

"How wonderful for you, Petra."

"It is. I love your new wastebasket. Is it sweet grass?" The basket has been tugging at her mind and won't let go.

"Sweet grass and brown ash. Isn't it beautifully done? It's called a barrel basket." Good Gertrude, dancing with every turn. Petra stares at the basket. It's like a stout little person, like a toddler with a tummy. How right this seems.

"Is it Penobscot?" She's shy, almost embarrassed to use the word which makes her think of Raymond, who comes too readily to mind.

"Yes," Gertrude says. "I went up to Indian Island, to the Penobscot Nation Museum. There was an old barrel basket. I'd never seen anything like it. James, the curator, led me to a woman who still makes them, full-sized and the smaller ones like this."

"I mean to go up sometime, but I don't do it." Gertrude nods. Busy women don't do the things they mean to do. They sit in silence. There's no reason to believe Raymond is Penobscot. *I don't know my tribe.* That was in the beginning, when she was running from Raymona's will.

"I'll be right back," Gertrude says. "Bathroom break. If you want, we can talk longer today. I had a cancellation." Petra touches the basket, the bent strips, the finely woven rope circling the center. It would be satisfying to have the basket-making skill. Or do they hate it? What must the harsh fibers do to their fingers? Are their minds dulled by the repetition? Some must love it, though, following the tradition, proud of the cuts or calluses. But then selling, to whites. Not easy. On the other hand, money pays for what's needed. Nothing's ever simple. The basket itself is simple. Strong and simple.

"What next?" Gertrude asks, sitting down. She does want to take more time, though she didn't know it until this moment.

"I do want to tell you something, Gertrude. It's a little off that track, but not entirely. I was reading Simone Weil last night. *Gravity and Grace.*"

"*Gravity and Grace.* I read that way back, but *Waiting for God* more recently. Weil's compelling, isn't she?"

"I always intended to read her, but never did. Now I have. I need the stringency. I've memorized a passage, not an easy task. I was using a neglected muscle."

Gertrude nods, smiles. "The last time I tried to memorize something I failed utterly. Ricki's doing work on Marianne Moore. Well, you know, being in the reading group."

"I'm worried about Ricki."

"I think she's managing well enough, considering," Gertrude says.

"I hope she's as resilient as she seems. What did you try to memorize?"

"Ricki inspired me to look at Moore's poems. A friend gave me a collection years ago, thinking, I suspect, that one spinster would take to the work of another, and, in fact, I did. There was something about a katydid's wings and a composition by Scarlatti—such complexity—I absolutely could not memorize that poem. The thinking and the rhythms and rhymes—all impossibly unique. As I'm sure you know. But give me your Weil."

She feels nervous, a child at a recital. This is private, nothing to do with clinical supervision. She takes a breath and it comes: "'To accept what is bitter. The acceptance must not be reflected back on to the bitterness so as to diminish it, otherwise the acceptance will be diminished in force and purity, for the thing to be accepted is that which is bitter in so far as it is bitter; it is that and nothing else.'"

"Again," Gertrude says.

"It's dense, isn't it?" Petra repeats the quote, this time with less embarrassment. She wants—needs?—Gertrude to follow the twisting path.

Gertrude listens, nods. "The bitterness of Anya and Marian's deaths?"

"Yes, and then it got larger."

"Helga?"

"And Bright Star. And her brother and..."

"Everything," Gertrude says. "Everything bitter."

"Yes."

"And the acceptance can be complete only if the bitterness remains undiminished."

"I think so. I mean, that's what she says, and I think it might be true." Embarrassment again, as if she's out in public in her pajamas, but this particular embarrassment doesn't matter. Which is noteworthy.

"No denial, no pretending," Gertrude says.

She nods. Last night she caught herself pretending, or nearly so. Thinking she could understand what happened to Anya and Marian. But, yes, Gertrude understands.

217

"'Sin is Behovely,'" Gertrude says. "Do you know that quote?"

"I do. It's Julian of Norwich, isn't it? 'Sin is Behovely, but All shall be well, and All manner of thing shall be well.' I know it from Eliot's *Four Quartets*, but is that the same thought?"

"There's an echo, for me," Gertrude says. "Bitterness and sin, life's difficult elements, our possible responses. The tones are different, of course. Weil so severe, Julian such a comfort." Gertrude gets up and starts rummaging in a desk drawer.

Petra says to her back, "Both women insist. Both are uncompromising as they hold the two poles."

"Do you need that right now, Petra? A reminder to hold both poles?" Gertrude is bent to a lower drawer, still rummaging. Petra is distracted. Since Gertrude quoted Julian of Norwich, Raymona has edged forward, her presence solidifying, her final notebook open. After DWELL discussed Eliot's *Quartets* an adolescent alter, in perfect handwriting, copied out biographical information from an encyclopedia. "Julian of Norwich, a mediaeval English Christian mystic, an anchoress, wrote Showings, a description of her visions. I am brave and writing at the Public Library. Julian, this lady, says Sin is Behovely, but All shall be well, and All manner of thing shall be well. Behovely means necessary. Roo told us that. I was listening."

In bolder handwriting, taking the entire next page, comes: "*SO WE CAN KILL OURSELF AND STILL GO TO HEAVEN!*"

But she's here with Gertrude, *wants* to be here with Gertrude. "Interesting question, Gertrude. You'd think this work we do would keep me alert to—what?—the difficult and the comforting. But you're right. I feel a particular need right now, not to lose track of either. *So we can kill ourself and go to heaven.*"

"What?" What, indeed. The words slipped out.

"I'm quoting from her journal."

"Bright Star's."

"Yes, but I've been thinking of her as Raymona. That was her name originally. I want to say, 'That was her *real* name.'"

"The complex topic of naming. Should we go there?"

"No. Someday, maybe. You found something in your desk?"

"In a minute. What was that about suicide and getting to heaven?" Gertrude sits, making no fuss, her energy focused.

"The journaling suggests MPD. Young alters, in this case, I think. If sin is inevitable and all's well, then heaven awaits the suicide."

"Hmm," says Gertrude, clinical and skeptical and forgiving all in one exhalation.

"Exactly. A bit of suspect reasoning, but I can understand." Gertrude nods. They can both understand. "What did you find in your desk?"

"It's a notebook I keep. Quotes, passages. Something about being with you today..." Gertrude looks off to the side, stopped.

"What, Gertrude?"

"I'll just read this. It's more from Julian. One of her 'Showings.' Her visions. The 'he' is Jesus, or God. Jesus, I think." Gertrude opens her notebook.

> *He shewed me a little thing, the quantity of an hazel-nut, in the palm of my hand; and it was as round as a ball. I looked thereupon with eye of my understanding, and thought:* What may this be? *And it was answered generally thus:* It is all that is made. *I marvelled how it might last, for methought it might suddenly have fallen to naught for little. And I was answered in my understanding:* It lasteth, and ever shall for that God loveth it. *And so All-thing hath the Being by the love of God.*

"Again, please." Gertrude reads the passage again. This time Petra is almost prepared for the littleness, for the largeness. For gravity and grace. For dislocation into new comfort. No, it's *old* comfort. The years gyrate backward, blurring, shifting, stabilizing. Tekla, one arm around her daughter, reads from the Bible, the Christmas story. Witold, atheist father, sits across the room, tolerant, a believer in the Spirit of Literature wherever it might be found. She feels her own wet face. Gertrude, ever tactful, gets up and puts the notebook back in her desk drawer.

"You OK?" Gertrude asks, sitting, crossing her legs, arranging her skirt, clean emerald green against white chair cushion, making art. Making space, allowing.

"I feel...I don't know...reconstituted...and strangely relaxed." She looks at the basket. Sweet grass and brown ash. It's such a *little* thing, a wastebasket-size barrel. She has to touch it. She moves to the floor, looks up at Gertrude. "Do you mind?"

"Of course not." She follows the basket's construction with her fingers. The texture of the tiny rope around the middle is harsh, necessary, and comforting. She's self-conscious about acting like a child, but she's...happy. Paradox everywhere. And there's no need to stay on the floor forever. She moves back to the couch, amused, adult, satisfied.

"Interesting day," Gertrude says.

"It certainly is, but what are you doing with the writing of a Christian mystic?"

"Peculiar for a Jew, isn't it? I hope you don't mind. I didn't mean to bring God in, exactly, but it's one of my favorite passages from mystical writings. I hope you don't feel..."

"I don't feel preached to, but how is it that..."

"I majored in Religious Studies in college, along with Psychology. My parents were horrified. I was reading Catholics, *oy vey*! Their horror was greatly satisfying to me and Christianity was such a fascinating system of thought, completely unlike what I was raised with. I suppose even then I loved unusual minds, the Christian mystics being choice specimens."

"Have you ever sorted the pathology from the truly spiritual? Is there such a thing as the truly spiritual?"

"I used to think about that but now I just let myself take what pleases me. I go through periods when I'm doing focused reading, copying out prime bits. Not much lately. As you could see, the notebook was all but lost in that drawer. Something about your situation, how you seem to be right up against the boniest aspects of existence..."

"Boniest. Excellent word, Gertrude. But Julian's...what does she call it?...All-thing...is so tiny, so likely to slip out of existence."

"'...it might suddenly have fallen to naught for little.'"

"I can hardly bear that. It's so *tender*. And then her sense that it's love, in some radical way, that keeps anything at all in existence. And how sufficient that is, that large love. What a thing, to believe in a God like that. Because it is God, after all, that she's talking about."

"Well, yes, she was inside a belief system," Gertrude says.

"Belief systems. I don't take to them. I like the story about the blind men and the elephant, each so sure he knows the whole animal from whatever part he happens to get hold of, the trunk or whatever—a toenail, even, if elephants have toenails. I suppose my own belief is that we're all blind when it comes to spiritual reality. If there's such a thing as spiritual reality."

"I like that story, too. Doesn't it hold for everything? I know I've clung to the hind leg of many a client and imagined I had the whole person," Gertrude says.

"The image of you, taking hold of a client's leg is, well, just a tad incongruous." *How good this is.* She and Gertrude might have stepped barefoot into a fast stream on a sunny day, two girls together, she feels so fresh and, yes, happy.

"Believe me," Gertrude says, "often enough I'm desperately holding on, getting dragged. By the way, your idea for salvaging the treatment of that couple is helping. I let go of being neutral. We made a nice mess last week and thrashed our way out of it, all three of us together. It's the least cool work I've ever done with a couple, and now, finally, I like them. A little."

"You're a brave woman, Gertrude Benstein. I had an impulse to call you and take my idea back. It seemed too risky. Life managed to distract me. I'm glad it worked."

"Me, too," Gertrude says. "But back to the blind men and the elephant. It just occurred to me that the story offers a nice little opportunity for hubris."

"Oh, I see what you mean. If the storyteller and the listener get to feel wiser than any of the blind men who jump to conclusions."

"Yes. And then there's this: at least the blind men are touching an elephant, instead of standing back and wisely understanding that touching can't give complete knowledge."

"Like the mystic? Allowing that experience, letting herself believe it's God, even if it's distorted by a limited belief system?"

"Oh, that's very smart. I wasn't making the link." They sit, letting the idea grow roots. Petra looks at the clock. Almost time to end.

"You gave me something, Gertrude, reading the passage."

"It's evocative, isn't it?"

"I keep seeing the little ball, the size of a hazelnut. I know we need to stop, but when you were reading, I thought of my mother, how she would read..."

"Petra Kalinowski, you're so fine when you let the tears roll. This has been a time, hasn't it? I feel honored."

"Well."

"Really, I've been let in on something special with you, and Ricki —and I must say I don't mind that it's not *my* drama. I just listen and observe and go to play the piano. Tchaikovsky or Mussorgsky. Mozart, if I need the brightness."

"You read poetry and the writings of mystics *and* play classical piano?"

"I'm single, Petra. I have to do something. You're single, too. What do you do?"

"I get involved in terrible human dramas, apparently. And fail to find my writing mind."

"You write? What do you write?"

"I don't know."

"Oh, dear," Gertrude says.

"Right. Oh, dear."

"Time of transition? Something new coming?"

"Maybe. That's a more benign thought than my self-recriminations."

"Good. Self-recriminations are so unpleasant. We do have to stop."

"I know. This has been..."

"Yes," Gertrude says. "It has."

Leaving, out in the brisk air, Petra has the strongest impulse to cup her hands in front of her own belly lest it all slip away. *God-Cup for Sweetly-shredded Certainties.* She puts her hands in her jacket pockets. There are limits to how ridiculous she's willing to be.

*

The world outside has a shape but it's blurred and it changes repeatedly as she, Ricki Harding, drunk inside an old van, is driven once again to the trailer of the woman who was her first lover and who, incidentally, died by her own hand. As they say. For the perfectly good reason that if she didn't do it herself some unnamed illness would do it for her. Perfectly good reason. The driver of this van is good old pal

Lionel, currently in cowboy clothes. Must recite demonstrable and salient facts or might vomit again; important to face facts; some of which are fine. Lionel, for example: one fine fact; definitively finer than the fact of suicide. Note the punctuation. A colon has authority, balance: period over period, never slipping down. Semicolons are less orderly, but necessary at times; when you need to reorient yourself. Never slipping down.

She's seeing her sentences. The mind loves them and thus distracts.

Breathe. Observe facts. Such as Lionel in the front seat, good place to drive from; and Ann Marie Redfeather, not his old lady; and oneself back in the section reserved for those who require the option of lying down; but at the moment sitting up on the mattress—or, to be accurate, on the tattered quilt that covers the mattress—looking through the window at the world, which appears and disappears. Never been drunk before, though excellent father Peter, husband to mother Mary— relationships matter—did once allow a bit of beer, enough to feel it. *Under controlled circumstances, Ricki, just so you know.* It wasn't like this. Why Bitta served beer after beer after beer is a question. Answer: perhaps she saw a need. The world is repeatedly repackaged—nice alliteration—while Lionel drives. With Lionel comes Ann Marie Redfeather, part of the package, it's a package deal, who happens conveniently to be twenty-one years old and therefore someone whose I.D. Bitta could safely request. Because Bitta *knew*, it was obvious she knew, but if Ann Marie acted as group representative, then everything would be dandy should some authority arrive from beyond. Must be authorities beyond Bitta; the world is full of authorities, hierarchies, structures, some of them kind, like facts; the sudden presence of good old Lionel being one of those. A kind fact. Facts and structures. It is imperative, or at least advisable, to get a grip on both; especially when drunk. Besides, that conversation about structure at Bitta's, developing piece by piece, beer by beer, was one of the most interesting in her life. Wait. Something needs remembering. About this Ann Marie person. The handshake. The jolt of inner command, *Watch this lady.* Damn near sobering to remember: unexpected, undeniable confidence embedded in that handshake; also, when the woman talked about art: confidence about art; and some other thing, some Indian thing. The proper designation might be Native American, though she just shrugged when the question came up: didn't care, the good word Indian suiting her fine, though some felt otherwise. Indian or Native American, Ann Marie was Penobscot. That was important. Named Redfeather, not Mitchell or Neptune or Dana, so the question slid out, why Redfeather? This was at Bitta's. Ann Marie, unsober, turned away, looked off, took her time. "A bird. May-May, the redheaded woodpecker—from the old stories—who helped the people in the oldest days. I thought a new name would be..." Voice almost disappearing, but then came a footnote: "I liked the sound. Soft. Redfeather." Wouldn't have been right to ask for more. Even drunk, a person knew that. Hand rubbing now. Allow it. Just for this drive. In the art of Ann Marie Redfeather the structure of the human face is crucial, a fact revealed by Lionel. Who appears a little off balance today, though the only one sober. Sober because of his Promise, his Decision, his Plan. A plethora of capital letters attends the matter. Lionel's decision: to swear off, unbelievably, sex; and, by the way, less important but still significant, mind-altering substances including alcohol. Swearing off those, too. Which Ann Marie revealed, possibly in retaliation for Lionel's revelation about the importance of the structure of the human face in her possibly private art endeavors. Excellent Lionel. Not drunk. Good thing, because someone needs to drive them to the trailer of Bright Star, also apparently called Raymona Weeks, a fact not divulged prior to her death, along with other salient facts not divulged, such as the one about Petra not having agreed to or even known about her designated role as Next Mom.

Of Baby Chippie.

Whose paternal parentage is an interesting question, another matter undivulged, but perhaps beside the point. Best to think it beside the point lest you feel confused about that swell fellow, Raymond. Lest. How literary the drunken brain is. Raymond, whom everyone looks upon as a nice man. Whom: objective case; as if there were any of those left.

The van lurches.

"Sorry. Tried not to hit the crow snacking on roadkill. Succeeded, too. You OK back there, Ricki?"

"Yes, Lionel."

"Good," says Lionel.

Ann Marie says nothing.

Getting the stomach back under control, breathing, breathing.

To continue: luckily, Danny McGuire appears on the scene ready to catch the baby ball and thus a happy ending can be anticipated in this complicated and fateful, but whether it's fate if someone just plain commits suicide is a question, life being a stage of unpredictability, or maybe it's a tale told by an idiot strutting and fretting, I hope not, hello, Shakespeare. Lovely, when one phrase leads to the next and the sentence deserves its period. Who deserves a period more than Shakespeare? Or good old Gertrude Stein, the period being the one and only punctuation mark she had patience for. All question marks, colons, and semicolons looming here in this van—thoughts are structured by them or is it that they, the living punctuation marks, are structured by thoughts?—would not have pleased Stein, who cherished the world as it went by, dissolving into dearness, fresh deep downness, or was that someone else? Hopkins. Gerard Manley. Who had a hard time being a priest. Might be good to lie down for a while. How handy, to have a mattress while being transported drunk to a dead lover's home.

Structure.

That *was* a fine conversation and it was inspired, downright inspired, to pull out the book itself, Ms. Stein's book, *Tender Buttons*, conveniently carried in the back pack from the Bears Den where Lionel showed up like an apparition, but he'd better not be an apparition, to Bitta's in Bangor. The world is replete with alliteration. Bitta's in Bangor. Where the pulling out of the book was done. Necessary: to walk back in, after that time with Stella. Walk into Bitta's and sit down this time in a booth in the far corner accompanied by Lionel and his package-mate Ann Marie, woman of worn and unassuming appearance and startling demonstrations of confidence. Impossible to sit at the table where Stella, crocheting, pretended not to hear about the bloody puddle made by the dripping wrist of her darling dying daughter, which is possibly an excess of alliteration for there is no indication, none, zilch, that Bright Star was regarded as a darling by her mother. Delete the darling. And then the gesture, Stella's, her arms achieving stasis, good word, stasis, holding her crochet-work up and letting slip a strange whimpering sound, prolonged, wild whimpering like a baby animal's cry, most likely a rabbit, desperate, then dropping the crochet hook and the black unfinished thing she calls a doily and the skein of attached yarn and slamming her hands flat against

225

the table and yelling for Bitta. Who came. But Stella didn't come, to Bitta's, today. No matter how much she was needed. Just the sight of her alive, needed. Didn't come.

Sit back up. Breathe. Do not tell Lionel who is careful as the day is long and this day is definitely long that he's driving too fast.

After drinking enough at the booth farthest from where Dave the insurance man gave his bloody description, *double entendre* intended, how educated we're becoming, and farthest from where Stella made her terrible gesture, after that: showing them, Lionel and Ann Marie, how when the structure appears to be most lost, the sentence in *Tender Buttons* was an example, *Listen,* and they listened, but which sentence, an unremembered sentence but no matter, the point could be made with any of them: that when the structure seems to be lost, of language, which is the same, it must be the same, as the structure of thought, which must be the same as the structure of life itself—large thoughts coming with the third or fourth beer—that's when, paradoxically, it's most there, still in place, odd juxtaposition of words by Ms. Gertrude Stein notwithstanding. In fact, unexpected word choice makes the point; the point being that the underlying structure, subject-verb-object, is indestructible, so it's all right, for example, if your first lover is removed from your life and replaced by strange absences and unexpected others.

Which is how she told them the basic facts of current reality: that she recently discovered she was a lesbian, that she had a lover, that she lost the lover; one, two, three; all in a short period of time but it's fine, she told them, insisting, it's absolutely fine. It's just ducky, as the woman herself would say, "Just ducky, Dicki dear, indeed it is." Very fond of alliteration herself, that lady now dead. Then she told them the name. Bright Star. Ann Marie looked up—she'd been looking down, being in the behind-herself mode—looked up and said, "Was she Penobscot?" Which stopped everything. It was and is a confounding question and part of why they're on their way to the trailer. To see the Fallen Goddess, in case it gives a clue to artist Ann Marie. But no, it seems unlikely she was Penobscot, though perhaps spiritually; perhaps she was Penobscot spiritually. "She was awfully white looking." Then, after a silence, "Why do you ask?" And another silence. Then, Ann Marie: "Watawaso." Lionel looking on like a fond uncle, his two drunk and dear girls with him in a bar in Bangor, a thing that after a while he said or perhaps this was only an imaginary transaction. As in psychology class: transaction. Then Ann Marie again: "A performer from the tribe. Watawaso. It means Bright Star. Back a ways. I think she's my relative somehow. Was." And went back behind herself. So it was Lionel who said, "Ann Marie does portraits. Get her to talk about the structure of her portraits. More like chaos to my weak and ignorant eyes, but the intersection of the two, structure and chaos, is perhaps what's playable here." *Playable here* is what he said, and he not even drunk. So then it was structure and chaos and hilarity and sorrow and then Lionel: "When did she die?" About Bright Star, this question, somewhat displaced from context but she, Ricki Harding, college student and near adult, understood and even replied. "Two weeks ago last Saturday." A fact. The other fact, that it was a suicide, not yet divulged. It will take the trailer for that.

"Is this it?" Lionel asks. She can't make meaning of the question.

"Is this the turn, Ricki?"

And oh, God, yes, this is the turn.

Chapter Twenty-one

A gust of wind pushes at Petra's back as she climbs the granite steps. Brittle brown leaves fly. November. These are library steps as they ought to be, wide and shallow, and they bring back the old stone edifice in Winona where she went regularly with Witold and Tekla, this being the Kalinowski family's idea of a good outing. What could be better than heading home, each with an armload of books? Even quite sick, Tekla would carry one or two of her own. "This, I don't give up." Raymond might be working, or not. She hardly knows which to want. The huge door opens out. An elderly woman, somehow familiar, exiting with her own armload of books, says, "Hello, dear. How is that baby of yours? Such a sad thing for a family, a suicide. What was your name again?"

"Petra. Petra Kalinowski." She can't quite...

"I'm Margie, of course, dear. Margie Stokes. You may tell Raymond he was most helpful. I'll soon understand why Galapagos turtles"—she displays the book's cover—"so fascinate the American public." Petra obediently examines two turtles, one of them stretching its head toward a tourist, a curious or friendly turtle, its prehistoric appearance notwithstanding. The other looks away, indifferent, or interested in something other than tourists. The shells are higher, or deeper, than she'd have expected. The legs might be miniature elephant's legs. How comforting: bare, aged matter, undecorated, reliable. Like a large rock beside the Penobscot River, for example. She smiles.

"I'll let you go to Raymond, dear," says Margie Stokes, making her way down the steps, noticeably upright, abruptly gone. Petra remembers now of course: the woman in the back pew with Stella; who has kindly let her know that Raymond is working, but not at the front desk. She heads downstairs to the pay phone in the children's section. There might be work messages and she ought to call Danny. No Raymond down here. She has one message. A male voice, older, probably gay: Patricia's been admitted to BMHI and won't be at her appointment. "I'm so *sorry* to have to tell you, dear..." Bangor Mental

228

Health Institute. A euphemism. The old hospital is a place for the chronically mentally *un*healthy, of which, face it, Patricia is one. The voice continues. Patricia in the form of Patsy, "the *alter*, you know, dear," went to a bar, got belligerent, threatened suicide. The bartender is not forgotten in this report: "*poor man,* Patsy went a little *wild,* if you don't mind my saying so..." Patricia hasn't been to therapy since she tried to burn "heaven" into her arm and stopped because, lo and behold, it hurt. A good moment, but now this. "...she *will* call when she earns points...tomorrow if she's a good girl, which I *certainly* expect...now *quite* miserable...unsteady tummy...sends apologies...does *seem* contrite..." At least Patricia has learned enough to feign contrition instead of raising a ruckus and getting herself locked in the Quiet Room. Maybe she *is* contrite, that would be a change.

So no Patricia today. No more appointments at all. Freedom. She looks around. A serious young reader stands quietly, intent on what he's pulled from the shelf. In the far corner a scuffle erupts. A matronly woman materializes, restoring order with impressive efficiency. No Raymond. She dials Danny's number. "How is she?"

"Fussy, but she had some good hours today."

"I'm afraid to go down there."

"Better come, then."

"I have an idea. It came while I was dialing, tell me if it's imprudent."

"OK." She can hear Chippie, little squawks of complaint. She'd rather hear contented cooing. She *is* afraid to see this baby.

"I thought I might ask Raymond if he'd like a ride down. His truck's still there, right?"

Just a hint of a pause, then Danny says, "Has to happen some time."

"Oh, Danny."

"What about you? Are you all calmed down about him now?" Hint of a pause on her part. More than a hint. "Petra?"

"No."

"Well. So there are two of us."

"This is stupid. We don't even know him."

"Yes, we do. Bring him." She puts the phone back on its hook, turns around. There's Raymond, down on his knees at the lowest crammed shelf, helping an angry blond preschooler look for the book she had that *other* time.

"This one?"

"No." She's scornful.

"This one?"

"I *told* you, two red boats."

"You're absolutely right, you told me. What about this one?" She scowls, but accepts the book. "Anything else I can do for you?" The child stares at him, the book tight against her chest as if he might steal it, then shakes her head. Her mother gives an apologetic look, says thank you. Watching the little girl march away, her mother trailing her, Raymond looks amused. He turns and sees Petra. He smiles.

"Nice work," she says, nodding toward the departing backs. *He's not sorry to see me.*

"Thanks. I don't come down here much, but Mrs. Knowles needed a break and here I was and here was this tyke with a definite idea of what she wanted."

"You're good at it."

"Thanks."

"I just talked to Danny. I thought...I guess your truck is still down there."

"I need to deal with that," he says.

"I'm going down."

"Oh."

"I could wait until you get off work."

"It's more than an hour. 5:00. I hate to make you wait."

"No, it's all right. I have some books to get and I can sit and read. I don't mind. Really."

Mrs. Knowles—apparently it's she—approaches, thanks Raymond for the break, goes off with the next young patron in need. Raymond turns back to Petra. "I'd be obliged. I have some things to ask you. It would be a help, to have the chance. And my truck. I have to get back upstairs but I'll..."

She can't ignore the sensations spreading through her as he climbs the steps looking so thoroughly set inside himself, so permanent, this man whose sister just killed herself. But it was only courtesy to offer a ride, wasn't it?

230

When she approaches the front desk, Raymond closes his book and sets it aside. *Life and Traditions of the Red Man*. The man who doesn't know his tribe reads Native literature. He checks out her books. She says she'll be back at the desk at 5:00.

"That'll work." He looks at her. What happened Sunday, how they were helpless together, how they turned Chippie over to Danny, is in his eyes. If he were someone else, he'd use words. She doesn't want him to be someone else.

On the second floor she finds an unoccupied table, old, dark, large, rectangular, a proper library table beside a big window. Outside, Bangor: Franklin Street angling off Harlow, pedestrians, a stream of cars and trucks, the city parking lot. Above the street, above the parking lot, above the low commercial buildings, above the half-stripped November trees, a good gray sky is alive with gentle light. She meant to read philosophy, not religion, when she picked up Weil's *Gravity and Grace*. She intended to rejuvenate her own labor-loving mental equipment. She wouldn't have said she had a real need, that she was *looking* for something. But there was that day on the rock when she definitely needed something firm—or stern?—to set her mind down into. Chippie had entered her life posing as an occasional visitor in need of occasional care. Helga had arrived, having shed the role of daily parent. But Raymona Weeks had not yet killed herself. It was a particular pocket of time. Just a dip in, she'd thought, to see what would happen if she exposed her mind to philosophy again.

Dip. The word brings Stein's carafe to mind. DWELL was reading *Tender Buttons*. There it was on the first page, the term traceable to *gharafa*, to dip, and then something about a spectacle...*nothing strange...an arrangement...a single hurt color...not ordinary...not unordered in not resembling*. Bright Star was still part of DWELL, alive and irritating. Chippie was a baby in her mother's lap, generally bright-eyed, looking from woman to woman to woman as conversation proceeded apace, but at the final meeting Bright Star turned strange and Chippie slept too much and then came the suicide and Bright Star's will and her own sentimental acquiescence: yes, she'd take this baby, of course, why not?

Two weeks of parenting, a mere dip in. She remains Petra Kalinowski, not meant for motherhood, and Danny McGuire gets a baby.

231

A new arrangement, *not unordered in not resembling*. In fact, quite ordered, quite fitting and proper. Can this be true? Yes, because Danny's ready. Beautiful George, sick and dying, readied him. Chippie's going to be fine. Surely this is true.

As for herself, it's time for her mind. She chose to start this rejuvenation project with Simone Weil, Jewish philosopher. Who was also, by the way, a Christian mystic. Behind philosophy, lurking, not innocent, not even truly hidden, was mysticism. Gertrude, another Jew, has routed out the half-hidden thing by rooting around in a messy drawer and coming up with Julian of Norwich to read aloud, to give comfort, during a *supervision* session. It's so unlikely it has to be honored.

She looks at the books she just checked out. Weil's *Waiting for God* will wait, patient as its title. She's drawn to Julian, opens *Showings*. On the first page is an old vocabulary. *Trinity. Incarnation. Passion.* How unexpectedly familiar the words are. And of course they are. Tekla insisted, Witold acquiesced, and she, Petra, is therefore the product of a Catholic education. "His dearworthy Passion...His precious crowning with thorns...the scourging of His tender body...plenteous shedding of His blood." Julian reveals a compulsion to join herself to all of this, to become ill, to suffer. Sounds sick, thinks Petra the therapist, but in her latest and least recognizable incarnation, newborn in Gertrude's office, she feels an irresistible attraction to the words, as if vitality danced behind the gore, pulsing stronger than the images or the dogma. She reads on. She dips in, here, there, fascinated. This document, after all, contains the ball of All-thing, the assertion that All Shall Be Well. She likes the voice, the often muscular prose, the evidence of a working philosophical mind stirring visions to meaning. Julian writes theological philosophy, *religious* philosophy, but somehow this isn't an obstacle. Both poles are held. Life is steeped in the acid of suffering; still, all shall be well. Sin and pain abound; nevertheless, all manner of thing shall be well. Not just in heaven, either. Here. Here and now, because the ground of being is so reliable, so *courteous*. Vision after vision unfolds and she samples bits of each. Julian gets a visitor, a priest, who asks how she's doing. She is, after all, supposed to be dying, having gotten her longed-for illness. She answers the priest: "I've been raving." So. The saint is a liar, taking the most profound experience of her life and labeling it insane. Petra's heart is wrenched: the pain of it. Though it might *be* insanity, thinks therapist Petra. This is a thin, rote response. Petra the seeker—can this be? that she's now a seeker? seeking what? surely not medieval Christianity—has been *inside* with Julian, striving, enduring, adventuring with God. Julian knows what she's done. It was an act of bad faith—the Sartrean language is as good as any—to doubt one's own truth; to distort or deny or disown it. In Julian's terms this is sin. Writing about it twenty years later she is still contrite. The next vision, the final one, is all reassurance. From the Lord, no less: "Wit it now well: it was no raving." In other words: Julian, my dear, the visions were real. Well, good, thinks Petra and lets herself breathe fully again. As advised by her courteous Lord, Julian will now fasten the visions firmly in her heart and keep them there for the rest of her life.

She looks at her watch. *5:20.*

"I'm so *sorry.*"

"No problem," says Raymond. "Gave me a few minutes for my own reading." She knows he's been waiting, though. He'd have been ready at exactly 5:00. Like Julian's Lord, he'd be courteous.

They drive through Bangor's little version of rush hour, hitting the red lights on Main Street with predictable regularity. Neither speaks. The stopping and starting is rhythmic, not irksome. Petra feels strangely comfortable. She believes Raymond feels the same way. At the third red light she says, pro forma, "I hope you're not in a hurry."

"No," he says, as expected. They pass through Winterport and both look toward the wide Penobscot, gray under gray sky. Lovely, thinks Petra. The river, the sky, this silence. Finally, Raymond speaks. He's been worrying about Ricki.

Petra sighs and agrees: "She thinks you're Chippie's father."

"I know. I saw that. I can't figure what to do about it."

"I told her you're not. Not the father. She didn't really believe me."

"You told Danny, too, which was a favor to me. Thanks for trying, with Ricki. You've been doing my work."

"Maybe it was my work. I'm the reader of Raymona's writings. I have a kind of proof. Which I told Danny, but not Ricki. We should talk about that. She doesn't know about the notebooks. Maybe we should tell her. Or maybe not. But as for your not being Chippie's father, my word is marginally better than yours." She looks to make sure he's not offended. He nods, undisturbed, but his mind is elsewhere. She waits.

"Her writing convinces *you* I'm not the father?"

"Her way isn't always straightforward," she says. He offers the rueful smile she expects. "She gets it across: Chip is the father. Not that I needed to be convinced, Raymond. It wasn't a question for me."

"It could be. You know enough." She hesitates. She's been treated, courtesy of his sister's journals, to the story of his refusal to become father to the Savior Child. Should she...? But he says, "There's a whole list of things we should maybe talk to Ricki about." Saved. No need to bring on fresh embarrassment. It's enough that he had to disclose adolescent incest the first time he talked to her.

"She believes that Raymona—I hope you don't mind if I call her that—had a fatal illness."

"It's fine, you calling her Raymona. Nice, in fact. I didn't know that version of things, the illness, until Ricki told me the other day. I had to think it through—about the consequences—before I said anything to her."

"I know. It would rip away a protection to raise doubts. Are you OK, talking about this?"

"It might do me good. And we need to."

"Yes, we do. I haven't given enough thought to Ricki." She sighs.

"It's not easy to think about her."

"I've been too wrapped up in my own dramas."

"Dramas that got imposed on you," he says. She looks at him. Is he angry with Raymona? They've passed the apple orchard. She speeds up because of the cars behind but she'd rather prolong this drive. So much to talk about. Something else, too, makes her want more time with this man. She's deciding it's got nothing to do with sex.

"I played my part," she says. "In the drama."

"I suppose, but Raymona sort of wrote the script, or at least the beginning of it. She gave you a big part. Complicated."

"What's it like for you, Raymond? Now, I mean." She hadn't planned to ask. She thought she'd be watching her words.

"Blank," he says, not hesitating. "And sad. Maybe not knowing what to wrap myself around is the main thing. I don't mean physically."

"You wrapped your life around hers."

"I'm learning that I did."

"I did that with Anya. My little girl."

"You mean when she was with you?"

"When I was doing the daily parenting, that was one way. Then she was with Marian, her second mother, and it changed...and then again after she died, yes. From when I knew I was carrying her, there was her presence. Or her absence. Chippie got mixed into that. I'm sorry."

"Don't be sorry."

"It's a powerful thing, when another person is at the center," she says.

"I'll need to find a different way of living, with Raymona gone. My mother can't be it."

"How is Stella?"

"She's avoiding me, but I have a key to her place. I've gone in, just to check. Her doilies are where they should be."

"Her doilies. You mean that crochet-work she does?"

"Oh. I guess Ricki was the one I talked to about that. Stella makes herself give it up if she takes a drink. Goodwill gets the doilies. I suppose they don't look much like doilies anymore. They used to lie flat."

"Stella's not your everyday person. I guess no one is." She pauses, thinks how the man in her passenger seat is certainly not an everyday person. She says, "I noticed what you're reading." Raymond is at this moment holding *Life and Traditions of the Red Man*, but is he even aware of that? This should be an awkward silence. It's not.

Finally, apparently calm, apparently willing, he says, "Raymona wanted to be the Indian in the family."

This is so easy. How patient and unworried she feels. How unusual it is, to feel this way. "So now that she's gone you have a kind of freedom about that? About being Indian?"

"That might be a way to put it. To tell you the truth, I'm not sure what it is. Someone gave me a book and I read it and that book told me about this one and I'm reading it. Following."

Following. She's doing the same thing. Following, through reading. "You saw the books I checked out." This might be presumptuous. He checks out hundreds of books. He probably doesn't notice.

"They looked like religious books. Is that what you're interested in? Religion?"

"Not usually. I'm...I'm following something, too. A friend read something to me..."

"I don't mean to..." They cross over the dam at Frankfort. She follows the turn in the road at twenty miles per hour, good citizen, and parks on the shoulder and turns the engine off.

"Raymond, I think something's happening here. I mean...I think we should be friends...or something. Is there a spiritual aspect to your book? Are the traditions in the title spiritual traditions?"

He looks at her for a while, then says, "There are ways you're like her."

She says, "Raymona."

He says, "Yes."

She takes a deep breath. "OK." She starts the car and makes a U-turn. He looks at her, interested. "We're going to the trailer, to get the crib," she says. "Then we'll go to Danny's. He needs the crib and we need more time for this drive. You're right that there's a list of things we need to talk about, about Ricki, and I'm going to tell you about my books, the ones I checked out. This might be the strangest way I've ever gotten to know a person, this way I'm getting to know you. Is it all right with you, backtracking to get the crib?"

"Sure," he says. "Tell me the items on your list. About Ricki."

She laughs. "That's it? On with business?"

"You're the one who set the agenda." He produces a subtle grin. Is she wrong? *Is* this sexual attraction?

"All right," she says. "My list. Four things. One, Raymona left writings; from which item all others follow."

"OK," he says.

"Two, Raymona appears to have had multiple personality disorder, or she was so entranced by the concept that she lived as though she had it."

"That's an interesting way to put it."

"Three, Raymona had no fatal illness."

"The writings prove that?"

"They do."

"That's got to be the worst one. For Ricki. What else?"

"You're not the father."

"That's not very important. When you look at the rest of the list, I mean."

"Anything to add?"

"I don't think so. I'd like to be friends, Petra. It would mean a lot to me." Unexpectedly, as if it's a natural phenomenon having little to do with her, she finds herself crying. She keeps driving, wiping her eyes for adequate vision.

"God, Raymond, I feel so crazy these days. There's a word in my profession for this. I'm labile. It means I cry easily, and often. It's not my usual...do you really want to be friends?"

"I never had the experience before, of being approached like this. Maybe I don't even know what you mean, but it's fine. It feels fine." She looks over at him, several times. She has to keep her eye on the road, and they're almost at the turn for the trailer.

She says, "Why?"

"Why?"

"Yes, why? Why does it feel so fine? I mean, do you know something I don't know?"

"Maybe we just got tossed together. Or it's Raymona's doing. Well, it *is* her doing, but you changed the script on her so it's not exactly..." He stops. They're turning into the road. It won't be long before they're inside the trailer. Will that be unbearable for this poor man? What is she *doing*? But Raymond goes on. "She had an instinct she could draw on at times. Other times, not."

"Do you have the instinct, Raymond?" Long silence. They're almost at the trailer.

"I don't know."

"Oh, dear," she says, because there's a van at the trailer. "Is this right? Should someone be here?"

"No." He sighs deeply and opens the car door and gets out. He climbs the steps and she follows him, thinking how they've gotten no further with their task. When they see Ricki, whenever and wherever they see Ricki, what will they tell her? And who's here and should they be frightened? Someone's broken into this trailer and here they are, entering as if this were just one more task to do. As if nothing could harm them. Except that Raymond's still carrying his book, so maybe they need it, as protection, but what a superstitious, frivolous, unfitting thought. The book has been in his hand through the whole drive and remains there, forgotten, while his mind is on the trailer and who might be in it. An appropriately focused mind. Whereas her own has been jarred off kilter by the sudden danger they might be in, by the contrast to the moments before when she felt so profoundly and unexpectedly comfortable, so *safe*.

Raymond opens the door to the trailer. Ricki stands there smelling of alcohol and toothpaste, holding a small ceramic sculpture, a contorted little man sitting on a turtle. She says to Raymond, as if he's just come in from another room, as if they've been together all day, "Did you know his name was Patchwork?" Raymond offers no immediate response. Ricki hiccups and says, "Hi, Petra. Meet Patchwork."

Chapter Twenty-two

He can feel the adrenaline, how prepared he was to take a stand, tell whoever it was they had to leave. Couldn't let them stay even if they were kids, homeless. Too many of Raymona's art things around. But it's only Ricki with Patchwork, one of his favorites. Ricki looks blurred and smells of drink. Poor kid. Is she staying here now? He'd be glad to know the trailer hasn't been empty. Hasn't been *lonely*, is what he really thinks. "Come in, come in," Ricki says. He has to smile at her playing hostess. "More glasses, we have company," she yells. Two heads crane at the kitchen door, a white-haired kid and an Indian girl. The heads disappear. He and Petra sit on the couch. Ricki stands behind the crib, elbows propped on the headboard. Inside the crib, like orderly companions, are the little art objects Raymona had lined up on the floor. They've been put to bed.

Petra says, "Is it OK if I use the phone? Is it still hooked up?" She's asking both of them, looking back and forth between Ricki and him. She doesn't know who's in charge here, which is amusing because she seems to know most things, this lady who wants to be friends.

"In the kitchen," they say, Ricki and himself together. Ricki starts to giggle and it gets out of control. It's not a contagious thing, she's by herself in this.

"Ricki," Petra says. Ricki's crying hard by the time Petra gets to her. They stand at the crib, Petra holding Ricki, not making her phone call. The other two come in, the boy carrying a tray he recognizes, Raymona's Minnie Mouse tray. Cookies on it. Two glasses. Cans of beer.

"Um," the boy says, looking around. He goes to the old stereo console, puts the tray down. Then he's standing in the middle of the room alone.

Beside the couch is where the girl and he, Raymond Weeks, are standing, recognizing the Indian in each other with no words. This has happened before. He'll meet one and there's a feeling. They don't see his white part. Petra's busy with Ricki, so it's up to him. "I'm Raymond. Raymond Weeks." He reaches out to shake her hand.

"Ann Marie Redfeather." She gives a warm smile, a little too warm. She's been drinking, too. "This is Lionel," she says.

Lionel comes forward. "Pleased to meet you, Raymond. Sorry to hear about your sister. Ricki told us." Something sweet about him. Ricki's been with friends her age, at least she has that. She finishes her cry, blows her nose.

Petra gets introduced and excuses herself to call Danny. Lionel offers the tray around. Raymond takes a cookie, declines beer, but he's thirsty. He goes to the kitchen for water. Petra's hanging up the phone. "Ricki's not so fine," she says.

"No. What about Chippie?"

"Sleeping at the moment." They go back to the living room.

"So, Raymond, how've you been?" Ricki asks. She's back behind the crib, leaning on it with her elbows. Her tone is not entirely friendly.

Lionel says, "Are you sure you want to do this, Ricki?"

"What, Lionel? What am I doing?"

"OK," Lionel says. "It's your business." He turns to Raymond. "You can see she's drunk, right?" The kid is trying to protect Ricki, but she ignores that. She's looking at him, Raymond, half-pleading, half-accusing.

"What, Ricki?"

"Are you or are you not Chippie's father?"

He almost wishes he could lie, give her a target. "I'm not her father." Ricki looks at Petra.

"I suppose you'll back him up, dear loyal Petra. How's a girl supposed to know what's true?" It worries him to see her bitter and helpless like this.

Petra just says, "Oh, Ricki," but she closes her eyes for a minute. By the time she has them open she's made her decision. She looks at him. He understands, nods. They'll talk to Ricki. They can't do it while she's intoxicated, though.

"I'll make some coffee," he says. "Will this be OK with Danny?"

"Yes." She explains to the others, "We just stopped by to get the crib." Ricki looks down into the crib with its contents and starts to cry again. "They can stay there for now, Ricki. It'll be all right," Petra says softly.

"OK," Ricki says. She sounds young.

He gets up to go to the kitchen. He's amazed when the others follow him. They sit around the table while he makes coffee, Petra keeping the conversation going, getting the young folks talking about how they came to know each other. He's glad to hear there's a real history with the boy, something solid for Ricki. The girl, Ann Marie, wanders off and comes back with his book. *Life and Traditions*. He must have brought it in with him, left it on the couch. He wasn't aware.

"You're reading this," she says.

"Yes."

She looks at him for a long time, no words. Tears run down her cheeks. The others must be watching but it doesn't bother him. He feels sorrow for all the human pain. This has been happening, sorrow coming over him.

"I have a quest," Ann Marie says. He nods. He understands. He's not pretending.

"She can't go home," Ricki says. "To Indian Island."

"I can," Ann Marie says. "Just not yet."

"She has to stay with white people a while longer," Lionel says.

"It's OK to pick up the book," Ann Marie says. "To have it in my hand, I mean. Because I didn't do anything to acquire it, it just came. And you're OK, Raymond Weeks. When someone comes close just by chance, I can look at them. It's fine."

She wouldn't be talking like this if she were sober, but he's glad for her, that she can say it. He can feel the pressure she's been under, keeping herself to whites. Strange quest, but maybe she knows her own track. Petra pours coffee, offers sugar, apologizes for the lack of whitener. No one cares about that. She gets them into the living room, in charge now. He likes her like this. When she cried in the car he was uneasy. Not as much as he would have thought, though. Maybe they can be friends. Or something, as she said.

"I only talk about it in special circumstances," Ann Marie says. She's putting her words into the silence where everyone is drinking coffee. The main thing is to get Ricki sober enough.

Lionel says, "Her quest, she means. It's a private thing." Protective Lionel, who doesn't seem to be drunk. From their place on the couch he and Petra, the older generation, nod. The young ones sit on the floor, Ricki in the middle. Solidarity.

Ann Marie's quest is almost over, after two years. She's stayed away from the Island, lived among white people, observed their faces, painted them. An artist. Like Raymona, or maybe not like Raymona. She's explaining how she needed a female quest, something different from going to a wilderness. Or it was a wilderness she went to, white and urban. As she drinks her coffee and gets some sobriety she comments that maybe she's been away too long. She wouldn't have expected to pour this out, and to people she never met before. She was taken by surprise. Ricki didn't tell them he was Indian. She's embarrassed. She apologizes.

"You should see her work," Lionel says.

"It's not all white faces," Ann Marie says. This is for his benefit, justifying herself to another Indian, or he fears it is. "I did a Molly Molasses series." At least he knows who that is. *Feared by all she frowned upon.* He almost says it, but Lionel jumps in.

"You should see her Molly faces. Cheek bones end up everywhere, and pulsing eyes. A pointed hat takes over sometimes, just takes over the whole thing. Still, the old shaman lady is there, you can see her, her ancient self, tension between old truth and Ann Marie's mind, scrambling toward the future."

"Lionel, shut up," Ricki says. She must see it too: Ann Marie's shrinking inward.

"Ricki's mad at everybody, not just you, Raymond," Lionel says, not upset. "Everybody except Ann Marie. She can't think of anything to be mad at Ann Marie about yet."

"You have reason to be mad," Raymond says to Ricki.

"But he's not Chippie's father," Petra says. "Ricki, we have some things to tell you. Now or later. Do you think this is the right time?" Ricki looks scared, but Petra sounds clear and strong.

Ann Marie enters in. "Your sister was good. Her work. It's good."

It's a quick turn, but Raymond goes with it. "I'm glad to hear that. I didn't know how to tell."

"She was good." Ann Marie sounds different. Sober. He can see what's she's doing, engineering a little time for Ricki to think about what

Petra asked. These young people take care of each other. It's a relieving thing to see. He's sitting in Raymona's living room, feeling all right. He didn't expect this. Ann Marie keeps talking to him. She looks at the book lying on the couch between him and Petra. "There's a sentence in *Life and Traditions* about art, or that's how I think about it. The First Mother says, 'I have brought all the color of life on my brow.'"

"I don't remember that part. Maybe I didn't get to it yet, or didn't know to pick it out. It's beautiful." Was this the right thing to say? What he remembers about the Mother is that she brought love and then talked about her body getting eaten. The book keeps two hands out, one for beauty and comfort, the other for harsher things. It heats and freezes his blood and there's no predicting what the next sentence will do. He's afraid Ann Marie Redfeather needs him to be more Indian than he is but she just nods.

"You'll get there," she says, looking right at him. He'd like to close his eyes against this, but then he only wants to sit, let her look. She turns to Ricki, though. "We could take a walk, Lionel and me, so you can learn what you need to know—if that's what you want." Ricki and Petra look at each other.

"No," Ricki says. "It's best if you're here. Tell me, Petra."

*

Ricki lies on Bright Star's bed holding Patchwork. There was no fatal illness. It was an ordinary suicide she helped with. She's supposed to get used to that. Ann Marie is wrapped around her, soft arms, soft belly to back up into. She backs up further to get more. Lionel sits in the little chair, their chaperone. He loves the idea that they need a chaperone, that he's it. Is Bright Star watching? *Fine, Ricki. Fine with me.* The bedroom window is a blank dark rectangle, shiny. Did she wash it before she killed herself? Maybe she couldn't help it, all the ways she neglected truth. The ceramics are back on the floor in the living room. Raymond and Petra took the crib with them. She believes the things they told her. She could read the writing for proof but the thought freezes her mind. Another thing she's supposed to get used to: her first lover had a mental illness. Multiple Personality Disorder, for example. "Maybe," Petra said. "We can't be sure it was MPD." Raymond: nodding. A team, the two of them handing out reality, helping her through. Kindness all around. Ann Marie and Lionel holding on to her, one each side. All of them on the floor, even Petra and Raymond once they started telling the truth, which is that she didn't do one single thing to stop a suicide that didn't need to happen. "Not your fault." Petra and Raymond putting that in, over and over. Lionel and Ann Marie holding onto her. *Not your fault, Ricki Dicki Darlin'*. There was evidence. Everything looks like evidence now. All the shaking and sobbing and how, after a spell like that, she'd quote Eliot. "Humankind cannot bear very much reality, Ricki Dicki. So says good old T. S." Or she'd go suddenly bright—too bright—like a five hundred watt bulb. And the same quote. "Humankind cannot bear very much reality, can it, Ricki Harding?" Mocking and hard-edged, then. Was that different personalities? Maybe. Was Bright Star Who Smokes an "alter"? Maybe. She sighs.

"At least Raymond's not Chippie's father," she says.

"Right," say Lionel and Ann Marie. Ann Marie's hand smoothes her hair. So kind. She closes her eyes. Lionel fidgets. She opens her eyes. The night light low on the wall shows him looking around and around, his feet all over the place. He's on the low padded chair with the rose-patterned material, a piece of furniture that doesn't fit the trailer. It could be from Stella, who got it from her own mother. There could be something passed down like that. Lionel needs a break. "Take a break, Lionel. He can take a break, can't he, Ann Marie?" She can feel Ann Marie nodding, yes.

"I just have to pee," Lionel says and gets up and leaves.

Maybe Ann Marie has to pee, too. "Do you have to take a break, too?"

"No, I'm fine. Go to sleep."

"It was nice of Raymond, wasn't it? To offer you guys the trailer." She *is* starting to feel sleepy. How late is it? Does that matter?

"It was more than nice. We owe him. We won't abuse the privilege."

"I know."

"We'll be out of here as soon as student housing comes through."

"It's good you don't have to live in the van. I had the idea I'd ask Gertrude if you could stay with me in my room but this is better."

"That was generous, Ricki. You're almost asleep. Go to sleep." When she wakes up, Ann Marie is gone. Lionel is asleep in the little chair. How does he do that? It has no arms to hold him. She gets up. The bathroom door is open. Ann Marie is sitting on the floor with Fallen Goddess. There's the bathtub, where it happened. Ann Marie doesn't hear her, or doesn't seem to. Everything that seems might be untrue. She stands in the doorway watching tears run down Ann Marie's face, a shining trail lighted by the night light. Ann Marie is beautiful, her shining tears are beautiful. Maybe this is what it's like to go to church, this quiet deep feeling. The floor, when she sits, is cold and hard, separate. "Hi," Ann Marie whispers, not turning toward her.

Chapter Twenty-three

"You get it this time."

"Fair enough." Petra watches Raymond from the couch in Danny's living room as he goes to the kitchen where the black rotary phone sits on its rough wooden stand. How agreeable he is, how sweet. It's 3:00 a.m. This will be Danny again. He'll say the doctors still don't know what Chippie's problem is, it might be a while, they should go home unless they really want to wait, Chippie will be all right, they'll both be all right. Raymond's voice will at least provide a small difference in the routine. "We could make breakfast...I'll tend Chippie, you can sleep...no, I'm off tomorrow, or I guess it's today now...Petra had jumper cables...yes, more prepared in that department than we were...got the crib up...maybe the little one will recognize it...they know what they're doing, don't worry...letting you hold her in between times?" Coming back, he says, "They're narrowing it down, almost sure it's just an ear infection. Might be a stranger type than most kids get."

"That would fit," she says.

"With the strange beginning to her life."

"Yes."

"You still mad at Raymona?"

"Apparently." They've been talking for hours, talking and waiting. There was a note taped to the door when they arrived. Another note. This one frightened her. Danny had tried to soften it: "Just a precaution, I'm sure she'll be fine." Still: "She's too hot for my comfort." Danny doesn't panic easily. She should have given him the trailer's number, but fever wasn't even an issue when she called, and they couldn't have left Ricki. No use going up to Bangor now, they'd probably pass Danny and Chippie coming home. She *hopes* they'll be coming home. She's been running around this circle all night. Here with Raymond, though, even worried and waiting, she feels a hum of comfort. She can hardly believe how much ground they've covered. Witold and Tekla, Minnesota and San Francisco, Anya and Marian. How she became a therapist who paints houses and, in the off season, writes. Writes what? Ah, good question, Raymond. As for him, the poor man decided as a teenager that he had to guard against becoming a child molester because when he was young, six, seven, eight years old, he complied, did the sexual things his stepfather forced him to do to his little sister. So he "knew" from the moment Raymona told him she was pregnant that he'd have to keep clear of the baby. So she had to ask, couldn't keep herself from the questions. Which he of course answered. No, he never wanted to touch a child sexually, the idea made him feel sick, but he'd wanted the sex with Raymona when they were teenagers. It was Raymona's idea but he was just as interested once they got started. He liked how she had things to teach him, so didn't that make him a danger? It gave her great and illicit satisfaction that the adolescent incest was in fact Raymona's idea, but she kept prudently quiet about this. Raymond made decisions, set up guidelines, after he shot Bede. Always give a true and complete answer to a direct question. No smoking. No drinking. No bodybuilding. No sex. He felt unfit for a normal sex life and anything else was unthinkable. She didn't ask if homosexuality qualified as normal. She would, though. She's inclined to facilitate a little something between him and Danny, being clear about her own feelings now. She might love this man, but sexuality would be irrelevant to that.

When Raymona got pregnant, Raymond repeated, he knew right away he'd have to stay away from the baby. Had he ever been aroused, she asked, even by the *thought* of this baby, or any other? Or any child of any age? Well, no. But what if? *If*, she said, *then*: he wouldn't act on the feelings, he'd talk to someone, he'd decide what he needed to do.

"I made the fence around myself too high, is what you're saying."

"That's what I'm saying." Now she's heard him offer to take care of Chippie, give Danny a chance to sleep. That fast, the turnaround. Such solid and unlikely mental health. His biological father must have had superb genes.

"You heard what I said to Danny," he says.

"That you'd stay here and take care of Chippie. Make you nervous?"

"No. It felt good. Did it make *you* nervous?'

"It felt good to me, too, Raymond."

"Thank you."

"Hey, it's in my interest."

"You mean the more Chippie gets from other folks, the less guilty you'll feel."

"Yes."

"I'd say I'm sorry about this whole mess except that it got the little one to Danny," he said.

"He sound OK?"

"Tired, but he has faith they'll find a way to help her."

"Where were we, before he called?"

"You know where we were, Petra."

"Oh. Right." The books. They'd both acknowledged reluctance. She doesn't feel ready. "One question, Raymond."

"One stalling question permitted."

"Why no bodybuilding?" He doesn't answer immediately. If he vowed always to answer direct questions, does this mean he can't protect against trespassing? Is she trespassing? But she feels fine, waiting for his answer. This odd calm, even with Chippie in the Emergency Room.

"Of all the things I decided," he says, "this is the hardest to make sense of, even for myself. Maybe I decided I should give it up, like we gave up things during Lent when we were Catholic, but I don't think I liked bodybuilding, so it couldn't have been much of a sacrifice. Maybe I was worried about my older self, about violence. I don't remember, is the truth. I'd say it was about accepting myself in my natural form, but that might be what I made of it as years passed."

"We do that."

"Make things different after the fact."

"Yes. You were Catholic? Temporarily?"

"Bede got on a tear about it. Then he got off it. Oh. I just remembered. After Catholicism came calisthenics, with him being the drill sergeant. Lasted about two weeks. He was a tiny guy and didn't really want us strong. He started to work out himself. We weren't invited to join, not that we wanted to. It could be I turned against bodybuilding then. That could be part of it."

They sit for a while before she points to his book and says, "Who starts, you or me?"

"I never had a conversation quite like this one, Petra. Is this what therapy's like?" She catches the glint in his eye. Teasing.

248

"OK. That's *your* one permitted stalling question. No, this is not what therapy is like because this is not designed for the good of one of us with the other at-your-service. Just for that, you start. Tell me about *Life and Traditions of the Red Man*."

*

They sit, Ann Marie looking at the sculpture, Ricki trying to see what Ann Marie sees. Ideas about the Goddess might need revision. Everything to do with Bright Star might need revision. "Ann Marie. What are you seeing?"

Ann Marie looks at her, then says, "Let's find out what Lionel's doing." Lionel is asleep on Bright Star's bed. They stand in the doorway and watch like parents. Here he is, their sleeping boy. Ann Marie takes her hand, leads her to the living room. They sit on the couch, one at each end, leaning their backs against the arm rests, facing each other. It was easier not facing each other. In bed it was easier, or when there was the Goddess to look at. "Ricki..."

"What?"

"There's something..."

"What, Ann Marie?" Silence and tension.

"Ricki, Lionel..." *Lionel has AIDS.* She can't stand to hear it. What a cowardly thought, and not even true.

"Just tell me, Ann Marie." But she's almost crying. Ann Marie moves toward her, puts her arms around her.

"No. No, Ricki. He's all right. He's fine. It's just...he had a rough time." She's crying hard but with Ann Marie instead of Petra, sober instead of drunk, so maybe it won't last forever. *Nothing's wrong, Lionel's all right.* If she doesn't stop crying she'll get Ann Marie's shirt soaked and snotty. She stops. Ann Marie moves back to her end of the couch.

A rough time. How could Lionel not have a rough time? She feels so irritable she could spit. "He did so much stupid sex, Ann Marie."

"He *did* do stupid sex, but he never got HIV. Miracle, huh? He got into a bad situation, though. He wants me to tell you." Pause.

"So tell me." Through grit teeth. She shouldn't be taking it out on the messenger.

249

"It's not as bad as AIDS. There was a guy into...control...and sadomasochism and...well...more."

"More?"

"Abuse."

"Somebody *hurt* Lionel?"

"He's ashamed, so he asked me..." Ann Marie is back next to her, holding her, apparently she needs to be held. These *damn* tears. "It's over, Ricki. It's really over."

"I can't stand it, Ann Marie," she says, blowing her nose. "No one should hurt Lionel."

"I know, Ricki. I know."

"He's so..."

"Innocent?"

"Yeah." They look at each other and laugh because obviously their friend Lionel is not exactly entirely irreproachably innocent and next they're kissing, gently, so gently it might not be happening, but it is.

They stop. Ann Marie says, "Um...I didn't mean to..."

It's Ricki's turn to smooth back some hair. "It's all right, Ann Marie."

Ann Marie moves away, but not far, and says, "Well..."

Ricki says, "That was unexpected, huh?"

"Yeah. Sure was."

"Tell me more about Lionel. Did you know this creep?" *Lionel's all right now. We can talk about him.* Which is easier than talking about what just happened. What did just happen, though?

"I met him," Ann Marie says. Her eyes are full of what they just did. They both know what they did. They kissed. "He came into the bar where I was working. I saw them together a couple of times. It didn't last long. Lionel got out fast, as these things go." She smiles a little about Lionel getting out. Inside the smile is shyness, about kissing.

"What did he look like, who was he?" *It's all right, Ann Marie. I think it's all right.*

"Oh, just some guy. White. I don't know. Ordinary. His name was Mitch. He did hurt Lionel, but then he'd kneel down and beg forgiveness. Lionel talked to me about it when the bar was empty, said he couldn't hold back when a person was crying and begging. Mitch would end up bringing flowers—right into the bar one time. Lionel was thrilled. 'Roses! I got roses!' Wanting me to be happy with him. Fat chance."

"I'm glad he had you."

"I'm not the only one he had. There's this great older guy. James. White hair, but not as white as Lionel's." They smile. Softness between them. They both love albino Lionel so much. "A gentle guy, sort of like a loaf of white bread. Lionel would be with him, then go to somebody else, then back to him. James heard about Mitch and reached out, helped Lionel walk away, or drive away. Our van—it comes from him. He signed it over to us, both of us, for a dollar, all legal. One condition, we had to get our asses into UMO, get our degrees."

"So this all just happened?"

"Yeah."

"Those resolutions he made, to give up sex and drugs and alcohol..."

"All new. He needs something, to make sure."

"Is he going to be all right?"

Ann Marie moves closer. They hold each other. Nobody knows if anybody's going to be all right, but the three of them, Ann Marie and Lionel and a tired person named Ricki Harding, are together, if only for one night. Together.

*

It wasn't so bad, telling about the books. He started with Etta, how she handed him *Old John Neptune* like a new priest giving out Communion, nervous and serious. That made his reading, or maybe it's his Following, into a story. Once he got going he just kept on. John Neptune and the others, their ways with magic. Clara telling Mrs. Eckstorm the old stories for supper and a bit of money. Mrs. Eckstorm writing it all down, not trying to make smooth what came rough out of Clara. Petra nodded right then and said in an undertone, not exactly talking to him, *rough exhalation preserved.* When he looked his question she shook her head as if she'd been foolish and motioned for him to keep talking. He left out the part about bare electrical wires crossing inside him but she knows it's not an ordinary thing, this reading he's doing. She listens between words, like Raymona on a good day. By the time he got

251

to this next book, *Life and Traditions of the Red Man*, the one he's holding in his hands with Petra sitting close enough but not too close on Danny's couch, holding just because it feels good, they'd already been around again to the idea of Raymona and how she took up the Indian place in the family. Petra commented that Raymona making him into her Special Indian set him "inside her narrative." "Narrative?" "The story she made of your lives." That sounded close to his own thought, how the family's attitude toward his Indian look was bent like a tool not quite true, whether it was Raymona and Stella adoring, or Bede hating. "Besides, I'm at least half white," he said.

"I know," she said.

She keeps the complications in mind. He himself leans too far one way, then the other. Most of his life he forgot to be Indian. Reading these books, he can forget to be white. It sounds strange, put that way, but it's true. Somewhere in this long night Petra stopped being mad at Raymona. She switched to being interested, just purely interested, in anything he had to say about his family or his life or his reading. He decided he could tell her how the words of *Life and Traditions* have been dropping down into him like cool rain, how the directions are in this book, East, West, North, South, and a familiar feeling from reading the words of Black Elk comes to him, but there's a difference, too, because it's a Maine story, so these are local people, Maine people, taught by the one called Klose-kur-beh and then left by him, left alone to make life into whatever they could, having their happenings, good and bad. He even told how he spent some time in his mind with this Klose-kur-beh, the first man, the man from nothing. They were lying on the ground, himself and Klose-kur-beh together, with no thought yet. Step by step the world of realness and wonder came visible around them, the shining beauty of every living thing. Then their abilities came to being. They could think. They could stand up. He offered Petra one word after another and she listened. She didn't take his thought and run around holding it high shouting, "This is *mine*." Raymona never did exactly that, hold something of his high in her hand and declare it her own, but the picture is so distinct it might as well be a memory. He's comfortable and uncomfortable, both, with Petra. He wouldn't be reading this book by Mr. Nicolar if Raymona were alive. Life with Raymona wasn't easy, but it was known. This new life isn't known. Here he sits with a lady who's a therapist and a house painter and a writer and not even a Mainer. A woman from Away, who wants to be his friend. She's quiet now but she'll talk soon. Chippie's in the background of everything. The three of them, Petra and Danny and himself, are carrying a worry about Raymona's baby through the hours. Petra keeps this conversation going, though not right now. Maybe it's both of them that keep it going. They talk a while, then stop and let the words settle. More words rise up or one of them goes to the toilet or gets something from the kitchen and they start again. The strangest thing about it is how it just keeps going and he's not afraid it will take a bad path. He's almost sure Petra won't run to bury her head under Danny's covers.

When he said "Your turn," Petra said "Give me a minute" but it's been more than a minute. He hopes he can find a way to help if she needs help. Back toward the beginning, it must be hours ago, she told him about her Polish parents who came to America after World War II, how her mother Tekla died when she was only nine, how her father Witold is a book-reading farmer who likes philosophy above all. She told about the death of her daughter and it was like Etta, another white woman handing over to him a holy thing. They kept going back to Chippie, their worry, and he told about the rule for keeping her safe, from him. Before he realized, Petra got him past that, just pulled him along. He stood up and walked to a new place. It was like Klose-kur-beh, how he got up and walked, after his time of lying on the ground. Now he can help out with Chippie, take Raymona's place in a small way.

"Read that part to me." It's a sudden start, a little loud. She's pointing to his book. He has a protective feeling for the writer, Mr. Nicolar.

"It's not usual, how he breaks up his sentences."

"Maybe he wrote in a transitional time," she says, "straddling the two languages. Maybe writing itself was a challenge. I'm not sure the Penobscot language was a written one."

"I thought it might bother you since you're a writer."

"That would be off to the side, Raymond."

So he reads: "*When he opened his eyes lying on his back in the dust, his head toward the rising of the sun and his feet toward the setting of the sun, the right hand pointing to the north and his left hand to the south. Having no strength to move any part of his body, yet the brightness of the day revealed to him all the glories of the whole world; the sun was at its highest, standing still, and beside it was the moon without motion and the stars were in their fixed places, while the firmament was in its beautiful blue. While yet his eyes were held fast in their sockets, he saw all that the world contained.'"*

"That's before he could stand up?"

"Yes, before he was much, in himself. Because he's still lying down and next it says, '*While the body clung to the dust he was without mind, and the flesh without feeling.*' He has to go through a lot before he can stand up. The heavens have to come alive and come at him and he has to go to sleep, maybe enter a trance. He has to see the Great Being and express trust. Then he can rise up and go on his way."

"It happens over and over. And continuously," Petra says.

"Starting from down in the dust?"

"From anywhere. Getting made from nothing, but with everything all around. I don't know. I lost my thought." So they sit again. Then she says, "When I first took care of Chippie, I needed to go back to a kind of reading I hadn't done in decades. Philosophy."

"Your father's interest."

"All right, yes, but mine, too. In college I studied philosophy."

"You were looking to understand something? Because of another baby coming into your life?"

"I didn't see then how the two things were connected. I started with a woman philosopher. Maybe you've heard of her. Simone Weil."

"No. You're out of my league." He doesn't mind telling her this. He'll try to follow her thought but if he can't she'll find a way to make him understand.

"She wasn't just a philosopher. She felt she had a personal— mystical—experience of God."

"Like Klose-kur-beh. The Great Being was visible to him for a while."

"Right. I haven't had anything to do with religion for a long time, or God, separate from religion. Then along comes Chippie, and I get all stirred up and start to read a Jewish philosopher mystic who was drawn to Christianity. And now I find myself reading a book by a very Christian woman, Julian of Norwich. She had what she called 'showings.' Visions."

"All of a sudden you're knee-deep in religious topics."

"That's right."

"Me, too, but it's not really the religious part."

"For you it's about being Indian. Part Indian." He likes it that she doesn't pretend this is an ordinary thing to say. She looks at him and he looks at her and they both know they're not in everyday territory. Maybe this is how friends are with each other. He's kept away from making friends, his family being the way it is.

"Yes, it's about being Indian," he says.

"I can't believe I'm having a conversation with the word religious in it, Raymond."

"Is it a wrong direction for you?"

"It's the direction that is." This he understands. He waits for her to get going again. It takes a while. "So the children are woven in," she says. "Old Catholic ideas are coming into it. You know Catholicism."

"Well..."

"I just mean the basic ideas, Jesus being God, becoming human, suffering and dying for our sins. The crucifixion."

"I never did understand how it saved us, him suffering."

"Well, me neither, Raymond, but I do understand, and you do, too, that somehow suffering is integral to this life."

"Unavoidable if you live on this earth, you mean?"

"Yes. So Julian—this sounds crazy when I try to say it—had this desire to experience the pain of Jesus' crucifixion."

"OK."

"I guess to join with him, not be separated off from the worst of what he went through. Did you ever feel that? When you saw Raymona having a hard time?"

"It didn't work that way with me. I just did what she told me, tried to help. Well, not always."

"I know," she says. It should make him squirm away, what she might know from Raymona's writings, but it doesn't. Whatever she knows, it's not making *her* squirm away. "When I was reading Julian's book...where are we now?...Wednesday?...so it was yesterday, in the library...it didn't seem so strange after a while, the things Julian was saying."

"You got inside it."

"That's right. So the desire to *experience* Christ's suffering was like any other thing a human being could be passionate about. So to speak."

"So to speak?"

"Passion. The Passion of Christ. His crucifixion. Passionate about."

"They call it a passion?"

She nods and laughs and asks, "How long were you a Catholic?"

"Just a little while. Maybe I forgot."

"Maybe you never knew. Yes, they call it a passion. The word sounds stranger every time we say it."

"Like *kitchen*," he says.

"Did you do that when you were a kid, say kitchen over and over until it sounded meaningless?" She looks happy. They're happy together right this minute, laughing a little about a childhood thing that was the same for both of them. Human beings find their way, is the thought that comes to him.

"Last night...no, Monday night," Petra says, serious now, "I tried to imagine the end of Anya's life, and Marian's, her second mother, how they got raped and killed. Maybe I wanted what Julian wanted, to experience it myself, to join that close."

"A brave thing, maybe," he says. He hasn't tried to imagine things Raymona went through. He knows he can't.

"No, it was just time to do it. I let every detail I could think of come right into me. I did my best. I don't expect to get further than I got last night."

"You're calm, talking about it."

"That's what happened. Because I learned I couldn't do it. It's not in me to know and I don't have to. Some weight I carried slid off me, and maybe it happened that way because of the reading. Julian worked hard to make meaning from her visions. There was the suffering of Jesus, which was just plain gory, and then there was the other side. She had visions that gave her the strongest conviction, the experience really, that nothing is wrong, ever, anywhere, on the deepest level. 'Sin is behovely but all shall be well. All manner of thing shall be well.'" *Behovely*? He looks his question. "Necessary. The mess we're in, it's a given, but..." He nods. "Raymond, I don't even know why I need to..." She looks helpless all of a sudden, so he does what he can, telling his own thought.

"There's beauty and comfort and power and the idea of the Great Being and everything alive being sacred in this book here about the Penobscot thinking. Then there's the story about winter, the boy named Frost who keeps cutting out the tongues of children, killing them, or the First Mother who makes her husband kill her and drag her body over the ground until all the flesh is gone. That's gory enough. But from her destroyed body corn and tobacco come, to feed the people and give a quiet spirit."

"Holding the two poles."

"Opposites, you mean?"

"Yes. So it's the same thing. The paradox."

"Raymona talked about paradox a lot for a while."

"Well, she'd know." They sit with that for a minute. He thinks how her voice just then sounded gentle and forgiving and how much he likes it that she's not mad at Raymona right now, how it eases him. "I wonder what it is," Petra says. He waits until she's ready to say more. She looks at him in the overly direct way she has at times. "How it is that we can talk like this." He just waits. She'll come up with an interesting thought if he gives her time. "Raymond, do you feel like a criminal?" Now it's his turn to ponder. No one ever asked him. After that first night, when he was back from the Youth Center and Raymona wondered if he blamed her, they never talked about it. No one else would raise the topic of Bede, ask him what he felt. Stella never would. It isn't long before he has his answer, though.

"When you kill someone I suppose you're a criminal. But no. In a deep way I guess I don't feel like one."

"Neither do I," she says. He knows she's talking about giving up her little girl Anya, and maybe Chippie, too. She makes it easy to know things.

"You think that's why we ended up here tonight, Petra, the two of us and our books?"

"It might be more tangled than that, or woven. Maybe woven, but who'd be the weaver? Raymona? God? Anybody but you or me." She moves her head back from that, a sudden movement. She might be trying to get a good look at the words she put into the air, how Raymona and

God ended up side by side. She shakes her head and looks amused. "Do you know what I mean?" It's the first time she's asked that. It comes to him that he has to take her thought in his hands and be careful with it while he's freeing the parts from each other.

He says, "We can talk to each other in a way that, well, we wouldn't expect to. We're walking into private territory, I guess you could say holy if you wanted to. We'd expect to keep quiet about things like this, especially with a person unknown to us until recently. Maybe there's a link, you to me and me to you, because we stepped outside of what good people do." She's nodding, so he keeps going, feeling his way along. "We wouldn't change the thing we did. We can't find the guilty feeling we're maybe supposed to have, or maybe we're not supposed to feel guilty, we don't know. We live with what we did." She's waiting for more, so he goes ahead. "It's not plain or easy, living with what we did. We both built something around ourselves afterward. I made my rules, though you just did away with one of them for me, for which I thank you. You...well, I'm not sure. You didn't allow yourself to observe the children, enjoy their ways." He waits to see if she wants to put something in here. No. She's patient with all these words, she likes words. "That's just one part of a more complicated design, or maybe it's only a mess, something a weaver made or something all tangled, that brought us to tonight. It's easy to see how Raymona made a mess, or maybe it's a weaving, by killing herself and leaving her will, not even asking you about your part. Or God, it's always sensible, maybe, to have God pulling strings..." Right there he can see he's gone off her track. She's been nodding and nodding but she stops when he mentions God pulling strings, and shakes her head, but so slightly he might have been mistaken. He got clumsy with her idea, maybe. He stops talking.

"Don't stop," she says.

"You don't like God that way."

"I don't know how I like God."

"If there is one, is what you might be thinking," he says. She smiles.

"If there is one, a god of some kind, then I don't imagine he, she, or it pulls strings. If I'm ever going to think there's a god it has to be one that likes us free first, everything after that being secondary. But you do understand what I'm saying."

"You're putting together the reading we're doing," he says, "how it's a Following, I guess that's our word for it tonight, and how we can talk, and you're bringing in the strange outlaws we are, both of us. Weaving it all together. This time you're the weaver."

"Or we are," she says and sits upright on the edge of the couch and looks at him. She's pondering, but only for a minute. She says, "Now I'm back to my thought, the one that escaped me."

"About Klose-kur-beh, about getting brought to life."

"Over and over, constantly, and *now*."

"More new than most times," he says.

"Yes, that's it. More new than most times." She looks happy, relaxing back against the couch. Something got completed. They're both in the silence when the phone rings. It sounds loud. Petra says, "My turn." It only takes a minute for him to understand this is Stella calling Danny in the middle of the night but having things to say to Petra since it's Petra she reached. "She's not *here* right now, Stella. And she's a baby. Well, I guess that doesn't matter, though the conversation might be one-sided. I know, she's a good little talker in her own way, but she's not here. Danny's not, either. Raymond is. Raymond and I..." When would Stella call in the middle of the night? When she's under the influence, that's when. Petra listens and sighs. "You're right. We should have. We didn't want to worry you. She seems to have an ear infection and it got away from us. At St. Joe's. I'm sure they'll be back soon." Maybe she had one of her intuitions, though. He should've known she'd call. "How strong, Stella?" The feeling, about Chippie, that's what they're talking about. He hopes. "Well, I think you might be right. Yes, serious if we didn't get her help, but she's getting help. What about now? Is the feeling any less intense now that..." Petra nods and nods. "Good," she says. Then, "I would, too. What about this weekend? Good, I'll call you. Do you want to talk to Raymond? OK, I'll tell him. Can you sleep now? Yes, one of us will call you in the morning. Good night, Stella."

"She's not drinking? Just worried?"

"Right. She says hello. She didn't feel it 'necessary' to talk to you."

"She's off me right now. It happens. This is normal, her having a feeling about the baby."

"She wants to see me."

"I heard you mention the weekend."

"I wonder what that's about. Sounded rather formal. Therefore daunting."

"I suspect she's just found herself with a set of thoughts."

"That's what I mean. Daunting." He can see she isn't really scared by Stella. She's relaxed now, yawning. The kitchen door opens. In comes Danny with Chippie, a quiet entrance.

"Oh, you're awake. I thought I'd just come, not call, in case you decided you could sleep. But here you are, um..." Chippie's waking up with little squawks and blinking eyes. Danny's hands are full with the baby and extra things that go along with a baby who travels away from home. Petra's right there, unburdening him, taking Chippie, feeling her forehead, smiling her relief. She hands Chippie over to him—to him, Raymond Weeks—as if giving him a baby to hold is an entirely normal action. Then she's hugging Danny and whispering in his ear and it's plain to see what's between these two, how they have a history beyond friendship. And here's Raymona's baby, surprised to find herself in the arms of her uncle. It only takes a minute for her to decide the situation deserves a wobble-headed half-sleepy smile.

*

"B-e-n-s-t-e-i-n," Ricki says.

Ann Marie runs her finger down the page of Bright Star's phone book. "Got it."

"You're sure it's her work number? I'd hate to wake her up."

"Benstein, Gertrude, psychotherapist. It's in the business section, Ricki."

Ricki forgot about Gertrude, how she might worry if a person stayed out all night, especially a person who helped her lover commit suicide. It was Ann Marie who said "Will your landlady worry?" and went in search of a phone book though that meant letting go of Ricki who couldn't stop shaking. Ann Marie dials and hands her the phone.

Ricki manages to produce a message apologizing, reassuring, apologizing, "...and, well, good-bye. Thank you, Gertrude."

"Good," says Ann Marie, putting the phone back.

260

They sit. Time passes. What happened to the shaking? It's gone. "I wonder what I meant, *Thank you, Gertrude*." The phrase strikes them as hilarious and they are in the grip of the giggles.

Which pass.

"We must be so tired," says Ricki.

Ann Marie agrees, wiping her eyes.

"Ann Marie."

"What?"

"We have to wake Lionel up."

"OK."

They tiptoe in, as if they had no plan to wake him. There he is, their sleeping darling. "Lionel." They whisper it, touching him softly, Ann Marie at his shoulder, Ricki at his hip. Lionel opens his eyes and looks at them, back and forth. He moves nothing but his eyes. "What am I seeing?" She and Ann Marie look at each other. What is he seeing? "We don't know." The giggles threaten to erupt again. Deep breathing helps. They sit on the bed, not too close to each other. "Ah, my girls," says Lionel. He sits up. They make a triangle on Bright Star's bed, symmetrical and human.

"Ann Marie told me," Ricki says. "Are you awake?"

"I'm awake." He looks at Ann Marie—did she really tell, is everything known?—and she nods.

"That Mitch. What a creep," Ricki says, and looks to make sure she hasn't said the wrong thing.

"It was complicated, Ricki. I just wanted you to know. I want you both to know everything. That's why I told the old lady here about your dying Indian, his wink."

"*What?*" The wink was theirs. No one else's.

"I'm sorry about your girlfriend and how she wasn't really sick," Lionel says.

She looks at him, hard. "Are you going to change the subject every second, Lionel?"

"You should say something to Ann Marie about how it's OK if she knows about the dying Indian, Ricki."

"Jeez, Lionel."

"I know, but I tell her everything."

Ann Marie will go back behind herself any minute. "*Dammit,* Lionel."

"Ricki, you have to be better about this."

"I'm tired of being better about everything."

Silence.

Ann Marie gets off the bed. It's not a fast move, it's more like a slow bear move, a big quiet move by someone who has to get to a different place, not in a hurry. But she's leaving. By the time Ricki gets herself moving, Ann Marie is out the door. "Ann Marie!" No answer, but Ann Marie is only a few steps beyond the dooryard. "I'm sorry, Ann Marie."

"I don't appreciate observing other people's business."

"I'm sorry."

"Don't say that any more."

"Come back in."

"I don't think so."

"Ann Marie. Come back in." Ann Marie sighs and starts toward the trailer but she stops.

"Go get Lionel. We'll go for a walk."

"You and Lionel?"

"No, Ricki. You and Lionel and me. Can't you feel how good it is out here?"

She hadn't felt the night, only the tension and how she had to keep them all together. Ann Marie's right. Being outside is the next thing they need to do. "You won't leave?"

"I won't leave. Go get Lionel."

He's right there in the doorway and now he's coming down the steps and putting himself in the middle and striding along, they're all striding along, Lionel and his two girls, their arms in the crooks of his elbows, and they might be in a movie. The rising moon slides between layers of clouds, a tiny part of it shining, the night still mostly dark. They might be silhouettes, three humans going down the road, the camera following at a distance, but now the camera is close up, on Lionel's feet.

"Lionel, you don't have shoes on," Ricki says. He stops, which means they all stop, and look down, and burst out laughing because of course no one has shoes on. It's not warm enough for bare feet but they keep walking and breathing, walking and breathing.

A thought arrives.

"I should call Stella."

It's a sudden imperative, not just to call, but to *see* Stella, which might or might not be like a categorical imperative since she never got around to looking that one up and can't even remember whose idea it was. Some philosopher.

"Stella?" Ann Marie and Lionel say. She must not have said anything about Stella yet. What should she say now? They're almost back at the trailer. When did they turn around?

"Her mother. Stella is her mother."

"Oh," say Lionel and Ann Marie in perfect unison as they march up the steps, herself in the middle, another little parade.

Chapter Twenty-four

Petra sits on her rock, reviewing. It is Friday, less than three weeks since Raymona Weeks killed herself. Less than one week since Danny, excellent Danny, took Chippie. Less than a week since she tried to relive Anya's last moments and discovered it was an impossible task, not merely a task delayed out of cowardice. And since the little ball of All-thing entered and altered her mind. And since she sat with Raymond fearing for Chippie while discussing the creation of Klose-kur-beh, Penobscot First Man, and the visions of fourteenth century English mystic Julian of Norwich and other improbable matters as well as solidifying her impression that unusual energies between new friends such as herself and Raymond are not necessarily sexual. And since she realized—resolved—that her writing is about to become something it hasn't yet dared to be, though she can't say what. Life hasn't been this overfull since early adulthood, since Anya and San Francisco and the seventies and change, change, change. *Intense*, they all used to say and look at each other and nod—whenever anything at all happened, she thinks now, amused—as if life had never before in all of human history been so packed with meaning. How young they were. How fond she feels of them, her former self and her old friends. She's already talked to Danny this morning. Chippie thrives on the exotic antibiotic or perhaps on the wonder of being held by Raymond. Whatever the cause, Danny swears the wattage of the baby's smile has jumped levels. Danny himself transmits the sound of a smile through phone wires but No, he says, he and Raymond are not sleeping together, how can she even imagine such a pace? Yes, it's true Raymond's been "around." Yes, that's nice.

"Perhaps now we'll change the subject," said Danny.

"Does the matchmaker not have a right?" said imperious Petra.

"The matchmaker has no rights," said noncompliant Danny.

Silently she took note: she was permitted to call herself matchmaker. Silently she smiled.

Now—it's still early morning—she sits on her rock beside the rising Penobscot. This is a writing day, no clients. She's glad for the break. She has no pen or paper with her, having learned. She's here to muse and prepare her mind. Or her soul; she might almost say her soul. The writing itself needs the kitchen table, fresh coffee, several pens, and books; some stacked, some lying open to just the right pages.

The sun shines, the air is cold, and the world smells salty, essential. Behind her the November woods are evergreen dark and deciduous dry. The clinging leaves have gone to brown and the ground is crunchy with their fallen comrades. She tests the width of the rock's long crack. Even her baby finger can't fit in. The piece will break off, but not soon. She doesn't need Nat to tell her such a thing. She's headed toward poetry, though she's never written a poem in all her forty-nine years. Inspired by Marianne Moore, she'll scavenge, piecing together her own mind. She feels radically unafraid, a contrast to the last time she sat on this rock when she feared her writing would be ragged or damaged, a thing dragged out of her. That was one day after Danny took Chippie, how could she have imagined any writing at all? How can she now? Nevertheless, she does.

She gets off the rock and starts toward home, choosing the long way. She'll pass a sight she doesn't like to see but feels compelled to see from time to time: a small abandoned house. It was a salvageable little house. Last year, along came a new owner. He made a good start on restoration, but his work took a turn. Maybe it was temper, frustration. Out walking, she found the poor structure battered. The guy must have gotten into his big machine—replica of a Tonka toy he had as a child no doubt—and rammed. Foundation stones had fallen inward, the first floor had buckled, the roof was skewed. Even the topsoil was plowed into piles, the path blocked by mounds of dirt clumped with uprooted grass and weeds. The only way through was around, a rough walk through wild brush, no path. Going home after her first shocked sight, she felt waves of strange, intense grief—for the house, for the hurt land, for the state of humanity.

Here it is, the sad ruined place. And here's something new: a sign. She stops. *For Sale.* A price. A phone number. The sign is hand-painted. She finds herself touching it, tracing letters, feeling thick dry new paint, feeling a cool pulsating aliveness. The sign is speaking to her.

Silly. She doesn't have that kind of money.

The house itself would have to go, it's beyond fixing, a hazard. More battering. *All fall down.* Or burning, people burn unwanted structures. So sad. *Ashes, ashes.* Maybe the fire department would do it, God knows they need the practice. The land itself could be returned to a sweet meadow, in time.

Absurd.

In her kitchen now. Hot coffee, open books, pen in hand. Her friendly wallpaper vegetables, subtle abstractions of themselves, leaning into each other. Tomorrow DWELL will discuss Moore's "An Octopus." This was Roo's idea, an attempt to do something, anything, for Ricki. Will this help poor Ricki with her paper, though? Petra has read and reread the poem, done a bit of research, and learned that Marianne Moore, poet supreme, was, as a voracious reader with odd and varied tastes, a thief. Moore took copious notes, circled what caught her fancy, stole phrases, changed facts, transformed ideas, found fragments of her own thought, and got thereby a skeleton on which to hang a poem. This information was electric, liberating. In the past Petra had the blank page and her own uncertain mind. She remembers the first day she wrote down a thought instead of telling it to Frederick, inadequate listener. Frederick, who was possibly the first person in her life to commit suicide, but she'll never know. Did he engineer his own "accident" that night? At least Raymona left no doubt. Which reminds her: she wants Raymona's notebooks here on the table, a random two or three, along with Marianne Moore, William Carlos Williams, T. S. Eliot, Simone Weil, Julian of Norwich. She gets up, pours herself more coffee, and heads toward the bedroom where the notebooks wait. Frederick was a good man with a good, if somewhat overly discursive, mind. She rarely thinks of him or of the time when she was a young wife trying not to dislike the smell of her husband. She feels no such distance from her early writing, it was a good beginning. Now though, today, the thought of poetry, and the possibility getting it published, have come tromping into her mind. There is, of course, no actual poem. She sits down, sips coffee.

She is not without ideas. In fact, she's a cornucopia of ideas, filling and spilling. At the center is Anya, turning a handspring in a circle of light; the black horse, the green, green field, and Anya executing her eternal handspring. But this first poem can't be about Anya. She knows this. Today, apparently, she knows things. In the back of her mind as she picks up first one book and then another, sampling, not ready to focus, not ready even to copy a phrase onto her very own blank page, is the poor piece of raped land with its ruined house, suddenly for sale; land which someone could, over time, work back into a lovely meadow; land which she can't afford, and therefore can't have. A flood of associations, though, she can have. The word raped. The sudden knowledge that integrity could be restored to a piece of raped land. The sight of Anya, raped and murdered child, acrobatic in a circle of light. "The Rape of the Lock."

What?

She gets up to find the book she suddenly needs. Here it is and she could swear it's is the same edition Witold had. Probably still has, he'd never discard a book. Black cover with dark red lettering. How did she know she should check it out at the library? Too bad Raymond wasn't working. She would have liked to get it over with, their first meeting after all that intimacy. It could be awkward, as if they *did* fall into bed together and now have to face each other across the breakfast table, strangers. But there's that odd comfort with him; she has to keep reminding herself.

The first time she read Pope's poem her mother had just died. Now here it is again: the rejected Baron, the scissors, Belinda's lock of hair. *The meeting points the sacred hair dissever / From the fair head, forever, and forever!* The Baron gets his revenge, one lock of the virgin's hair. The triumphant "rape" is accomplished despite the tiny wonder-beings of the air, little sprites, attending Belinda, trying to protect her. *Transparent forms too fine for mortal sight, / Their fluid bodies half dissolved in light.* A super-rational philosopher father who, stunned with loss himself, gave his child fairy-light in her dark time, gave her *poetry*, deserves a phone call, and soon. Not right now. So. Here is "rape," the word scrubbed clean.

And here is William Carlos Williams, exulting over Marianne Moore: "With Miss Moore a word is a word most when it is separated out by silence, treated with acid to remove the smudges, washed, dried and placed right side up on a clean surface. Now one may say that this is a word."

267

And here is Simone Weil with her bone-clean sentences, her stringencies. And Julian with her hazelnut-sized little ball of All-thing that won't slip from existence because the courteous love of her Lord prevents it. *This is it. This is how her mind will work.* She takes her pen and begins carefully to copy, like a school child.

"...fluid bodies half dissolved in light..." (Pope)

"...treated with acid to remove the smudges..." (Williams)

"Originality is the byproduct of sincerity." (Moore)

"At the first turning of the third stair..." (Eliot)

"...methought it might suddenly have fallen to naught for little..." (Julian)

"An Eskimo story explains the origin of light as follows: 'In the eternal darkness, the crow, unable to find any food, longed for light, and the earth was illumined.'" (Weil)

Scavenging, she is happy. It's almost noon. She looks at the notebooks that contain the rambunctious half-crazed, half-brilliant writing of Raymona Weeks, hesitates, then opens one from several years past. Her eyes catch the word she didn't know she was looking for: *steps.* She finds a description of the inner architecture of a woman with multiple personality disorder, or perhaps—she reminds herself not to know more than she knows—something else, not MPD at all. The handwriting looks like that of a twelve-year-old. The notebook is dated only a few years back.

How It Is Inside, an Essay

Inside is different, not like outside where all is seen by regular people. Today I will write about Mama Dragon because last night we had to go there. This won't get handed in to Miss Ouellette who is the Best Teacher because this is about Entirely Private Matters, that's what Martha says, and anyway Miss Ouellette was a long time ago which I don't understand. Mama Dragon stays in the cellar, down cold gray dirty cement steps. In the cellar you have to be terrified but you will never be Truly Harmed because Mama Dragon who breathes fire is only loving you away from worse. That is how it is inside. Today, after, is a good day. I will make this story be "Unsigned."

Petra looks out the window. Here is Raymona Weeks expressing, with perfect pitch, the uses of her own inner torture chamber. Her eyes fill. *Sometimes, brightness:* that they, any of them, all of them, the raped

268

and the rapists and those like herself who are spared, have existed. Sometimes—now—she loves: her daughter, her mother, her father, her not-quite-friend Bright Star, all of her friends, and her clients, every single one. She feels it: the essential *it*.

It—existence?—is fragile and terrible and lovely and full of holes and in need of being saved like old lace. It—life?—runs up and down some eternal set of stairs, reaching the shimmering highest air, visiting the deepest horror-ridden cellar. She takes her pen and writes. *Stairway Lace*. She sees again what she saw the night she decided to give up her second child, a woman descending a flight of stairs who is, to the sudden poet mind, her self-possessed paternal great-great grandmother, counterpart and counterpoint to the peasant woman collecting items on a windy cobbled street, *Vanished Babushka*, maternal great-great grandmother, apparition of a steamy bath who turned a Polish corner and disappeared. Petra laughs, amazed and delighted at the human mind, one of which she seems to own—and the phone rings. It's Nat. They'll get together after tomorrow's meeting, it's been too long. She makes one more note before stopping for lunch.

"That is how it is inside." (Raymona)

*

So Stella Weeks is an alcoholic who lives above a bar, thinks Petra, climbing stairs that smell none too good. It's a busy Saturday. After this—interview?—with Stella comes the DWELL meeting, then time with Nat.

What *is* on Stella's mind?

Before she can knock, the door opens.

"Right on time, dear. I appreciate that in a person." Stella turns and walks to the stove and pours two cups of coffee, leaving her to do as she pleases, which means she stands awkwardly in the middle of a very clean kitchen, then holds a cup of coffee, still standing, facing her hostess and, in perfect simultaneity with said hostess, takes a sip. They might be mimes, but they lack an audience. Another sip, together, still standing. The linoleum is worn to black at the sink and stove. It's been waxed and the worn places shine as bravely as the geometric designs, red and white. Stella speaks. "I've looked up and noticed. The century will soon turn.

The millennium. It's given me a jolt. Perhaps the living room is our place."

So they sit on serviceable slightly worn beige living room furniture. Crochet work is everywhere, doilies on end tables and furniture arms, framed samples behind glass on the walls, colorful, varied, skilled work. One photograph: Raymond. It has to be Raymond, age twelve or thirteen, looking like a good boy. None of Raymona. Stella says, "I hadn't expected to see it, you know." *The millennium, she must mean.* Petra herself has said not a word. The same odd calm she feels with Raymond has come over her. Maybe she'll stay all day, the coffee's good.

"A longer life than expected imposes obligations, don't you think?"

Does it? There's no need to decide. Stella will tell her.

Stella goes to the kitchen and returns carrying a plate of sweet rolls. "I've always been partial to lemon. You're wondering why I've invited you here and I don't blame you, I've been wondering myself. A conversation, I thought, when I invited you, but I've lost the topic."

"That's all right, Stella." The filling is just tart enough. She lets herself sink more deeply into the couch.

"Well I knew you'd say that. I have a little gift for you, I remember that much." Gift? She's holding both a cup of coffee and a sweet roll and has no hand free when Stella returns. Stella gently lays a large red doily across her lap, and pats her on the knee, motherly. The thread shimmers in the morning light. This is a flat piece with raised edges and raised replicas scattered across it: a pen and a bottle of ink; a typewriter; most endearing, a random spray of letters falling into the bottom right corner.

"Stella, this is wonderful." Stella beams. "But how did you...?"

"You mentioned it, dear, the night we found the right home for our baby."

"I did?"

"Yes, you told us Nat Levesque would probably say your writing deserved a consideration."

"I did? How odd. That *is* what Nat said."

"It was a small element, dear, in a large night. I wouldn't be surprised at anything at all from that night disappearing from your mind.

I do know a thing or two about stress. I remember my topic now. We both yielded, you see, you and I."

"Stella, this is so beautiful."

"Well, I thought a little boost."

"Thank you. Yielded...?"

"That was the topic that came to me. Then I worked day and night, you know, because it occurred to me a gift..."

"Day and night? You shouldn't have. My stress can't compare..."

"I have enough insomnia to permit good production. Your stress compares quite well."

"I suppose I shouldn't argue."

"That's right, dear." They fall silent, sip coffee, finish their rolls, as if they've completed phase one and deserve a rest. Stella produces napkins and they wipe their hands vigorously and smile at each other. *So companionable.* "I plan one for my son, should he ever again see fit to appear."

"Raymond hasn't been around?"

"His will be red-brown, and a rougher thread than yours. Lying flat because he likes that. Two flat ones, for you and for him, but it doesn't mean I've given up shapes."

"How could you? It's such interesting work. Did you finish your series in black?"

"You ought to know, dear, that a series such as that is never finished."

To which there can be no reply.

Stella takes away the used napkins and returns with the coffee pot. Petra accepts a refill.

"In the matter of motherhood," Stella says, after a while.

Yielding to one's nature? To one's incapacities as a mother?

"And then of course they're gone," says Stella.

Our daughters, thinks Petra. And Chippie. Though Chippie's not really gone, she's with Danny. Good Danny.

"So I thought perhaps a little chat," Stella says, but she looks away so determinedly that mere chatting is out of the question.

Petra waits like a therapist, but she's not a therapist. Here with Stella she is, apparently, a mother who yielded.

"Not many do," Stella says finally, looking at her, or into her. She can't remember ever feeling so examined.

"I did, with Anya. You're right, Stella. I yielded to..."

"Well, yes, I know you did, dear." Stella is gazing off again. This conversation won't be shaped in the usual ways any more than the "doilies" are. Petra fingers the lovely gift that honors her writing. "I thought perhaps it was my fault," Stella says, still looking into some private distance. When she turns back, tears are running down her lovely cheeks.

"Raymona's death, Stella?" She wants to get up, walk across the few feet separating them, and hold this beautiful woman. Which is of course out of the question.

"Well." Stella has a small white handkerchief. Petra's heart jumps. They're a club, Nat and Stella and herself, the handkerchief ladies. *No Kleenex for Us.* This is ridiculously irrelevant, they are talking about a mother's guilt over the suicide of her daughter. Or not talking. Stella's silence reigns. An urge toward honesty rises up. Petra focuses on the remnants of her coffee. Even lukewarm, it's good. She uses the occasional tissue herself, she's not entirely a handkerchief lady.

But the urge is irresistible. "Stella, she was hard. Not an easy person, I mean." Stella is set into a soft distance, unmoving. Did she hear? "What I mean is, I can imagine how alienation could come about. She was...unusual." No change in Stella. "Stella, I was so angry when she killed herself." She can't believe her own determination. Is this what Weil meant by being impelled by God? If there is a God. "In the last few days, though, I've felt something different. Something gentler. Stella?"

Stella comes back, as if she reenters the room, and says, "I'll reach for that, then, since it's possible. Thank you, dear."

Another silence. Meditative, Petra thinks. We are meditating on these matters, mothers together. Time passes. Such leisure, thinks Petra.

Stella smiles and says, "I had it in mind to thank you, for trying to take on the raising of that baby. It was a generous attempt."

"Attempt, indeed. A mere attempt, with no oomph to it, Stella."

"Well, yes. What possessed you, dear? Though I'm grateful, as I said. A path to that nice Danny is what you made."

"It was sentimental of me, Stella."

"I've never understood what that word was meant to communicate."

"Well, give me a minute because I'm just getting clear about it myself."

They sit. Abruptly, Stella speaks. "She happened upon a particular way of hurting me."

"Raymona."

Stella nods. "I let her go to the world when she was far from ready. That was my yielding. Yours would have been different, of course. I yielded to her will. It was a habit, I believe. Then she was gone and I found no further way. I've told my friend Margie but she's childless. I thought I'd tell you. I do hope you found time for your writing this week. Have you come upon a definition of sentimental?"

Like sleight of hand, this. Quick shifts, impossible to follow, at least with any competence. Stella's eyes are now bright with intelligence and warmth and, yes, humor. *This woman knows exactly what she's doing.* Petra waits for several more topics to be thrown into the mix. But no, it's her turn to speak.

"When Raymona's will announced that I was to be a mother again..." She stops. Her tone is almost flippant and she's talking to the mother of the recently dead Raymona.

Stella says, "Oh, I know what you mean, dear. She did have a tendency toward making announcements." They smile together over Raymona's tendencies.

"My reaction to what the will said was to get all stirred up."

"I should think so."

"Excited, and honored."

"I'm sure she meant it that way. Then, too, she was just bouncing the baby against you, Petra, you know that."

"Do I?"

"Of course you do."

"Maybe. But what I mean by sentimental, what I think I mean is that there was nothing solid in me, nothing real."

"Nothing that would help you on the long road."

"That's right. It was all...I don't know...fantasy..."

"A remnant, dear. I suspect it was a remnant." This stops her, but only for a minute.

"You mean something left over from my time with Anya but too small to make a new thing out of."

"Yes, it worries me."

"Worries you?"

"That my own remnant might be too scanty for the job."

"Of being Chippie's grandmother."

"I do appreciate how you work to follow, dear. Not everyone is willing. Afterward I can see what I require, you know."

"I don't doubt it, Stella."

Going down the steps, red doily in hand, she feels as lightheaded as if she's had a glass of champagne on an empty stomach—an inappropriate metaphor, for there's Stella, valiantly sober in the wake of her daughter's suicide. She herself must be drunk on something because it occurs to her that she and Nat together *could* afford to buy the land with the ruined house.

Chapter Twenty-five

Saturday afternoon. Petra's living room. Chopin's music fills the room, warm and delicate and powerful, but Ricki feels chilled and clumsy and fragile. Overexcited, frayed. By now she should know everything there is to know about Marianne Moore and she should have "The Octopus" rebuilt inside herself like the engine her brothers put back together after an entire summer of parts laid out on the lawn, parts as intricate and useful and *multitudinous* as the ideas and images of this poem. Ever since Roo called—*Would it be a help with your paper? We could stay with Sappho, it's up to you, I just thought maybe*—she's been crazy with energy, doing research, taking notes, reading and rereading the poem, still failing to comprehend, all the while swimming, or drowning in confusion over Ann Marie. Well, not quite drowning. At least Moore's been useful as a distraction; and intriguing, even if her mysteries are uncrackable. She hasn't seen Lionel and Ann Marie since the night of the kiss. Tonight they'll be cooking spaghetti and absolutely unqualifiedly need her presence, so says Lionel. Which would be only sweet if it weren't for the complications with Ann Marie. Who could have expected a kiss? What does it mean?

Roo and Jessie are fussing with Petra's broken vacuum cleaner. "It's stuck." "No, it isn't, if you'd just—" "I *am*." They giggle as they squabble. For no good reason, this brings up the Indian's wink. She has forgiven Lionel for telling the secret. In fact, she's glad Ann Marie knows about this thing that happened to her, that's *in* her, that keeps her...what?...safe when it comes to death. Which is certainly a strange thought. Maybe Bright Star was right and she can't be rearranged. Bright Star is dead from a plain old unvarnished willful suicide. She needs the meeting to start, to save her from her own mind, but her mind and this meeting are like Scylla and Charybdis, as they say at school; or a rock and a hard place, as they say at home. This meeting sets her up as the expert she's not, and her mind sets her onto useless tracks, one after another. Ann Marie, Bright Star, Ann Marie, Bright Star. The vacuum cleaner starts. Petra and Nat yell *hooray* from upstairs.

Now, finally Petra is standing near the stereo, apparently waiting for the right moment to interrupt the music. The moment comes. Petra sits down. This is it: time for Ricki Harding to be The One Who Knows. But Roo has another idea. "Ricki, I thought maybe if the rest of us talked and you just listened for a while..." Salvation. She nods, yes, yes. Roo says, "Or if you'd rather..." Jessie reaches over, touches Roo's arm. "She likes the idea, sweetie." Roo laughs and manages to stay quiet.

The chance to watch Roo and Jessie is a benefit of DWELL. They get cranky sometimes, or Jessie does, she's the one who adds grit to things, but they like each other. And respect each other. Being with them has been part of her Introduction to Lesbianism. The other relationship here, Nat and Petra's, is more confusing. They used to be lovers, that much she knows, and they're still good friends. Mostly they seem to belong in the old shoe category, worn and comfortable together. Just now though, when they came into the room, they looked tense, and Petra, standing at the stereo, took a lot of deep breaths. Is something wrong?

But Petra's the one who gets them started: "I don't know if I love or hate Moore, but I got something..." She stops. Her eyes are wide and Ricki recognizes the effort to keep tears from falling, but they do fall. Nobody says anything. Possibly nobody's breathing. Petra swears and says, "I thought I could just say it. Apparently not. It's about my writing." Her writing? Petra takes a couple of obvious deep breaths. "If anyone laughs I will stand up and run screaming from the house."

Nat says, "Petra." She means, Petra, no one will laugh. She's scolding and supporting, all in one word. Relationships are complicated. What does Ann Marie want? Even with the confusion, though, she, Ricki Harding, age nineteen, understands suddenly that she's more comfortable with the Gleesome Threesome—that's what they're calling themselves— than here at DWELL. With Lionel and Ann Marie she's at home. Here, she's in The World of Adults. One of whom is announcing she plans to write poetry this year, which must be momentous because Roo says, "Wow." Jessie says, "Good woman." Nat says, "Amazing, truly amazing." All at the same time. She herself is so busy trying to understand the significance she forgets to say anything and then Petra is sort of shining while she smiles and wipes her eyes and asks a dumb question: "Do you think I can?"

Nat says, "Of course you can," and everyone firmly agrees, and Petra laughs and comments on the inevitability of their response.

"I'll take it anyway. Thanks. Now let's get on with the discussion." Jessie wants to be told, though, what the connection *is* between Marianne Moore and Petra's plan to write poetry. "Oh. Well. I found out Moore took notes from whatever she was reading. I guess that's obvious from all the quotes in this poem. And then she'd go through her notebooks and circle salient phrases, that's what she did here, with this octopus which is not an octopus at all, of course, but a glacier on Mount Rainier, where she went with...maybe you all know this?" They quickly sort out: yes, Ricki and Roo know the background, but Nat and Jessie, both of whom are grumpy about their ignorance, do not, so would Petra please just spill it? "OK, OK. She went to Mount Rainier with her family, which is a whole story in itself, her mother and her brother, they were insanely close and had these animal identities, Marianne was called Rat, if you can believe it, as well as being, in the family, male, which is a thing a lesbian literary group ought to know, I suppose, though she seems to have been a true celibate, sexual identity irrelevant, but in their letters they all refer to her as *he* and, oh, this is good, the octopus is a symbol for the *mind* so maybe that's relevant. Lord, I'm about as wound up as Roo gets, though with you, Roo, it's more of a *wandering*, I suppose..." Roo just smiles. She's squeezing Jessie's hand. Ricki has the sudden embarrassing thought that they made love before they came today. This makes her face hot but everyone, thank God, is looking at Petra. "So, back to my point," Petra says. "I do have a point, I *am* going to answer your question, Jessie. Moore kept working with these fragments she gleaned, and she'd been to this mountain with its glaciers and trees and flowers and animals and human guides, and she looked into her own mind which was of course quirky and capacious, and she put the pieces together this way and that until she...made something...out of words...that no one else could have made..."

Petra stops. Nat is saying, as if she knows, as if it's a thing she takes for granted and at the same time a thing that has to be said carefully and clearly, "You'll do it, Petra. You'll make something no one else can."

Petra lets her breath go, she must have been holding it. She says, "Thank you, Nat." She looks at Nat. It's a complicated look with old shoes and something new and sharp all mixed together. It's a loving look. Nat sighs, then smiles and sends the same look back.

Petra wants to make something no one else can.

She, Ricki Harding, wants to fall down and worship this woman. So maybe she really *has* forgiven her for not being perfect.

Petra takes a breath and turns a corner, suggesting they try to do something with "this damn poem," and smiling crookedly at everyone. Before they can start, though, she looks over and says, "This was supposed to be your day, Ricki. Sorry."

Ricki says, "It's important, about the poetry," She feels shy telling an older woman what's important. The age difference between her and everyone else is wide today. Bright Star was a bridge but the bridge has been blasted away. *Damn.* But she decides to be brave and ask the question that will make Petra say exactly what she means. "Are you going to do it the way Moore did, Petra?"

"Yes, Ricki. That's what I'm going to do. Now, let's see if we can get to the poem."

Suddenly Ricki knows what she wants: "Would someone read the poem aloud? I need a new way to hear it." Petra looks at Nat. Nat nods and gives a little grin and starts to read. She's a wonderful reader, sure of herself and very, very smart. Today her voice sounds more resonant than ever.

AN OCTOPUS

of ice. Deceptively reserved and flat,
it lies "in grandeur and in mass"
beneath a sea of shifting snow-dunes;
dots of cyclamen-red and maroon on its clearly defined
       pseudo-podia
made of glass that will bend—a much needed invention—
comprising twenty-eight ice-fields from fifty to five hundred
       feet thick,
of unimagined delicacy...

Grain and ginger. Nat's voice is full of grain and ginger. Ricki suspects Nat understands every single thing Marianne Moore intended to do with this poem. Petra is letting tears run down her beautiful face and drip from her chin while she looks at Nat as if Nat is...what? A visitation, that's what. Ricki didn't know Petra was beautiful until this minute. As for herself, she wants to stand up, leave the room, and *run*—not screaming, but whooping—all the way to Winterport. She wants to take the road over which trees protectively bend and burst into the trailer and kneel down before Ann Marie who'll be standing in the living room doing nothing but waiting for her and she, Ricki Harding, will say "Let's love each other."

*

"Beer?"

"Definitely," says Petra. The meeting has ended. It's only the two of them and the wallpaper vegetables. The vegetables are behaving themselves. Petra watches Nat's clean capable sexy hands get glasses and pour. *She's is so utterly at home here. Now we have no brake, the others were a brake.*

"Still mad at me?" Nat asks.

"Hardly."

"Hardly?"

"I fell in love again. You *know* that," Petra says, and the train is moving.

"You're right. I do. It's what makes me ask."

"Jesus, Nat."

"See, you're mad."

"I'm wild, somewhat, in a contained and cool sort of way, which is different from being mad, if mad is a synonym for angry. If, on the other hand, mad means nuts, well..."

"Petra Kalinowski, you *hypocrite*. You know being in love with me is your only sane option."

"Is it?"

"Yes," Nat says.

"What about you? Are you still mad?"

"I dropped the last remnants when I saw you shed tears at the sound of my wondrous reading voice."

"It was unexpected."

279

"Seeing through to me again."

"Yes, Nat. Seeing through to you again."

"You wanted me to read."

"I know. All of a sudden I *had* to hear you read."

"It's because you've cracked yourself open."

"Is that what I've done?"

"You're writing, and writing with this new desire."

"Well, not quite. I haven't actually *written*."

"You're writing, whether you have words on the page or not. You've started. You're all broken open. It's not just the writing, it's everything."

"There's more to tell, Nat."

"Is there? Well, I have a thing or two, also."

"Oh, God. I hope it's not complicating."

"It's complicating. Or could be. Or maybe not at all. I didn't expect what happened today. How *could* you?"

"*You're* still mad, Nat Levesque."

"Well."

Petra did know, before the meeting started, that she shouldn't talk about the land with the ruined house, not impulsively like that—*Should we buy it, Nat?*—with the others waiting downstairs, no time to smooth and shape things, no time to say what she meant. Not that she understood precisely what she meant. All these years she and Nat have taken care not to damage what they have and now she's done this raw thing. It's no wonder Nat was furious and called her a damn tease. To which she responded badly of course, but listening to the Chopin, waiting for a moment when she could interrupt the piece without doing violence to it, she was entranced by beauty. When Ricki asked that someone read the poem, she only wanted more beauty, in the form of Nat's voice. "Don't be mad, Nat."

"We'll see. Speak."

"It was Moore's opening lines, the glacier, the depths, the delicacy, the impossibility of ever *seeing* it all, but the attempt could be made, a person could...I don't know. You were reading a portrait of *yourself*, and of me, because I've been 'deceptively reserved and flat.' I understood suddenly. I could be 'glass that will bend.' I *could* bend."

Nat is quiet. Finally she says, "Can you, though?"

"Bend? I don't know. Maybe. Yes?"

"Yes with a question mark. Petra, Petra."

"I know."

"Meanwhile..."

"Meanwhile, what? What, Nat?" Silence. The sudden terrible thought occurs: "Are you sleeping with someone, Nat?"

"No, I'm not. But..."

"Who?"

"Well."

"*Who?*"

"It's only a phone call. I only made a phone call." They look at each other. Stalemate. But Nat's grin, suppressed, then escaping off the side of her face, gives her away.

"To whom did you make a phone call, Nat Levesque?" She's behind Nat, her hands in strangling position. Her gangster voice is pathetically ungangsterish.

Nat hangs her head and gives a strangled Brando-impersonating response: "*S-t-e-l-l-a.*"

"*What?*" The stranglehold loosens.

"Well," says Nat, standing up. What happens next is a confused melding of kissing orgy and fits of giggles. It ends with Nat leading them to the living room where they collapse on the couch. For the first time in many years Petra finds herself on top of the entire sexy body that is Nat Levesque. She stays there. They almost fall asleep but she has to say it.

"I don't think she's a lesbian, Nat."

"Oh, probably not," Nat says sleepily.

"She's wonderful, though."

"Isn't she?"

"If odd."

"That's part of the appeal, Petra."

"I suppose."

They do sleep, but Nat has to move, her arm and shoulder are all pins and needles. She stretches and yawns and reminds: "Didn't you have more to tell?"

"I have to pee," says Petra. They both pee. They zip up. They hug.

Nat whispers. "Petra, my dear, you have to tell."

281

"Aren't you hungry?" Nat sighs, admits she's hungry. "Eggs with things in?"

"I'll cut up the things. What do you have?"

"I must have celery, I always have celery. Olives? I think there's half an onion. No mushrooms, sorry. How many eggs?"

"Two. Start talking, Petra."

So Petra starts: "I'm not sure you'd be getting the same woman."

"I'm not sure I want the same woman. She was a bit unreliable when it came to remaining involved."

"No, really, Nat. Something's happened to me."

"Tell me, then. I want to know."

She tries to explain what she herself doesn't fully understand. She's committing the fault of wishing to be understood before making herself clear to herself. Simone Weil wouldn't approve. Still, she proceeds. "It has to do with Anya. Possibly. That's the safest way to put it."

"And the least safe way?" Nat is gentle and perfect now.

"Something about God."

"God. You're afraid I'll hear that word and run, chaos theory tucked under one arm, dropping fractals as I go."

"God might not be the right term."

"But something."

"It's easier to say it in the negative."

"So do it that way."

"We forgot toast."

"Do we need toast?"

"We absolutely do." Making toast, she ponders. Does she want to be talking about this? Why is it so easy with Gertrude and Raymond, and so difficult with Nat? But she knows: Nat is essential. No one else, not even Danny, is indispensable.

Nat comes to embrace her from behind. "Petra, this is going to be all right." Buttering toast, comforted, she tries not to spill tears, for soggy toast is an abomination. Back at the table, Nat prompts: "In the negative, then."

"All right. In the negative." Because it's necessary, it can be done. "It's not the God of any particular religion. Not the God of religion at all, or possibly it's the God of all religions. Not the God of sin and virtue. Not the prescriptive God and certainly not the punishing God. Not the God of faith, unless it's an existential, leap-of-faith kind of faith. Not a God who requires allegiance. Not a God who *requires* anything."

"No God of limits," Nat says.

"I don't know what I'm talking about, do I?"

"You do know what you're talking about, Petra. How did you get here?"

"You're right. I do know. Sort of. I stumbled upon...or followed. That's the word that came when I was with Raymond."

"With Raymond? You've had this conversation with Raymond?"

"Don't worry. Yes, but don't *worry*."

"Then say something explanatory."

"I suppose I shouldn't start with how I thought I was sexually drawn to him." She was trying to tease but Nat has put her fork down and gone rigid. No one's tough enough today for teasing. She goes around the table and embraces Nat from behind, resting her chin on Nat's head. "I'm sorry, Nat...all these years...it's been awful for you. I couldn't. I'm sorry I couldn't. Let me talk about Raymond, it's not a threat." Nat turns around. She's been crying in her quiet Nat way. "Oh, Nat," Petra says gently. "Please, just listen."

Nat wipes her eyes and blows her nose and says, "All right. Just tell it straight, Petra. No pun intended. Absolutely no pun intended."

"Come in here," Petra says, and leads Nat to the couch because obviously this is more important than food. They sit down and Nat allows herself to be held. She tells about the energy she felt when she was with Raymond, how it was confusing at first but it got sorted out. She knows now it had nothing to do with sex, with wanting sex. At least it had nothing to do with wanting sex with Raymond, though it might have been essential to getting here, to this moment, when she...well...wants sex with Nat. "I do. I want sex with you, Nat." Nat doesn't react. She keeps going, determined. She says Nat is right, the whole complicated experience with Chippie, which of course is all about Anya, has broken her open. Freedom is what it feels like and she's almost convinced it's true, freedom from constrictions that she placed on herself almost without knowing it. It took the conversation with Raymond, who did his version of the same thing. "The same thing, Nat. It was amazing.

There we were in the middle of the night..." Nat breaks away and moves to the other end of the couch.

"Nat."

"I'm listening. I'll keep listening."

This is called Necessity. Help me, Simone Weil. "We were at Danny's, waiting. Danny had Chippie at the emergency room."

"All night."

"It was important to me, Nat, and it wasn't sexual."

"It came close, but you found another way to be with him, or convinced yourself you did. Is that what you're saying?"

"No. Yes, in a way. No. Damn it, Nat. It was intense energy and I interpreted it as sexual at first and I learned I was wrong about that and then it became what it was."

"Which was what?"

"I'm on the verge of not being able to talk to you about this."

"Well, step back from the verge and talk to me. Get it together, Petra."

A few deep breaths. She can do this. "We were two people, Nat. Two people who were following something. We both found ourselves reading these *books*, spiritual books from old traditions, and we were both in this *time*, after the suicide, after everything with Chippie, and we had both long ago, as young people, done something, something wrong and not-wrong. No, I don't even believe that. Something outside the bounds, you know what I mean. For Raymond it was the murder and for me it was what I did, or didn't do, with Anya. We both survived by limiting what we could expect from life afterward."

"So now you've got this non-prescriptive but deeply rooted liberating spiritual bond with your new soul-buddy?"

"Nat. Please."

"I'll try."

"Can I come over there?"

"Not yet."

"What will it take?"

"Time. I just need some time, Petra. Right now, over there at your end of the couch, you look sort of condensed, as if you're in another...I don't know...dimension. You and your pal Raymond, I suppose he's there, too. I can't..."

"Nat..."

"Petra, you're not trustworthy about what you want." In the past this would have led to a conflict with higher and higher decibels, but Petra feels suddenly calm.

"That's what's changing. I'm almost...different...about that very thing. Maybe."

"Almost? Maybe? *Dammit*, Petra."

"Well, I wouldn't want to overstate it."

"Right."

"Nat, stop it."

"OK. I'm listening. You're different. What do you mean?" It's a real question. Nat will try to listen. Kind, smart Nat is almost here again. Take a deep breath.

"I know I'm going to write poetry. Maybe a lot of poetry."

"That's nice. That's...well...wonderful. But it's only you and you, Petra. You've always been sure inside yourself. It's relationships that confuse you, sweetie." Honest words, honestly offered. Petra doesn't even feel defensive. She dares to hope for a decent outcome to this conversation.

"That's true, Nat. I know that's always been true, but..."

"What, my dear exasperating Petra?"

"Nat Levesque. I love it when you get nice again."

"Nevertheless, you must tell me about being different." Nat comes close and puts her arms around her. The relief is intense.

"Mmmmm," says Petra.

"Not that relaxed," says Nat.

"I know. Nat, it's so *embarrassing* to be turning to God, or whatever it is I'm doing. And you're so...scientific."

"You're deluded about me and science. My interest in science is very unscientific. Tell me about turning to God. Just talk about it. And at some point please try to get around to how this makes you a more reliable bet in the relationship department."

"It *does*."

"It may well, but I need tutoring."

"I loved what you said today about Moore's poem."

"Is this relevant?"

"I think it is."

"What did I say, Petra?"

"That Moore gives us the vertical and the horizontal in one poem. I thought it was very smart of you to bring in Stein's level field, her democracy, how she insists on the equal importance of every word, and then Bishop's Man-Moth climbing the side of the building and falling. Up and down. The Man-Moth isn't hurt when he falls. Don't you love it that he's not hurt, having climbed and fallen?"

"I love it. Keep going."

"And then you convinced us, or at least convinced me, that Moore somehow gives us *everything*, the vast and the infinitesimal, all approached with equal interest and care in a Steinian sort of way, but at the same time we're going up this mountain, up, up, up, and the poem itself is this mountain to climb so that's a bit like Bishop's vertical vision, not that Bishop's vision is essentially vertical, but in 'The Man-Moth'..."

"I said all that, did I?" Petra twists around to view Nat's poker face. She knows it's there, she just wants to see it.

"I *know* you know what you said, but I'm getting at something. First, it was so smart and right to bring our recent reading in like that, as if you were giving us back our story after it got blasted apart by Bright Star. But also, do you remember when I was reading Polish writers and I found Czeslaw Milosz? He wrote something in one of his memoirs about a shining point."

"I remember. 'Nothing could stifle my inner certainty that a shining point exists where all lines intersect.'"

"You memorized it?"

"It was important to you, Petra. Also, I liked it."

Petra has to stop to absorb this. She takes an extra breath, shakes her head, and says. "You are one astonishing woman, anyone ever told her that?" Nat just waits. Petra continues: "So: Moore's poem— horizontal and vertical, as you said, and even multidirectional, as I think Roo said—brings us to that point. Maybe. With one kind of reading."

"Petra."

"OK. I know. You want me to just *say* it."

"That's right. I won't snarl."

"Right. OK. That's the God I'm talking about, that shining point where all lines intersect." She stops.

Nat says, "I'm listening."

"I want something, Nat. I want something I never knew I wanted and I'm reading *mystics*, old-fashioned religious mystics, and there's something there for me. I don't understand it, but it's there, even if weirdly expressed. And if I can want that...I didn't know this was where I was going...but if I can want some tiny personal hint of what God is, some actual experience, I mean...if I have that kind of *chutzpah*, then..."

"What, Petra?"

She takes a breath. "Then I can want you, Nat Levesque."

Nat just holds her. This is a complete holding. She, Petra Kalinowski, unreliable in the relationship department, does not break away. Nat's heartbeat is regular and sure. She can breathe with Nat's arms around her. She leans back. She lets herself feel the spaciousness of the old bond, relaxing further and further into confidence despite her sense that Nat is thinking, thinking, thinking.

"OK, Petra, let's see where this takes us."

This is enough, she thinks. At the same time she's greedy for more. More of Nat and more of all the rest. Which she knows will come. Such luck she has. Also, on the merely physical plane, she's starving, "Let's dump those cold eggs and start over," she says.

"Good idea, my dear," says perfect Nat as they head to the kitchen together.

Chapter Twenty-six

Sunday morning. Ricki steps into the dimly lit, graffiti-filled, piss and vomit smelling hall that leads to the stairway that will take her, unannounced, to Stella's apartment. She remembered to stop on the sidewalk, ready herself. The wink, the kiss, and the list are what she has for courage. Think of the wink, said Lionel. So she did. And felt it, the gift from the dying Indian, alchemized. Felt, too, the careful, tender kiss Ann Marie gave her last night. It was a kiss with a promise. *For now, just this,* it said. *More later.* In her hand is the list, *What Ricki Needs To Know from Stella Weeks,* composed during the Gleesome Threesome's spaghetti event. Ann Marie was the secretary. Her touch is on the page. Up the steps, then. One, two, three. Fine. Four, five. Good. Six. She's on her way to talk to a mother about her daughter who shot and killed herself. Seven, eight. As well as slicing her wrists and killing herself; twice-killed, this daughter. Nine. This is crazy, she should turn around. Ten, eleven, twelve. Maybe Stella won't be home. Thirteen, fourteen. She knocks. Stella is home.

"Why, Ricki Harding. Imagine your appearing at the very moment I need clarification. I suspect I haven't found the essence. For Raymond, you know." Stella holds out a half-finished deep brown—or dark red?—doily. It's normal and flat, not like the ones done for spite. Is that good or bad? Stella leads her through the kitchen to the living room and invites her to sit on the couch as if she were an expected guest, then leaves her alone for too long. Which is just Stella being Stella. Finally, here she is, with coffee. "I plan one for you, too, dear. Of course, Petra's is completed. Perhaps we'll find our way today, you and I. Petra was plain to me but you and Raymond are...well...I do like a cup of coffee, don't you?" They drink good coffee. Time passes. A dreamy silence reigns. The list with Ann Marie's warmth still on it rests in her lap. Did Stella mean she wants to make a doily for all three of them? It would make sense. Besides Stella and Chippie, they're the ones most affected by Bright Star's...

"A piece of paper can be a help," Stella comments. She feels found out, captured and pinned to the board like a butterfly. A butterfly with a list in her lap. But, no. This is the Stella who takes charge, who can handle whatever comes. This is the Stella she needs. She takes a deep breath.

"I have some questions, Stella."

"Well, of course you do."

She picks up the list. "First, how are you?"

"Is that on your piece of paper, dear?" She nods, embarrassed, helpless. Lionel dictated the question, afraid she'd forget her manners. Ann Marie wrote it down without hesitation. Stella sits up straighter. "I'm doing quite well, Ricki Harding, and thank you for asking."

"It's just that I didn't want to get nervous and forget to ask, so my friends suggested..."

"That you write it down, a reminder to yourself. Well, you're a bit young to be handling things that way but I imagine you're stressed. What happens to be next on your list?" She'd like to crumple the paper and just *talk* with Stella. Is such a thing is possible?

"Raymond."

"What about Raymond, dear?" For one agonized instant she can't remember, but it comes to her.

"He's not the father."

"Of Persephone. Well, I know that, dear." She *knows* that?

"I thought..."

"I did have a misapprehension, perhaps following on the comment of my friend Margie who jumped to a conclusion, but Raymond assured me and he wouldn't lie. He has a little code, is my observation. Lying doesn't come into it."

"But Raymond thinks you..."

"I myself have a different code, I suppose."

"But why would you say 'my son's child'?"

"At that diner. Well, yes. That was plain embarrassment, I'm ashamed to say, but it's passing. I'll clarify myself to Raymond when he deigns to visit me again. I can do that, you know. Clarify myself."

"Embarrassment? About thinking in the first place...?"

"Oh, I know I can be a task to follow, but who'd be embarrassed about a misconception? No, it was the wanting."

"Wanting?"

"Having a desire. You know, dear, what a desire is. I imagine you had one in relation to Raymona Weeks."

"Raymona?"

"Raymona Weeks. I understand she came to call herself Bright Star. Were you wondering about my drinking, dear? Perhaps that was the purpose of your call. You needn't worry. I have Raymond's doily in progress and my Alcoholics Anonymous meetings and my new friend Margie." Stella's eyes dart off but she brings herself back quickly.

"I'm glad you're not drinking, Stella. I did worry because a person's daughter..."

"Oh, she was no longer my daughter, dear. That was the cause of the embarrassment, you see." But she doesn't see.

"I don't..."

"Perhaps a straighter line, then. Excuse me for a moment, dear." Alone again. Is this visit even possible? Sound of the toilet flushing. Stella returns, settles herself with the same fussing ritual she used at Bitta's. Finally she's ready, crochet hook in motion, eyes on Ricki. "Now, where were we, Ricki?" Perfectly composed. A normal person. A person who can answer questions, explain things.

"Something about embarrassment. Then you said Bright Star wasn't your daughter. 'Any more' is what I think you said."

"Yes. Well. The two are nicely linked. We had a falling out some years ago. I found myself embarrassed to acknowledge—to Raymond, I suppose, since no one else could have a concern—that I would want to carry out the duties of a grandmother. If the child belonged to Raymona, you see. Whereas Raymond's child would naturally become my grandchild without complication. Is that what you want to know, dear?" Is that what she wants to know? "Perhaps your list would help you, dear." Would it? She glances at the list. *How Stella is. Raymond. Why Bright Star wouldn't talk about Stella. Why Bright Star killed herself.* "More coffee, child?"

"No. Um. Thanks. I have to go soon." She crumples the list.

"No, you don't, Ricki Harding. It wouldn't be an easy thing, coming to visit a relative, even a former relative, after an event. You had no way of knowing the exact situation and besides, all that time we spent driving, it makes a little bond, don't you think? I have a debt of gratitude

I'm not repaying well today. Raymona was once my daughter, you're right about that. It has an effect still, such an inconsiderate death, and you and I are together in that, as is Raymond who avoids me these days, and that nice David Robichaud." Is Raymond really avoiding her? Who's David Robichaud? But she wants to keep things on track. If there is a track.

"I thought I could understand better if we talked, Stella."

"Why she took her life, dear?"

"Yes."

"Well, she had good reason, we know that." We do? The statement sounds final, as if the subject has been dealt with quite completely, thank you. Stella looks toward the corner of the room, toward what Ricki failed to notice earlier, a pile of flat doilies in many colors neatly piled on the floor. On top of them are the familiar soft black sculptures done for spite, looking precarious. They might slip from the pile at any moment. She looks at Stella. Stella looks at her.

"She lied to me, Stella."

"Oh, that would be her way, dear, but she was good with truth, too. She was good with both, in the sense of being an expert, you know. Lies had many uses. Truth was for hurting others. She was a piece of work, that girl."

"Petra thinks she had multiple personality disorder." This is a blurt, not intended, or not quite.

Stella nods and says calmly, "Oh, she did indeed."

"You know that?"

"It was one of her truths."

"A truth she used to hurt you?"

"I hope she was kinder to you. You seem to have appreciated her. Except perhaps for the ending."

"She told me about her plan...when we first..."

"Well, that was only fair."

"Except she said it was because she had a fatal illness."

"Oh, no, dear. She planned her suicide when she was quite young. If I remember correctly, she was eight years old." Eight years old? How could that be? Stella puts her crochet materials on her chair's arm and rises stiffly and walks into the kitchen. Eight? And Stella knew? Stella is moving around and muttering to herself. Then she's back with fresh coffee. They sit drinking coffee, strangely relaxed, as if their topic has gone away. Which it, or she, has. That's the plain truth about death. The person is gone. It's not complicated. There's nothing to talk about. Stella gets up—not suddenly, but as if some sign, some direction, has been given and she's happy to respond to it—gets up with no difficulty, almost fluidly, and approaches her and leans over and kisses her on the top of her head and says, "What nice hair you have, dear." Then the gesture is finished, it might never have happened, and Stella is carrying cups toward the kitchen. She stops in the doorway and says brightly, over her shoulder, "Did I mention the fact that Nat Levesque called me?"

"Nat?"

"You know, dear. That lovely Nat Levesque who spoke so movingly to you at Raymona's service." Which turns out to be the gift Stella has to offer today. Ricki had talked herself out of the idea that Nat, reading the poem about the kind of love that doesn't last long, was speaking to her in particular. It was pure and unexpected that Nat would do this, a great comfort and honor, but she decided she must have misinterpreted. How embarrassing. Now Stella says the poem *was* meant for her. And Nat, who can steady a person like no one else, has called Stella. These are good things. She can almost hear Bright Star saying, "Ricki Dicki Dear, don't worry your handsome little head about *anything at all*." Almost, but not quite.

*

Tuesday afternoon. Raymond would rather be at work but it's his day off and he's gotten a summons. He stops before he enters the hall, closes his eyes, opens them, takes a deep breath, goes in, starts up the stairs. The odor's worse than ever or maybe it's that he hasn't been here for several days, not even to knock and get no answer, use his key, check on the doilies. He can't shake what he left behind today—Danny's invitation, his shy-bold manner, how he went about communicating that a difference was possible, giving the menu, spaghetti and meatballs, salad, apple pie, putting in the idea of candlelight to make things clear, nervous all the while. Stella gave him an excuse for delaying his answer. Can't make plans until he sees what her situation is. He's taking these steps one at a time and there are a lot of them. He means the steps he's climbing to get to the apartment but he could mean steps he's taking in this new life. He doesn't have much of a shield around himself. Raymona's angled-back head keeps bringing sex to his mind along with the fact that she shot into her own mouth and then he's back to when he's the one holding the gun and Bede is dead and they're waiting for the police. He's sitting on the bare mattress with the body, Bede's blood seeping, and Raymona sits on the floor next to him, her chin propped on her knees. Was he so confounded by what he did that he couldn't move? He thinks he wanted to give a kindness to the body, stay there with it, not leave for a second, but that might be a whitewash. The climb from street level up to Stella's has never felt so steep. He's stalling, is what it is, going slow like this. That conversation with Petra at Danny's went to Bede, too, and to how the two them, himself and Petra, found themselves in unusual territory— territory beyond the boundaries—past what most people would say is right. But they don't feel like criminals to themselves, that was Petra's point. Then there was Klose-kur-beh and Petra's idea that everybody is created new every minute. That was a unique conversation. Raymona would hand out big thoughts but she wasn't inclined to listen for his. Everybody's different. Where Petra weaves things, trying to work out her own thoughts while she listens, Danny's eyes sparkle from the pure adventure of hearing. Having a man's eyes on you like that, a person feels how it would be possible to step over a line. Another line. So he'd better say it to himself. He could turn gay, though he never thought about such a thing before. Even with all these topics rising up, there's still Chippie tumbling along, a baby doing somersaults in the middle of his mind, or maybe it's his heart. This is the best thing, how he likes the baby so much, and it's thanks to Petra. He'd say his debt to her is getting bigger all the time except that she lectured him about mutuality.

Only a few more steps.

But he doesn't get his steps, at least not in privacy, because here she is, opening the door. "You are dragging your feet, Raymond. Never has a person taken so long to arrive at this landing. I thought I'd allow you your own pace but there's a limit to waiting."

"Hello, Ma."

"Hello, yourself. Now come in. I have your coffee poured and it's nearly cold with the waiting." The apartment is a mess. It's been a long time since he's seen it this bad. He doesn't smell alcohol, but the idea of it is heavy in the air. The kitchen table hasn't been wiped, dishes are helter-skelter in the sink, pieces of a broken cup lie in a puddle of what looks like coffee on the floor. When they get to the living room he sees the doily situation. The ones piled on the carpet aren't orderly and those on the furniture aren't placed right. Stella seats herself and picks up a black piece of crochet-work that has a long way to go to become anything but he can tell it will never lie flat. She starts her hook going as if there's a deadline. For all the attention she's paying him, he might not be here. Nothing to do but wait.

The minutes mount up. He tries to remember what it feels like to hold Chippie against his chest, but he can't. He can remember her bright little eyes, though. All his life he was the one looking at situations, trying to see what was needed, trying to do what was called for. Now people are looking at him with a pure intention that shifts things. He has to stand off from himself a little to tolerate it but he wants it all the same.

"You have a good capacity for silence, Raymond."

"What?"

"You heard me, dear." He looks at her and she's got a smile for him. With Stella you never know. He feels like crying but of course he won't do that. The crochet hook keeps on going. He drinks his coffee. He starts to relax and his curiosity rises up. What road will they take today? Maybe she'll let him bring her back from where she's been.

"Once we get our business done I have something for you, son." Son? First time he's been called that.

"What business, Ma?"

"We'll get to that. Not that it's complete yet."

"The business?"

"No, dear. The gift. It's happening in stages and requires a rest between. I see from the window that you got your truck going."

"I did, the night Chippie was at the emergency room. Petra had jumper cables." He hopes it's not a mistake to mention Petra. He knows she's been here but not what happened when she came. He knows Ricki visited, too, from trying to call her and getting Gertrude on the phone. He's part of a series.

"I understand that baby has improved."

"She's much better."

"Of course she is." She puts her crochet-work down and takes his cup to the kitchen. He can see her in there, hesitating about where to put it. She chooses the table. Who's stalling now, he wants to say, but you don't tease Stella. She comes back and picks up her work. "Now, Raymond, I'm in the middle of it, as you can see." He certainly can.

"Hard time, isn't it, Ma?"

"Well, yes, it is. I'm going to drink, it's been decided. Right along with that is the intention to remain sober. You can observe the result and imagine the degree of disarrangement in my mind. I don't blame her because it might be a good turn she's done me but that little Ricki Harding has started a train of thought in me and I don't easily find the brake switch. Is that right? That a train, to stop it, needs a switch?"

"I don't know, Ma."

"Well, I suppose that's a side question. My idea was to tell you some things but now it occurs to me that..."

"Ma?"

"I do have the writing on my mind. You are not my sole concern."

"Writing?"

"As a way. To try to make up for what Raymona did to that young woman."

"I don't..."

"I know you don't. Just be patient with me. I've come to realize the amount of patience I require. From those I talk with, I mean. I've come to understand a number of things, but it's a hither and yon proposition. As for your father, his name was Raymond which you might have guessed a long time ago, I don't know why you didn't."

"My father?"

"That would matter less to Ricki Harding than the rest of it."

"Are you going to tell me about my father?" He knows it's the wrong thing to say, it's not patient. He doesn't feel patient.

"I'll get to that. I suppose it's what's important to you but I would think you might be interested in how to give aid to that young woman's mind."

"I'm interested, Ma. Go ahead." He didn't derail her. It's the best he can hope for. His father's name was Raymond. She's right, he should have guessed, and it does tell him something. She liked his father, at least at the time of his birth. Or maybe not. Maybe his father was a tyrant and she was forced to name his son after him.

"Trying to write it all down has been a chore."

Write what down? But all he says is, "I suppose it has."

"So I thought you could help me."

"I'll try." Does he even want to know about his father? Getting a first name alone feels like a sock to the gut. She said *was*: your father's name was Raymond. Does that mean he's dead? But he can't think about this now because he's looking at Stella and she's looking at him and a phenomenon is in progress. His mother is crying.

"She was named after you, of course, dear. To keep that line going." She blows her nose.

"Raymona," he says. He says it as carefully as he knows how to. She nods like a five-year-old, nodding and sniffling. He'd like to give her a hug, maybe he should. But right away she pulls herself up.

"You were not around when it came out." He waits. She might be able to say whatever this is. "You were at the Youth Center just then as I recall." She looks around the room. He almost thinks she's counting doilies, she's giving such careful attention here and then there, wherever the doilies are. "I don't know what to do about them," she says.

"The doilies?"

"One minute they're one place, the next minute I see that they've moved. They don't settle."

"You'll find your way, Ma."

"Call me Stella for a while, Raymond. It might help."

"OK. You'll find your way, Stella."

"She named herself after me, though I can't be sure she knew it."

"Raymona?"

"My name means star, Raymond. Margie told me that. All this time and I didn't know it. Do you think she did?"

"Taking that name, you mean. Bright Star. I only know she said it came to her in a dream."

"Did it now? Well, that's nice."

"You said I was away."

"She got it out of me. Her lineage, you know."

"Oh."

"She started calling me Sister."

"Sister?"

"Because we shared a father, of course. So there was a basis and I remember thinking it was clever of her but that thought came years later. She was bright, wasn't she? I birthed no stupid children. At the time, however, I could feel nothing but the cruelty, an arrow into my heart every time she said it. Sister, she'd say, with that mockery in her tone. So she had to go, Raymond, though she was young for it. You think I don't know but I do know." Know what? But he can't interrupt her now. She looks around the room again, but she pulls herself into her dignity and looks right at him. "I imagine she told you all of this, Raymond. Sometimes I think about the two of you, talking. I do understand you've lost your sister." She's looking at him clear-eyed. He has the sudden feeling that she knows him and it takes his breath away.

"I don't know what to say, Ma. Stella."

"You can call me Ma, Raymond, now that I got this much out."

"Ma. I didn't know any of this."

"She never told you, then."

"She told me the two of you had a fight and she decided to leave."

"Well, that's not accurate."

"I guess not."

"My question is about Ricki."

"Whether it would help her to know some of this?"

"I thought it might. She got drawn into a whirlwind of great proportion."

"Stella—Ma—are you saying your father is Raymona's father?"

"Yes, Raymond. Perhaps you've wondered why we had no extended family but now you have the reason."

"And my father. He was somebody else?"

"He was that nice boy I met at the roller rink. Indian, of course."

"Ma, would you tell me his last name?"

"Oh, I wouldn't know his last name, dear." So that's all there is. A first name. "Yours isn't finished, Raymond, try as I might, so I've gone back to what has to do with Raymona. Even this I can't be sure of. What shape, I mean. I have a certainty about the color."

"Mine? Something you're crocheting for me?"

"I had to unravel it. Partially. Words are difficult, but you deserve what I'm intending." She's looking down at her work, very busy. His heart goes soft.

"Thanks, Ma."

"Do you think it would help her? I'm asking you, Raymond." Moving along, then. He shakes his head, helpless before her various intentions. Later he'll have time to think about fathers, how his grandfather was Raymona's father, how his own father has a name, Raymond.

"I don't know what Ricki needs, Ma. Petra and I tried to figure what information would help her. I can't say we came to any solid ground. We told her there was no fatal illness. Did you know Raymona convinced her she was about to die from some illness?"

"Ricki and I visited the topic. It's my impression facts help that young woman, but the writing gets tangled. I wanted to be sure it was worth the effort."

"I don't know. It looks like it might be too hard on you."

"That is not my question, Raymond." They look at each other. She, challenging, he, meeting her with his plain unknowing. We're pretty well matched, he thinks.

What he says is, "Maybe I could do some dishes."

"You can't help with my question, can you, dear?"

"I wish I could."

"Well, then, you wash and I'll dry. A companionable time might be an aid to my mind. I do crave a drink, Raymond."

"I'll stay, Ma." Danny will wait, and Chippie, and his new life. Also, sorting through his old life will wait. Bede wasn't the first perpetrator of incest in this family. *My grandfather was my sister's father. Stella was...what?...raped? By her own father?*

Chapter Twenty-seven

Wednesday afternoon. Petra sits in Gertrude's waiting room, early for supervision. No one else here. She's made herself comfortable, shoes off, jacket and carrying case on the chair next to her. She has Martin Buber's *Ecstatic Confessions* and Gertrude of Helfta's *The Herald of God's Loving-Kindness*. The library was busy. Luckily, Raymond was at the desk. He checked out the books and while he did it they checked each other out, exchanging a look, smiling. It was enough, the comfort is still there. When she called to tell Danny about developments with Nat she could hear his ungoverned grin. She imagines he told Raymond. As for Danny and Raymond, she assumes they'll get together whenever Raymond can stop spending nights at Stella's. How good that would be for Chippie: two parents, besotted with each other and with their baby. The work week so far has been unique but not distressing. Who could predict she'd calmly say good-bye to Helga so soon? It's possible she has no clinical judgment left, but she feels relaxed, even serene, about Helga. It was the return to subtle, tasteful makeup, the cared-for cuticles, and, of course, Helga's own serenity. She will make a new life, living with her generous cousin and her little girl, Ingrid. She feels better, having told the story of the group rape and Ingrid's conception; feels better and doesn't wish to dwell there. *I don't wish to dwell there, Petra. I hope you won't be disappointed in me. I know others might go deeper.* Petra, therapist with the light touch, nodded and felt like chanting *Go, Helga, Go*, but only smiled and wished her client well. "The door is open, Helga, if ever..."

"You wouldn't mind? If I had to come back? I know this is the right decision, but..." They shook hands and said good-bye. All very gentle and, of course, in good taste. Also, there was a warm glow. Truly: a warm glow. Let no one call Petra Kalinowski sentimental, for the cliché is accurate. What a good mood she's in.

She said good-bye to Andrew, too. It helped him, to talk and cry. He wanted to test himself, come a second time "just to see," but after five minutes he knew this would be his last session. Iris couldn't tolerate living with her parents, she's back with the children. *The kids are back, Petra.* This was the essence. She listened with no interference from personal static. "And Iris?"

"In the guest room."

"She still wants to explore her sexuality?"

"Yes."

"And?"

"And we'll see. For now it's enough to have them all back in the house. I'm eating, I'm sleeping. Can I go, Doc?" Yes, he can go. The door is open, of course, if he needs to comes back. They hugged good-bye. He simply stepped forward and they were hugging. It was brief. Appropriate, she thinks, despite the tiny question in her mind. If Iris leaves again and Andrew returns to therapy, she'll be alert. She wouldn't want to confuse him, raise hopes that she might be his next woman. On the other hand, he's a very attractive man. If it weren't for Nat, and, of course, professional ethics...

But she's just playing. The theme here is lightness, a spillover from the last meeting with Gertrude. And here's Martin Buber, Jew who collects mystical writings of all faiths, like Gertrude. If Gertrude doesn't know this book, she needs to be introduced to it. Buber led to Gertrude of Helfta, Gertrude the Great, who has to be read for the very good reason that her name is Gertrude. The sentimental strain of mysticism owes much to this Gertrude: devotion to the Sacred Heart of Jesus, those terrible holy cards with the exposed heart, thorn-pierced and dripping blood. Maybe someday she and Gertrude will talk about these matters, try to sort wheat from chaff. She'd like to do this immediately but they really ought to return to clinical supervision after recent irregularities. Besides, it's Gertrude's turn. But here are the books, just in case. Maybe they'll play hooky. Being with Nat again encourages these frivolous impulses. She'd almost forgotten about the possibility of pure pleasure. Now she's inundated, knocked off her feet, and happy to be laid flat by the wave. Or happy to be laid, period; a sentiment she will not express to Gertrude Benstein, whose office door opens at this blushing moment. A tall thin black man emerges. He looks familiar. It's the wire-rimmed glasses, the white hair, the supple body. Another attractive man. There are a lot of attractive people in the world just now. Even Kiki this week, who has a new FRIEND, looked downright pretty in purple and red. As the man takes his jacket from Gertrude's lovely antique coat rack, she remembers: he was in line at the Shop and Save in Bucksport. Unusual sight, a black man in Bucksport. He looks happy, emerging from his therapist's office. Well, good. She wants everyone happy today. But Gertrude isn't happy. Fussing with papers at her desk, her back turned, she seems nervous, or vulnerable. "Are you all right, Gertrude?"

"I need to talk, Petra." Since talking is their reason for meeting, this declaration should strike them both as funny, or at least ironic, but Gertrude is too tense for that, and too quiet. "I don't want to talk about clients today," she says, finally.

"No problem." Then, thinking she's been abrupt when she ought to be sensitive: "Really, Gertrude. Talk about whatever's on your mind."

"It's us. There are two distinct aspects to my concern, Petra." So formal, this tone. Anxiety-producing. Curiosity-producing, too. The silence has risen up again. Gertrude could use a set of Helga's worry beads, she's kneading a dry tissue into a ball. Does she expect to cry? Gertrude? Unlikely. It could be she only wants to talk more about mysticism and feels it would be inappropriate.

Or she's finally appalled at the idea of a therapist who gives her kids away.

Gertrude speaks. "I worry that I stepped out of my role, that it was wrong, to bring in Julian of Norwich."

"But it was perfect, Gertrude. Just what I needed. We're fine. At least with aspect number one, if that's aspect number one."

"Are you sure? I've never done anything like that in a professional context and I know it might change things and..."

"It's fine, but you're driving me crazy. What else?"

"Oh. Well, that's harder."

"Just give me a hint."

"A hint won't do it. I have to tell this whole thing, and it's complicated and I don't even know why it's so crucial. No, that's not true. I do know why, but I don't want anything to..." She's never seen Gertrude so unsure of her footing.

"Gertrude, I think we're pretty solid." Gertrude says nothing. "Is this about my giving up Anya?" Gertrude looks astonished.

301

"Oh, Petra. No. I'm sorry. No, not at all. It's...it's about our backgrounds."

"Our backgrounds?" Gertrude just nods. She looks almost helpless. "Gertrude, we can make this be OK. Please. Tell me."

"I saw my parents this weekend."

"Your parents. I'll listen, Gertrude. I'll listen as well as I can."

"They're survivors. I don't think we've talked about that at all."

"Your parents? Of the Holocaust?"

"Of the death camps, yes. In Poland." *Death camps*. Why has she never wondered about Gertrude's parents?

"I didn't know, Gertrude. But of course I should have thought—"

"Well, Benstein. You'd have assumed Germany, but my mother's people—"

"No. The fact is I didn't think at all. I never even wondered."

"You're not required to. That's not important. I'll just try to tell you this thing and we'll get past it." What thing? This is something between us? "I mentioned you to my parents. I was feeling so good about...well, I treasure you as a colleague, Petra, and then...I was telling them I had a friend who was a therapist, how rich it could be, how we talked about Simone Weil. They respect Weil, this political intellectual Jew, even though she identified in her own way with Christianity and wasn't exactly sanguine about the Jewish State. They admire her mind."

"But..."

"Sometimes they feel sorry for me because I never married. They imagine I'm lonely. Telling them about you—"

"You mentioned that my people are from Poland?"

"It's worse than that. I told them your last name." Gertrude is crying now, just a little.

"I don't understand, Gertrude. My last name?"

"I'm sorry. It's not your fault. I can't stop thinking about Jedwabne."

"Jedwabne?"

"You weren't even born."

"Gertrude, what's Jedwabne?"

"You don't know? I thought your parents came from Poland, after the war."

"They did, but—"

"So I thought...but, no, why would they talk about it?"

"I know the Poles could have—should have—helped the Jews more. Is that what this is about?"

"When my parents heard your last name they froze. Jedwabne was only a few miles from where they grew up. It's a terrible story. I thought you'd know it."

"What story, Gertrude?" But Gertrude is looking into a distance all her own.

"Gertrude, please."

Gertrude sighs, and says, "It'll give you nightmares."

"Then I'll have nightmares."

"It's all hearsay, really. My parents weren't there."

"OK, it's hearsay. Tell me."

"My parents lost relatives there."

"This doesn't sound like hearsay."

"I mean the details. Maybe it was the Germans' idea. Some say it was. Others, not. Let's say it was, let's say the German soldiers gave the Poles of Jedwabne a deadline, until nightfall. So in the end they—the Polish townspeople—herded the remaining Jews. There was a huge barn and they...locked them in."

"Oh, God, Gertrude."

"Half the town was Jews, Petra."

"Imprisoned them? The Poles imprisoned the Jews of their own town? I always thought of Poles, all of us, Jews and gentiles together, as victims. Victims of Germany, but also Russia. Of course it was worse if you were a Jew, of course, I know that, but—"

"My parents think seven or eight Jews survived. I suppose they found good hiding places."

"What?"

"I think it was just seven or eight."

"Are you saying all those people in the barn died? That they were never released? Or taken care of?"

"Petra, they were killed."

"Killed? This was a mass murder?"

"The Poles poured gasoline around the barn and set fire to it." Gertrude is pale, telling this. Petra's never seen such a pale person. Well, other than Ricki's Lionel. This pale person goes on talking. "I don't know why this is so...big...for me. I know about atrocities. All my life, I know about atrocities." Petra isn't sure she understands. Her people massacred Gertrude's people? "It was your name, Petra. My parents stopped talking about the camps a long time ago, and the war. They made a decision to put it in the past, *decades* ago. But your name..."

"Kalinowski." Petra pronounces it carefully. She's always loved this name. It has to do with a cranberry bush that grows in Poland. She can see the springtime flowers, delicate and white, and the tart red berries. But do cranberry bushes flower? Are the flowers small and white? She never troubled herself to do the research.

"There were Kalinowskis involved in getting gasoline, Petra. Gasoline for burning the barn." Gertrude is saying this carefully. Gertrude is telling the story and it's a terrible story, just as she warned. "Two brothers, or cousins. Kalinowskis. It won't make any difference once I absorb it. I'm sorry, Petra. I just..."

"God, Gertrude. I don't even know how to...what to...say." This is radically true. Not-knowing is her radical truth. She can barely grasp what their topic is. A town named Jedwabne. Her possible relatives.

"The story goes on and on. I just need to tell it to you, Petra. I thought...I imagined...that your parents left Poland because of it. Which is irrational, it was a middle-of-the-night thought. My parents and I...we kept going back to Jedwabne all Sunday afternoon, Sunday evening. They were inside it, it was a horror. Can you stand this?" The question is a good one, a bracing question, she can brace herself against this question. Can she stand it? To hear a simple set of facts that a colleague and maybe also a friend needs to tell her? How can this even be a question? What's the matter with her? She looks at Gertrude who looks so vulnerable, whom she loves.

"Of course I can stand it. We can stand it, you and I. It's fine. Well, it's not fine, it's horrendous, but we'll be fine. I'll be fine. I guess I can't say your parents will be fine, how could they be fine? Or you. But yes. Please. I want you to tell me."

"If you're sure."

"I'm sure." And she is. Something will happen to her sense of herself today; to her sense of her Polish self at the very least. And she feels ready. "Talk, Gertrude." But now Gertrude isn't ready. Petra waits. Finally Gertrude bites her lip. Then she talks.

"That day at Jedwabne...the details are so monstrous, Petra. It was like a celebration, a grotesque celebration, all day. It couldn't have been that way for every Pole, but there was so much...*glee*. That's what my parents got focused on. Jewish women were trying to drown themselves...a story of a woman trying to drown her baby to save it from the Poles during the roundup, and the Poles...but it can't have been all of them, it just *can't* have been all of them...egging her on, from dry land, having a wonderful time...while she held her baby under water. As if it were a sport, drowning babies. Mockery, so much mockery, Jews made to sing and dance on their way to the barn and the Poles clapping and laughing at them. And bodies hacked apart. They had axes, hooks of some kind, knives. Those who weren't dead by late in the day got put in the barn. Hundreds. The bodies in the barn were found crushed against the door, as if they had hope, as if they believed they could get out. Our relatives...for some reason my parents are convinced they were in the barn, not killed earlier, though they went vague when I..." Gertrude stops. She squeezes her tissue into a smaller, denser ball. Petra isn't sure she'll be able to remember this story, but of course she's not allowed to forget it, ever. She and Gertrude sit together, tears running down their faces. After a while Gertrude says, "You really never heard this story?" Petra shakes her head. Gertrude blows her nose. "I thought I'd heard them all, but never this. It poured out of them. My mother's favorite cousin was killed that day, and an aunt and an uncle. She cried and cried, telling me. Your parents didn't talk about what happened in Poland, the war, any of it?"

"Some. Of course, some. Not this. My mother was raped by Russian soldiers who were supposed to be saving Poland from the Germans. My father was a young Polish patriot, a partisan. There was something about my mother teaching him to think better of Jews. This, about Jedwabne, doesn't fit. I'm not sure I'm hearing it well. You're saying German soldiers might have been behind it, forcing the Poles to do it, but at the same time at least some of the Poles, many, had a monstrous enthusiasm for the task, as if it was a relief to be wildly and openly anti-Semitic. But the term anti-Semitism seems mild."

"Not to a Jew. This is what anti-Semitism means, or this is part it. It all clings together. The tiniest slight is connected to...this. To things like this."

Petra nods. She feels humble, ignorant. She feels embarrassed. "Your parents just kept talking, once they started."

"They didn't even disagree on the details, which was one of the stranger parts of the day for me. To see them united like that."

"In pain," Petra says. "United in the pain. Or horror."

"It was terrible for them, but it had a compulsively satisfying aspect. You know what I mean. It gave them something, I think, to recover the details, together, and to pass it all to me. Though my mother says they haven't slept well the last couple of nights."

"And you?"

"I just want you to tell me it's acceptable for us to talk about it."

"It's imperative that we talk about it, Gertrude." They sit silently, not talking about it. Finally Petra says, "I feel a little sick. Stunned. I don't think of myself as Polish all that much. I've never been to Poland. I haven't paid a lot of attention to my 'roots.' There was a period, though, when I read Polish writers. I was planning to...this is so strange...I was going to show you a quotation today about a point where all lines meet, just a little footnote to add to our talk last time, which was more important to me than I can tell you. We were going to have this very normal supervision session and then I'd tell you about the shining point because it seemed mystical to me and I really am trying to understand..."

"The shining point where all lines meet. Yes. Czeslaw Milosz. He's wonderful."

"Have you read *everyone*?"

"Petra, you are so precious to me. Just don't put me in a barn and burn me."

"It's not funny, Gertrude."

"I'm not joking."

"I won't put you in a barn and burn you."

"It's like a tide, when it comes."

"You mean when anti-Semitism takes over a country?"

"Well, that. But I meant when paranoia takes over a Jew."

"Oh." This stops her. "You actually get scared like that?" Gertrude nods. "Oh, Gertrude. But it does make sense, it could happen anywhere. I know that. We shouldn't call it paranoia."

"Well, I don't think it's entirely realistic to fear you, Petra." A slight smile changes Gertrude's pale face. A bit of color, too.

"Maybe not. I certainly hope not. I'm one of those homosexuals, you know. I'll get thrown into wherever you get thrown."

Now they can both smile, a little. Gertrude says, "I forget that sometimes. How you live with homophobia."

"So do I. I've had such a lucky life."

"But you *are* socially unacceptable. More so than I am, I think."

"It's odd. It's easier for me to come out as a lesbian than as a woman who gave up her child."

"Really? But, Petra, you only wanted what was best for Anya. And to survive with your mind intact."

"Not everyone is as tolerant as you are, Gertrude. Still, I've been lucky there, too. It's fear, not any actual bad treatment I've gotten."

"The same could be said for me. People treat me perfectly well. But we're alike. We choose our friends carefully, don't we?" *Gertrude says we're alike.* Relief washes through her. She can't predict, of course she can't, what this story of Jedwabne will do to Gertrude, to their friendship. Nevertheless: relief.

"We do choose our friends carefully, Gertrude, a fact that's relevant to this hour. But don't you have a client?"

"What? Oh. Look at the time. Yes, I have a client, one who gives me hell if I'm one single minute late."

Being disciplined professionals, they stop, just like that.

*

And, she thinks later, sitting in her kitchen with books, notebook, pens, what more could have been said? It all had to be absorbed. They had a quick hug and Gertrude hurried to the bathroom, apologizing to the woman in the baseball cap who must have been in a good mood because she grinned at Gertrude's being flustered, rather than scowling over having to wait. The woman obviously has a crush on her therapist. Which crush, Petra would be willing to bet, her therapist knows nothing about. Any dyke could see it. All very entertaining. The fact remains: Kalinowskis played a key role in the slaughter of hundreds of Jews at Jedwabne in Poland. What to do with this information? Her mind keeps veering to the books. *Ecstatic Confessions. The Herald of God's Loving-Kindness.* Can they help? While she was with Gertrude she held them, never letting go through the entire hour. She had no awareness of this until she stood up to leave, but it was as if her hands knew: here was something to hold onto. Raymond did the same thing. When was that? She has the sudden thought that Gertrude has read the book by her namesake saint and doesn't find it sentimental, that Gertrude Benstein, daughter of Polish death camp survivors, isn't alienated, isn't embarrassed, by spirituality rooted in emotion. In heart. Gertrude of Helfta resisted writing and had to be goaded by her God. After the first disastrous try, during which she was unacceptably overwhelmed, God agreed to titrate: "I will only lean you against my divine Heart and pour the word into you softly, mildly and gradually, according to the measure of your comprehension." This meant Gertrude received inspiration for one day of writing at a time. What would be written the next day was unknown. Petra's own brain is overcrowded, she wouldn't mind a bit of divine titration—or triage. Before she knew about Jedwabne the plan for this writing hour was to sit quietly with the quotes she copied out last time, let the ideas and images play with—or against—each other, and see what happened. She had a particular zest for watching her imagined great-great grandmothers: *Stairway Lace* and *Vanished Babushka*. She wanted them to meet, in a poem. And now? One of those grandmothers, the one descending the staircase, married a Kalinowski. Which means what? Should she be calling Witold? She tries to imagine asking him about Jedwabne. Too soon, she thinks. Has to happen, she thinks. She opens her notebook and writes. "Just don't put me in a barn and burn me." (Gertrude Benstein) She sits and looks at the sentence, a real sentence. A real person said this sentence. Just above: "That is how it is inside." (Raymona Weeks) Another real sentence. The night she tried to imagine Anya and Marian's last hours, she learned the limits of her own empathy, or perhaps the limits of the human capacity to know. She looks for the relevant lines in "The Octopus." She writes: "...complexities which still will be complexities / as long as the world lasts." (Marianne Moore) Moore took her quotation from a book titled *The Saints' Everlasting Rest*. The juxtaposition of irreducible complexities and everlasting rest rouses a distant and untrustworthy sense of irony in Petra Kalinowski, possible relative of Jew-killers, but she keeps reading "The Octopus." She needs to bring herself, she hardly knows why, to the final lines:

the glassy octopus symmetrically pointed,
its claw cut by the avalanche
"with a sound like the crack of a rifle,
in a curtain of powdered snow launched like a waterfall."

Sound of a rifle. In other words, a gun. Last sound Raymona heard. Did Ricki make the connection? Did it upset her? She gave no sign. Roo would have noticed even if Petra didn't, and done the right thing—spoken, soothed, hugged. Or the right thing might have been to allow Ricki her privacy. The young woman has lost her first lover to suicide; another reality she, Petra the Pole, has limited capacity to imagine.

Simply because of the word *point*, which is at the heart of something she cannot yet grasp, she writes: "symmetrically pointed" (Marianne Moore)

And: "Nothing could stifle my inner certainty that a shining point exists where all lines intersect." (Czeslaw Milosz)

Lines, and lines, and lines. Geometry. Genealogy. Poetry. The old image comes: the universally inclusive, infinitely reflecting, spinning globe of a God, with its bright points reaching out in every direction. She was driving Chippie to Danny's to get permission to say yes when she last thought of it—permission to take the baby tossed at her, tuck her under an arm and run with her, dodging all obstacles. She wasn't feeling kindly toward Bright Star just then. Still, she wanted the baby, wanted to receive the baby and carry her, joyfully, skillfully. Wanted to make the touchdown.

Football?

Nevertheless. She wanted the baby. And then did not. Would she have participated, at Jedwabne? Would she have gotten caught up in the energy? Shouted and mocked, urged the men to hack at terrified dying Jews? Hacked at them herself? How compelling to think of herself as the exception, to think she would have, oh so bravely, welcomed the panicked Jews running by, hidden them, fed them. "...complexities which still will be complexities / as long as the world lasts."

Two grandmothers, who possibly never met, about whom she knows nothing, existed. One could have descended a staircase. It's possible, permissible, to imagine. The woman is the lady of the house. This is Part One. There is lace. She has cut into her wedding gown, a sacrilege, and taken a piece of the lace, sewn it into the bodice of her elegant but masculine shirt. She wears pants, though this is not acceptable, not done by any woman she knows. At the bottom of the staircase waits a woman in peasant dress. This is not a humble woman though she's been a servant in the house and has many times scrubbed these very steps on hands and knees. It is after the great man's funeral, the husband. In some war, there was always a war, he has died, his bland soul finally achieving a single moment of intensity. Oh, this is very cruel, very wicked, thinks Petra, writing down every word. They're released, finally: two women. Down the steps comes the lady of the house, slowly, slowly. At the bottom waits the former servant, ardent and self-contained. No story, only this lesbian moment. Light shines on this moment. Lines of light stretch out from this moment. They come to a point here, at the end of the twentieth century, in this kitchen. They light up the vegetables on the wallpaper. Look, the vegetables receive the light, ardent and self-contained. Part Two: Jedwabne. All whimsy gone. And yet: existence, event. She can almost see it on the page, how rough the diction becomes, how irregular the lines. She can't write this poem, certainly not tonight. Nat will arrive any minute. But to include. To *include*. Does she know what she's doing? Yes. No. Yes. Does she know where this will lead? Certainly not.

Nat knocks, enters, opens her arms.

Chapter Twenty-eight

Saturday again, driving up Route 15. Dave's been down to Bucksport, delivering a basket to a friend of Etta's who's been sick, as her daytime bathrobe and worn-out look testified. The basket held a variety of what Etta called "long-ago borrowed things," but the point was the flowers, bought flowers, that covered all the rest. Etta's been putting in more hours at the laundromat due to the suicide but she tries to keep up her good works. The friend brightened at the sight of flowers, and then the vice-grips. "Oh! I forgot all about these." A good smile. He'll tell Etta and her beautiful eyes will tear right up with pity and happiness. The Penobscot sparkles between houses. A lot of houses here, where there used to be only a few. Even if he had money he's not sure he'd build on the river side of 15, the land is too narrow. The way the houses sit high over the river is good though, no flood worries and yet the water's right there. On the other hand, the river being down so far could almost make you dizzy, especially if you think of the bedroom window on the second floor when you get up in the morning. The floor's cold but you have to walk over and take a look just to prove to yourself that you live on the water. Maybe you get used to it. Maybe Etta likes it, a definite plus.

Not too bad a day for mid-November. The sun still warms, at least a little. Etta has it in her mind that Stella Weeks and Raymond might like to join them on Thanksgiving. His Etta. Never was a man so lucky with a late life find. Even if you have a good woman loving you though, life can throw a curve. Every Saturday's a reminder. Four weeks now since he drove to that trailer thinking he might sell a policy. At least he's been privileged to learn the baby's OK. Chippie. Cute name for a little girl. Good people watching over her, too. Information from the family is a help, something to put around the event as padding. The kind movers use for furniture is what he's picturing here. When something big gets moved it needs special attention. Protection is what it needs. No matter what happens, things move along. Even him. Etta calls it making progress, says he's doing fine, considering. He's almost used to Saturdays and he can eat his breakfast or drive down the road, like now, without too much trouble. Terrible, what a person can get used to. Etta still gives him extra hugs, a bonus he doesn't mind, but she listened when they had their talk, him telling her he has to start finding his own customers. Or clients. The company wants you to say clients. Right now he's going to meet a possible client in Brewer. He sold three policies in the last ten days, and them from cold calls. Surprised himself. Of course there were about fifty that didn't pan out. Still. Etta says he's letting his old charm out. He hasn't been out on a Saturday looking to sell since that day. This appointment is the very same time, 11:30. Couldn't happen twice, could it? The fellow will be there and he'll be interested. You can tell on the phone what your chances are. That's what's coming back, his feel for the business. It's slow, but it's coming.

Orrington. Won't be long now. He'll be walking up to the fellow's house, his adrenaline rising, taking a breath, ready. He knows his intro and he's not too bad at tinkering with it the minute he gets the flavor of the customer. Or client. It's not like an ordinary conversation where he's flummoxed by the least blank space. In his work he has a set of things to get across. He doesn't have to worry about what to say, just how to say it. There's where charm comes in. Maybe Etta's right and he has a supply of his own. His own charm. Maybe it's ready at hand and he can dip into it on a good day. Maybe this will be a good day.

Coming into Brewer. Not the most beautiful town in Maine, but if it gives him a customer he has no complaint. He hasn't been playing the radio, didn't even notice. Well, either he's in worse shape than he thinks, forgetting to give himself a little Johnny Cash or Merle Haggard, or he's happy enough in his mind even with that movie of suicide pictures going on in the far back of his mind. It's like a nighttime dream now, doesn't have much pizzazz in daylight. Maybe there'd be some Dolly Parton on. He likes Dolly, she has a good spirit. He reaches for the radio just to see if one of those little miracles will happen, Dolly singing to him right this minute, the announcer's choice matching his own, but he pulls his hand back. Better concentrate on the road or he'll miss the turn. He notices the pedestrian because she's not too steady on her feet. Then she stumbles.

He's out of the car as fast as he can manage. She's stuck on all fours, can't get down and can't get up. He stoops to talk to her but she's already talking. He recognizes her now. "Ignorant," she's saying. "Downright ignorant, Miss Stella Weeks, and you'd do well to admit it." Now he's down, too, hands and knees in the dirt. They're facing each other like a pair of animals or like kids pretending to be animals. He hopes his pant legs won't look too bad after this, for the customer. He can smell the alcohol. "You know quite well that you have a mission to complete," Stella says to the dirt. "This delay is unwarranted." How long do they have to kneel here? He left himself extra time, but not more than twenty minutes. "Hello, David Robichaud. Nice to see you." She's looking right at him now, finished with the dirt. She gives a strange nod and her voice has a twist to it beyond the slur of alcohol. She's making fun of their situation. She doesn't want a hand up. She almost slaps his away, but he gets the message before she has to. They spend a while brushing themselves off. By the time that's accomplished she has her posture in good order. It occurs to him he never answered her hello. He's not so good in this kind of situation. What kind of situation, though? He can't classify it. She doesn't look like she needs help now.

He says, "Um," and feels like a kid. She might scold him in a minute. She hands him an envelope instead. He almost drops it, not having fair warning about receiving it. He takes a quick look. *To Ricki Harding by way of Mary her mother in Bucksport or thereabouts since I do not know her address.* Is she planning to mail this?

"A mission is a serious undertaking, don't you think?" She looks at him. She wants an answer.

"Yes, Ma'am." He looks at the envelope again. Maybe it explains her mission but he can't see how.

"I decided I'd walk, David." She's giving him the glowing eye. That's what his father used to say when his mother would look at him in her extra serious way. *She's giving you the glowing eye, son. Better listen.* Not that Stella's his mother's age. More like an older cousin, just enough older so you have to attend. Maybe she's not older at all, maybe it's the gray hair and what drinking does, or a hard life. She has the softest wrinkles he's ever seen. A good looking woman in her own way. He's supposed to carry his part of the conversation, that's what the glowing eye means.

"Nothing wrong with going for a walk," he says. That sounds good. It brings a strong nod from her, too. They have a little pause. Would she notice if he checked his watch?

"Raymond was against it." Oh, boy. He didn't mean to get in the middle of a family dispute. Why would Raymond be against a walk? He'd better keep his mouth shut, if he's allowed. "In my dream, I mean," she says, after more of her eye is beamed at him. He nods, pretending he understands. You have to do that with a customer sometimes. Client. "Since Raymond hasn't had the courtesy to say it aloud, I feel justified." She feels justified? He really has to go. Would it be all right to say that? She's looking off into the sky and her lips are moving. It wouldn't be right to interrupt. He sneaks a look at his watch. "I'll be on my way now, David. Thank you for your attention, it's been a help." She starts off, carrying herself like a lady. A little careful, like they often are. Not weaving or falling. She must know what she's doing. But when he gets in the car he still has the envelope. He hauls himself out and runs after her. He's winded. One of these days he'll start exercising. "Why, thank you very much, David."

"You're welcome, Stella. Have a good walk." Her son wouldn't mind plain courtesy, would he? He gets behind the wheel. Stella's unusual, that's for sure. He shakes his head and turns the key. He looks at his watch again. He'll make it. Wait a minute, her son only disagreed with her in a dream. You can't take sides against a dream. Should he have asked if she was hurt, though? He turns and looks at her, walking along, head up. No, she needs to keep her dignity.

This must be the house. Two puppies behind the fence, golden retrievers, frisking around. Good sign. Maybe this is his morning.

*

Yesterday at sunset she went down to the land with Nat, who saw immediately: yes, the house would have to go; yes, the land could be worked, made into a meadow. The Penobscot running by, the surrounding woods: yes, it would be lovely. "Good investment, too," Nat said.

"But how could we sell it?"

314

"Excellent point. Might feel like selling our baby." They stood, held hands, let that sink in.

Nat said, "You're OK with that, aren't you?"

"I didn't exactly *sell* my baby. Or babies."

"Petra. I didn't mean that. What I meant was..."

"Oh, you meant am I OK with a reference that makes us sound so married."

"Right."

"I'd want wildflowers, a proliferation of them. It *would* be our baby." Which led to a long hug. When they pulled back and looked at each other they were both letting tears run down. On the way back to the house she told Nat about Jedwabne, about Gertrude, her parents, the Kalinowski part. She was still a beginner with this story. The place it had found in her mind was tentative, no real place at all. And her heart? Her heart just kept clenching and unclenching.

"Have you called your father?"

"I've picked up the phone."

"And put it down again?"

"And put it down."

"You're not ready."

"I'll get there."

"Are you and Gertrude all right?"

"I think so. I don't want to assume."

"Should you call her?"

"What?"

"It might be helpful, for both of you."

"We never call each other." She was afraid to call Gertrude, afraid of doing the wrong thing, of offending. She knew this was not the best possible set of feelings.

As they were taking their jackets off, Nat said, "Maybe you're nervous. About Gertrude."

"Probably."

"Maybe she's nervous, too, Petra."

"Oh. Maybe so. What a self-centered bitch I can be."

"Attractive, too," Nat said, and gave her a hug, with some distracting little pelvic movements added in. The question of Gertrude was put aside. They went to bed. It was well nigh unto perfection.

Now this meeting. Sappho on the agenda. Also, they plan to tell. Disclose. Come out. Jessie and Roo are in the bathroom as usual. Weak bladders. A bond, as Roo cheerfully puts it. Ricki's preparing a tray, glasses and cups. The wallpaper vegetables are at ease. Petra says, "Let's tell Ricki first."

Nat says, "Good idea."

Ricki says, "Tell me what?"

"Nat and I are officially lovers again, after a little hiatus."

Nat says, "An eighteen-year hiatus."

"Seventeen and a half."

"Um. Congratulations. Is that what I'm supposed to say?"

"That's the appropriate response. Especially if you mean it for me in particular," says Nat.

"Nat didn't like waiting seventeen and a half years."

"Eighteen." It occurs to Petra their hiatus spans nearly Ricki's entire life, an astonishing fact.

"You both look happy." They beam and nod.

Petra remembers to ask: "How are *you*, Ricki?"

"It helps to have Lionel back in my life." Pause. "And Ann Marie." Hmmm, thinks Petra, virtuously holding her tongue.

"Petra told me about your friends, Ricki," Nat says. "Showed up just in time, didn't they?" Ricki looks worshipfully at Nat. Fine role model, thinks Petra: smart, sexy, lovely, just butchy enough. She wonders: if she and Nat had been a couple all these years, no hiatus, would she be so ridiculously in love at this point? Unanswerable question. Is Nat worthy of such ardor? Absolutely.

Everyone sits. She and Nat disclose their status. "So we're a couple now. Again."

Jessie grins: "Well, thank the Lord and pass the mashed potatoes. About time." Roo beams through her tears: "This makes me so happy, you can't imagine how happy this makes me, you two, so long, God, I'd say I was getting my period if I still got my period, what's the matter with me?" Nat clears her throat. "Drum roll, please." Ricki produces a fast staccato, spoons against the bottom of a pan. When did they plan that? Nat continues in a solemn stage voice. "I have a little something for the occasion, courtesy of Mr. Robert Duncan, pioneer gay poet. The poem's title is 'Often I Am Permitted to Return to a Meadow.'" She pulls a folded piece of paper from her hip pocket, faces Petra, and reads: "'as if it were a scene made-up by the mind, / that is not mine, but is a made place, / that is mine, it is so near to the heart, / an eternal pasture folded in all thought.'" Petra listens, crying cool quiet tears. "'...a place of first permission, / everlasting omen of what is.'"

"All right!"

"That's *beautiful*."

"You two..."

Petra just smiles and dries her tears and looks at Nat. What a woman.

Nat says, "So, tell them."

"What?"

"Tell them. I dare you."

"Nat Levesque, how old are you?"

"I dare you."

"You dare me? Oh, my. Well, then: apparently Nat and I are going to buy a piece of land. Together. It's like deciding to have a baby." Nat just sits there, pleased with herself, clearly not intending to say a word. Petra tells about the land, the ruined house. "So it will be returned to a meadow. Us, too. We'll be returned to a meadow." That last bit slipped out. The censor appears to be off duty. She gets up, kisses Nat on the top of the head, sits back down. "Anyone for Sappho?"

*

When he's not at work, Raymond is at Stella's. He's been home to get fresh clothes and his books, that's all. It's been four nights of sleeping on her couch, Tuesday, Wednesday, Thursday, Friday, and calling Danny every day, checking in, saying he can't get away yet, hoping Danny believes him. He's aching to see the baby, but also, if he's honest, Danny. He tried to get Stella to go with him over to Blue Hill. "It would do you good, Ma, to see Chippie." "It wouldn't be right just now, Raymond. I have work here." Her work is divided between a letter she's trying to write to Ricki and her doilies. It doesn't include keeping order. Every day when he gets back from the library she has the place in a mess. He's allowed to clean up the kitchen and a little beyond. Maybe part of her work is to make these messes. Items get pulled out of drawers, off

317

shelves. She's grudging with information as to where things belong, but will give it to him if he insists. She's sober, but barely. He can feel the knife edge of it. Most of the time when he's around she's working on the doily meant for him. It makes her cranky and happy by turns. She pulls out rows and starts them over. Here's where some humor comes into their life because she makes a game out of showing him the progress and asking him to guess the outcome. So far the letters are G-o a-h-e. The *h* and *e* keep disappearing and then coming back as she pulls the red-brown thread out of its pattern and then reworks it. It's a businesslike dismantling most of the time, but it can be slow and dreamy, or it can be so fast you think she'll break the thread. She never does. She knows the strength of it and takes it to the limit, but not past. Putting her design back together requires some sighing and maybe a trip to the bathroom. He knows better than to suggest she let the whole thing drop. When Stella feels her necessities a person does well not to interfere. He'll get his doily before long. *G-o a-h-e.* It looks like a foreign set of words, maybe from an Arab language. He thinks of goats. He doesn't work overly hard at his guesses because he likes seeing the sparkle in her eye when she defeats him. "Try again, Raymond." "*Go ah-e*. I don't know, Ma. Have you learned a foreign language?" "You know very well I have not." "I never know with you, Ma." And the sparkle in her eye. As for family history, they appear to have gone as far as they're going. He's left to his own thoughts. The first thing is incest. More incest than he already knew about. Stella's father was also Raymona's father. He can't sort out whether he's stunned by the fact or just surprised to learn any fact at all from his mother. Then the next thing. Raymona found out about her father years ago and never told him. *That* makes a shift in his mind. And the final thing, information about his own Indian father, Raymond-with-no-last-name, a nice boy at the roller rink. Did Raymona know he was named after his father? How much did he miss, not being home those years? He's at the library now, shelving books and pondering the elements of his life. He'll call Danny soon. They both benefit from the calls, or maybe that's his imagination. Danny puts Chippie on the phone and makes her produce a goo or gurgle for the benefit of Uncle Raymond, trying to get Uncle Raymond's heart beating fast. Succeeding. Why does he believe Stella this time? She's told stories about the past before, drunk and sober. This is different. How? He wasn't begging to be told, that's how. He gave up begging a long time ago.

Margie Stokes walks by the doorway at the end of the stacks. She's on one of her missions, he can tell. Maybe he'll be back at the desk to check her books out in a while. That would be fine, he won't be nervous now. They've established their way of meeting, friendly and not overly conversational. He has the sudden idea he could say his new sentence to Margie Stokes. *My father's name was Raymond, an Indian who went to a roller rink at least once in his life, a nice boy.* He knows he'll do no such thing. As Stella would say. *You'll do no such thing, Raymond.* He's been full of tenderness for this mother of his. His heart is active in a number of directions. Stella. Chippie. Petra. Danny. The exact meaning of this extra activity escapes him. He's trying to watch and wait like a good hunter, alert and patient. What he wants to catch is his own self in its new mode. For study, not for killing. A sentence came to him while he was falling asleep last night on Stella's couch. *My amazements are many.* He liked the sound. He was thinking in particular about Chippie and himself, both of them named after Indian fathers, surnames unknown, both of them with mothers who are Stars. It gives him a feeling hard to put words to. You could say the baby and he have acquired an extra degree of relationship. A bond. It was an amazement to see Stella so pleased to find out her name means *star* and, furthermore, pleased to notice Raymona took the same name. Stella's been doing some hard thinking which is a good thing and a terrible stress on her, both. He hopes it won't take her to alcohol. When he left this morning she was already at her letter writing. How many crumpled up papers will he find on the floor tonight? Is she getting anywhere with that? Reaching up to shelve an old history of Poland, which makes him think of Petra, he feels like crying over how hard Stella's working to compose a good letter for Ricki. This is when Charlene comes toward him with the young officer.

319

Chapter Twenty-nine

Break time at DWELL. *The women come and go / Talking of Michelangelo.* Ricki Harding from Bucksport, Maine can quote a major modernist poet. Who'd a thunk it? But these comings and goings aren't sophisticated or ironic or whatever they are in Eliot's poem. They're uncomplicated and innocent. The atmosphere's fine today among the Dykes Who Love Literature. The air is like a substantial thing a person can ride on. Maybe it's a carpet under her, magical. Maybe she's a witch, the good kind, with powers. Petra and Nat are in a fairy tale, that's for sure. A real one. *And they lived happily ever after.*

Her turn in the bathroom. Good.

Down in the corner of the last page in tiny letters a new story might start. *Once upon a time, two lucky women, Ann Marie Redfeather and Ricki Harding...*

Stand up. Flush. Warm water over your hands. Petra's soft old purple towel, ragged around the edges. Homey.

She stands there for a moment, remembering. Savoring.

"We're starving. Lionel, go get us something," Ann Marie said.

"You think I don't know what you're up to?"

"Get out, brother Lionel."

"Blessings upon you, my children." He danced out, a stately waltz. Then they were alone.

Back to Petra's living room, trying not to grin too much. Schubert keeps the magic carpet floating. Petra told her: Schubert today. Someday she'll be able to hear the differences herself: Chopin, Schubert, Beethoven, Tchaikovsky.

They were in the bathtub when Lionel got back. He opened the door and gazed. "Lovely," he said, tracing a cross with his hand's edge into the air of the steamy room, their priest. They got out of the tub as if it were any other tub. She looked at it. No blood. Ann Marie toweled her dry. Lionel had the table covered with treats. "Here are your healthful foods. Here are your sweets. Here is your salty fatty variety which

320

sounds worst and tastes best. Dig in, ladies." A white bath towel folded neatly over his arm, a black bow tie clipped to his T-shirt, him bowing. She and Ann Marie sat, allowed him to push their chairs in. Extravagant toasts with Pepsi, no alcohol for anyone. They'd be saner without it, at least for a while. Lionel confessed it would be a help, though he had previously insisted it didn't matter, his resolutions were Tough Little Things, unbreakable.

In the bathtub: "Are you sure this is OK, Ricki? Being in the bathtub, I mean." Was she? She knew what happened here. Suicide, but more than suicide: the champagne night, sexy and fun, and other times that were simple and loving. Now she was in the tub with another woman, a softer and rounder woman, resting against the softness and roundness, telling herself, *It's all right with Bright Star.* Believing it.

"It's all right with her, Ann Marie."

"Do you talk to her?"

"Not exactly. She sort of talked to me, at first, but not really. Just for a while. I know she's getting a kick out of this. She wants me happy."

"That's nice," Ann Marie said, and picked up the small hand and kissed it. *Use the damn tub*, Bright Star would've said, grinning, challenging. *Love the ladies, Ricki Dicki Doodle.*

Sappho fits right in with the mood of this day. Roo gave a little introductory lecture, for which Ricki was grateful. With classes, visits to the trailer, and her paper—it did help that DWELL discussed the complicated "Octopus"—she found no time for research on Sappho. Correction, Psappho. Psappho, or Yapfoi, said Roo. In other words, everything changes as the years pass, even simple things like how to spell a name. Psappho is what they settled on, trying to work the p in, laughing because they were spitting, deciding the damn p was probably silent anyway. Still: Psappho: late seventh century and early sixth. Before Christ. Also, before Plato and Socrates and Aristotle, before Pythagorus and Euripides and the Delphic Oracles. All of whom she'll someday learn more about. The names flew around her as she rode the carpet. A woman who loved women—as well as men, but that's OK—was writing her own mind into history way back then. Not-knowing was the theme of Roo's little talk. Psappho comes to us in fragments, part-poems, half-lines, guesses. Torn strips of papyrus. Quotes inside the writings of Great Thinkers of Western Civilization. *Fragments.* Roo kept repeating the word. Ricki decided to add in *valuable*. Valuable fragments. Because all the not-knowing brought Bright Star to mind and Bright Star was a collection of valuable fragments. This thought was a good one, not even painful. *Fill our gold cups with love / stirred into clear nectar.* High on her carpet, Ricki sipped the clear nectar. She was living in the time of the gods and goddesses when

incense
smokes on the altar; cold
streams murmur through the

apple branches.

She's safe here with these longtime lesbians. She's tucked into a big safe pocket, so big the whole air is inside with her, carrying her. She's a little nuts with happiness. Maybe she's in love with Ann Marie and maybe this time being in love will be different from what happened with Bright Star where it was hard every minute even if it was fun. Maybe it will be like what Sappho's poem promises—

and quivering leaves pour

down deep sleep; in meadows
where horses have grown sleek
among spring flowers, dill

scents the air.

How Petra loves it that meadows keep appearing in the poems. Maybe someday, far in the future, it will be Ann Marie Redfeather and Ricki Harding buying land together. Here they all are. Petra. Nat. Roo. Jessie. This is her lesbian family. Add in Ann Marie. Stir lovingly. Is this a normal response to loving a normal woman? It's possible she should be getting more sleep. Jessie says, "Break time over, lovely ladies. Let's go!" And raises both arms up and out to the world at large. Jessie loves Sappho. Psappho. But there's a knock at the door. Petra gets up to answer it. It's Raymond.

Time breaks to pieces. Look at his face, it's the same face he brought here last time. Except there's no look of relief at seeing the baby. The baby's not here. Petra and Raymond stand at the door talking quietly.

322

She, Ricki, watches the two of them, Her ears aren't working well, she can't hear much.

"I'm..."

"It's..."

There's only one reason Raymond comes here. There's only one person whose death he can be reporting. Petra and Raymond glance her way, trying to disguise the direction of their look. Or no, she must be imagining things. *He's just here to borrow a cup of sugar, sweetie.* Shut up, Bright Star, you're dead. *Ah, what is death, Ricki Dicki Darlin'?* I don't know. I don't want to know. *Cup of sugar, babes. Just a cup of sugar.* Petra and Raymond sit down. Raymond sits down right in the middle of a DWELL meeting. Petra says, "It's Stella." Raymond says, "My mother was hit by a car. Around noon." Petra says, "She probably died instantly. Not knowing what hit her." Nobody else says anything. Maybe they knew this already so there's nothing to say. No, that can't be right.

Now the grownups are expressing condolences to Raymond. Very appropriate. But Stella had a *car* hit her. Think what that feels like. So big and hard and fast, and nothing you can do, not one single thing and no time passes and it takes forever. She died instantly. Inside an instant eternity hides. Who said that? Bright Star said that. *Inside every instant eternity is hiding, Ricki. That's what this guy I'm reading says. Fascinating, huh?* And she went back to her book. She loved her books. "Ricki?" Petra has her arm around her. How did Petra get over here? What does a person say? Sorry, sorry, sorry, that's what.

"I'm sorry, Raymond."

Raymond receives the words. He has his kind eyes. Stella was his mother.

"I'm sorry to have to tell you about it, Ricki. I...I brought this for you but you don't have to look at it now." He gives her an envelope. *To Ricki Harding by way of Mary her mother in Bucksport or thereabouts since I do not know her address.* The envelope is dirty and a little torn. No blood. That's nice, no blood.

"Address?" is what comes out of her mouth. She's looking at Raymond, pleading. Her mind is working very clearly and very fast because if Stella knew the address it might make a difference. There's a puzzle here to solve. Stella needed an address. She was in the road where cars are, looking for an address, but whose? My address or my mother's? Tell me, Raymond.

"I'm not sure what she meant by that, Ricki." OK, fine. We don't need to know that right now. What we need to know is inside the envelope. Or maybe not.

"Should I open it?" She's asking Petra. Petra will know.

Petra says a stupid thing. "Do you want to, Ricki?" Nobody can help. They're all a mess. Raymond's the biggest mess of all, of course he is. He just hides it good. *Well, babes. He just hides it well, not good.* Shut up. You're dead. Petra's holding her even though she, a therapist, can't find one intelligent thing to say. No one can say a single intelligent thing.

Give the envelope to Petra, Ricki.

OK.

You can't be rearranged, sweetie.

OK.

Now, Ricki.

OK.

She hands the envelope to Petra. "Should I read it, Ricki?"

"Yes, please."

"Out loud?"

"Yes, please. If it's OK with Raymond. Is it OK with you, Raymond? I'm sorry." Raymond nods his Raymond type nod. He just lost his mother. I bet he knows where to find her. In the morgue. "Is she in the morgue, yet?" She probably shouldn't have said that. What's a person supposed to say?

"Yes. I had to identify her."

"Was it hard?"

"Yes." He's telling a truth. Petra's squeezing, almost too tight. Roo's offering something to drink. Warm milk. How did that happen? It tastes good. The cup feels nice. Even a small hand can hold a warm cup. That sounds like the title of a short story. Even a Small Hand Can Hold a Warm Cup, by Ricki Harding. Except Ricki Harding isn't a writer. She's a reader and a student and someday she'll be a teacher. When her mind is OK again.

"Maybe it's too soon to read the letter. Would you rather wait, Ricki?" This is Nat, stooping down right in front of her. Kind, wise Nat. A flash of her dying Indian. His wink. On the way out he gave her a present. Stella, too. This envelope. I should open my present now with everybody here, like a party. A going away party.

"A little more milk, Ricki." That's Petra. "Good. A couple of deep breaths, sweetie." That's Petra, too. Calling her sweetie. Like Bright Star, who's gone now. She takes her breaths as instructed. She's trying to be good. Poor Raymond. It's his mother, dead on the road. What road?

"Where?"

"South Brewer," he says. It's hard for him to say this. No more questions for him right now. How patient everyone's being. Her mind is coming back. She feels a little more ordinary. Stella died, though.

"I'm sorry," she says. Here they all are. Petra, holding her around the shoulders. Nat, squatting down in front of her, warm hands on her knees, holding things together from that angle. Raymond right across the little bit of rug in the comfortable chair holding himself together. Poor Raymond. Jessie, tears running down her face, her hand reaching up to dry them, a tattoo showing at the edge of her sleeve. Jessie was so happy today. Poor Jessie. And Roo, her favorite teacher of all time, looking love at her, with red eyes. Everyone's here. "OK, Petra." Petra opens the envelope. She has to take her arm away to do it. She brings her arm back when she has the piece of paper opened flat, and starts to read in her nice voice. Petra has a nice voice, too, not just Nat.

"'*My dear Ricki Harding, Raymond and I have decided it's best to lay out a solid path. To walk on, I mean. Into your future. After what's been done to you. She had her reasons and they preceded you so no guilt is in order. On your part that is, dear. She was a sprightly child. Raymona, I mean. No. Lively. No. Determined. That's better. Never plodding. You could follow her, she made a wake. There. The path I mean is one of facts. Clarity in writing is not my strength. I hope understanding is possible. You have been a good girl through all this time. I did see blood on the underpants, don't think I didn't. Multiple Personality Disorder has its sources, I've listened to the news about that. And the ignoring mother. She was far too young for her menstruation. I knew that. It was wrong of me to make her wear pads. I believe she was seven at that time. In her underpants, you know, dear. The kind that stuck on. At least she never had to use the belt, well, you don't know about the belt that held the pad in place, or that was its stated purpose not that it was achieved, because you are young. I never blamed them for killing him*" *and you shouldn't either. I don't suppose you would but I thought it would do, to write it out. Sanitary napkins is what I mean by pads. They were good children except for the clash later between her, a bitter teenage girl, and her mother. Myself. She was always bright. I imagine you think so, too. And good with her clay work. It started with the first box. Strips of soft clay in clay colors, dusty clay pink and clay yellow. Gray too of course. I do not recall a blue but I might be mistaken in that detail. Possibly there was brown. She made her little shapes and called them what she wished them to be. It was her way. She liked bowls and her bowls were bowl-like. But her elephant, for example, was only a lump. Well, she was young. Three, if memory serves. Now that I look back I see it was ambitious of her. The elephant, I mean. Cruel is what Bede was. His was a dried-up cruelty. The wicked stepfather. More stories should be written. I was unable at the time. To contemplate, I mean. It might have been a case of hubris. I heard about it on the radio this very morning after Raymond left for work. He's being good to me. Hubris, thinking I could draw the cruelty onto myself only, and drink it away later. She drew some to herself. Or he had to put it all around, not just into me. He was a pathetic case. Shriveled. I was a pathetic case, wrung out and ragged before I left my teenage time. Onto the children came the results. I do not forget Raymond. I will try not to drink after I write like this. I hold it in mind that you are young, Ricki Harding. I hope to do no more damage, this is my best effort, dear. May you enjoy a fine day and may sorrow reduce as time passes on. May the road rise up to meet you. I believe they say it that way. The Irish, if I'm not mistaken. I multiply my wishes. I apologize for the harm. Yours respectfully, Stella Weeks'"*

Silence in the room. Stella's last message. Petra kept her voice soft and tender. Petra did not cry, reading. Every word came forward, clear in meaning, and then disappeared. Strong clear disappearing words from Stella to her, Ricki Harding.

Raymond says, "She worked hard on that letter. I thought she'd want me to deliver it." He sounds soft and tender, like Petra. His mother died.

Petra says, "I'm glad you came here, Raymond."

Nat says, "Yes."

Roo says, "It's good."

326

Jessie says, "A privilege to have you come. And the letter." Raymond nods. He's feeling humble.

Petra says, "Ricki?" So she says her sentence.

"The letter feels holy." The truest words she can find. Stella died today. Bright Star is silent.

Chapter Thirty

"I know this is an awkward plan but it's better if you don't drive."

"I appreciate it, Petra."

"Danny will reunite you with your truck."

"I know. I came to the end."

"No wonder, Raymond."

No wonder at all.

After the reading of Stella's letter, she watched Ricki and Raymond sit there, dazed. They started to tremble when required to move. They followed directions like good children up long past bedtime, putting on jackets, climbing into cars. Now she, Petra the Unscathed, is driving Raymond to Danny's house. "It was the letter," Raymond says, "and what Ricki said."

"I know." They drive along without further conversation. Nat is at this moment taking Ricki over the bridge to her parents home. Are they silent, too? Stella's body, hit by a car, lies in the morgue. There was a terrible, generous effort in her letter to Ricki, but, God help us all, *sanitary napkins for a seven-year-old whose underpants showed up bloody in the laundry?* Stella, Stella, Stella.

She takes the road to Blue Hill, refusing to imagine damage done to Stella's face, seeing instead Ricki holding the sacred letter. They're close to Danny's when Raymond says, "You were right. I need to see Chippie. She's my family now, I need to see her. Thank you." His words coming one by one, thick, but at least there are words.

"You're welcome, Raymond. You know that."

"Yes, I do."

Danny is outside, waiting, holding Chippie, when they get there. She has to tell herself: *This is the best we can manage.*

But driving home alone, Petra feels something beyond concern for Raymond and Ricki, beyond stunned shock over Stella. What she feels is impermissible: a surge of adrenaline, her pumped-up cells singing at the top of their little lungs, declaring their ongoing being. In back of that ruckus, or in the interstices, between and around mere cells, another thing, seeping and flooding. *Joy.* She can't stop it. It's stronger than her feeble will, larger than her limited self. Joy, at every curve in the road, as her eyes and brain and arms and hands work in perfect accord with the steering wheel, with the faithful engine, with the intact, air-filled tires. Joy for every sun-struck rock in every hilly little field, for every tree limb reaching into the blue sky, for every remaining dry clinging leaf. Joy for the three young boys leaning against the worn red barn as if nothing can touch them and for the way one of them raises his hand to his mouth and takes a quick puff and drops his cigarette and snuffs the fire with the toe of his boot, but awkwardly, his heel too far off the ground, it might be the first time he did this. And for the sturdy white cat and the old mongrel dog lying side by side, watching traffic; for the raucous crows flying up; for the man walking his pair of unruly black labs; for the bald skinny runner and his expensive running shoes and his silver sun-caught outrageously large crucifix and his deep-rooted loneliness. Joy. *We both yielded, you see.* Yes, Stella, I do see. *Now, with this little accident, comes another way, Petra. Of yielding, I mean. I've had good practice, year by year. You understand, dear.*

It's not that Stella is actually in the passenger seat, not quite. It's not that Raymona is actually flashing a grin from the back seat. It's the flicker of possibility, simple and gentle. *This will be my way*, says Petra to herself. She means: to experience God. Whatever God is, he, she, or it will be evident in little flickers of possibility.

Under the daytime sun, says Raymona.

And why not? Whyever not?

When she gets home she'll call Witold. Nat will be there, but she'll call her father anyway because if Stella and Raymona can share a ride in this car then she and her father can talk to each other. Flickers of possibility.

Nat opens the door. She was watching, waiting.

"Oh, Nat. My dear Nat. How's Ricki?"

"She has a good mother. Mary just folded her up in her arms. Peter will be home tonight. They'll take care of her, she'll be all right. What about Raymond?"

"He has Danny and Chippie who will also do their best. Are you OK, that I went off with him?"

329

Nat takes one step backward, away. "Should I be OK?"

"Yes."

"Well." They stand inside the door.

"I mean it, Nat."

"It's just that anything can get smashed to pieces."

"I know, but we're not smashing to pieces." Petra still has her jacket on. She can't do anything until they have a hug. Nat's breathing becomes regular, she steps toward Petra, and they hug. It's a brief hug. Petra takes off her jacket and hangs it up. They go to the couch and sit and hold each other for a long time.

"It's exhausting," Nat says, finally.

"All of it?"

"Death."

"Tell me what it was like for you when Raymond came. I don't forget you had your eye on Stella."

"You won't like what I have to say." Nat's voice is dull and flat.

She can't feel this thing I feel, this inappropriate, providential joy. Just get her talking.

"Were you planning to leave me for her, Nat?"

"I was not planning to leave you for her, Petra, as you well know."

Irritation is better than nothing. Keep pushing.

"Right. So tell me what you felt."

"I had her on my list, still."

"Oh. Your list. Oh, well."

"You're not supposed to like it that I still had a list."

"Had?"

"It was a short list."

"Stella was the only one on it?"

"Yes, pitifully."

"Well, maybe you can start a new one in a while. Or maybe you won't need it."

"You're awfully calm."

"I know you won't need it. Unless I die."

"Jesus, Petra."

"I'm not planning to die."

"I'd like not to need a list."

"What did you feel, Nat?"

"Socked in the gut. I didn't want her to be dead. We were going to have coffee. She was a little nuts but she was from way back, significant...and it's so soon after Bright Star..." Nat cries for a while, blows her nose, looks up. "What did *you* feel, Petra?"

"Stunned. Then worried about Raymond and Ricki. Then this other thing."

"What other thing?"

"It won't sound normal."

"Oh. You felt good instead of bad."

"Right."

"That's just you, Petra. I love you anyway."

"I have to talk about it some time, not now. Are you hungry?"

"No."

"Then I have a phone call to make."

"Gertrude?"

"Two phone calls. I forgot about Gertrude. You're right, she has to know why Ricki isn't showing up tonight."

"Unless Ricki's in the habit of not showing up."

"Do you think she's been sleeping at the trailer?"

"She's certainly been doing *something* at the trailer."

"Are you better, Nat?"

"Maybe. Do you really love me?"

"I love you, Nat Levesque. You're my woman."

"Good. Keep it that way."

"I hope Ann Marie is sane."

"Me, too. Is your father the other call?"

"Oh, you are so very smart, my beloved."

"Should I stay or go?"

"Stay, definitely. I'll make the call in the bedroom. Put some music on so you can't hear me. And be ready to pick up the pieces."

"How nervous are you?"

"Very."

"I'm glad you're still alive, Petra."

"Nat, you really are my best buddy. I'm happy about buying the land. Are we doing that? Did you mean it?"

"I meant it. I even..."

"What?"

"Maybe it's a bad idea."

"What? Nat?"

"I...it's about Stella...I thought maybe..."

"What?"

"I thought we could get a bench...have a stone bench, or it could be wrought iron..where we could sit and look at the water...and you could think of something that would go on a plaque...you might write a poem..."

"Commemorating Stella? I love that."

"It came to me while I was waiting for you. It was strange here in the house, before you got back. I thought I'd be OK, but..."

"You were alone."

"Stella was dead and I didn't know how long you'd stay with Raymond."

Nat starts to cry again, hard. Petra holds her and says, "Nat, Nat, Nat, Nat."

After a while Nat says, "This is crazy." She blows her nose, but doesn't break away. Petra holds on.

"Oh, babes, oh, Nat." She loves this woman. This is obvious, absolute.

"You need to call your father. And Gertrude."

"Sh-sh-sh."

"Just a minute more, then."

"Sh-sh-sh."

It must be literally one minute later that Nat sits up straight and says, "Petra Kalinowski, go make your phone calls."

"Hi, Dad. It's Petra."

"Well, Petra. Good. Let me put my hearing aid in. I was having some thoughts." Hearing aid? He has thoughts? Something to say? Unprompted? The sound of his voice affects her. He's himself, but the texture is new. More present, more *particular*.

Or it could be a change in me.

"This damn thing."

"Can you hear me now, Dad?"

"Wait. There's supposed to be a phone mode. That's what they call it, phone mode. "

"When did you..."

"There, that should be better. Say something, dear."

Dear?

"Can you hear me, Dad?"

"I think we can converse now."

"Good. When did you get a hearing aid?"

"Two. I have two of them. Expensive annoyances. I don't know, a month or so ago." Has it been that long since she called?

"You said you'd been having thoughts."

"I'm sitting here reading Spinoza." He'll be in the high-backed wooden rocking chair, no cushion, facing the wood stove. He might allow a lamp, reading glasses. Victorian, upright, proper. At regular intervals he'll have stood up, gone to the bathroom. He'll have stopped at the sink on his way back to his reading for a full glass of water. After rinsing the glass and placing it upside down in the dish drainer he'll have returned to the rocker. But how easy, or difficult, is it for him to get up, to walk? How truly old is he?

"Spinoza," she says.

"Have you read his *Ethics*?"

"I know I should have." At least she's heard of Spinoza. Brilliant rebel Jewish philosopher, seventeenth century. Some call him a rationalist, some a mystic. How unexpected that her memory would offer this. Must be reacting to the emergency: essential, that she keep up with her father. Also impossible.

"I'd think by now, Petra..."

"I tend to read more poetry, but I've picked up Simone Weil."

"A long time since I looked into her. No system, as I recall." Her father knows Weil, who postdates Kant by a long, long time. Her philosopher father did not stop at the eighteenth century.

"Does Spinoza have a system, Dad?" Of course he does.

"Well, yes. A fine system, but also a following among the poets, I hear. Goethe, Wordsworth, Coleridge, Shelley."

"Romantics."

"Yes, dear."

"Interesting."

"Paradox is at the core of any worthy philosopher's work, if my current thinking is correct."

"I like that, Witold."

"I thought you might." Has her father developed a sense of humor? Very dry it would be. Still, she suspects their entire history is acknowledged in those four words. *I thought you might.* Meaning: I know you and I have not always agreed, daughter, I'm reaching toward you, please reach toward me. Witold's hand reaches out from above. *Witold on the Sistine Ceiling.* In the past this would have been a cynical image. Now? Something more generous. On whose part? Hers. His. Both.

"Tell me about Spinoza, Dad."

"We could come at this in a number of ways. The range of responses is impressive. Novalis famously called him a God-intoxicated man. Hegel said that to be a philosopher one must first follow Spinoza. Then, of course, many have thought him an atheist. Or, on the other hand, a pantheist."

"That *is* a range." She must remember, she's not allowed to forget, Jedwabne.

"Three things interest me, Petra. First, he uses the methods of geometry to express philosophical thought. Your Simone Weil was fond of geometry also. Spinoza tries to surpass ambiguities. He fails, of course, but the attempt is valiant. Second, he believes everything is held in existence through continuous intimacy with the divine. A powerful concept with an abundance of implications. Third, the only knowledge worth a pin is intuitive knowledge of God, knowledge which can be a prism for all else and which brings joy. As the years add up, I've found that joy has great value."

She calls to ask about Jedwabne and Witold gives a philosophical lecture and his endpoint is...joy?

"Petra, are you still there?"

"That's...beautiful," she says. This is called understatement.

"Exactly. It's aesthetically pleasing to a certain kind of dry truth-seeking mind. Also, comforting. I've discovered the hand of God in my later years. I feel as though I'm carried in it. I thought you should know, but you'll find your own way. You might say that each of us is small speck in the Great Hand. I tend to call it God, a convenient shorthand, now that embarrassment has become irrelevant."

"It will take me a while to absorb this, Dad." Can she bring up Jedwabne now? Could she *not* bring up Jedwabne now?

"Yes, I imagine it will, dear. I only regret that I can't discuss this with your mother. She'd have a hearty laugh at the old atheist, but she'd be kind."

I am to be kind. He's vulnerable.

"Dad, these ideas aren't...well, they aren't far from some things I've been thinking. I've done a lot of that lately. Thinking."

"Well, good. Sincere thought is a good." Sounds like a closing declaration. He doesn't want to know my thoughts. We're about to end this conversation. I can't let that happen.

"Dad. Witold. I need to ask you something." Long pause. "Dad?"

"Are you still there, Petra? I can't hear you."

"DAD."

"Oh, I see. Wait just a minute, I think my battery's run down. I knew it was close." She waits. A break might be good. "Petra?"

"Can you hear me now, Dad?"

"Batteries are expensive. I overuse them. Emma scolds me regularly."

"Emma? Who's Emma?"

"My Scrabble partner."

Scrabble?

"Where do you play Scrabble?"

"In the kitchen. It's the only table, as you know."

"I meant..."

"I don't go *out* for Scrabble, dear."

"Of course not. I have to ask you something, Witold."

"Yes, I believe you said that."

"It's..." But how to proceed?

"Petra? Are you there?"

"Yes. I heard something the other day. I have to ask you..."

"What is it, Petra?"

"I know. I'm being difficult."

"Perhaps your topic is difficult." How kind. Truly, my father is being kind.

335

"But before I...Dad, I want to tell you how grateful I am that you had me read poetry, after..." She stops. She doesn't know what to call her mother. Can it be true that she and Witold have never referred to Tekla?

"What, dear?"

"After Mother...after Tekla...after she died, you encouraged me to read poetry. I read 'Rape of the Lock.'"

"Oh, yes. Pope. You were a bit young for him. I must not have been thinking clearly."

"Witold, I'm thanking you."

"Oh. Well. You're welcome, Petra."

"But that's not...do you remember a town called Jedwabne?"

"What town, dear?"

"Jedwabne. J-e-d-w-a-b-n-e. In Poland."

Silence.

"I remember Jedwabne," he says, finally. He sounds small. She was supposed to be kind. He was vulnerable. What is she doing?

Chapter Thirty-one

Raymond makes his way up Stella's steps. Someone should clean them. He should have. Maybe he will. Would it do any good? Danny and Chippie are behind him. In case he falls? He's leaning forward, he can feel the forward tilt of himself, as if there's a strong wind coming at him from above and he has to compensate. The key still fits the lock. The door still opens. She managed it: in the short time after he left for work she got things into a mess. "I apologize for the mess."

"No need," Danny says, and right away he's looking for a place to settle the baby. He goes ahead and makes one, a blanket on the carpet. He knows what to do, Danny does. He gives the baby a selection of toys to grab for.

"It won't take long." He's apologizing to Danny for his crazy need to strip and make the bed. *Beds matter* is the set of words behind the need.

"No hurry," Danny says.

He heads toward the bathroom where the clean sheets are. It *is* crazy, coming all this way just to make a bed. He couldn't rest in his mind without doing it though. According to Danny he doesn't have to understand why. He starts to strip the bed and makes a decision not to put his face into the sheets to get the smell. Danny comes to take the bundle away, not asking where to stash it. The baby talks blurred singing baby talk alone in the living room just loud enough to hear. She doesn't mind being on Stella's floor. He has trouble getting the clean folded sheet to open out but Danny enters in and somehow it's ready to put on the bed, except there's a discovery to be made, a secret she had, tucked under the mattress but showing itself now. Pulling out the dirty sheet must have displaced it. It's a tablet with her writing on it. Wait. Not so much writing as drawing. Diagrams. "It's her plans for her doilies."

"Oh," says Danny. "Private stuff, huh?" Danny sits beside him, not too close. They've been closer on this day already but Danny won't presume.

337

"She gave one to Petra." Danny doesn't say anything. "Petra's is red. She was working on one for me, having some trouble with it. We'll find it if we look around."

"We'll stay as long as you want to."

"I know. Look, here it is. She was teasing me, not telling me her plan, but here it is."

"Is that a book, in the middle? She planned to work that in?"

"Looks like it. And her words, this is what she teased me with. *Go ahead, then. I was wrong.* No wonder she had trouble, it's a lot to fit in."

"What's she apologizing for?"

"I don't know. Oh, here's more. She wrote to herself about it." They look at the page together. They're reading words his mother wrote, Danny and himself. *"Will he see it's that book from Etta? Maybe some words. All around the edges, the words, repeating themselves. 'Go ahead, then. I was wrong.' Again and again. On the book cover I can put 'Etta's Book.' No, it's his now, but what's the title. He's bound to like this one, it lies flat. Why shouldn't he be Indian? Maybe just along the bottom, once being enough to give him the thought. 'Go ahead, then.' The apology is a mistake, putting myself in. Who ever wrote to herself like this? No. Better put it in, about being wrong. But just at the bottom. Around the edges a space for him to fill with his own mind. Would he do that? My baby boy."* Danny's arm comes around him. They sit there. It's a long time. This is another bare mattress. This one doesn't have that old look of ticking, nor a patch of fresh blood spreading. It's old, but more like worn satin that used to be sky blue but got pale with years. He runs his hand across it and thinks of Stella's face, her skin soft from the years adding up. His whole family is gone except for Chippie. Persephone Star Chip Weeks. Or maybe McGuire, maybe she's called McGuire now, Danny's little girl.

"Do you think about changing the baby's name?"

Danny picks the topic right up, but with a turn. "I've been thinking about the future. A girl called Chippie. I've been wondering about that, worrying away at it to tell you the truth. It might not be the best thing for her. Maybe your sister never intended that part to go past babyhood. I've been wondering about Persephone, thinking Sephie for short. It's up to you, though." He nods his head, he can feel himself nodding his head. Change what she's called in the everyday way, then. Sephie. Because the whole of life is changed now.

So he says, "It's up to you, not me, but I like it. I was meaning McGuire, though." He adds that, about McGuire, so as not to have a little place of secrecy between them, a misunderstanding that he let go uncorrected. He's trying to do right by Danny and maybe this is one way, being careful with how information is handled.

"Oh. McGuire. I hadn't thought about that. What's wrong with Weeks?"

"She's yours now."

"Mine. What a strange thought." They sit with that, then they look at each other and acknowledge strangeness beyond the idea that a person owns a baby. Strangeness is sitting on this bare mattress with Danny McGuire, a baby in the other room. She's quiet now. Maybe she fell asleep, happy enough in her grandmother's place with her grandmother's smell all around. He'd have to smell the sheets but a baby might have a better sense, might know right away whose air she was breathing. Danny's eyes are ready, full of possibilities for what they could start talking about but not set on any particular direction. The baby is a possibility, and Stella, anything at all about Stella. Also, the two of them, Danny McGuire and Raymond Weeks. It's wide open, the door they could walk through. In comes Raymona.

So he says, "I'd like to tell you that I slept with my sister." Danny is quiet, receiving it. It isn't too long before he talks.

"Was that part of how your family was, when you were growing up?"

"That might be a way to put it. I'm telling you because..." But he doesn't know the end of his sentence. He finds himself out of words.

Danny waits a respectful time, then he says, "Let's make this bed." Before the bed is made, Stella's tablet has to get a place of honor on the dresser. Danny waits while he, the son, clears an area for it, carefully putting things back in drawers. Stella's messes are familiar by now, he knows where things go. When he puts the tablet where it wants to belong it looks square and orderly on the bare wood. A hairbrush is the only other thing that stays on the dresser. He and Danny stand looking at the dresser, then they look at each other. They're satisfied with this part of things. The bed-making isn't as smooth. They don't observe each other's work. Maybe it's an embarrassing thing, to make a bed together. When they stand back to look they see the mistake. On Danny's side everything hangs down untucked, the sheets and blankets showing like a slip that's too long for a lady's dress. One of them says, "Oh," and the other one says, "Well." It doesn't matter which of them says which. Then Danny bows and makes a sweep of his hand, ushering him over to do it the Weeks way. He tucks the sheets and blankets under. That feels good. What now?

Danny won't let these blank times grow into a problem. He says, "The living room." So they go into the living room where Chippie's sleeping on a blanket on the floor. Maybe that blanket was supposed to go on the bed. Will Stella be upset? No, wait, she's dead, she can't get upset. He'll have to get used to the idea. Now Danny has the baby in his arms, bringing her back to the couch where they sit side by side. He missed the minute when Danny got up to get her but at least he's catching this one. "Want her?" Danny says.

"Do you?" They look at each other because the question got big. Danny's holding the baby out to him, but it's one of those times when a person can't move. Do they have to talk again about who'll be in charge of her? Isn't that settled? Danny pulls back a little and makes a place on his own lap for Chippie who is maybe now called Sephie, but he and Danny don't stop looking at each other. Tears are filling Danny's eyes and he blinks and the water spills over. He pulls the baby toward himself with one arm and wipes his eyes with the back of the other hand. The baby joins in the looking. She looks out from her place on Danny's lap at him, her uncle. She has an ease about it though. Danny doesn't.

"Raymond..."

"No." That stops things. Danny looks down. Everybody sighs, including Chippie who is maybe Sephie. She's right in tune with them, or he could be imagining that. Nothing happens for a while except that the baby twists herself to look at Danny and Danny takes her to his chest and gives her a hug. She likes the hug.

"Raymond." That's Danny, trying again.

"OK. What?"

"I don't know what you meant by No." Well, neither does he. Is he going to say this, though?

340

When he doesn't say anything, Danny says, "Maybe talking isn't the right thing."

"It's a big job, taking on a baby. Maybe you're tired of it."

"What? Why do you say that?"

"I was thinking about the night at the emergency room. Maybe you got a big taste and found out."

"I don't think that's really what's on your mind." Now they stop again. Is this a fight? Danny's right. The emergency room wasn't really on his mind. It just rose up in the jittery atmosphere that's been filling the room. He has to think hard to find a thread to pull on here, maybe unravel the mess he started to make.

"You're right. It would calm my mind some, though, to hear your thoughts about her. About Sephie."

"I think you know," Danny says. "But, OK. I don't have any doubts. I don't mean I can see the future, or what it will be like with her. It might be rough. She's having a hard start, and the genetics, we might as well face it, are possibly not the best."

"Genetics?"

"What she inherited," Danny says.

"Alcoholism."

"That, and maybe other mental problems."

"You can inherit those?"

"Petra says yes. Depression, for example. A tendency not to be stable in your mental make-up. I don't know a lot, but enough to know there might be a chance, no matter what I'd do as a parent..."

"I see." What he sees, really, is how Danny didn't say *we*. How *we'd* do as parents.

"Maybe you want to know if I'll do what Petra did after a few more weeks or months or even years."

"I didn't know I wanted that, but yes." This is another track, the one about Chippie and not about their relationship, but it's a true track.

"As far as I'm concerned, I'm doing this. The last time I understood my purpose so well was when I was nursing George through to his death. I told you about that. You know what it meant to me. But by now, with your mother gone, you might want this baby yourself. Not having to watch out for your mother, I mean. Or just the change a death can bring to a person. How could you know that already, though?"

341

But he does know. He says, "We're doing a dance here we don't need to do. I'm sorry about it, my fault. You want to be her father and I can see how good you are at it. I'm her uncle. I want to be the helper, not the main person." Danny nods. It's plain he isn't surprised. He wasn't expecting to lose the baby, not really. They sit for a minute, side by side, not looking at each other. The baby yawns. She's wearing one of her little Indian outfits, very cute. Raymona sewed those. He misses Raymona a lot right now.

"There's another dance going on behind that one," Danny says. His voice is careful, a little tense.

"I know."

"Your mother just died. We'll take our time. We would have anyway."

"I know." He does know. Danny won't push ahead, about the two of them.

Finally Danny looks straight at him, kindness and concern in his look. They'll talk about Stella now, a little. "All I meant was did you want to hold this little girl. I thought it might help. Being here can't be easy."

"It's easier than I thought it would be, or maybe I should say more natural. My mother is still here. Well, not really. But what she left here—look at the mess—it's how we've been living this last little while. She could almost come in right now from another room and comment what a hard time she's having with my doily." Danny listens. The baby listens.

"I'd wander into George's room, just to make sure," Danny says.

"Yes, it's like that."

"Even with the mess I can see how Stella kept a nice place, underneath."

"She liked to wax a floor. She liked beauty and order when she could find it." This makes him want to cry. Will he? "Maybe I could hold her for a while." The handover is easy. The baby won't mind if tears come down on her, it might feel like rain. Not a cold rain, he'll keep her warm. Here's Danny, very close, while this little one is sucking on his own finger, the finger of Raymond Weeks who was never going to have such things as a baby to hold and a person next to him who's interested in loving. *Look, Ma. Look what's happening.*

342

Chapter Thirty-two

Here it is Monday morning again and here she is in Roo's office with another death completed, Stella's this time, death being an expected and natural part of life, absorbable, as the philosophers tell us. So says any educated person. Why is she in Roo's office? Because Roo managed to locate her at the trailer and strongly suggested she come in. So here she is, as requested or possibly ordered, first thing Monday morning, 8:05 to be exact, an obedient student or maybe friend, it's a little confusing, in Professor McGuire's office. No shower, no breakfast, and maybe a hint of alcohol underneath the mouthwash, but she's here. Roo's gone in search of "real food" and left her sitting in an office that fits the mode of current times. Changed. Yesterday Jessie and Roo spent the day sorting, tossing, and cleaning. There are places not wrecked yet, a few shelves where books and papers make a familiar mess, but mostly there's order and strong-scented unwelcome cleanliness. Maybe it helped Roo, making order. As for Ricki Harding, she goes in the other direction, toward a little more chaos with every new event. Look at that, a chocolate stain on her shirt. Oh, well. The latest news is at least from another front, not the Weeks Family Front. Ann Marie, it turns out, can't go home—*yet*, she keeps saying—for more reasons than that her Quest is incomplete. The newly revealed reason is that Ann Marie Redfeather is plain scared to go home because if she does she has to face the music she left playing behind her when she called the authorities and reported being molested by an uncle. Reported finally after years of dithering, motivated by signs that another girl was becoming friendly with this pathetic man and was therefore possibly—or probably—in danger. The family was not pleased to have the report made. The world, it appears, is full of dangers and other unpleasant aspects, as well as a variety of formerly unfamiliar liquors. Ann Marie, having disclosed personal history, decided it was time to stop being sober and proceeded to mix drinks. "A body has to indulge in Major Consumption from time to time," said this Ann Marie. "Agreed," said the new Ricki, leaning against her on the couch. Thus, last night she and Ann Marie drank. All night. Lionel, sitting cross-legged on Bright Star's living room rug with Patchwork, ran his thumb repeatedly over and around the little grotesque's limbs, too stunned by his own near-miss to scold them. He'd gone home with a man, not a very nice man, and almost had sex. "It's a miracle, Lionel. You escaped. Maybe you should have a drink." This was Ann Marie. "The only miracle is that not a drop of alcohol or any other Forbidden Substance entered the picture," said Lionel. "I disagree," said intoxicated Ann Marie. "You got your pants back on and drove your sweet little ass home to us." Ricki drank and listened. Eventually Bright Star and Stella came to sit on either side of Lionel, for support. They, however, were not real.

"This is the best I can do," says Roo, offering lemon custard yogurt and a plastic spoon. She looks terrible.

"You look terrible, Roo."

"You don't look great yourself, Ricki." They sit for a while. She's supposed to eat, so she eats.

"Why did you call me?"

"Oh, the usual. I was worried." Ricki nods. They sit for a while longer. "Maybe you don't want to talk," Roo says.

"I don't know." Silence again. Two silent people. Roo looks truly terrible. Death has undone her. Or maybe the poet meant the dead people were undone.

"I keep thinking about Stella's letter, Ricki." Well, yes, don't we all. The problem being not all of us can remember it and one of us, me, has been unable to read it to revive the undone memory though she does keep it in her back pocket just in case.

"Me, too." She looks at Roo. Roo looks at her.

"It seems big, that letter," Roo says, after a while.

"I know."

"I keep going over it."

"The letter?"

"Well, that. And the way Stella died. How much we don't know," Roo says.

"Did it help?"

"Help?" Roo says.

"Did it help to clean up the office?"

"Oh. No."

"That's too bad."

"Well, it helped while I was doing it. And having Jessie here, being my cheerleader, that was good. Kept me going."

"Good."

It looks as if Roo wants to keep things going right now because she says, "Jessie has a head for organizing. She made me buy this new file cabinet." They smile a little over bossy Jessie. It's her turn to say something.

"It feels strange, Roo, like somebody else's office."

"I know. Everybody's going to give me a hard time about it, ask if I've had a personality change."

"I wish it had helped." Roo nods but they sag again.

A few minutes pass blankly, then Roo says, "I wish we could help you."

"I maybe look worse than I have to. Smell worse, too." Roo waits. "We were up drinking all night, Ann Marie and I. Lionel has joined the Temperance League." This is a feeble joke, but an educated person's joke, or maybe not a joke, maybe just a clever little reference. Roo ignores the clever little reference.

"Are Ann Marie and Lionel at the trailer?"

She nods, yes. It's a fact. One of the good ones. Friends at the trailer.

Another silence. Stella might be haunting this conversation, or non-conversation. Silent Stella. Go away, Stella. *An effort toward speech on your part might do some good, Ricki Harding. I cannot do that for you given my current situation.* She sighs. Roo sighs. It's not Stella's fault, or even if it is, what difference does it make? So she finds something to say. "Lionel is my oldest friend, back from the land of Big City Faggotry. He got hurt there."

"Oh, Ricki. I'm sorry."

"That's OK. Ann Marie is my new lover. She got hurt right on Indian Island."

"Ricki..."

"That's OK. People get hurt." She can feel herself staring, her eyes stuck on nothing, her words flattened out. She looks up after a while. Roo is crying. Just sitting there, her face wet. Well, people cry.

After a while Roo says, "I don't think this is right."

"What?"

"This. How we're sitting here."

"I'll go then."

"No, that's not what I mean."

"Oh." They have to sit for more minutes, both of them down in the hole, but then Roo makes her effort, starting with a question.

"Did you know Raymond has been staying at Danny's?"

"No."

"Well, that's good gossip. I thought good gossip might be a way."

"Oh. You mean..."

"I think so," Roo says.

"Just like me, then." They sit for a minute with that. Roo was trying to get them out of the hole. Raymond and Danny might be a couple. Right after someone dies, try a bit of sex.

"Ricki?"

"I'm sorry. It's interesting, what you said about Raymond and Danny."

"I'm pulling teeth here."

"I know. I'm sorry."

"Well, I think I'll pull harder. I don't know what else to do and you're not walking out of here until something better happens. I'll just talk, you don't even have to listen. I'm worried about what that letter is doing to you, so I thought if you heard about life in Blue Hill, which is sort of sweet right now even with all the sadness, it might be a good thing."

"Roo, nothing is your fault." This is always a good thing to say to Roo.

"I know, but I keep thinking I could have done something when Bright Star was young and I made it possible for you to meet her and look what happened and now Stella." Roo is crying again. Stella is over in the cleaned-up corner. Not really, but her spirit could be. Bright Star is absent or at least very tardy. Roo blows her nose and apologizes.

"Tell me about life in Blue Hill. I want to hear." So Roo tells. Once upon a time there were two houses, a big house and a little house. Roo lived in the big house and her life was good. Danny lived in the little house and his life was good. Along comes a baby after death number one. Danny is happy to have a baby to take care of and Roo is happy to

346

have a baby to visit and fuss over and once in a while take care of. Then death number two happens, which is not so much fun, but along comes Raymond. Raymond is added to life in the little house with Danny and the baby. Danny and the baby are happy and Roo is happy, too, because just like everybody else, Roo loves Raymond. And they all lived happily ever after.

Which is not exactly the way Roo tells it. This bitter little edge to everything is not nice. Still, even with the bitterness stirred in, this is almost a comforting story. Something good might be happening to Raymond. About time. "I'm glad if something good is happening to Raymond, Roo."

"And the baby and Danny."

She nods and says, "Sephie." Trying it out.

"Yes," Roo says. "I'm adjusting to that."

"Does she know her new name?"

"I think she does."

"Is she OK?"

"That medication was a miracle."

"I mean about Stella."

"Who knows? I'm glad she's got Raymond close by, at least for now. I make a hopeful story when I can, I suppose. So I'm making a hopeful story out of this, that the baby will have her uncle. Not that he's moved in for good. I don't mean to imply that." Ricki nods. Roo asks, "Is there anything, Ricki? Anything you have to hold onto, with two deaths coming at you? Do you have a way of thinking about...?" This is a quick switch but Ricki follows it the way she would in her truck, not even a squeal of her tires. Just hold the road.

"Thinking about death?"

"Yes," Roo says.

You have the wink from the dying Indian. This is the voice of Bright Star, and a very irritating voice it is. I never told you about the wink, Bright Star. *No secrets from me now, babes.* Sometimes she wishes she never met that woman. She must have left a gap because Roo is saying, "Ricki? I'm sorry. I don't mean to pry." Change the subject, she thinks, and finds herself able to do just that.

"I can't remember everything Raymond said. Maybe we could go over that." Because this is better than answering Roo's question.

347

Roo nods. She'll go along with this. She starts talking in her kind Roo way and the facts come marching into the cleaned-up office. Raymond said Stella was walking south on 15 and, according to the driver of the car, stepped out into the road looking unbalanced in her stance and her mind, weaving. Then she was down. Raymond doesn't blame the driver. Of course not, being Raymond. She was a new driver, a teenager, very undone.

"Death has undone so many," she says, and gets a sharp look from Roo, then a long nod of the head.

Then they go on to that other fact, the final fact Raymond decided to tell. They had to pry the letter out of Stella's hand, she was dead and still holding it.

"I remember Raymond told us that," she says.

"I thought you'd remember that," Roo says.

Ricki has a thing to say now. She decides to say it, why not? "So I guess it was my letter that caused her death."

"That's why you're here this morning, Ricki. I was afraid you might think that."

"Well."

"You're thinking she got drunk after she wrote the letter and started walking toward Bucksport, trying to deliver it to your mother because she didn't know where you were, how to find you."

"That's probably what happened, isn't it?"

"We can't know, but I want you not to blame yourself. Are you blaming yourself?"

She looks at Roo, the person most prone to guilt of anyone she knows. This is almost funny. But Roo is so earnest, out of her hole now, doing what she does, trying to help. She's a good person. There are good people. A thought comes: she can at least forgive Roo. Then the next thought, the miracle thought: that she might as well forgive everybody, even Bright Star and Stella, even herself. She looks at Roo. She wants to give this to Roo but it's not ready for handing over yet. "I'll work on it, Roo, I really will." She means it. Also, Roo will let her go now.

She has another thing she could give to Roo, but it's not ready either. The Gleesome Threesome, even with two of them drunk, tackled the problem of What Ricki Should Say at Stella's memorial service. They came upon an idea, but agreed it might be a crazy one and should be subject to changes made under the influence of sobriety. The idea is that she would get up in front of God knows how many people, the whole AA community might show up, and tell how she's been trying to alchemize in her mind or maybe it's her heart the wink of a dying man, tell about the flashing blue neon and the knife coming down and how a big Indian with a long black braid looked at her and winked, and how crossing over to death is something besides a tragedy even if violent. A gift was given to her to help her through these times, maybe it could help someone else. She might be able to do this when the time comes. Inside the trailer it seemed possible. Drunk, she felt up to the task. Here with Roo a glare is on the whole idea. It's exposed and naked and ridiculous. It wants to hide in a corner, an idea ashamed of itself. A glare *is* on them. Roo must have washed the windows in her marathon cleaning, the sun is overly bright. She needs to get back to the trailer in the woods. "I need to get going, Roo," she says. And Roo lets her go.

Chapter Thirty-three

"I'm in the HOSPITAL, Petra."

"Hi, Kiki."

"I'm supposed to be there with YOU, but I can't."

"What happened?"

"Nothing." The voice going tiny; Petra's heart unexpectedly touched.

"Please tell me, Kiki. I want to know."

"I'm sorry, Petra."

"OK, Kiki. But what happened?"

"I cut myself with Daddy's fishing knife."

"On purpose?"

"Y-y-yes."

"Oh, Kiki. Did something make you feel bad?"

Heavy breathing.

"Kiki?"

"My new friend isn't a friend to ME." Anger surging through the primitive, volatile, vulnerable being.

"Do you feel like you lost your new friend?"

"Not FEEL. I truly REALLY lost her."

"That's terrible. Things can get pretty hard, can't they?"

"THAT'S RIGHT. REALLY, REALLY, REALLY HARD." The decibel level sets a record. Petra loves Kiki.

"Do you have a good therapist in the hospital today?"

"YES, I DO."

"That's good."

"GOODBYE, PETRA."

"Goodbye, Kiki. I'll see you when you get out."

"OK, PETRA. I LOVE YOU, PETRA."

She should probably have made an anti-cutting statement, but what would be the point? She's shaking her head over Kiki's ongoing predicament: life. Also, she's glad to have the free hour to add to her lunch break because her poem for Stella's memorial service is not yet firmly begun, much less finished, and here is some *time*. She takes out her sandwich and her notebook. The service will be Saturday. Roo is organizing it, coordinating with Raymond. They'll display the crochet-work, a parallel to Raymona's art. They'll enlarge Stella's high school graduation photograph. Nat will be amazed. Petra imagines Roo and Raymond working together, deferring to each other. Somehow decisions will get made. Raymond has let himself fall into the arms of Danny, than which there could be no better place to fall. In Raymond's own arms: a baby now called Sephie. Watching Raymond hold Sephie, she felt a depth of unfamiliar peace. So there it was again: joy-and-peace, her very own gestalt of responses to this time of Stella's death and sundry other developments such as learning that her relatives, her father's cousins, did in fact, and proudly, produce gasoline for the burning of hundreds of Jews locked inside a barn at Jedwabne, Poland in 1941. This fact is horrendous and when she thinks about it she feels nausea, shame. Witold answered generously, revisited his own intense dismay at his cousins' crime, did not flinch. She learned there was a split in the Kalinowski family and that Jedwabne was, more than any other single thing, the reason Witold and Tekla left Poland. Every careful searing sentence Witold spoke was a formidable, precious gift. She now has moments of feeling completed, rooted in fresh ground, and strangely beyond suffering. Witold, by chance not in Jedwabne at the time, was horrified by the massacre and worked for some months afterward with Zegota, doing what he could for local Jews. How relieving to hear there was an organization like Zegota, to learn that Polish anti-Semitism was not absolute, that it had cracks through which a better humanity could escape and exercise itself.

After the phone call, in bed with Nat, clinging to Nat, Petra was overtaken by the memory of her mother's death. In the days before she died, Tekla seemed far inside herself. *Already gone*, thought nine-year-old Petra. Perhaps Witold even spoke to her about it. Then one day came Tekla's return. Her face shimmered with astounding reality as she whispered *Look at you, just look at the two of you,* eyes moving from husband to daughter, back and forth, back and forth. No further words, only labored breathing. Witold asked if she, nine-year-old daughter of dying Tekla, wanted to leave the room. No, she had to stay. Soon there

351

was a mother on the bed but nothing coming from her. She stood watching, curious. There wasn't much to see and Witold was just a statue, a church statue, stone, so she went and did the dishes. She could use the stool or not by then, her choice, because even though she was the shortest kid in class she was tall enough. That day she didn't use the stool. It was hard to reach the faucets, but she could do it.

"My mother saw something before she died," she said to Nat.

"A vision?"

"No. Well, maybe. Something in us. Maybe just us, not something in us. Maybe just...us."

"You and your father."

"Witold and me. Yes." Nat rocked her. She cried herself clean and fell asleep. In the morning she said, "We all think it was alcohol, but Stella could have had a stroke or something like that. A heart attack." Nat nodded. "It was probably just alcohol," she said, and Nat nodded again. "She was beautiful, wasn't she, Nat?" Nat agreed, Stella was beautiful.

Now, in the office, she eats her sandwich. She has an idea but fears its ambition. Three generations of Weeks women have entered her life. Stella and Raymona are dead, but Sephie lives. Anya comes shining in dreams and visions, bringing energy and permissions. Tekla also, finally. And she, Petra, is the Kalinowski who survives. Her idea wants to reach into the plenitude: the generations, life and death, the two families. A mandala. A verbal kaleidoscope. Impossible, of course. She's brought with her one of Raymona's notebooks, for the entry that startled her last night: *"Here is a name, Persephone, Queen of the Underworld, cold queen made from meadow child. Persephone, daughter, lost and returned inside the cycle. Bend, child, bend to pick the flower created by the gods. The earth opens and encloses into dark strictness. The earth opens and receives backward into the light. This is the forever daughter forever about to be separated, forever to be joined with the forever sad mother, Goddess mother Demeter who mourns and seeks. Ashes, ashes, all fall down. Thus are the Native Peoples saved by the Queen who knows death in the meadow."* The passage was written ten years before Chippie was born. The layers of meaning and feeling embedded in such a fact are inexhaustible. She copies Raymona's words into her notebook and turns to Robert Duncan's poem, thinking of Nat's voice and of Nat's pledge. The pledge held. They meet with the realtor tomorrow. She writes:

352

"Duncan's poet mind: 'Often I am permitted to return to a meadow...' Duncan's Persephone: '...Queen Under The Hill / whose hosts are a disturbance of words within words / that is a field folded.' Duncan's ashes: '...whose secret we see in a children's game / of ring a round of roses told.' Is Stella Demeter? Forever sad mother whose child has been taken to the Underworld? Goddess whose bright power can't be seen because sorrow is too heavy a disguise? Sephie, your mother and grandmother were like your own small self, goddesses in disguise. Raymona, you heaved and pulled and now your mother is in the great place of the dead where you are. Stella, your daughter sorrowed in secret at the loss of her mother. Can you know this now? To whom is an elegy addressed? Thick scarlet lace with a tumble of alphabet. Stella's doilies. Gift-giving Stella, grandmother Stella. The goddess ungrieving attends to the harvest. The child is restored in new form, newborn Persephone. But blood in the panties. A pad to catch future spills, to keep the child clean. What can be done with an unbearable history? This sorrow and this brightness. Stella is Demeter who lets the crops die. But only for part of each year. Stella's cold child is Queen of the Underworld. The baby is Persephone. Ergo, Raymona is Demeter. Circles and confusions. Goddesses abound. Facts are interchangeable. Meanwhile: Tekla, Petra, Anya."

She hears the waiting room door.

The session begins. Patricia, recently violent in a bar, recently hospitalized at the State's expense, somewhat less recently presenting in therapy as a child alter who tried to burn h-e-a-v-e-n into her skin—but she was stopped by the pain, remember that—this same Patricia, in the form of an alter who tends toward the flippant, Patty Jay, paces the room and eventually speaks.

"So, Petra Kalinowski, what would you say to a bit of integration?"

"Integration?"

"You know. A couple of us get together, make a single." Flirting, teasing.

"I don't suppose you're serious, Patty Jay."

"Ah, Petra, dear, you would be not-supposing incorrectly." Petra waits. Patty Jay sits down. They look at each other.

Petra did get supervision from Gertrude this week, and about this very client. *I expect her to throw me a curve. That's what she does after hospitalizations.* And Gertrude: *Are you inclined to try to catch it? Or bat it over the left field fence? Or perhaps duck?* This was after she reported her conversation with Witold. "So they were my relatives. They really were." She and Gertrude looked at each other. They said "Well" a few times. She asked Gertrude if they should worry about their relationship. Gertrude said they should not. She believed this. Then Gertrude said Witold was right, she should read Spinoza, but only when her mind is at its finest; Gertrude of course having read him long ago. "In fact, I have a quote—" And she went to her bottom desk drawer and took out her notebook. "This is from Somerset Maugham, *The Razor's Edge.* 'I've been reading Spinoza the last month or two. I don't suppose I understand very much of it yet, but it fills me with exultation. It's like landing from your plane on a great plateau in the mountains. Solitude, and an air so pure that it goes to your head like wine and you feel like a million dollars.'"

"Hmmm," said Petra.

"Doesn't it make you want to do as your father says, good daughter that you are?" Which question she did not see fit to answer. But she'll read Spinoza, how could she not? What she was inclined to do about the curve thrown by Patricia, if it came, was stand steady and hope not to get beaned.

"Beaned?"

"Right. Beaned," said Petra. Gertrude smiled.

After considerable silence Patricia becomes collaborative which probably means she's switched from Patty Jay to Trish. The hospitalization was a good one. Hard as hell, but good. She's tired of falling apart at regular intervals. Either the System used to work better or she was too numb to notice when it didn't. Either way, the System needs an overhaul. No, she isn't thinking all parts will now be sweetly united in mind, heart, history, habits, and names. Step by step is what she wants. Some pairs of alters are buddies already. They remember together, forget together, go to work, have sex, listen to music, whittle a damn stick, you name it, together. How about starting with Mikey and Pat? Work might go more smoothly if those two were one. Sometimes one of them types a report and the other one repeats the task. Wasteful. Yes, everyone is scared shitless. So, what?

"I'm flabbergasted."

"Good. If that means what we think."

"It means you're surprising me."

"Good."

"Who's here right now?"

"Everybody. I'm talking—Trish—but everybody else is close, listening. Well, except for the contingent in the tower." Petra nods. The contingent in the tower are infant personalities who know nothing but contextless pain and terror. The only thing to do with them for now, and maybe forever, Patricia decided a while ago, was lock them into safety and hope not to hear their constant screams more than occasionally.

"Will they make trouble?"

"The tower babies? We don't think so."

Trish is trustworthy. Petra is inclined to support this, not that she could stop it.

"I'd like to talk to everyone," she says.

"No problem."

Petra allows a minute for the personalities to ready themselves for listening.

"Ready?" She receives a nod. "OK. As you probably know, Trish is talking about integration and she thinks Mikey and Pat would be a good place to start. If there's anyone who has a question or complaint about this, now would be a good time to let me know." Patricia sits, quietly receptive, apparently passive. "No questions? OK. If anyone has questions or anything to say at any point along the way, let me know. I'd like to talk to Mikey and Pat, but everybody else should stay close and listen. Except for the babies in the tower. Let's keep them where they are." She waits. Patricia shifts a little on the couch. She looks like a very young adult, very alert.

"OK. We're here."

"Are you OK with being co-present right now?"

"Sure. We do it a lot at work."

"What do you think of this plan?"

"Makes sense to us. Might make work easier."

"Is there anything you're afraid you'll lose, if you become one?"

"We—us two—used to think if the one who had the front got scared then we needed the other one to take over, but it's different now. We're usually both in the office unless one of us is just—well, it's sort of like playing hooky—just not feeling responsible, not wanting to be at work. We don't think we need to have a backup any more. Another thing. We do understand, you've pounded it into us, that in reality we're all here all the time, which means, logically, we've all handled the tough situations all along. We have a question, though."

"OK."

"Can we change our mind?"

"You mean, if you want to go back to playing hooky with half of your working self you'd like to be able to do it?"

"That's not very funny."

"Reality-based, though. I think you could split again into the alters you are now, but I can't guarantee life would be unchanged. Of course, I can't guarantee life will be unchanged by what you had for breakfast this morning."

"You seem awfully happy today. Almost silly."

"If you take your therapist by surprise you have to expect consequences."

"You like the idea of this integration, don't you?"

"I think I really do."

"Well, the truth is it scares us but we're more excited than scared."

"Makes sense. Me, too, I think."

"You? Why would you be scared?"

"Good question." But Anya appears wearing red corduroy pants and a bright white shirt, shakily riding her new bike. *Thank you, Anya.* "I guess I feel like a mother watching her kid learn to ride a bike. Not that I'm your mother, but scared and excited like that, about a new thing. You could fall but I think you'd only skin your knee. Mostly I think you'd love being able to go fast with the wind in your hair."

Patricia nods maturely and says, "Everyone likes that."

"Have Pat and Mikey gone back inside?"

"Yes. They're getting ready."

"Are you going to be here to communicate with me and act as a bridge?"

"Yes. It's Trish back again."

"I thought so."

"You'll help us, right?"

"That's my job."

"We don't know how to start."

"Let's find an image. We need to think of things that are separate, but they can be transformed, they can become one thing."

There is a pause, then Trish says, "Everybody likes fire. We never got hurt by fire and it's so beautiful and powerful."

"OK. Let's work with that." Another pause.

"Metals. Somebody inside says metals are good."

"Interesting. Say more."

"What's the word when metals aren't hard? They're not liquid like water, but..."

"Molten?"

"Right. Someone's saying, 'We love you, Petra.'"

"Because I thought of molten?"

"I think so. They like the word."

"It's nice to be loved for one's vocabulary."

"Nice to be loved for anything," Trish says.

"I agree."

Trish focuses, appears to be listening to voices inside. Slowly she brings out words. "Gold...and silver...that get molten. Mikey's gold...and Pat is silver. In the fire they get molten and...mix into...silvery gold."

"That's lovely, Trish."

"Can they be called Pat afterward? That's what they want. It's practical because that's what they're called at work. Nobody there knows about Mikey."

"It's up to them, to all of you, to you as one person."

"We'll ignore that little reference to one person. We know the theory you operate from. So there won't be a Mikey any more."

"No. Does that bother you? Or anyone?"

"It's just a change. Harder for the rest of us than for Mikey and Pat. We like the molten metals in the fire. There's no problem."

"Is there anything that needs to happen before we go ahead with this?"

Trish—Patricia—shakes her head no. Petra takes a breath. It's not every day she facilitates an integration. Always this has felt spiritual to her, always she has felt her own privileged position. Now, in this time when she's doing something—but what?—with her own spirituality, there is added weight, or perhaps lightness. When she sleeps alone—she and Nat spend every other night together—she dips into *Ecstatic Confessions*. Last night, an Indian mystic, something called "Conference of the Birds": "*To love, one must have no mental reservations; one must be willing to throw a hundred worlds into the fire.*" Message from the demanding mind of God, she thought, and went to sleep. Now, this integration. Never before has a client chosen fire for the alchemy of the mind. Clouds have united. Streams have flowed into oceans. Never has metal been put through fire, but here is Patricia.

Worlds into the fire, then. Wishing her client and herself best luck, Petra begins.

Works Consulted and/or Cited

(An unconventional addition to a work of fiction—but my debt is too great and too various to ignore.)

Bishop, Elizabeth. "The Armadillo" in *Elizabeth Bishop: The Complete Poems 1927-1979*. New York: Farrar, Straus and Giroux (1979)

Buber, Martin. *Ecstatic Confessions: The Heart of Mysticism*. Edited by Paul Mendes-Flohr. Translated by Esther Cameron. Syracuse University Press (1996)

Duncan, Robert. "Often I Am Permitted To Return to a Meadow" in *The Opening of the Field*. New York: Grove Press (1960)

Eckstorm, Fannie Hardy. *Old John Neptune and Other Maine Indian Shamans*. Portland, Maine: Southworth-Anthoensen Press (1945)

Eliot, T. S. "Ash Wednesday," "Four Quartets," "The Love Song of J. Alfred Prufrock," and "The Wasteland" in *T. S. Eliot: The Complete Poems and Plays 1909-1950*. New York: Harcourt, Brace & World, Inc. (1971)

Gernes, Sonia. "Waitomo: The River under the Earth" in *Women at Forty*. University of Notre Dame Press (1988)

Gertrud the Great of Helfta. *The Herald of God's Loving-Kindness*. Translated, with an introduction and notes, by Alexandra Barratt. Kalamazoo, Michigan: Cistercian Publications (1991)

Gross, Jan Tomasz. *Neighbors: The Destruction of the Jewish Community in Jedwabne, Poland*. Princeton University Press (2001)

H.D. "Sigil" in *H.D. Selected Poems*. Edited by Louis L. Martz. New York: New Directions Books (1988)

Hopkins, Gerard Manley. "God's Grandeur" in *The Norton Anthology of English Literature*. Major Authors Edition. M. H. Abrams, general editor. New York: W. W. Norton & Co. (1962)

Leckie, Robert. Chief Joseph's formal surrender speech in *The Wars of America*. Victoria, British Columbia: Castle Books (1998)

Julian of Norwich. *Revelations of Divine Love*. The Christian Classics Etherial Library @ http://www.ccel.org/ccel/julian/revelations.ii.ii.html

_____. *Showings*. Translated, with an introduction, by Edmund Colledge, O.S.A and James Walsh, S.J. Preface by Jean Leclercq, O.S.B. Mahwah, N.J.: Paulist Press (1978)

Maugham, Somerset. *The Razor's Edge*. New York: Pocket Books (1946)

Milosz, Czeslaw. *Native Realm: A Search for Self-Definition*. Garden City, N.Y.: Doubleday (1968)

Moore, Marianne. "The Octopus" in *The Complete Poems of Marianne Moore*. New York: Penguin Books (1982)

_____. *The Selected Letters of Marianne Moore*. Bonnie Costello, general editor; Celeste Goodridge and Cristanne Miller, associate editors. New York: Knopf (1997)

Neihardt, John G., *Black Elk Speaks: Being the Life Story of a Holy Man of the Oglala Sioux*. University of Nebraska Press (1988)

Nicolar, Joseph. *Life and Traditions of the Red Man*. No publisher given. No original date given. Reprinted by Penobscot Nation Museum, Indian Island, Old Town, Maine (2002)

Owen, Wilfred. "Strange Meeting" in *The Collected Poems of Wilfred Owen*. Edited, with an introduction and notes, by C. Day Lewis. Includes a memoir by Edmund Blunden. New York: New Directions Books (1963)

Pike, Donald. *Anasazi: Ancient People of the Rock*. New York: Three Rivers Press (1986)

Pope, Alexander. "The Rape of the Lock" in *The Norton Anthology of English Literature*. Major Authors Edition. M. H. Abrams, general editor. New York: W. W. Norton & Co. (1962)

Ryan, Kay. "Poetry in Review: The Poems of Marianne Moore" in *The Yale Review,* Volume 92, No. 2 (April 2004)

Sappho. *Sappho: a New Translation*. Translated by Mary Barnard. Forward by Dudley Fitts. Reissue edition. University of California Press (1999)

Smith, Stevie. "Not Waving but Drowning" in *The Norton Anthology of Modern and Contemporary Poetry: Volume One: Modern Poetry*. Edited by Yahan Ramazani. Third Edition. New York: W. W. Norton & Co., Inc. (2003)

Spinoza, Baruch. *The Ethics, and Treatise on the Emendation of the Intellect, and Selected Letters*. Translated by Samuel Shirley. Edited, with introductions, by Seymour Feldman. Indianapolis/Cambridge: Hackett Publishing Co. (1992)

Stein, Gertrude. *Tender Buttons: Objects, Food, Rooms*. Los Angeles: Sun & Moon Press (1991)

Stern, Daniel M. *The Diary of a Baby*. New York: Basic Books (1992)

Weil, Simone. *Gravity and Grace*. Introduction by Gustave Thibon. London: Rutledge and Kegan Paul (1972)

_____. *Waiting for God*. Translated by Emma Craufurd. Introduction by Lesle A. Fiedler. New York: Harper and Row (1973)

Williams, William Carlos. "Marianne Moore" in *Imaginations*. Edited, with introductions, by Webster Schott. New York: New Directions Books (1970)

About the Author

Shirley Glubka is the author of *All the Difference: poems of unconventional motherhood* (Blade of Grass Press, 2012) and *Green Surprise of Passion: Writings of a Trauma Therapist* (a collection of poetry and creative prose, Blade of Grass Press, 1998).

Her poetry and prose have appeared in such journals as *2River View, Conditions, Feminist Studies, h.o.m.e. Words, Narramissic Notebook, Puckerbrush Review, Seems, Sinister Wisdom,* and *Sun Dog: the Southeast Review*; and in these anthologies: *Lesbians at Mid-life: the Creative Transition*; *Mothers Who Leave: the myth of women without their children*; and *Women in Culture: a Women's Studies Anthology*.

Shirley is a retired psychotherapist. She lives in Prospect, Maine with her partner, Virginia Holmes.

For the Curious: Author's Note

Readers often wonder what facts lie behind the fiction. Such readers might be wondering: is Petra a slightly disguised version of Shirley Glubka? The answer is probably predictable: yes and no. Everything in this novel is fictional, though large elements grew out of what life offered me "in reality."

Petra and I share much. We are both from Minnesota, spent time in San Francisco, and have settled in Maine. We know the deep satisfactions and challenges of working with severely traumatized clients, some of whom have Multiple Personality Disorder (Dissociative Identity Disorder). We love to tackle difficult poetry and are interested in spiritual/philosophical questions. We have made our ways, not entirely parallel, to an increasingly serious writing life. We are both lesbians. And we are mothers who chose to give up the daily parenting of a child.

But Petra and I are not one person, not at all. I am seventy years old, a long-retired therapist. None of Petra's clients is based on any client of mine, though I could not have written about Petra's work life, or about Bright Star, without the privilege of working with the women and men who came to my office. There is no real Dykes Who Love Literature but the fictional group charmed me so much that I invited a few long-known and well-trusted women (straight as well as gay) to create, with me, The Pleasures of Difficult Poetry Group. We have a very good time. Unlike

Petra and Nat, my partner and I have been together—in cherished domesticity and mutual satisfaction—for over three decades.

As for motherhood: my son, raised by his second mother, is alive and well. I never had a baby thrust into my unsuspecting arms, never had to wrestle with the decision Petra faces.

Danny is based in some essential way on a beloved old lover, still my dear friend, but my friend is not gay, lives in completely different circumstances from his fictional counterpart, and has never found himself with a baby to raise. Also, he's thin and eats an astoundingly healthy diet.

Bright Star, Raymond, Stella, Ricki, and various other characters all brought their own stories with them—stories unlike mine or those of anyone I know.

*

Here is an excerpt from the preface to my chapbook, *All the Difference: poems of unconventional motherhood*:

> When my son Kevin was three years old his day care teacher came to me. He was very angry, this beautiful boy—a biter, a bit of a problem, though a charismatic one. How she loved him! She herself could not achieve a pregnancy, a sorrow in her life. We talked and talked. He went to live with her, his new mother. I became a shadow mother, a visitor, a sometime babysitter. I felt unsuited for the long work of daily parenting, though exactly what "unsuited" meant was, and still is, more mystery than explanation.

It is perhaps obvious that *Return to a Meadow*, while certainly not an "explanation," is one attempt to confront the mystery.

www.ingramcontent.com/pod-product-compliance
Lightning Source LLC
Chambersburg PA
CBHW051445260626
47162CB00001B/254